THE ALIEN RING

ROBERT ZOGBY

Copyright © 2023 Robert Zogby
All rights reserved
First Edition

NEWMAN SPRINGS PUBLISHING
320 Broad Street
Red Bank, NJ 07701

First originally published by Newman Springs Publishing 2023

ISBN 979-8-88763-373-2 (Paperback)
ISBN 979-8-88763-374-9 (Digital)

Printed in the United States of America

To my beloved father, a gentle, kind and funny man,
who taught me patience, acceptance and humor.

ACKNOWLEDGMENTS

A special thanks to three of my former Language Arts students who have already had published works, a situation of the students teaching the teacher:

- Corey Rosen (*Your Story, Well Told: Creative Strategies to Develop and Perform Stories That Wow an Audience*), who read the very early draft, editing for content, consistency and flow;
- MB Caschetta (*Miracle Girls* and *Pretend I'm Your Friend* and *A Cheerleader's Guide to Spiritual Enlightenment: a Memoir in Essays*), who read for theme and overall likability of the characters; and
- Kimbra Leigh Tabechian (*With a Stroke of the Pen*), who edited for grammar, spelling, punctuation and sentence structure.

Each of them used their talents as published authors to help me understand the nuances of novel writing.

An extra special thanks to my wife, Carol, who read and edited, reread and edited and reread and edited again—almost to ad nauseam—a science fiction novel even though it is not the type of book she enjoys reading.

CHAPTER ONE

The Removal

Walker Air Force Base, outside Roswell, New Mexico, Area 55

The annoying buzzing of the three fluorescent lights' ballast on the ceiling was steady, with one light beginning to flicker, indicating that it was approaching the end of its life span. General Charles Ruppel was a forty-year-career military man who was serious about protecting the nation as an American patriot. He believed that without our fighting men and women of the military, our country would fall to alien forces. Diplomacy was foreign to him, and only the use of force in world or extraterrestrial conflicts was effective. He loved using weapons as tools to defend individual liberties and freedoms. He followed orders from his superiors without hesitation even if he disagreed with those orders.

Addressing the various doctors assigned to operate on the recently found patient after they had updated him on their progress, he was steadfast on his commitment to his assignment. This wasn't the first extraterrestrial that the military had encountered over the decades. Following the Roswell Incident of 1947 in Area 51, rumors swelled and spread among the most fearful and suspicious of nearby residents that Area 55 would be conducting overhead espionage. But instead of monitoring activities by the Russian government, it was used as aerial reconnaissance for foreign air technology belonging to aliens and was entirely designed to capture, reverse-engineer and study alien aircraft and the aliens themselves. Doctors who had participated in the examinations, dissections and eventual secret interments of the numerous creatures they encountered over the past years were sworn to secrecy. Before being discharged from the military, those doctors briefed the incoming specialists on the history of their alien encounters, the required procedures and the necessary protocols. As a result, recent doctors assigned to the current patient of Area 55, despite having another alien lying on a gurney in front of them, never gave them a second thought. But they wondered why the military's intensive scrutiny of the alien was not focused on its biological structure or place of origin. They were only interested in its only adornment: its ring.

"What do you mean you can't remove it!" yelled General Ruppel. "We have the smartest scientists in America working here, and you're telling me you can't remove a simple ring off a finger? Why are we paying you the big bucks if you can't accomplish this simple task? Do you realize how important this research is here at Walker Air Force Base? This artifact on that being's finger may be the key to curing cancer or maybe the common cold."

However, Dr. Harold Hinek knew that was not the purpose of the research since an unknown benefactor controlling military brass was paying for the research, not a medical facility. Hinek was a timid, by-the-book fifteen-year veteran scientist who tended to panic in pressure situations. His colleagues were surprised he ever made it through medical school. "General, we've tried everything. Soap and water, WD-40, olive oil spray, dry silicone spray, white lithium grease. Nothing will loosen it! Nothing is allowing us to slip it off," Dr. Hinek frustratingly replied.

"Keep trying! I don't care if you have to use K-Y Jelly. Just get it off its finger. We need to analyze it."

"Umm, we used that too," the doctor embarrassingly replied.

"Then cut the damn finger off if you have to. Just get the job done. And next time I check in, I want to see results!" General Ruppel stormed out of the examination room where the alien body lay motionless on the sterile sheets of the gurney. Dr. Hinek looked at the alien and sighed, feeling less of a doctor of science and more

THE REMOVAL

like a frustrated mechanic who can't get a nut loose from a rusted engine bolt.

The life-form was gray-skinned, about five feet and six inches tall and hairless, with a head slightly larger than a human's. Its black pupil-less, almond-shaped eyes indicated it might have a wide peripheral vision. The nostrils were simply small holes on a very small protrusion indicating a nose. The slit for a mouth was only accented by minute upper and lower lips. On each side of its head, there were comma-shaped holes for ears. Its four unusually long thin fingers including the thumb completed the picture of a creature that resembled a deformed human than an extraterrestrial.

The three-toned wooden-like ring was located on the left hand's third finger and resembled a combination lock dial, all movable but with complex white pictograms instead of numbers. Each dial was a variation of brown—one mocha, the second coffee and the third peanut. There was one silver band between each of the three dials and one on each end of the set, totaling four. Dr. Hinek and his team were able to rotate the dials but could not remove the ring for further examination. The purpose of the dials or why it could not be removed by conventional means confounded Hinek.

"Maybe it's a combination of symbols that, when aligned, will release the ring."

Dr. Hinek, who was becoming more frustrated with his inability to remove the ring, wanted to try other options before resorting to the general's extreme suggestion of amputation. As he walked away from his comatose guest into his office cubicle, he used his military-issued cell phone and punched up a secure line to his colleagues, who were observing the procedure from an adjacent office via a CCTV camera system that allowed them to zoom in and out for detailed recordings. He asked them to come to the surgical area for assistance.

In his absence, the alien body morphed from its previous gray form and shape to a larger greenish-silver body with an elongated neck, thicker lengthened fingers, gnomelike ears and eyes that now displayed sparkling crystal pupils. The ring, however, remained on its finger, resizing itself like a jeweler rescaling wedding or engagement bands.

Upon returning to their alien cadaver, Hinek's mouth was wide open at the change. Thinking his eyes were playing tricks on them, he rubbed them as if irritated by smoke or fine dust, then scratched his head and stared at the body with confusion. Dr. Helena Stewart, one of Dr. Hinek's closest colleagues who was assigned with him to examine and fulfill the order to remove the ring, arrived late from a meeting as Hinek was in the process of changing the position of the surgical lighting over their patient, thinking it was an optical illusion brought about by light refractions. Of course, that did not work, and it left the bewildered experts another mystery to solve.

"Fill me in. Why the puzzled look?" asked Dr. Stewart. Dr. Helena Stewart was a remarkably tall, reserved, forty-something female. She tended to keep her hair wrapped up in two carefully braided dirty-blond ropes pinned to each side of her head. Her bespectacled face was light-colored, with very fine freckles around her nose. In situations she had not been briefed on, she wore a serious countenance. But her seriousness was also mixed with déjà vu after her husband had died in the bombing of a combat support hospital in Afghanistan years ago and she wasn't informed immediately. She wondered what the military was hiding and why this ring was so important. Even though she was devastated by the loss and missed him immensely, she stayed on to assist in different capacities to honor her fallen spouse.

As the medical scientist with the most surgical experience in the group, she was assigned to Area 55 to study the anatomy of alien beings that were brought to them.

Joining them were Dr. Peter Capell and Dr. Bruce Ganland, arriving after only a few minutes after Dr. Hinek had called them. Hinek briefed them all on the current situation. As they entered the room after the creature's first transformation, Dr. Capell inquired, "Wait! Wasn't this creature gray?"

"Yeah, and weren't his eyes larger and blacker and not hanging to each side of the head?" questioned Dr. Ganland. "And what's with the dark-blue-green liquid dripping from its, umm, penis?"

THE REMOVAL

Dr. Stewart responded, "I'm guessing this is their form of rigor mortis. Let's work on one mystery at a time, please. And someone please get some dry towels to soak up the urine."

"But shouldn't we review the video recording to confirm that it did, indeed, change form?" questioned Dr. Ganland.

"Look, I don't care if it changed to an oversized pomegranate. Our main focus is to get this damn ring off its finger. Why this ring is so important is beyond me, but let's just do what the general ordered. So let's start discussing options," Stewart sternly dictated.

One of those options was to find the proper sequence to dial on the ring. "That would take a computer weeks to calculate the thousands of possible combinations, especially with these unknown symbols," Dr. Hinek stated. All nodded.

Hours had passed as they formulated hypotheses. More hours passed as they tested those hypotheses, such as injecting the finger with cortisone to expand the finger, then wait for the finger to shrink back, thus loosening the ring. They thought extracting the fluid of the finger to reduce its width would be another possibility or even cutting the skin and ligaments surrounding the ring to try and slide it off a thinner area. No matter what they tried, the ring would match the reduced circumference of the finger. Each time they tested one of their postulations, the alien would twitch as if the surgical procedures hit nerves within it.

All the doctors were at their wits' end. They needed to seriously consider General Ruppel's recommendation of amputation. The procedure needed to be done carefully, as amputating an extremity from a human, but with fewer precautions since the subject was presumably dead.

As Dr. Hinek turned toward Dr. Stewart, he said, "This is beyond anything I have been trained for, so I will leave this conundrum to you, Dr. Stewart."

After Dr. Hinek passed the baton to Dr. Stewart, he left the room. Stewart rolled her eyes in disgust and whispered to herself, "Coward." There was no discussion about who would perform the amputation, which angered her. She and the remaining doctors exited the observation room to the pre-op area of the facility to prepare themselves for the surgery, leaving two physician assistants—Carl and Susan—to stay with the patient. "Please watch the patient carefully. Notify us if anything unusual occurs," instructed Stewart.

All three doctors moved into a designated scrub room. As they all started sterilizing their hands and putting on new protective goggles, face shields and fresh sterile disposable nitrile gloves, Dr. Stewart was not shy about showing her annoyance at the lack of professional courtesy in discussing the procedure. "What medical professional would leave a patient on a gurney, unattended? No pre-op team would ever leave a patient unwatched. Did anyone even check its vitals?" She was concerned that the creature might not be truly dead and, if so, escape, or it might be in a self-inflicted coma, trying to heal. These were uncharted waters for her not only because her patient was an alien but also because she took the Hippocratic oath, the earliest expression of medical ethics in the Western world. "It is morally wrong to be forced into operating on a being that may still be alive. That's what doctors are supposed to discuss prior to surgery. Did all those professional courtesies disappear when they entered the military?"

While she vented about the difference between private practice surgical procedures and what she has experienced at this facility, one of the medical assistants, Susan, screamed as the creature silently morphed again, this time with less subtlety. It now had no conventional nose, as in standard medical anatomy books. A small indentation appeared above the mouth, with a thin breathable skin over it, similar to a window screen at one's home, and two cephalopod eyes protruded about three inches from each side, drooping to the sides of the head, indicating that the eye muscles could not support them unless the owner was conscious. Its skin transformed to an aqua-blue color, and its ears resembled gills. The fingers thinned and elongated but formed round suction cups at the ends. Between its legs, through what looked like its phallus (indicating the male of the species), passed dark-blue-green urine onto the gurney sheets, which overflowed onto the floor, sounding like a showerhead dripping water after the water had been turned off. Carl ran to get a bedpan to place under the trickling.

THE REMOVAL

Upon returning from preparation and garbed in personal protection clothing, Dr. Stewart, seeing one assistant staring and shaking, asked, "What's wrong?" as she was rushing into the room. Then she looked at the alien on the gurney. "Holy shit!"

Susan fainted, and Carl decided he had enough of this bizarreness and bolted for the exit of the observation room, leaving Dr. Stewart and colleagues—Dr. Capell and Dr. Ganland—to assist in the procedure. Dr. Capell lifted Susan from under her arms and placed her on a chair against the tan brick wall.

Normally, prior to amputation surgery, a surgeon would do a careful examination of the hand and have x-rays of the area or other imaging studies to assess the area to be severed. Dr. Stewart knew the amount of bone and tissue that needed to be removed would normally be based on the extent of an injury and the health of the remaining body part. Well, since the alien might be apparently alive, evidenced by its morphing, she felt it necessary to check whether the creature was breathing. She moved closer to the extraterrestrial's mouth and placed her ear near the screenlike covering over what looked like its mouth to check for airflow. She felt a very faint breath. She then watched the screened mouth for a sign of air moving in and out.

"Oh my god! It's still alive," she gasped. "I felt it breathing. I can't amputate the finger of a creature that still has life. It is unethical. When it is revived, we can simply ask it to remove the ring." She called General Ruppel on the two-way radio located in the adjacent office near the surgical area. "Hello, General! Listen, we have a problem. I cannot, in good conscience, amputate on a subject who is still alive. I will have to put it under anesthesia, and since we don't have an anesthesiologist available on the base, I would have to do it myself, which I refuse to do since I have not been certified in that field. Without anesthesia, the pain to the creature would be excruciating. And if it is still alive, once revived, we can simply communicate with it requesting the ring's removal!"

The general told her to prepare for the procedure regardless and that he would be right over.

While she, Dr. Ganland and Dr. Capell stood over their patient, it began to murmur as if suffering from laryngitis. Dr. Stewart could barely hear the sounds, so she placed her ear once again above its mouth. It murmured with more articulation. She thought she heard the word *water*, but how could an alien being speak English? She decided not to worry about that and get some water for it. Rushing over to the faucet in the scrub room, she filled a beaker halfway, then quickly but carefully walked over to her alien patient and began pouring methodically over the screened mouth. The creature seemed to be swallowing as its cheeks were moving. After it drank, a few minutes passed until she saw more of the dark-blue-green liquid drip out of its penis. Dr. Stewart instructed Dr. Capell to get another larger bedpan under the gurney to collect the drippings for analysis. Dr. Stewart presumed their patient was dehydrated, so she continued feeding it water as Dr. Capell caught more of its urine with the larger pan.

The creature showed slight signs of movement as Dr. Stewart continued to supply water to it. The alien's right hand was shaking in an attempt to flex. As she tried to revive the creature, the general burst into the room, looked at Stewart feeding her patient water and yelled at the top of his lungs, "WHAT THE HELL ARE YOU DOING?"

"IT'S ALIVE! IT'S ALIVE!" she shouted back. "I think we can revive it and ask it to give us the ring voluntarily. There's no need to amputate the finger. Plus, we can learn so much from it if we can resuscitate it. I actually heard it ask me for water in ENGLISH."

"We will not negotiate with an alien. This creature invaded our world and should be treated as an intruder. What happens if we revive it and it becomes violent and kills all of us?" the general questioned as he shook his head. "Or worse yet, try to penetrate our bodies and impersonate us in their pursuit of world domination?"

"You've been watching too many sci-fi movies, General. I cannot morally or ethically operate on a creature I know nothing about or how it will react to anesthesia if we need to put it under."

The general looked down at the creature, who was visibly beginning to breathe, and replied, "Well, maybe you're right." Then he suddenly pulled out his military tactical knife from his side holster and fiercely plunged it into where he presumed was the area of the creature's heart. Dr. Stewart, along with Drs. Capell and Ganland, gasped in horror at the general's vile actions as the creature convulsed violently, bleeding phosphorescent light-gray blood. It shook, trembled and collapsed on the gurney. Without remorse, the general stated, "Now it's dead. Proceed, or I will have you court-martialed with a dishonorable discharge along with the rest of you! Do I make myself clear?"

Dr. Stewart, visibly shaken by this assault of this guiltless creature, knew that a dishonorable discharge was like a scarlet letter when looking for jobs after the military. She would be labeled as uncooperative in the eyes of an employer and would lose her credibility as a doctor if she received one. It was a decision between her morals and her future employment. She was raised to place her morals and values above all else, but if her future of possibly remarrying and raising and supporting a future family was at stake, her morals would have to take a back seat to her forthcoming aspirations. She had to be realistic about her decision, and she would have to live with that choice for the rest of her life. As a doctor, she knew she would have to break the Hippocratic oath. But as she further contemplated the decision, she came to the realization that she did not break that oath. She did no wrong or harm. It was the general who did the harm. There was no way to have prevented the general from stabbing the victim since it happened quickly and unpredictably.

She decided to proceed, knowing of the guilt she would endure for a lifetime. With only three days before her military service would be complete, she informed the other doctors of her choice. "It is against not only my oath as a doctor but against my own morals as well, but I will perform the amputation." Empathizing with her, they understood the consequences of her decision.

Dr. Stewart had performed amputations before on soldiers wounded in battle. The procedure, for her, was routine. She needed to cut directly behind the ring to avoid cutting near the knuckle of its longer-than-usual extremity so it could simply slide off or fall off after the finger was amputated.

All surgical tools were laid out neatly and in order of need on a separate table beside the patient: a scalpel with blades; dissection and cutting scissors; retractors and handheld clamps; needle holders;

suture material; fine and toothed forceps; a diathermy device and, most importantly, bone instruments—a saw, bone nibblers, osteotomes, a mallet and curettes.

To avoid all the technical and medical terminology applied to this procedure, let's just simply say that the removal, with minimal phosphorescent light-gray blood excreting from the surgical cut, was complete, the stump on the creature's hand cauterized and bandaged. There was but one problem. Despite the finger being amputated, the ring still would not come off. All the doctors were truly baffled as to why a simple ring would not just fall off the severed finger, but Dr. Stewart had one more idea.

She carved out the inside of the finger from the end of the ring to the knuckle, pulled the bone from the inside and dropped it into the surgical pan. The skin of the finger buckled within the ring after the bone was removed, but the ring compensated for the collapse. She then hollowed it out like she was preparing to stuff a jalapeño pepper. Dr. Stewart grabbed a scalpel and inserted it between the skin and the inside edges of the ring to carve it out of the detached finger's skin. She discarded more pieces of skin into a surgical pan. The ring vibrated as she continued cutting along the inside circumference. But the movement was not loosening the ring; the vibration was causing the rest of the dissevered finger to wiggle, flapping up and down rapidly. Stewart was feeling success as she finally separated the object from the alien's dissevered finger, leaving a small gap between the circumference of the ring and the dismembered finger, enough to place a scalpel between. The inside of the ring was coated with the light-gray blood of the alien. As she attempted to scrub the blood from the ring, the vibrations intensified; and when the ring finally loosened from the extremity, instead of falling into the doctor's open hand, it floated above it, the dials on it spinning uncontrollably. When she attempted to grab it, it moved away from her like the ring and her hand were two negative sides of a magnet repelling each other. The other doctors clumsily lunged for it as well, looking like a pair of jugglers attempting to catch a descending ball. As the ring began to vibrate more violently, accompanied by a piercing high-pitched tone, it eventually disappeared in the air, slowly fading as it vibrated.

THE REMOVAL

All doctors just stood, staring up in disbelief and then at each other in bewilderment. They did not notice that the solitary finger and the being to which it belonged disintegrated, leaving gray phosphorescent ashes on the soiled white linen.

Dr. Stewart looked back at the gurney and the remains in ashes and said, "Shit!"

CHAPTER TWO

The History of the Themadorians

One day earlier

Handcuffed and unconscious from the chloroform that military officers used to quiet him, the creature was dragged into the office of Darius Crumb, CEO of Nanogenics, the most advanced technology firm on Earth, which was currently developing self-defense mechanisms for the military. Crumb—a large, oily, corpulent man—was dressed in formal military attire. He worked in the field of engineering and scientific research, specializing in computer software and mechanical engineering. Crumb knew that civilian companies sought out military veterans for their work ethic, dedication and leadership skills to fill key positions within their companies, but while Crumb served his twenty-five years, he did everything he could to fake those personal skills, simply changing and modifying his true nature without seeming uncooperative. He planned and schemed his way through those military years, secretly learning the military's technological capabilities as well as stealing some from others, and was able to leave the armed forces with an honorable discharge.

Even though he had very few characteristics of a successful CEO, he tried to mimic the persona of one. He never revealed his true nature as a narcissistic, untrustworthy tyrant in his business endeavors. From his military experience and other sources, he possessed intimate knowledge of technology needed to move the world forward, but only if that move included him as the ultimate leader.

He stole others' ideas and had little respect for his workers, especially the females and his board, and if someone disagreed with his thoughts, he'd fire them without consulting his board of directors. His dealings were coldhearted, and his friendships shallow. He'd rather throw an associate under the bus than take any responsibility for his actions. His prime objectives were to make money, be powerful, take over as many corporations as possible and always be in the news cycle.

"Sir, we searched the crash vessel and only found this creature working under a crystal console. It was not violent or aggressive toward us, but we sedated and cuffed it anyway. We were just taking precautions, sir," said Lieutenant Gallagher, the commanding officer of the military police.

Crumb spoke in a deep reticence, "I understand. Proactivity is preferred. Sit it down, take the handcuffs off and wake it."

Lieutenant Gallagher complied by lightly slapping the being's cheek several times.

"Water, please! I need water," the alien moaned in a whispered, barely audible tone as the ring he was wearing transmitted the proper language to everyone in the room.

"Get it some water, Lieutenant," Crumb demanded.

"Yes, sir!" Gallagher shouted. Gallagher had his accompanying officer, Second Lieutenant Jenson, fill his canteen with water from the CEO's office bathroom and hand it to the puzzled alien.

It sluggishly, with an outward hand shaking, took the canteen, looked at it with a puzzled expression and proceeded to drink all of its contents. He handed the canteen back to the second lieutenant, but Jenson refused to take it, saying, "Um, you keep it. I don't know what kind of alien disease you may be spreading."

Still weak from his sedation, he replied, "We are a very clean species, but if you insist. Now I need to relieve myself, please."

"No way that water went through you that fast! Besides, you'll answer some questions first," Crumb demanded.

"Then I will discharge my waste right here."

"No! No! Okay. Fine. Lieutenant, escort it to the bathroom and watch it!' Crumb shouted.

"Sir, um, I have to watch it pee?" Gallagher questioned.

"That's an order, Lieutenant. We don't want him to escape," Crumb retorted.

"Um, Mr. Crumb, there are no windows or doors in this army research office's restroom. The only door is in front of you, and the windows are on two sides of the army research office. So it would be hard to escape without us seeing him," Lieutenant Gallagher replied.

"Well, fine. Just leave the door open. Who knows what it's capable of doing!"

The extraterrestrial staggered to the bathroom, did its duty and left the blue-green liquid in the toilet.

"Gross, flush it," Gallagher said as he gazed at the excretion, which resembled a cleaning chemical.

The creature had no idea what "flush it" meant and responded, "Flush what?"

Gallagher showed him how to flush the toilet, and the alien jumped at the noise of the pressure-assisted flush of the toilet. It was fascinated by this churning vortex since Themadorians' eliminations were instantly disintegrated upon contact with their advanced commodes.

The strange creature staggered over to the chair in front of Crumb as he mumbled, "So primitive."

"Better?" Crumb sarcastically uttered.

Still foggy from the chloroform, he spoke, "Not really. I don't understand why I was cuffed, sedated and forcefully brought here. Are all your inhabitants this paranoid of visitors? Are you all so violent with guests on your planet?"

"Let's just say that trust is not in abundance on Earth," Crumb said pragmatically.

Lelak looked puzzled and asked, "Why is that? On our planet, we trust one another and have no reason to distrust. Well, until the Era of the Great Gasses destroyed that trust."

"Era of the Great Gasses? Interesting. First of all, do you have a name?"

"My apologies. It is Lelak."

"Tell me, Lelak, what is the purpose of your visit? From the result of your landing, I'll presume this was not your destination," Crumb genially referenced.

"It's a long story," sighed Lelak.

"I love long stories. Lieutenant Gallagher, leave the office and guard the outside entrance with Lieutenant Jenson. I'll call if I need you," Crumb barked.

As the MPs exited the facility, a female with a white lab coat was at the north side of the research office, listening through the half open window, one of the windows that were required to be open for air circulation, according to the US Army Corps of Engineers. About 19 percent of each office had to contain windows on the north and south facades, with each building having its long access east and west. In an effort not to be detected, she made sure she was on the outer edge of the pane. She had some suspicions about Crumb after reading past reports of alien encounters and the briefings from discharged medical personnel.

Darius Crumb sat back on his high-backed leather chair, swiveled around to look out the south-side window at the military facility and replied, "Please sit, relax and tell me a story, your story, your family's story, your planet's story! I'm intrigued."

"I'm really n-n-not sure I should t-t-trust you, especially since you admitted that trust on this world is scarce," Lelak stuttered.

"You are correct. You can't. But if you don't, I'll torture the information from you, fulfilling our cruel nature, as you called it, so you won't be disappointed. So educate me on the history of, umm, what is your species called?"

"Themadorians," Lelak replied hesitantly. "I don't care if you torture me. I will not share with a leader who violently captures visitors, then drugs and handcuffs them."

"Leader? Oooh, I like that. You know, I have a better drug than the one they used to knock you out. It will force the truth from you, but hey, it's a free world. For now anyways. So you can choose among three options. Share on your own, be tortured for information or be drugged. Torture is always fun, but it's rarely effective since the one being tortured usually passes out from the intense pain or even dies, which, of course, would defeat the purpose of torturing in the first place. So, as the expression goes, choose wisely."

Lelak asked, "Why do you want to know about us? What will you use the information for?"

"Research into the next technological marvel," Crumb excitedly replied. "I am presuming you have better technologies that I could, um, borrow to advance our military capabilities."

"We were always a peaceful species, so our military technologies were available but rarely used. Our species' history should be a model for all other species including this planet you call Earth," Lelak proclaimed.

"So let's hear it!"

"No!"

"Very well. I'll call my lieutenants to bring me the sodium pentothal. Do you know what that is?" Crumb questioned his captive.

"I am unfamiliar with the combination, but I believe, from my studies, that it is a mind-altering drug known as a barbiturate," Lelak answered.

"Aren't you a smart little alien? In the military, it is referred to as truth serum even though some scientists have claimed instead that it makes people feel like talking, and when they talk, they usually tell the truth."

"Whatever information you get from me will be of no use. It's more historical than technological. Your threats of torture mean nothing to me, for if I die, you will get no information from me."

"Aren't you the brave one? You have one more chance to enlighten me on your species, or I will use the sodium pentothal."

Lelak was hesitant. He was afraid that another drug in his system would do more damage than the chloroform did to him, possibly killing him. Themadorians kept their species free of harmful drugs and processed foods, which was why his family could not survive on synthesized food from their replicators for an extended period of time. He thought he'd tell him as much as he needed to know. He wanted to have complete control of his faculties when he shared his species' background. He finally, with reservations, agreed to Crumb's demand.

THE HISTORY OF THE THEMADORIANS

"We Themadorians were peaceful people, cooperative and welcoming. But for three hundred revolutions of our sun, we were also in a very productive, large-scale industrial period in agriculture, manufacturing and technology, a slight combination of your Industrial Age and your Digital Age but much more advanced, until the Era of the Great Gasses, that is."

"Wait! How do you know about your people prior to this Era of Gasses?"

"Era of the Great Gasses!" Lelak corrected.

"But you said 'hundreds of revolutions of your sun.' That implies that you lived through it."

"As did my parents," Lelak shared.

"How old are you?"

"Based on how you Earth creatures calculate age, about 349 years old."

"Wow! You look good for your age!" Crumb laughed.

Lelak looked at him, tipping his head like a dog, not understanding a command.

"How do you know so much about our world? Are you planning an invasion?"

"When I landed, I used our star maps to find out where I was and what this planet's history was like. You have a past of multiple wars, racial injustice, intolerance to diversity, discrimination and inequality along with environmental disasters. Your governments have self-serving politicians and do not care about their constituents. Why would we invade your planet and inherit those problems? We have our own.

"Prior to the Era of the Great Gasses, we ignored what we were doing to our planet's environment for hundreds of years. The misuse and waste of our natural resources caused problems with the core of our planet. We contaminated our atmosphere chemically, biologically and physically with pollutants from our factories. Agricultural practices polluted the soil with pesticides, chemicals, urban and industrial wastes and even some early radioactive emissions that contaminated the soil with various toxic substances. We neglected to reuse or replenish our resources and neglected to filter the smoke and waste water from our factories, and we never bothered to consider fewer toxic alternatives to powering our planet nor where our debris was being dumped. We simply ignored it because we were working so harmoniously that there was no one to examine what we were doing to our planet. The temperature of the planet was changing, making it more difficult to grow crops to feed our people. Our seasons began to merge from four seasons to two. Some sectors were seeing extreme heat, and others extreme cold. Other areas still had too much rain, while some areas saw dried-out rivers that used to supply fresh water to their towns and cities. Over time, the contaminants in the soil seeped into the core of the planet, mixing with the molten center. The combination of the toxins and the molten lava forced the volcanoes around the entire planet to begin quietly expelling invisible and odorless gas similar to your odorless carbon monoxide expelled from your vehicles, heaters or cooking equipment. Eventually, it spread all throughout Themadoria's atmosphere and added to our already polluted air.

"Unbeknownst to us, Themadorians were inhaling that unseen and odorless gas, causing our appearances to slowly transform. Each of our genders turned into two different colors. We used to be all light gray with a soft-blue undertone. But due to the volcanic gasses being inhaled by all of us, the males became fully gray, and the females a light blue. Not only had we changed colors, many but not all Themadorians developed severe personality changes such as depression, uncontrollable anger, anxiety and obstinance. Many but, again, not all the males became more aggressive, stubborn-minded and dominant over the females, who refused to be subservient to them since previously, they had all worked cooperatively together. The females retained their morphing powers, but most of the men lost theirs. We had no idea why, but we knew that the emissions of industrial gasses and the pollution in our waters and streams must have been the cause. Scientists theorized this after we advanced to our current technological status. The gray males who were affected worked together to force their dominance onto the females. The affected light-blue females became fierce warriors and fought valiantly to eliminate their repression.

"Those not affected by the gas chose to wear masks to avoid possible exposure just in case. But it made the Unaffected stand out, and they were frowned upon, criticized for living in fear. They knew they would have to find a place on our planet to gather as a commune and live their lives similar to the Co-op Era. To this day, our planet is consumed with greed, immorality and selfishness, uncaring to its neighboring communities and unwilling to help one another. Our inhabitants now eat processed or synthetic foods, which has caused medical problems among the Affected and Unaffected alike since our soils can no longer sustain organic produce."

"Sounds like our world," Crumb ecstatically exclaimed. "It's the way I like it! It's great for business!"

Lelak continued, "Eventually, the blue and gray Themadorians were unable to marry since blue and gray Themadorians were constantly bickering and fighting and lacked mutual trust and respect. This was when the Unaffected decided to escape the towns and cities in search of any hidden area of the planet where they could live out their lives peacefully and cooperatively and freely marry whomever they wanted without interference from the developing ruling factions. The Affected were glad to see them go, not seeing them as a threat.

"During the migration, unexplored caverns were discovered by my parents, Noj and Ahtram, who are archaeologists. They had, through their excavations, uncovered mappings of the entire planet prior to the Era of the Great Gasses. The maps revealed tunnels and corridors in underground caves where the Unaffected attempted to create a society that would eventually bring back the Co-op Era. Noj and Ahtram were in the process of uncovering the origin of those maps until the EGG occurred."

"Are your parents dead?" Crumb didactically asked.

"No! Of course not!"

"And how old are they?"

"My mother is 483, and my father is 492."

"Holy shit!" Crumb almost fell off his chair. "So where are they?" he inquired.

"They are still underground, waiting for my return with a possible cure." Lelak again avoided any mention of his family. "That's why I was traveling to Proteus 9."

"Proteus 9 has the cure?" Crumb asked.

"I think they may since they may have better technology than we do."

"How?"

"Maybe you weren't listening because your arrogance and your overactive ego was blocking your ears," Lelak sarcastically replied.

"Don't get brazen with me," Crumb yelled. "I demand respect!"

"You haven't earned it. Perhaps they may be able to share their cure with us or at least the means to create one. They are well-known for creating amazing medical and technological breakthroughs, and they were able to avoid Themadoria's situation. I was hoping to work out a mutual collaboration with Proteusans to share each of our planets' discoveries."

"Hmmm, mutual collaboration, eh? We have another word for it here. *Profiteering.* Anyway, go on."

"Eventually, in our new realm below the surface, we established a new society, which we dubbed the New Co-op Era. It's where the Unaffected lived secretly and where many mixed-colored Themadorians including my parents eventually married and had offspring. We were able to develop a light source from luminescent rocks, filters for drinking water and soil and an air filtration system so we would not be contaminated by the gasses that continue to seep underground. We used everyone's expertise to form a barrier that would keep the contamination at bay. Years went by on the surface of our planet, with continuous conflicts and environmental disasters that caused a schism between the males and females and infertility among the surface dwellers, reducing the population of our planet and its productivity."

Crumb began laughing.

"Why are you laughing? There was nothing humorous in my telling of my planet's history."

"New Co-op Era? Affected? Unaffected? What a bunch of crap! Let me tell you something. The only cooperation in our world is when someone, namely me, tells people, namely everyone else, how things are done, when they get done and never why they need to get it done. If you pay them enough, they will do anything. And your Unaffected sound weak. Maybe your people belong under the ground."

Lelak was beginning to clear his head and was contemplating a way to exterminate this sad example of this planet's inhabitants for his perverse attitudes toward the Unaffected Themadorians and others of Crumb's species. But Lelak was a noble, honest and kind Themadorian who had the morals and values of his parents and his grandparents.

Crumb noticed Lelak fingering his ring. "So tell me about that ring. An heirloom from your ancestors, I presume?"

"I'd rather not share that information since I already told you more than I wanted to about our planet."

"Does it do anything special, like emit a death ray or something?" Crumb inquired insistently.

"Nothing so primitive and stereotypical as that," Lelak fervently denied as if insulted by the suggestion.

"Ah, so it does do something," Crumb replied quickly.

"I never said that," refuted Lelak.

"Take it off!" Crumb demanded.

Knowing that the ring would only come off if the wearer voluntarily took it off, Lelak defiantly replied, "No! Besides, it would not fit you."

Crumb laughed, "I wasn't going to wear it. I was going to take it for analysis. Then eventually, if it does do something that would be to my benefit, I would reverse-engineer it and mass-produce it for the military."

"No!" Lelak again declined.

"It must do something spectacular, or you would not be protecting it so vehemently. Shall I remind you what I can do to you if you refuse?"

"I don't care. It is not yours," Lelak vociferously refuted.

"Oh, but it will be mine one way or another, and I will use any manner at my disposal to obtain it."

"The answer is still no!" Lelak decreed.

"Very well," Crump said matter-of-factly. "Lieutenant Gallagher, take him to Area 55's research lab. Have our scientific personnel remove the ring from his finger by any means at their disposal. Have them report to General Charles Ruppel. He will monitor their progress. Then have him check in with me periodically with information on their progress."

Gallagher and Jenson grappled with Lelak, as he tried to break out of their grip, but his attempts were futile. They finally decided to a more lasting dose of chloroform to get him to Area 55.

"That should keep him out of trouble for at least a couple hours," Jenson told Gallagher. When they did, Lelak spasmed violently and passed out.

After notifying the scientists and doctors assigned for the task, Lelak was delivered to Area 55, where he was placed on a freshly prepared gurney.

CHAPTER THREE

Second Abduction

The day after Lelak's death
Dialogue translated from Themadorian

"You children all right?" Lah whispered as they emerged from their secret annex.

"Just scared! Where's Dad?" asked both Arak and Etak in unison, their quivering mouths adding to their worried countenances. Arak was the oldest of the two Themadorian offspring, female and a lighter blue than her mom. She had black slanted teardrop-shaped eyes that held very small light-blue pupils and two nostrils without an obvious nose, only a very small protrusion indicating the semblance of one. A slit for a mouth with very slim lips, comma-shaped holes for ears and four unusually long fingers including the thumb made up her unique appearance. Etak, a male of the species, was the smaller version of his father but was a lighter-gray version of his sister, with the exception of more rounded eyes and small white crystal pupils. His lips were present but looked more like a thin rounded eyebrow above the mouth and the reverse under it.

Lah was a more feminine version of her husband, with light-blue skin and fine aqua-blue ridges that formed from the back of her head to the front like converging branches of a leafless tree. Her prism-like pupils were centered slightly below her teardrop-shaped black eyes. Her other features were simply larger versions of her daughter's.

Lah was in the secret annex, in a small room with all the necessary monitors, computer access and a seamless door. She had access to the digital relay console of the ship, so she could familiarize herself with their current planet's geography, history and culture. "From what I can obtain from the surveillance cameras, he was taken by a few of this planet's inhabitants, dressed in blue-and-gold uniforms, possibly the standard attire of these creatures. According to our recorded video feed, they did not sound friendly, judging from their tone and attitude."

Etak asked, "Is he in danger? Can we rescue him?"

Lah hesitantly replied, "I don't know. I need to continue the diagnostics Lelak was working on. Hold on."

Lah spoke into the large atrium of their ship. "Talock, status report." Talock was the onboard AI navigation, diagnostic and information system, which was standard equipment in Themadorian ships.

"Fuel down to 5 percent, not enough to escape this planet's atmosphere. Cloaking device still in operation but has been damaged. Complete failure in about five cycles. Food replicators online but may be unreliable due to subroutines being damaged," Talock replied with Themadorian inflections. "No extensive damage to the outer hull except for the door, which would have revealed the interior of this ship, had our cloaking device malfunctioned."

"First things first. Use auxiliary power to keep that opening cloaked," demanded Lah.

"Auxiliary power transferred to cloaking of door," Talock confirmed. "It may not last long, possibly a few *mators* to a few *nelights* [equivalent to a few hours to a few minutes]."

"Why do we only have 5 percent of fuel left? We had more than enough fuel for the journey to and from Proteus 9. What happened?" Lah inquired with a shocked look on her face.

"Running diagnostics. Diagnostics indicate a very fine crack in the fuel tank, causing a slow leak of fuel during the journey."

"What caused the crack?"

"Assessing… According to our backlogged sensor information, fatigue failure of the fuel tank skin caused a crack growth of the skin structures. Self-sealing protocols failed. The proper maintenance of this craft was never regularly scheduled, which may have contributed to the sudden skin failure and crack path."

"Are your sensors functioning properly, Talock?" Lah asked. "Why didn't the sensors warn us so we could have initiated repair protocols?"

"Unknown. It's possible that the fuel sensor was inoperative due to faulty maintenance. I will do a self-diagnosis of my operating systems." After a few seconds, Talock responded, "My systems are working within acceptable parameters."

"Can we first find out where Dad is, please?" Arak asked desperately.

"Yes, of course!" Using the ring's built-in GPS system, Lah requested Lelak's location. A small light-blue projection displayed an image above them. It showed a forest with a sign at its entrance that read, Rosemont, New Mexico. "I am not familiar with the lettering of this sign until I can ascertain more about this planet and our location to this place."

"Well, this ship was never intended to be used so soon. Our aeronautical engineers had not tested the spacecraft for flight yet." Then Lah directed her comments toward Talock. "So it's obvious now that our low fuel caused us to crash on this planet. Begin working on getting the entrance closed again. If we are captured like Lelak, we want you to continue working on the repair to the entranceway. I don't want any of our crystal technology to get into their hands. There's no telling what they will use it for even though they are only cave crystals and are of little use in the military. Then try to find out how the sensors failed to detect the crack in the first place."

"Affirmative, ma'am."

"Bring up star charts of this solar system please, Talock."

As Talock brought up the 3D star charts of yellow-blue-and-white graphics, a depth map of round planets materialized in midair. He replied, "This planet is called Earth, and it is thirty light-years away from Themadoria and fifteen light-years away from our destination of Proteus 9."

"Since we will be here for a while, may I have more information about this planet called Earth?" Lah asked calmly, hiding her urgency so as not to frighten the children.

"Accessing... Earth is one of nine planets in this current solar system and the only planet in this system with plate tectonics. These tectonic plates have been broken up into regions. These are floating on top of the magma interior of the Earth and can move against one another. When two plates collide, one plate can go underneath another. The regions are called continents, which the inhabitants have divided into countries and provinces. Many of the regions are surrounded by water. Similar to Themadoria, which emits gasses and molten material, the continents have many active and dormant volcanoes.

"According to my most recent data, Earth takes twenty-three hours, fifty-six minutes and four seconds to completely rotate around its axis. If added to the little motion from the Sun as the Earth orbits around it and combined with the rotation on its axis, it totals twenty-four hours.

"Earth has only one orbital construct they call a moon. But there are two additional asteroids locked into co-orbital orbits with Earth. They're called 3753 Cruithne and 2002 AA29. The first doesn't actually orbit the Earth, but it has a synchronized orbit with the planet. It makes it look like it's following the Earth in orbit, but it's actually following its own distinct path around the Sun. When discovered in 2002, it was determined that AA29 travels in a horseshoe orbit around the Earth that brings it close to the planet every ninety-five years. According to current records, Earth is gradually slowing down. Every few years, an extra second is added to make up for lost time. Millions of years ago, a day on Earth would have been only twenty hours long. It is believed that in another million years' time, a day on Earth will be twenty-seven hours long.

"Their climate is changing due to industrial pollution of their waters and land, similar to Themadoria. The global temperature has risen six-tenths of a degree in the past twenty years, causing the waters to increase in temperature. Their population has increased by 1.7 billion inhabitants called humans. Sea levels have risen three inches, transforming their coastlines through erosion to where the local sea level rises, strong waves occur and coastal flooding has worn down and carried away rocks, soil and sand along the coast. Extreme weather on this world has increased by 30 percent. Their northern and southern poles' ice sheets have lost 4.9 trillion tons of ice, killing much of the indigenous creatures that live there, and more of their animal species are being threatened with extinction.

"The steady increase of extreme weather will eventually cost them not only lives and livelihood but also an increase of painfully slow hurricanes in some areas, deadly heat and droughts in other areas and floods and extensive rain in still other areas. These conditions will cause a major upheaval in the way humans live and grow food. Humidity and heat will collide to create 'wet bulb' temperatures that will disrupt the norms of their daily existence. If they continue on this path of ignoring the signs of these changes, the Earth will cease to exist in thirty of their cycles."

"This sounds all too familiar. Talock, what are their inhabitants like? Are they friendly or hostile?"

"According to my resources, this planet is quite diverse, unlike Themadoria. Even though they are of the human species, they look slightly different, speak many different languages and have very different cultural and political beliefs. Their planet is not as united as Themadoria once was in the Co-op Era. They seem to be constantly at war, trying to force cultural and religious beliefs on one another when neither faction is willing to compromise. There are extremists, terrorists, conspirators and power-hungry types, similar to our current situation on the surface of Themadoria."

"Talock, are there any redeemable qualities of these…um… humans?" asked Lah as a feeling of hopelessness consumed her from Talock's analysis.

"The information I currently have in my database indicates that there are many kind, generous, understanding, thoughtful and honest types, similar to our current situation in the underground caves of Themadoria, but it will take me hours to fully calculate the numbers. Shall I begin calculations?" asked Talock.

"No, not if it compromises the energies we have left on this ship. Work on the duties I previously ordered. Our priorities are to get off this ship undetected, find Lelak, return to the ship, repair our damages including the cloaking device and fuel leak and find some biofuel or some other organic alternatives that may exist on this planet," Lah despairingly noted.

Before Lah could gather her thoughts, she heard noises from the outer hull that sounded like the same voices she heard earlier when Lelak was captured. "Talock, are your sensors picking up anyone around the outer hull?" But before Talock could reply, bright-red lights and a warning sound much like the security horn sounds on a car blared within the ship. "Warning! Warning! Cloaking device compromised! Doorway is now visible."

"Oh, *Gnikcuf tihs*! Sorry, children. Didn't mean to say that! Quickly, get back into the annex," yelled Lah, but before they could, three military soldiers stormed the ship through the now visible door entrance and grabbed Lah and the children. Struggling to get out of the grip of the soldiers, Lah roared, "How did you disrupt our cloaking device?"

The soldier holding Lah replied, "Crumb technology, of course."

"Who the *dratsab* is Crumb?"

"You'll soon find out little...um...lady, um, blue alien person. Umm, never mind. You're coming with us! Come quietly, or we will use the same method on you and your children as we did on your husband...um...mate...um, the gray guy."

Lah thrashed to free her hands so she could use her ring, but she could not wriggle her fingers free. But because of her continuous struggle, the soldier, Lt. Flanagan, could only handcuff her hands to the front of her. As the soldiers pushed the struggling family out the ship's doorway, Lah remembered that she could use her thoughts to activate the ring to get herself out, but that would not help her children. Arak was a forward thinker and had already made her ring invisible. It was too powerful a tool to fall into the wrong hands. With her hands cuffed in front, she took a chance at moving one of the three dials on the ring. She was unsuccessful, so she inaudibly whispered the request to the ring. "What did you say?" the lieutenant snapped.

Lah did not answer that question but asked him a question instead. "I said what did you use on him?" Lah feared that whatever it was might have killed him.

"Trichloromethane, but you probably have no idea what that is," replied Flanagan.

Lah knew that he meant chloroform, and she also knew that if enough was used, it could be deadly to Themadorians.

Arriving in Crumb's office, the soldiers released them. "Ah, it's the Lelak family. How pleasant. He never mentioned he traveled with family, but I had my suspicions."

"What do you want from us? Lah angrily asked.

"Your mate was not very cooperative when last he and I met."

"What did you do to him?"

"Me? I didn't do anything. He simply refused to tell me about the ring he was wearing, so I sent him off to Area 55 to have it removed."

"What did they do to him? Is he dead? Did you kill him?" Lah stuttered as her eyes watered.

"Let me put it this way. Unless you want to suffer the same fate as your companion, you'll need to tell me about the ring. Lieutenant Flanagan, check her fingers and then her person for any similar ring," Crumb demanded.

Flanagan instructed the other soldiers to examine all three Themadorians for rings, none of which could be found.

"It was the only one of its kind. It's just a family heirloom. Why do you want it so desperately?" Lah asked.

Crumb explained it the same way he did to Lelak, "Research into the next technological marvel and advancement."

"What happened to Lelak?" Lah cried.

"Oh, he's dead. We have his ashes. Would you like them? We are currently analyzing them to see if we can replicate his morphing abilities, which our scientists have discovered while trying to get the ring off your partner's finger."

"He's d-d-dead? You k-k-killed him?" Lah stuttered.

"Oh, I did not kill him. According to my scientists, he died on the operating table. But the report has not been completed yet, so I do not know exactly how he died," Crumb unemotionally responded.

Lah, Arak and Etak wept.

"Tissue?" Crumb offered the grieving family. Lah took some and handed them to her children.

"Now, preliminary reports tell me that the ring was removed by cutting Lelak's ring finger off, but once they got it off the severed finger, it floated in the air and disappeared as your husband, I presume, turned to ashes," Crumb analytically explained.

As Crumb was interrogating Lah, Dr. Stewart was once again on the east side of the research office, listening through the same half open window as she did when Crumb interrogated Lelak.

"Which one of you is the son, gray or blue?" Crumb asked politely.

"I-I-I am, sir," Etak sputtered.

"Ah, such a polite boy. Lt. Flanagan, put this alien boy in the brig," ordered Crumb.

"Wait! No! What do you want from him?" Lah shouted.

"Ahh, collateral. Do you know what that means?" Crumb sarcastically asked, treating Lah like a child.

"I'm alien, not stupid," Lah explained as she gave him an eye roll. "Collateral for what?"

"For giving me information about that ring. First, what does it do? I know it must do something. Otherwise, your deceased husband would have told me, yet he was willing to die to protect its secret. Now, what does it do, and where did it go when it disappeared?"

Lah was afraid that Crumb would kill her son or torture all of them until he got the information he was seeking. "Fine, I will tell you since there is no way that you'll be able to use the ring. It is one of a kind."

"Very well. I'm listening," Crumb replied as he crossed his arms tightly, making his face look like a balloon ready to burst.

"First, the wearer must be righteous and noble, which would exclude you from those characteristics," Lah sarcastically declared.

"Your sardonic humor is appreciated. Proceed!"

"The three dials on the ring will impart three powers, upon request, to perform a task. The wearer would simply turn each dial, thus imparting a particular power to the wearer. One, two or three powers, depending on the wearer's request. It is limited to three. It was designed to help others in need. However, it will not work if the wearer is performing a task for his or her personal gain, which would apply to you as well, since I believe you want to be able to gain control over your adversaries," Lah enlightened her abductor.

"Quite perceptive, dear, um, lady! I knew it did something fantastical! And when I obtain it, and I *will* obtain it, I will modify it to conform to my needs. So with this knowledge of the ring's abilities and since it's the only one of its kind, I now have a little assignment for you and your daughter," Crumb calmly reassured himself.

"You said you would release my son if I gave you the information," yelled Lah.

"Oh, my dear, you did not let me finish my requirements for your son's release," Crumb imparted.

"You are a *nimaddog* liar," Lah erupted.

"I don't know what that word means, but I'll bet it shouldn't have been spoken in front of your impressionable children. Anyway, since you claim it's the only ring of its kind, your mission, if you choose to accept it—" Crumb laughed. "I always wanted to say that."

"I have no idea why you are laughing, but what about this task you want my daughter and me to complete?" Lah angrily growled with teeth clenched.

"Is to simply locate the ring that disappeared, return here and surrender it to me. Then, as agreed, I will release your son, and you can leave on your ship. I'll even offer to repair it, refuel it or provide whatever it needs."

"How do I know you are being truthful?" Lah questioned.

"Oh, you don't. I guess you'll just have to fulfill my demands and find out." Crumb sneered.

"I will get the ring for you. It will never fit you anyway. It will sense your evil immediately," Lah bellowed.

"But maybe it will fit. I'm sure I have ways of tricking it into thinking I am a noble and righteous being. How do you think I got into the position I am in now?" Crumb said unruffled.

"As for repairing my ship, I will never allow you to go near it. I have no trust in a human who finds pleasure in threatening me with the life of my son. If you are an example of the typical human on this planet, we will gladly leave this planet and warn others of the cruelty and viciousness of you…Earthlings. Upon our return, we will commence repairs on our ship, refuel and leave as fast as Themadorianly possible."

"Good. You have a fortnight to return with the ring. You can figure out what a fortnight is on your own since you're not, as you said, stupid," Crumb stipulated.

"I cannot return with just the ring. Its wearer must voluntarily take it off. I cannot guarantee that the wearer will do that. And why would a human just hand it over to me?"

"That's your problem, not mine. Get it to me in fourteen days in any way possible," grumbled Crumb. "I will also be gracious enough to give you this travel money—um…funds so one of the personnel here can get you transportation." He handed them a stack of currency. "Oh, and I advise that you two morph into something that will not bring attention to you."

Lah and Arak complied with his suggestion and began morphing. They both had seen humans on the database provided by Talock. So they had some ideas of what to morph into.

Lah chose a green-eyed, mid-thirties human female about five foot seven with brown cropped hair. She was a strikingly attractive female with a finely curved athletic figure. Crumb, of course, objectified her appearance. "Wow! If you weren't an alien, I'd do you!"

Lah replied with disgust, "Whatever that meant, I'm sure it was repulsive!"

Arak decided to morph into a seventeen-year-old petite young lady with brownish-black hair cut in a pixie style.

As the two finished morphing, Dr. Stewart walked in as if she had not heard a word.

"Oh, I'm sorry, sir. I told the soldiers out front that this was urgent, so they let me through. I apologize for the intrusion," Dr. Stewart explained.

"Is that the official report?' asked Crumb.

"Yes, sir, and my discharge papers that need to be signed."

"What? Why are you leaving? Has it been four years already?" Not waiting for an answer, he looked down at the discharge papers. "Hmm, why did General Ruppel only give you general discharge under honorable conditions and not an honorable discharge?" Crumb asked.

"We had some, let's say, professional and moral disagreements about the surgical procedures I performed."

Stewart knew that she could easily have General Ruppel court-martialed under the Uniform Code of Military Justice for killing the alien visitor, but Crumb would probably cover for his murder by claiming the alien was already dead or became violent during his capture. But since Lelak was now in a jar of ashes, it would be considered exculpatory evidence, the type that serves to either justify, excuse or introduce reasonable doubt about the defendant's alleged actions or intentions.

"Ha, morals! That's a joke," Crumb chuckled as he signed the discharge papers.

Dr. Stewart looked at the two disguised aliens in front of Crumb's desk. "Hello, I'm Dr. Stewart. And you are?"

Lah and Arak had to think quickly, but Crumb cut them off. "These are visitors taking a tour of the facilities, umm Olivia and her daughter, um Christine."

"Where are you both from?" Stewart asked.

Crumb again answered for them, "The same place you live which is...ahh..."

"Oh, Rosemont, New Mexico?" Dr. Stewart energetically said. "Would you two want to ride with me? You can give me directions as to where you live."

Crumb again interrupted, saying, "That would be greatly appreciated."

Lah and Arak, now officially Olivia and Christine, nervously nodded.

"Good! It's settled! Dr. Stewart will drive you to her hometown, and there you can begin searching."

Dr. Stewart looking puzzled asked, "Searching for what?"

Lah replied quickly, "An apartment to rent. We are new to this world…um…country and only have temporary housing, so we are looking for a forever home."

"Well, I'm recently single, living in a four-bedroom house. You are welcome to stay with me while you find an apartment. I have plenty of room," Dr. Stewart exclaimed.

"That's very generous of you. We would like that," Olivia gracefully accepted.

Crumb acknowledged, "Good, and as soon as you find what you are looking for, let me know, um, so I can send you an apartment-warming gift."

"It's about a two-hour drive from here, so we should get going. If you are hungry, we can stop to eat. By the way, how did you get here?"

Again, Crumb answered for the two aliens: "By Uber."

Dr. Stewart knew why Crumb kept replying to her questions but was not going to show her hand to Crumb or to the two visitors.

A military jeep took them to Dr. Stewart's vehicle, located in a special military parking lot near the base. All three exited the vehicle and entered the doctor's navy-blue SUV. Olivia and Christine were not sure how to enter the car, but Dr. Stewart opened both the passenger and back-seat doors for them. Smiling, they both entered, Olivia in the front and Christine in the back.

Once they were on their way, Dr. Stewart, knowing who they really were, conveyed to them what had happened to Lelak and what she witnessed in the lab. "I was shocked at what the general had done and vowed to myself that he would eventually be brought up on charges. I've had my suspicions even before the general murdered your husband. Oh, and don't worry! I know your secret and what you have to do for that creep Crumb. While you are living with me, your name will be Olivia Stewart, my sister-in-law, whose husband, my brother, died during a surgical procedure. And your daughter will be Christine Stewart, my niece, who will be starting at Rosemont High School as soon as we get back to town."

Olivia spoke, "Why are you doing this for us?"

"I want to work with you to find the ring Crumb is after and develop a plan to make sure he never gets it. While I was eavesdropping, I had heard your conversation with him about the ring having special abilities that you do not want Crumb to use."

"That's correct. That ring is very powerful when used to help, but I am afraid Crumb will convert it to use as a way for him to gain more power. The ring was not designed for personal gain, but this Crumb character seems smart enough to pervert it."

"Well, we will not let that happen, okay?"

As the three of them drove through the Chihuahuan Desert and eventually along the El Capitan to their destination of the small suburban town of Rosemont and, finally, to Dr. Stewart's apartment in Rosemont Estates, Olivia explained to Dr. Stewart how the ring worked and how only those who were morally just and righteous could use its powers.

"How will you ever locate the ring? It could have traveled thousands of miles away or maybe just a few miles away," Dr. Stewart inquired.

Olivia explained, "I'm not familiar about how the ring travels after the death of the wearer, but it has a tracking device similar to your GPS devices. The rings are calibrated to keep in sync in case one ring is lost or, in this case, was surgically removed, as you said."

"But you don't have another ring," Dr. Stewart emphasized.

As the doctor was driving, Olivia raised her left hand, which had no ornamental band. But slowly a ring materialized on Olivia's finger.

"So that's why Crumb couldn't see you had a ring. You made it invisible."

"Yes, I was able to instruct the ring to make itself invisible by turning a dial and whispering to it," Olivia acknowledged. "It was to protect us from the evil it had sensed in the military police and eventually Crumb. It would not protect us itself. It had to be asked for protection by requesting it to become invisible."

"You are very smart. Do all you…um…what do you call yourselves?"

"Themadorians," Olivia responded, helping the doctor complete her sentence.

"Themadorians have superior intellect?" Dr. Stewart asked.

"Before the Era of the Great Gasses, no one thought of themselves as superior or inferior, just equal," Olivia clarified. "We were simply Themadorians."

She explained their history to the good doctor to help her understand what had happened on their planet.

"We humans could learn from what you have experienced, but there are so many skeptics spreading conspiracy theories and disinformation that no one bothers to search for facts anymore, and anyone who tries to expose the facts is silenced by people of wealth and power, similar to Crumb," Dr. Stewart elaborated as she enlightened her two passengers. "But first, we have to create a story about you two so you can pass off as humans. I'll also have to quickly teach you the necessities of becoming independent so you can begin your search as I protect you both on your quest. You'll need identification, driver's licenses and school records, among other necessary certifications, and you'll need to learn some of the traditional American holidays and customs including the many diverse traditions celebrated by many immigrants this country. This will enable both of you to walk about freely without seeming suspicious. I'll have my work cut out for me, so as soon as we get to my house, we'll have to act fast. There is a lot to learn. Are you quick learners?"

Both Lah and Arak, as Olivia and Christine, looked at each other, smiled and nodded their heads!

CHAPTER FOUR

Discovery

Immediately following Lelak's death

Rob Shehan's journey to his version of the Fortress of Solitude—though not as grandiose or concealed and, of course, not in the Antarctic—had been an easy one. With a simple walk up a short paved road into a wooded area only a half mile from his house, he had arrived at his usual quiet spot. Rob sat on the same large rotted-out log he always sat on when he wanted to get his writing assignments done or simply simmer his anger from a bullying incident that occurred at school. The limited woodsy area had broken branches scattered throughout among piles of moribund autumn leaves, with the rustle of chipmunks and squirrels rooting in underbrush, insects humming and whirling in the decay of forgotten leaves and solitary unknown species of flowers strewn throughout the brown-and-orange arras, barely moving in the light breeze.

Rob had also frequented this serene area to get away from his mother's incessant belittling of his father, who had worked so hard for his family but had received no appreciation from his wife for the hours of intense labor he endured every weekday. However, his mother's harassment had extended to Rob and his sisters as well. It had reminded him of the bullying he had suffered from the same tormentor during middle school. Unfortunately, that same tormentor had continued pestering him even in his senior year. Rob had felt that he had not deserved this endless torture. Was it his quiet demeanor, his lack of high athletic ability or his lack of more fashionable attire? Rob had never really understood it. But why would his own mother brutalize him and his family?

Nevertheless, surrounded by the chirping of the birds, rustling of the leaves and the other harmonious sounds in his seclusion, he could try to clear his mind of all those worries. He needed it for full concentration of his task at hand: another senior elective writing assignment. He began, with a notebook of his incomplete mind mapping, for developing a two-hundred-and-fifty-word essay about a hero he wanted to study. Once that was completed, he could begin a rough draft on his laptop at home. Staring up at the myriad of tree branches crossing in front of the sun, he began.

In the world we live in, most guys, especially at my age, seem to pick athletes. I don't understand why. If they were overcoming fears or obstacles that they endured when they were younger, that would make more sense. But how do I distinguish a real hero from a phony one, especially in these complicated times? I guess the first thing to consider is their motive, I suppose. I think genuine heroes seek to first overcome a fear, then maybe help or serve others but not to acquire fortune or fame. True heroes are caring, compassionate, and moral individuals who want to save or improve people's lives, independent of what external rewards may come their way.

Then Rob's ADD kicked in. *Why is it always a 250-word essay? Maybe I can write about my dad or Uncle Bob. Then again, perhaps someone from the entertainment industry.* Rob's ideas were coming in too fast for him to write down. *How about Jim Henson, the creator of the* Muppets? That's when Rob pulled out his smartphone and started doing a quick search for Henson. He learned that along with *Sesame Street* founders Joan Ganz Cooney and Lloyd Morrissett, Henson had wanted to help prepare disadvantaged children for school. According to an article he found, it had been the time of the civil rights movement of the '60s and the war on poverty that had motivated them to create children's television. Maybe he could write about all three. But did they have obstacles or fears they overcame that made them heroes? Rob reconsidered.

DISCOVERY

Then Rob thought of Harry Chapin. He had learned about this singer and songwriter of the '70s when he had visited his grandmother once a week. His uncle Bob, who had always lived with Rob's grandmother, was always playing Chapin music whenever Rob had visited her. His uncle had told him about the singer, songwriter and storyteller and about the causes he was passionate about.

Once again, Rob conducted a preliminary search and found that Chapin co-founded, along with a radio DJ named Bill Ayres, the Why Hunger Organization in 1975 on the fundamental belief that access to nutritious food was a human right and that hunger was a solvable problem in a world of abundance. And after he read more articles about Harry, Rob realized that the singer and advocate had a lot of obstacles to conquer and that Harry would be a strong possibility for his choice. But Rob wanted to make sure he had as many options as possible before deciding.

Rob also thought of choosing a fictional character, most probably a superhero—someone who had powers to help fight crime, save people from disasters or prevent violence. But was his teacher only looking for real-life heroes? It had seemed to Rob that his Creative Writing 401 teacher, Ms. Mia Digit (whose name sounded like "my digits") would be open-minded to a fictional character, even a comic book character, as a person to embody. He could convince his teacher that he wouldn't be emulating superheroes for their special powers but for their moral stance and values. *Maybe that's what Digit was looking for.* The goal of this writing was to find a hero that he could use to focus on his own morals and values. He knew that he could never achieve the exaggerated physical attributes of a fictional superhero even though his uncle Bob told Rob that he looked a lot like Clark Kent with his thick, wavy blackish-brown hair. But maybe he could at least encapsulate the hero's character traits and moral compass. He recognized that his choice would have to be narrowed down from many superheroes of the innumerable characters in the comic books that he continued to read and collect even at seventeen. *I can thank Uncle Bob for that since, even at forty years old, Uncle Bob still bought and read comics.*

Rob remembered how he had become enthralled with comics as early as five years old. He recalled his uncle Bob bringing stacks of comics from his uncle's workplace, Key Drug Mart, to his grandmother's house where his family frequented every Sunday.

Whenever they had visited his *sitto*, his family's equivalent to a *Nana* or *Grammy*, the first thing Rob would do upon arrival was kiss Sitto hello and ask permission to get some comics from his uncle Bob's bedroom. Once granted, Rob would make a mad dash upstairs, bring a small stack down from the lopsided pile of comics on his uncle's bedside table and flop down in the family room's oversized chair at the bottom back corner of the staircase to delve into them. He had realized as he got older that those comics of yesteryear were not as vocabulary intense, plot-complicated or graphically violent as the comics on the comic racks now, but they helped him acquired his love for reading.

Enough daydreaming. Rob shook his head to clear out those fond memories for now. He added to his mind map some comic heroes he admired since he was familiar with them, and it wouldn't require much research. If Ms. Digit, who would need to authorize his choice, decided she wanted Rob to pick a real person, he would fall back on his other choices.

As he jotted down countless heroes that came to mind, he eliminated some of them for various reasons—anger issues, cockiness, impulsivity, violence or vengefulness. But he had questioned whether it had been necessary to pick a hero that was perfect. No hero was flawless, but he wanted to pick one that was as close as possible to one he would like to emulate.

Feeling frustrated with how to proceed, he decided to walk through the woods and talk to himself, weighing the pros and cons of his possible choices, hoping for a revelation. Watching where he was stepping, Rob had been carefully rambling through the woods of entangled vines, exposed tree roots and poison ivy since he did not want an injury prior to his upcoming theater performance at Rosemont High School.

Hollowed-out acorns had been scattered over the orange-red-and-brown decomposed leaves as he had heard the cracking undergrowth with each step through the fresh weeds growing right through the piles of compressed and flattened foliage.

As he continued his aimless journey, he noticed a small pile of dead leaves quivering like a scared puppy on his way to the vet. As he approached the pile, he heard a clicking sound accompanying the vibration. Rob, thinking it might be a hidden click beetle or some other insect, brushed the leaves and debris away to find someone's ring lying next to a hollowed acorn that had been vibrating in unison, causing the clicking sound. It was the same three-tone wooden-like ring on Lelak's finger, with the three brown variations on the combination lock dial, symbols instead of numbers and silver bands separating each dial. The only difference was that the interior's circumference had what looked like wet phosphorescent light-gray paint inside it. As it continued to vibrate, Rob picked it up and tried rubbing it off with his thumb. He succeeded in getting all of it off. However, the light-gray liquid attached to his thumb and then absorbed into his skin and disappeared like water being sucked into toweling paper.

"What the…" Rob thought out. "How the hell does paint get absorbed into skin?" *I've had paint on my hands in art class, but it never absorbed into my skin like this. It would leave a stain but not soak into my skin with no indication of it ever being there. In fact, I had to vigorously scrub regular art paint off in the slop sink in the classroom, and even then, some outline of it remained.* He tried shaking his hand and wiping his finger where the fluid had disappeared, but to no avail. The paint-like substance was gone.

At this point, the dials had been spinning rapidly with no perceivable pattern. Rob struggled to get the vibrations and the spinning dials to stop, but he was unsuccessful. The vibrations almost caused it to fly out of Rob's hand, but with his quick reflexes from playing video games at the local arcade, he was able to grab it before it got away. He held it tight in his hands, but the vibrations continued, tingling the inside of his fist, reminding him of how his elbow felt when he accidentally hit his funny bone. He thought that placing it on his finger would stop the vibration and keep it from escaping. He thought it would be implausible if it fit his finger or even stop the vibrating. He wiped off the debris of dried-bug-embedded mud from the outside of the ring and placed it on his left ring finger. As he tried to slide it on, he wondered who could lose a ring and not notice, unless it was too big to begin with. It slid on easily since it was about one size too large for his finger. *Ah, that's the reason it fell off! It was too large. But who would wear a ring that was oversized?* But once on, the ring shrunk to fit his finger perfectly, with a little wiggle room for comfort.

"Shit! What the hell?" *If Mom ever saw me place something on my hand that wasn't doused with a disinfectant spray, she'd bless herself and scream her go-to word,* Yeeeeee, *so loudly that it would decalcify my spinal column.*

Almost immediately his body tingled and ached as he had looked at the ring, but as he did, he watched something strange happening to his hand. There was movement under his skin that looked like small ball bearings on an assembly line traveling up and down, causing his hands and then his arms to shift and reshape in size, color and texture. He panicked, thinking he was infested with a flesh-eating bacterium and that tiny scarabaei were feasting on his innards. He felt the skin of his face tingling and moving as if he was purposely contorting his appearance.

As he looked down at the ring, the three dials on the ring spun, two clockwise and one counterclockwise. The dials stopped on a combination of strange white symbols. He had no idea what those symbols were or what was going on with his body. He panicked and started to shake it off like shaking off ants crawling onto him at a family picnic. That didn't help, so he tried taking it off. But he couldn't get it over his middle knuckle. *What the hell is happening to me?* That's when he nervously took out his iPhone, touched the camera icon on the home screen, opened the camera app and reversed the lens as if taking a selfie. He needed to find out why his face felt so funny.

Once he had looked, he screamed in disbelief. This wasn't his face; it was a mix between a half-shaven cowboy and a very tan Ken doll, which he actually thought would be more attractive to females, but this did not decrease his level of shock. *These aren't my hands.* He watched them hold his phone. He looked down at his legs and feet. His legs were more muscular than usual, causing his denim pants to expand as well. And his arms and chest had swelled, expanding his shirt without ripping it. *Why the hell aren't my clothes ripping?* He had become quite muscular, resembling the drawings of those superbeings in the movies and comics who miraculously got beefier when they received their superpowers. Rob had always thought that that was weird. *No exercise or weight lifting, just instant muscles and abs.*

While he felt his pants continue to expand without ripping, something else had been as well. This gave him an emotional mixture of fear and delight. His member was bigger as well, and a strange thought came to him. *Male superheroes seem to have no bulge in that area, not to mention flimsy to nonexistent groin protection.* He looked under his stretched-out pants and underwear to confirm that it was indeed larger. He had to rearrange his goods because his manhood began to feel uncomfortable in its current position and size. *I knew I should have started switching to boxers.*

Then, while still in shock at his appearance and still looking at his new face on his phone, a text message dropped down from the top of the screen like a news notification but in a bizarre language, a cross between computerese and a wingding font. The message sender's name was indecipherable as well.

He wondered if there was a remote chance that Google Translate could help decode the symbols. He tried, but of course, it did not. *How could it not translate the symbols? Are they hieroglyphics? Ancient unknown symbols from thousands of years ago?* He was panicking and had been trying to come up with some idea of what to do. Rob needed to find out if this message was for him or whether he was the recipient of a text message scam or maybe even a phone virus. The only other idea he had was to see if he could copy the message onto a text document on his phone, highlight the phrase and continually change the font until an understandable sentence appeared. As he proceeded, each of the fonts did not create any meaningful message. He continued pouring over more than two dozen fonts until he came across the second-to-the-last font named Visitor, which he never used before. When he changed the font of the message to the font Visitor, the message was being revealed: "Please place your communication device on the ground and prepare for a live transmission."

"What the hell!" Rob didn't just place the phone on the ground. He quickly opened his hands in disbelief and dropped it onto a small pile of dried leaves. Once on the ground, the phone's screen lit up with a distorted display of jagged lines combined with a snowy background, like the old TVs that people used to have when a channel went off the air in the early '70s. Then an image began to appear faintly through the flurry on the screen. A blue-gray ghostly projection similar to the hologram of Princess Leia projected by R2-D2 in the first *Star Wars* movie lightly projected from the phone and materialized in front of Rob. He had a difficult time focusing on the image since he could still see the trees and foliage through the blue aura. Rob squinted to focus on what looked like the stereotypically oversized alien head with black almond-shaped eyes with no pupils, a nostril-less nose and a narrow line for a mouth, but it was in a hoodie that covered its ears and a robe that shadowed some of the minuscule details. As the picture became clearer and the background decreased in translucence, the image began to speak.

"You have found one of the rings of Themadoria. I am Kralc Tenk, the guardian of the ring you have discovered. I am communicating with you through the ring in your native language using its built-in universal translator. I've been monitoring a community of Themadorians who specialize in methods of mutual cooperation and trust. I have watched and observed their activities from the tunnels and caves below the surface of their planet. The New-Co-op Themadorians, who now live below the surface of our planet, are a mixture of scientists, engineers, archaeologists, historians, builders and other specialists in their particular field. That ring you are wearing was accidentally discovered by Lelak Nadroj, son of Noj and Ahtram, and his wife, Lah. Noj and Ahtram are two of the archaeologists on their planet."

Rob was gasping for air in an anxiety-induced asthma attack from what was happening. He immediately reached into his side pocket to retrieve his inhaler and quickly took two puffs. "So y-y-you are, like, the g-g-genie of the ring?" stuttered Rob, still in disbelief in what he was seeing.

"No, not like a genie, so don't start rubbing it again or asking for wishes. Its last wearer, Lelak Nadroj, was one of the individuals who had to escape our planet with his wife and children due to the civil war between the blue Themadorians and the gray Themadorians who were affected by the Era of the Great Gasses and landed on your planet accidentally."

"Ha, ha! Civil war, blue and the gray. I get it. Great joke."

"I am not joking!" Kralc sternly replied.

Taken aback, Rob embarrassedly said, "I'm sorry. I thought this may have been some practical joke that my best friend, Tommy, would pull. He is a technological genius. I thought maybe he had hacked my phone."

"THIS IS NO JOKE!" Kralc yelled. "Now are you ready to listen?"

Rob stuttered, "Yes, sir, M-M-Mr. T-T-Tank, sir."

"It's Tenk, not Tank. May I continue, please?"

"Please," Rob timidly replied.

"As I was saying, Lelak Nadroj and his family unfortunately ran out of algal biofuel due to a leak in the fuselage when traveling at hypersonic warp and crashed on your planet. Since I am the guardian of the ring, I was able to follow them throughout their travels using a method you would not understand. They survived the crash, but the ship's door cracked open and would have revealed the interior, had it not been hidden by their cloaking device."

As Kralc projected images of the ship, Rob noticed that it was not the saucer-shaped type of vessels that he had seen on television. It looked more like a long, slightly flattened geode with shale pieces all over. Geodes usually crack open, revealing a sparkly crystalized hollow interior; however, the inside of this ship was more like a pop-out birthday card, where the interior expanded when opened. The center was sparkling inside like the interior of a macadamized rock but with flashing lights, various consoles of levers and buttons like his gaming system, but it was definitely not hollow.

Kralc continued as Rob kept watching the projection. "Lelak Nadroj, who hit his head upon crashing, was foggy headed and could not use his ring quick enough to avoid capture by your military police. They commandeered the spacecraft and placed it in something called Hanger 84. I lost contact with the ship once it was inside the hangar. While his family hid in a secret annex, whose door could only be seen with Themadorian eyes, Lelak was attacked and chloroformed. Since large amounts of chloroform are deadly to their people, Lelak Nadroj would not be able to be resuscitated properly unless he was given water to expel enough of the poison to survive. My sensors were somehow blocked when they took Lelak into the facility. Not sure what was causing it, but I lost contact with him. The ring was somehow removed, which I thought was virtually impossible since the ring does not come off the wearer's finger even upon death—unless the wearer removes it or it is surgically removed."

"So how did the ring end up in my woods?' Rob questioned. He called it his woods because it was never used by others to contemplate and relax. It was similar to friends calling a sports team their team even though they didn't have ownership.

"Do you always interrupt someone before they are finished explaining?" Kralc sarcastically asked.

"Oops! I did it again, didn't I? Sorry! I thought you were done." Rob apologized as his ADD kicked in. *Why am I thinking of Britney Spears right now?*

"Anyway, if the ring was removed in that manner, it would transport itself to a random location on the current planet the wearer was on in hopes of finding another deserving creature. This has apparently already happened since you have found it and placed it on your finger. If you were not worthy of the ring, it would have never fit on any of your fingers."

Rob spoke, "Wait! Is this a recording or a live transmission from outer space?"

"As I mentioned earlier, it is a live transmission, similar to your world's streaming services. So I can respond to your questions, and you can receive my answers when a question is posed in real time."

"From where is it being transmitted, and how do you know about streaming services?" Rob inquired.

The hologram sternly replied, "Besides interrupting, you are not a very good listener, are you? One of the rings of Themadoria, so I'm therefore transmitting from…"

"Oh, sorry, Themadoria," Rob replied stupidly.

Kralc Tenk responded to the second question. "How I know about your planet's streaming services is irrelevant to what the purpose of your mission will be. And since you don't seem to be retaining much of what I have said, I'd rather get right to the mission."

"Yeah, I have a moderate case of attention deficit disorder. On Earth we call it ADD. That's why… Wait, what? Mission? What mission? I'm seventeen! I'm too young to have a mission! If anything, my mission is to have fun, graduate, attend college, get a job, meet a nice girl, maybe get married and raise a family and hopefully be prosperous," Rob assumed. Of course, experiencing his parents' marriage, he was reconsidering matrimony or ever having children.

"This mission is so much more important than that. You can still fulfill those dreams, goals, quests or whatever you want to call them because you would also be helping people in need, saving your kind from accidents, dangers and other forms of bodily harm. This ring has abilities to help the wielder perform actions to protect, defend and preserve the health and safety of your fellow beings and oneself. Its powers are only limited by the user's imagination."

"You didn't mention this weird transformation that occurred when I put the ring on."

Kralc replied, "I can't explain that unless…"

"Unless what?" Rob questioned, frightened.

"Was there any unusual residue on the ring that you may have had contact with?" Kralc nervously inquired.

"Umm, yeah, some light-gray paint or something. When I tried to rub it off, which I thought came off far too easily for paint, it got on my thumb, and then it seemed to seep into it. Am I going to catch some alien disease or permanently be disfigured?"

Kralc looked down and sighed, "I was afraid of that."

"Afraid of what?" Rob's voice raised an octave.

"Themadorians have natural morphing powers that help them with adapting to changes in their planet's altering environment. It's a safety feature all Themadorians used to have in the Era of the Co-op, but after that time period, what is called the 'Era of the Great Gasses,' it was only used to hide one's identity through the morphing of one's face, body and even fingerprints."

"But I'm not a Themadorian. Why would I have it?"

"The ring never had that property before, but I theorize that if the ring was surgically taken from Lelak by your planet's military doctors, it was stained with his Themadorian blood, which stays wet for hours. Since it remained on the ring and you tried to rub it off, it may have leached into your skin, thus having your body absorb Lelak's morphing ability. Please understand that this is only a theory. Morphing may now be part of the ring's ability, to morph the wearer when necessary to conceal the wearer's true appearance. Similar to a defense mechanism of a chameleon when it camouflages its skin to hide from predators, the ring may deem it necessary to change your appearance, choosing any age, shape, size or gender it deems fit to protect its wearer. However, it also may not be part of the ring's ability. You may also have that capability without it."

"Cool, like a secret identity! That would be so... Wait! What? Gender? I could morph into a girl?"

Kralc once again cleared his throat. "I thought you people believed in being gender neutral or nonbinary."

"How do you know that?" Rob questioned.

"You seemed shocked that I have that knowledge. You see, I have already picked up much of your historical background, your technological advances and pop culture references telepathically since you put on the ring as it transmits your planet's information to me," Kralc responded.

"I don't have all the planet's information in my brain. You must have picked up all of it through my phone. At seventeen, I am still learning," Rob clarified.

"Nevertheless, it is information necessary for having the ability to relate to you,"

"Relate to me? No one relates to teens except other teens," Rob retorted.

"It's called empathy, and your people need more of it."

"You can say that again."

"It's called empathy and your people need more of it," Kralc repeated.

"Stop that! It was rhetorical!" Rob exclaimed.

"Oh, I figured that with your ADD, you needed it repeated." Kralc grinned.

"Not funny!" Rob told Kralc sarcastically.

"We do believe in gender neutrality, but that's a choice for us. And besides, I feel comfortable being a guy," Rob whimpered thinking of the Brad Paisley song "I'm Still a Guy."

"But if you wish not to have it decide a gender, it should pick up on your choice, or you can simply ask it. But I must warn you. Even though it will morph you when you request a power, it will not automatically protect you from attacks or other dangers that could be encountered unless a protection power is requested. That's where you come in. The three dials on the ring will impart three powers required to perform a task by simply turning the dial and requesting a power. You may turn one dial and use one power or turn two or three dials in any combination to call upon one, two or all three powers. If the bearer cannot determine the particular power needed, then the ring may determine the appropriate power to bestow. You can ask for the powers to protect you or others as well."

"But what if I can't turn the dials? Suppose my hands are indisposed?"

"The ring must be dialed in order for powers to be activated," replied Kralc. "However, I theorize that Lelak's blood combined with your human blood may enable you to use your thoughts to activate your requested powers, but again, it's—"

Rob interrupted with "Only a theory, I know."

"You may experiment with that possibility, but once again, be cautioned. The ring will not work if you are performing a task for personal gain, and since the ring allowed you to wear it, it felt you were noble and righteous and that you would not use its abilities for your own private use or profit."

"You talk like the ring is an organism," Rob stated.

"It may very well seem that way at times, but I have not run though any diagnostics to investigate that theory. Be that as it may, do you understand the power of this ring and how to use it?"

"I think so!"

"Good. Before I end this transmission, do you have any questions?"

"Yes, do all Themadorians have rings?"

"No, these were unique rings that were discovered by Lelak and Lah Nadroj. On Themadoria, Lelak and Lah were archaeologists like Lelak's parents, studying the Themadorians' history after the Era of the Great Gasses since most of the underground refugees had long passed on, and those born of these refugees had little knowledge of the crisis, similar to your lack of intimate knowledge of, let's say, your World Wars. They needed to impart that knowledge to each generation in their underground society."

"So kinda like school?" Rob interjected.

"Yes. Anyway, Lelak and Lah Nadroj had hoped to discover the mystery behind the two different colors of Themadorians and eventually a cure so that their people, the Unaffected, could return to the surface and share the findings for reversing the effects of the gasses.

"One day, while recording their findings with their fellow underground Themadorians and continuing their work with the scientists and other archaeologists living in their covert society, they accidentally came upon rings embedded in various hanging stalactites in an abandoned dig. Unaware of the rings' abilities, they spent one of your Earth's cycles freeing the rings from the hanging rock. While carefully and methodically chipping away so as not to damage the rings, they did discover something more important, their affection for each other through mutual cooperation and respect, what you Earth people would call love."

"That's really corny, don't you think?" Rob chuckled.

Kralc paused and stared at Rob with an expressionless countenance, then continued. "They eventually espoused in a clandestine hybrid union because Lelak was gray and his wife, Lah Nadroj, was a blue Themadorian. Lelak and Lah wore the rings as a sign of their union. During their time underground, they conceived two offspring, a blue daughter, Arak, and a gray son, Etak.

"Since all Themadorians on our planet had protective morphing abilities prior to the Era of the Great Gasses, Lelak and Lah remained part of the Unaffected after the EGG. To protect themselves in case they were exposed to the land above, Lah morphed gray, and surprisingly, her daughter did the same. Some offspring of a blended union may or may not have inherited their parents' transformational ability due to the EGG. These color transformations were to cover up their mixed marriage. It had not been determined whether Etak could morph.

"Their community agreed to sacrifice their only spaceship, which was built entirely underground, so that Lelak and Lah's family could have a future on whatever planet they decided to inhabit. Due to their experiences on Themadoria after the EGG, the Unaffected Themadorian family decided to look for a planet whose inhabitants were open to the art of a third alternative, had cleaner air, water and soil, and had the means to control their industry from making the same mistakes the Themadorians had made. The planet had to have righteous creatures displaying honesty, altruistic abilities, empathy and righteousness. After careful consideration, they agreed to set their sights on a planet thirty light-years away from Themadoria, the planet called Proteus 9, known for their hospitality, wisdom and cooperative nature. The planet had never seen war, pestilence or environmental strife. Proteus 9 had the closest characteristics of life on Themadoria. They had hoped to settle there until the inhabitants could share how they were able to control their industrial progress to avoid Themadoria's current situation.

"With the help of the communal family, they were able to negotiate its use even though it was a project that had never been tested for long journeys. To avoid the surface dwellers' detection, it remained naturally cloaked behind the once clear, clean Aragain waterfalls. However, due to the contaminated dregs of the soil erosion into the water supplies, the black oily Aragain waterfalls flowed over the cavern instead, effectively hiding the ship.

"Last-minute preparations were commencing by testing the cloaking device, setting up the backup battery generator, filling the fuel tank with algal biofuel using a fractional distillation system and checking the ship's replicators. The built-in replicators made synthetic food, which, unfortunately, lacked the nutrients of the vegetation of the planet on which the Themadorians used to thrive, but it sufficed for their journey. Thanking their community for sacrificing their only ship, now artificially cloaked, the four soared off the planet, undetected by the Affected Themadorians living on the surface.

"On their journey, I decided to contact Lelak and Lah the same way I am communicating with you, by lightly vibrating the rings and emitting the same projection you are watching in front of you. I, of course, explained the properties of the rings to them and how to use them."

Rob was enthralled. "Will I eventually turn into a Themadorian because I absorbed Lelak's blood?" questioned Rob in a very serious tone.

The projection responded, "I don't know. I believe the little amount of blood you absorbed would probably not transform you like in your vampire or werewolf movies, but—"

"Don't say it. Don't say it!" Rob begged.

"It's only a theory," Kralc finished.

"I asked you not to say that!" Rob sighed. Rob pondered whether he could make a difference by helping shape the future of the world—well, maybe not the entire world but his small part of it—with this ring's ability. "Can I get in contact with you if I need help or screw things up?" Rob timidly asked.

"I'm not Yoda, and you're not Luke. So, no!" Kralc smirked as he answered, proud that he was able to reference *Star Wars* from his empathic connection to Rob.

"Again, not funny!" Rob exasperatedly rolled his eyes. He then embarrassedly replied, "Sorry for my rudeness. This is a bit overwhelming! Actually, it's a lot overwhelming. Will the ring give me an idea of what powers I should ask for when helping people in need?"

"I believe I had explained that to you earlier. I sure hope the ring has chosen the right...um...human, I believe you are called. I will leave you now with this. There are others. Keep Roswell, New Mexico, in mind. I wish you the best for your sake and the sake of your planet. Good luck."

The blue haze of the hologram began to fade when Rob yelled, "Wait, don't leave yet. What do you mean others? Other rings? Other people with a ring? Are they located in Roswell, New Mexico? Why did I morph without even using the ring?"

But unfortunately for Rob, the hologram projection faded, and his phone returned to its home screen, covered in apps.

Crap! Leaving me with more questions than answers and no user manual. I can't do much without a user's manual, Rob angrily thought, knowing full well that he needed specific instructions for everything, including building a bookcase, cooking and sometimes using new software. *Well, not software. No one ever reads those manuals or their agreement policies.*

Rob sat back on a dead tree limb as he tried to wrap his mind around this whole occurrence. *This cannot be real. This did not just happen. And who is going to believe me? What do I do now?*

As Rob began fiddling with the ring, he observed his arms as they began to return to his original, less-than-muscular form. His pants, which were stretched out, shrunk to the size they were when he put them on in the morning. Rob exhaled a sigh of relief, looking down at his pants. *At least they didn't rip. How would I have explained my transformation to my parents if I didn't return to my normal shape and size? With someone else's face, they'd have probably called the police, thinking I was an intruder.*

I wonder if I should test the ring, questioned Rob, doubting the ring's ability. He was actually afraid to begin using it without an actual need.

He decided to leave the wooded area where he spent most of the afternoon, and foggy and unfocused, he began walking home. He had been looking at the ring and contemplating. *Maybe I should choose the Green Lantern as my hero for my essay. He fought evil with the aid of a ring that granted him a variety of extraordinary powers, all of which came from his imagination. But those powers only created constructs and didn't really give him superpowers. He did use it to protect others but also fight against aggressors. I have no intention of trying to do that with the ring.* Rob laughed how peculiar it was that all of Green Lantern's creations were green and transparent. *I guess it didn't really matter since he accomplished his goal.* He began doubting himself and was followed by a myriad of questions. *Would this ring do the same thing? Would I be able to create structures with the ring? Would it require recharging, like the Green Lantern's ring?* The Green Lantern had to decide very quickly the right type of structure to create for the situation. *Can I think that fast? Maybe I should think of it as ad-libbing onstage.* Then his ADD kicked in. *Do the dials need oiling or spraying with an emollient to keep the dials from sticking? Why didn't I ask these questions to Kralc when he asked me?* Rob scolded himself as he walked. *All I could think of was whether I would turn into a Themadorian! I have so many more questions now that I've had time to think about them.*

Rob had started speed-walking home, thinking about the possible uses of this ring, how he would know when to help people by using its power or what powers to ask for, but he worried more about his mom yelling at him for being late. He soon forgot about his creative-writing assignment. He now had new anxieties he thought he'd never have.

CHAPTER FIVE

Almost a Beta Test

By the time Rob arrived at his house—which was in the small village of Rosemont, New Mexico, in the county of Lincoln near the Capitan Mountains—he heard his mother from the kitchen.

"Wipe your feet, take your shoes off and wash your hands."

Rob replied, "I know. I know. You say it every time I come home. I'm surprised you didn't say 'Close the door. You don't live in a barn.'" *Since it's still quite light out, that phrase makes no sense to me because farmers often left the barn doors open most of the day in the spring until sunset for the livestock on pasture.*

"Don't get snide with me, young man. Do as I say," she bellowed.

While washing his hands and staring at the ring covered in soap suds, he thought of each possible maneuver to hide the ring as best he could. He thought of covering it with his right hand, placing his left hand on his lap while eating or even putting his hand in his pocket. There was a small possibility that his newly acquired ornament would not even be noticed.

His mother had finished cooking dinner while his father had been snoozing on the deep, cushioned, reupholstered flowery chair in the living room after an exhausting day's work as a carpet installer. His father was a hard worker, starting his own carpet business after working freelance at various companies for years. Not only was he excellent at his job, with so many people recommending him, but he was also amazing at math. He never used a calculator, to Rob's knowledge, when estimating a job. Even though his father was great with numbers, Rob's mother controlled the finances and what appeared to be everything else in their lives. But his father had been smart enough to place some cash in his wallet for himself.

Still, his father, Lou (or Louie), really was his hero. *Maybe I should write about Dad,* Rob considered. He had all the qualities Rob loved. He was kind, friendly, easygoing, nonjudgmental and physically strong, and he had a great sense of humor. His jacked arms had been developed from lifting rolls of carpet from the carpet warehouse to his truck, then from his truck to the job site, then into the room or rooms being carpeted. His almost-bald head and slight paunch did not deter from his pleasant disposition, as demonstrated by his wonderful whistling. He'd whistle whenever he was outside doing yard work, inside reading the newspaper or just getting ready for work. He loved whistling tunes from the radio, and Rob would frequently try to guess the song he was whistling as he joined along with him. They would even whistle together when they sat at the dinner table, but his mother had a dumb rule about whistling.

"No whistling at the dinner table!" grouched his mother.

Rob mumbled to himself, "Why? Did someone with lousy whistling ruin it for everyone else?" His father heard him and stifled a laugh. Rob had wondered why his mother had been so miserable all the time. As requested—or rather, demanded—he and his father stopped and quietly sat at the dinner table. *No need to upset She-Hulk. Actually, She-Hulk would have been an insult to Jennifer Walters, She-Hulk's alter-ego, since she was a lawyer. Mom is far from that!*

"Hey, Dad, how was work?" Rob asked, trying to lighten the mood.

"It was good. It's exhausting, laying carpet every day, but that's how I get my daily exercise," his father responded.

"Um, Dad, try saying 'installing carpet' from now on. You don't lay it!" Rob chuckled as his mother gave him a disgusted look.

"Ha! Ha! I never thought of it that way!" His father guffawed.

With that laugh, they finished dinner, and everyone went their separate ways. Rob and his sisters had gone to their rooms to work on the evening's homework assignments. It was a requirement from the matriarch.

As Rob sat at his old scratched oak desk, he considered his father as the subject of his writing assignment. After a few minutes, though, he felt uneasy about his father being his hero. Lou was very passive and quite henpecked. He didn't stand up for himself when dealing with his wife. And Rob's mother had not only been belittling to him but also to Rob and his sisters. His father lacked the emotional strength to deal with his wife, being so wearied from the physical work that was required each day. The insults that Rob's mother would use on his father were so demeaning that Rob wanted to yell at his mother to leave his father alone, but he knew if he did, it would make things worse. And it would probably result in his restricted use of the family car on the weekends. He couldn't risk that personal sacrifice.

Rob's mother, Tilly (whose real name was Matilda), wanted people to call her Lee for some odd reason. Even calling her by the wrong name agitated her. She constantly threatened Rob and his sisters if they didn't do what they were told, but she hardly ever followed through on those threats. Carmella, Mariam, Lou and Rob had been trying to learn how to tune her out since her threats were meaningless, but it had seemed as though only their father had been able to perfect that skill. That skill was demonstrated by his father every day as he read the newspaper in the living room. She would be screaming for him to do something, or she'd be loudly calling his name just to keep track of where he was. No one really knew for sure what her motivations were for her insistence, screaming out, "Louie! Louie! Louie!" Her voice would reverberate throughout the small ranch house, letting everyone know that she wanted him to get up off the couch and do her bidding like a subservient butler. All he had wanted was to relax after work.

I remember a funny incident when my friends since kindergarten, Tommy and Jim, came over to hang out after dinner one weekend. They experienced the frequent shouting of Dad's name for themselves. They were waiting for Dad's reaction. That night, Dad had his newspaper above his face. After the irritating repetitive shouting of his name, he lowered his newspaper so only his eyes could be seen, like a detective peeking over a fence, and said, "Doesn't that woman ever shut up?" He then returned the newspaper to cover his face. After witnessing Dad's reaction, they looked at each other in awe and started laughing quietly. When we left the house, both Tom and Jim looked at me and jokingly said in unison, "Whatever drug your dad is on, we want some."

Rob continued to think about his dad's situation. *The common phrase that Dad would use is "You heard what your mother said." Dad would parrot that phrase as he always does whenever his wife would deliver her commands. Dad is more a follower than a leader. His superhero name would have been Passive Man. With the characteristics that Dad had, criminals would pretty much get away with crimes easily. I think it's best not to use Dad as my hero. Yes, all heroes have flaws, but this one is a game changer.*

"What homework are you working on tonight, Robby?" his mother inquired in her customary vile tone, yelling from the hallway into his room. She always called him Robby as if he was still five years old.

Why does she always ask me and not my two sisters? "Nothing" was Rob's standard reply even though he had the essay for Creative Writing 104, word problems in precalculus, a lab report for physics and a reading for American history, which he had a new appreciation for since his encounter with Kralc. His senior year was supposed to be a lot less stressful than his junior year, which had been loaded with AP courses. Apparently, that had not been the case.

But Rob wasn't really thinking about his homework. Instead, he was contemplating how to use the ring to help people and even defend himself from bullies, specifically Tim Murphy and his gangs of goons at school. More concerns were racing through his head. *How would I get informed of the events where people need my help? The news would be useless if the occurrence had already transpired, resulting in casualties. How would I get there without the use of the family car? Would I have to get permission to use it? I can imagine what Mom would say if I asked.*

"*Hey, Mom, May I use the car for about an hour tonight?*"

"*Why?*" *Mom would shout in her usual nasty tone.*

"Oh, I have to save a bus full of people that's hanging on the edge of the Driving Park Bridge." Rob laughed to himself. *Yeah, that should convince her. Would I even need a car, or would the ring provide me with the ability to transport or fly? Or would I be given super speed to get there quickly? Would I address the ring like addressing Amazon's Alexa? Or do I just state the power I need, and it would suddenly be given to me?* But after attempting to remember everything Kralc told him, he finally remembered. *"If the bearer cannot determine the particular power needed, then the ring will determine the appropriate power to bestow."* The only thing Rob could do was get his homework completed and worry about how to use the ring later.

*****

Mornings had always been difficult for Rob, just like it was for any seventeen-year-old. Struggling to get out of bed at six in the morning to go to school had been a trialed ritual. He would shower the night before so he wouldn't have to get up any earlier the next morning. He would avoid breakfast because he had never really been hungry that early. But nevertheless, his mother would prepare sunny-side-up eggs, bacon and toast soaked in bacon grease, which his father would eat when Rob refused, which was most of the time. The only time he ever heard of soaking a piece of bread in bacon grease was when he read Jack London's "To Build a Fire," but that had been for survival. In this case, if his father had avoided this concoction as well, it sure would have helped in his survival against cholesterol. Of course, Lou didn't seem to care, adding that to his three cups of coffee before he would prepare to go to work.

The best part of the morning was when his best friend, Tommy Molinaro, would come over, riding his ten-year-old Schwinn mountain bike to escort Rob to school. Rob would walk while Tommy rode. Both Tommy and Rob didn't have a car to drive to school, and they were both embarrassed since most seniors had cars, presumably from their parents, for their senior years in high school.

Rob and Tommy were the Woody and Buzz of the neighborhood except that they had met in kindergarten, not in Andy's room in *Toy Story*. Tommy was the very first friend Rob had. Rob remembered the day he and Tommy met at Rosemont Elementary School after they had realized that they lived fairly close to each other.

It was in Mrs. Randell's kindergarten class. In kindergarten, I usually played alone, building something with worn-out and chipped wooden blocks or Lincoln Logs, which were missing important pieces for making an actual log cabin. Tommy would come over to the corner where I was and build stuff with me. We would start up a kindergarten conversation, pursuing a very limited dialogue since, at that age, there wasn't much to talk about.

A few days after meeting Tommy, Rob remembered that his father had actually picked them up instead of his mother since Lou had the day off. Since his father never met Tommy before and Tommy needed a ride to his house, Rob had wanted to introduce Tommy to his father during the ride. He recalled saying, "Hey, Dad. I made my very first friend today!"

My dad replied, "That's great! And what's your friend's name?"

Little five-year-old me looked at little five-year-old Tommy and said, "Hey, friend! What's your name?"

Tommy and I still laugh about it to this day.

"Mornin'!" announced Tommy cheerfully as he opened the dented white aluminum door of Rob's house. He typically entered the living room with some type of contraption in his hand, announcing, "Check this out!"

Tommy was the only seventeen-year-old electrical engineer in the neighborhood, and he was always developing some type of gadget consisting of toggle switches, push buttons and knobs that would supposedly make people's lives easier. In reality, his inventions were mostly useful only to Tommy, but they would have the potential to be amazing prototypes for future endeavors.

"What is it?" inquired Rob, with his face tipped sideways, indicating some thought process to determine the gadget's use.

"It's a light-flashing relay system for my bike."

"What would you use it for?"

"Beats me, but it gets everyone's attention whenever I ride down the street."

"Unless it can shoot destructor rays at Murphy, I'm not interested. Come on, we're going to be late." Rob was not really concerned about being late for school since the later he went, the fewer bruises he would have to suffer from the jabbing fists of Murphy. One would think that by senior year, bullies like Tim Murphy would have matured and realized that what they were doing was sophomoric in nature, but Tim's lack of brain power matched his lack of maturity.

As Rob walked alongside Tommy, who rode his bike, with his new invention below his seat, he was surprised that Tommy had not asked about the newest accessory on Rob's finger, but then again, what high schooler looks at another's hands?

The school bell rang, or more like buzzed, at Rosemont High School just as Tom parked and locked his bike on the rusted, mangled bike rack. Tommy used his own concoction for locking up his sole means of transportation. It was an electronic alarm system jerry-rigged with his lock that emitted an ear-piercing squeal if someone tried to steal the bike, much like the panic button on a fob that beeps a horn in a vehicle. Rob thought that that was a bit overkill since whenever Rob rode to his part-time job at the drugstore, he relied on a Kryptonite lock that he bought when he and his father shopped for bike locks. It was a combination lock with an eight-millimeter hardened steel shackle, a double-hardened deadbolt to prevent twist and cut attacks, a steel sleeve over the crossbar for double security, a pick- and drill-resistant disk-style cylinder and a sliding dustcover to protect it from debris and dust.

Walking to the blue double doors, Rob was feeling a sense of relief that homeroom was going to start, so Tim "Moron" Murphy wouldn't have the opportunity to put his grungy hands on him. But Rob's feeling of relief faded and was replaced with one of terror as an overwhelming chunk of hulking corpulence stood in front of the entranceway to his homeroom, the only safe place from "Mr. Moron" and his fellow agitators.

Tim stood a full five feet eleven inches, displayed enormous biceps of flab that were obviously never properly developed, donned a Beatles-type haircut and wore a pair of black Converse sneakers. And he had a face like the Creature from the Black Lagoon—scaly and pimply. As a matter of fact, it was difficult to locate Tim's eyes since some of the pimples he had could have easily been mistaken for extra eyeballs.

"Where ya going?" Tim questioned since he so possessed a keen sense for the obvious.

"LAY OFF HIM!" Tom shouted protectively. Rob knew that Tom wasn't scared of Tim. He was only afraid of getting too close to his pimply face in case one of his whiteheads burst. Tom's peach-colored face was so clear that it could have been used in an Ivory soap commercial.

"Stay out of this, Molinaro! This is between Little Robby and me!"

"I'm going to homeroom." Rob sneered with the thought of adding "you, numbskull" to his statement but knew he would advance to the next stage of pain if spoken.

Tim then grabbed Rob's eyeglasses from his surprised face, dropped them on the marble-colored linoleum floor and put Rob in a nearly choking headlock. That's when Rob thought of using the ring. But that thought vanished seeing that he wanted to get Tim in a situation that did not have such a captive audience. *Maybe this was the situation that Kralc was referencing when he said, "The ring will not work if you are performing a task for personal gain." But this isn't really for personal gain. It's simply self-defense, and the ring seems to know it, as it's glowing a pale light blue and gently vibrating.*

As Tim grasp tighter around Rob's neck, Rob rammed his shoe heel into Murphy's toe, which just happened to be located under a ripped and thinly cushioned sneaker. A samurai yell exploded from the villain's mouth, his grip loosened and Rob pushed himself from Murphy's perspiring body, picked up his glasses and ran into his seat in homeroom.

"You just wait until I get you after school. I'll be waiting," threatened Murphy as he always did when he didn't finish the attempted task. "I'll make you wish you—" Before he could complete his sentence, the homeroom bell rang out, and everyone stood for the Pledge of Allegiance.

Most students weren't very enthusiastic about saying the pledge since the phrase "with liberty and justice for all" did not apply to all people in America, but everyone stood and recited it without question. As Rob followed suit, his thoughts wandered. *Why do we sing "The Star-Spangled Banner" during hockey games? Are we supposed to be proud Americans while players on the ice violently beat the crap out of one another?* Rob had a tendency to daydream.

While morning announcements were being read, Rob turned his daydreaming gaze at Christine Stewart, a new senior who had just moved here and was starting her first day. She seemed smart, energetic and athletic. She was stunningly beautiful, and she certainly grabbed Rob's attention. Rob adoringly stared at her five-foot-five, pleasantly shaped petite figure; her silky-smooth pixie-cut brunette hair; creamy complexion with faint freckles and luxurious blue eyes. Rob was always noticing girls' eyes. Eyes could make or break a girl's looks, and Christine's comely eyes were comparable to no one's.

As Rob gazed at Christine's radiance, he remembered that his father had told him that it was what was inside someone—their personality, disposition and kindness—that should be attractive to a person. Rob never understood why he said that. *If Dad's advice was true, why did he marry Mom? Mom yells at Dad, insults him, and never gives anyone in the family positive pats on the back or rewards for doing something right. Maybe Mom's suffering from PTSD. I must remember to discuss this with Dad sometime.*

As homeroom ended, students began walking out of the room, carrying lighter loads than lower-level students since most seniors signed up for electives to fill college requirements. Rob tried to walk out at the same time as Christine but also had to avoid Moron Murphy so he wouldn't be embarrassed in front of Christine. Luckily for Rob, Murphy wasn't around, but unfortunately, Christine had already headed to her first class.

As he moved to his first class, he kept an eye out for Murphy. Rob was trying to wrap his head around the responsibility of using his ring. Should he start small, like help students at school or help people on the streets? But he had no clue how to start testing the power of the ring. He knew he couldn't change people's behaviors, like bullying, with the ring, but at least he could help in small ways to alleviate the victims' stresses and conflicts.

There was so much going on in his head that he felt someone was flashing a thousand images in front of his eyes, and he could only manage to distinguish two or three. How was he supposed to focus in his classes when he was distracted by his encounter with Kralc Tenk yesterday, his avoidance of Murphy and his attraction to Christine?

Rob shook his head in a futile effort to shake it off and focus on his classes.

"This is going to be a very long day!"

CHAPTER SIX

The Actual Beta Test

The last couple minutes of the final class of the week just reminded Rob of Moron Murphy's threat: "Just wait until I get you after school. I'll be waiting!" Murphy's voice echoed in Rob's head as he tried to write the last bit of information from class into his notebook.

Since Rob was in a lot of after-school activities, he felt safe that Murphy wouldn't try anything in front of club advisers. As Rob headed for play practice in the auditorium, he passed the glass display that exhibited trophies from music competitions to sports plaques to awards from debate tournaments and other bragging accolades of the high school. There he found Murphy bullying what looked like a freshman who was just trying to get to his extracurricular activity.

This may be the time for a beta test of his ring. Welp! Here goes nothing. "Hey, moron, it's one thing to bully me, but you've stooped even lower to bully an underclassman. Have you no pride?" Rob bravely said. *If this ring does not perform, this will be my death sentence.*

Murphy looked up from his current victim and turned his head to meet Rob's eyes. He furnished a sinister smile that could only mean one thing: Rob was going to be pummeled. "So little Robby Shit-*han* wants a go at it, eh? You were lucky last time. This time the bell won't save you." Murphy's latest quarry ran off after he let the freshman go and slowly approached Rob. Rob frantically fidgeted with the three dials, asking for superstrength and superspeed, but he couldn't think of another power he would need to defend himself against his archenemy. Then the third one, invulnerability, came into his head. As he asked the ring, it emitted a very light-blue glow and vibrated slightly, which Rob interpreted to mean that the powers were activated—at least he thought that was what it meant.

"This is for the foot jam earlier today, you butthead." Murphy approached Rob and wasted no time by leading with a direct punch to Rob's face. Rob knew that if his face was damaged, he would lose his part in the play, in which he was the main lead. The school was putting on *Fiddler on the Roof*, and Rob was playing Tevye. Even though he'd be wearing a beard for the role, he didn't want to take any chances. Without hesitation, Rob moved quickly behind Murphy as if he disappeared and reappeared behind him. The ring had actually given him superspeed. Unfortunately, Rob was not used to the ultra-speed the ring had bestowed upon him because he became instantly nauseated from the extreme speed that he was moving.

Murphy's missed jab surprised him, and he whipped around to see Rob standing behind him in a defensive position. "How the hell did you do that?" And with that, Murphy gave another jab to Rob's face, and Rob repeated the move he previously used, this time getting even more nauseated. He knew he could not keep doing this, or he was going to puke. But again, Murphy whipped around and tried to give the jab faster. Rob repeated the move even though this time, his nausea became almost uncontrollable. Murphy thought that this time, he'd swing around quickly and come across Rob's face with a left cross. With Murphy's offensive move, Rob held his right hand up, blocking the punch by grabbing Murphy's fist and squeezing it, causing Murphy's countenance to wince. Rob felt his flab-filled enemy's hand begin cracking and popping within Rob's grasp like popcorn slowly crackling and popping in a microwave, crushing the bones in Murphy's hand. Murphy yelled so loud from the pain that it could be heard throughout the length of the hallway—like a pig squealing in pain as it was taken in to slaughter. Rob released his grasp. Murphy clutched his broken fist and held it to his chest just as Rob's nausea caused him to spew out a massive stream of green-and-brown projectile vomit that covered Murphy's face, chest and broken fist. Murphy cowered and collapsed onto the hallway floor.

"Time to take off! Nice seeing you, Murphy. Next time, let's not fist-bump so hard," Rob said mockingly. Leaving a cool gust of wind and static electricity in his wake, Rob ran off. Thankfully, the hall was clear because students were to be at their clubs at this point.

He arrived at the boys' locker room to clean the stream of remaining vomit from his mouth and find a clean shirt that didn't have pea-green drops of vomit on it. Most of it had evaporated, leaving a cloud of green in his path. He hadn't stopped shaking from the experience and needed to check for any remaining athletes left. They had all left to their respective playing fields. Breathing heavily, he located his locker and nervously dialed the combination of his gym locker as his hand tremored like a car engine. He finally opened it and luckily found a blue clean T-shirt with, ironically, a lightning bolt logo on it—a spare he used when the other was too sweaty to wear. He then moved to the adjacent bathroom sink near the showers to rinse his mouth out with a small bottle of mouthwash he always kept in his gym bag. Of course, once again, he was queasy from the high-speed sprint to the locker room but not enough to hurl like before. As he popped a breath mint into his mouth for extra coverage, he smelled a rubber odor similar to the rubber blacktop sealers used on driveways. He continued sniffing like a dog seeking out and analyzing the source of the aroma. As he snuffled, his eyes saw light puffs of smoke directly in front of him. *What the...*

His eyes followed the trail of smoke toward the locker room floor. His eyes opened wide in shock to see the bottoms on his sneakers had melted and were smoking like a campfire after dousing it with water. It was caused by the friction of superspeed after racing to the locker room.

"Oh shit!" Rob sputtered, and he quickly took off his sneakers using the toes of his feet and ran cold water onto them in a nearby sink. The sneakers only sizzled slightly since the sneakers were not fully aflame. Looking around as he shook off the wet sneakers, he knew there was a stainless-steel bin that contained lost sneakers, shorts, sweatpants and other miscellaneous gym clothing. He knew he needed a spare pair of sneakers. Carrying the slightly dripping burnt sneakers, he walked to the bin. *Damn. It stinks.* The smell of sweat and athlete's-foot powder emanated from the squashed pile of assorted athletic paraphernalia in the bin. As he held his breath, he threw his melted sneakers as far down into the bin as he could, then began searching for a replacement pair his size. He tried to work as fast as he could to get the deed done without the assistance of superspeed. He finally found a size nine, which was about half a size smaller than his regular shoe size, but he quickly put them on anyway, checking to see if anyone was looking. The fit was actually good since this pair was wider than his regular size. *It's disgusting to wear someone else's sneakers, but I figure that with my socks on, my feet won't contract athlete's foot or other foot fungi. I wonder if there is a can of disinfectant somewhere in the locker room or some antifungal spray to apply on these new, well, old-new sneakers, but there's no time. I wonder how often the locker room floor gets fumigated. Damn, I'm starting to act like my mother.*

However, Rob was more worried about his mom finding out about the damaged sneakers and about him wearing someone else's sneakers since she frequently used the phrase "I paid good money for those," which, again, made no sense to Rob. He wondered if there a way to pay bad money for something. His mind once again was distracted. *Maybe bad money is counterfeit money.* He shook his head as if to bring himself back to his current situation. *I guess I'll have to buy another pair with the money from my upcoming paycheck.*

He quickly rushed off to play practice but not at the speed he was given by the ring since it was not necessary anymore and the ring had relinquished those powers once he arrived at the locker room. He had hoped that he wouldn't have to explain things to a teacher, administrator or a nurse as to how he left Murphy with a broken fist and puke-covered shirt and pants. Of course, Murphy probably wouldn't want to admit that Rob was able to defend himself, defeat him and lose his reputation as a badass.

As Rob ran, he wondered why the ring did not have him morph, as was explained by Kralc. Rob could only surmise that the ring did not find it necessary to morph at that time since it would have probably brought a lot of questions that he was not prepared to answer.

THE ACTUAL BETA TEST

Entering the somewhat musty auditorium to begin practice, his best friend, Tommy, who was the technical supervisor for stage lighting and sound, approached Rob. "What the hell happened out there?"

"Wait! You saw what I did?"

"I was coming in the other direction and saw you and Murphy having a moment, but then I saw you as a blue blur three times in front of him, then back, then front. I watched you block his punch and Murphy scream, which just about everyone heard because people's heads were sticking out of classroom doors, cafeteria doors and this auditorium door to find out who was screaming and why," Tommy explained.

"Dang!" Rob muffled with his teeth clenched.

"What the hell did you do to him besides puke on him? Nice move, by the way," Tommy complimented.

"I think I shattered some of his bones!'

"WHAT?" Tommy almost yelled but lowered his voice so no one would hear. "How?"

"Did anyone else see me?"

"No, you were gone by the time everyone's heads started sticking out of the doors. So are you going to explain how you did that?" Tommy questioned in anticipation of the explanation.

"Um, come on over Saturday, and I'll explain it to you. But you have to keep this in strict confidence, okay?" Rob earnestly pleaded as he put both hands on Tommy's shoulders.

"Okay! Yes! Of course, I will," Tom promised. "I've got to get back to lighting this dance scene. We'll talk tomorrow."

Rob's part would not require him to get onstage for a little while since Mr. Heathtree, the director, was focused on an all-girls scene. Rob grabbed one of the red corduroy cushioned seats that folded down in the auditorium and sat down. It gave Rob time to try and answer some questions that he should have asked Kralc but never did. How long would the powers last? Could he stop one power and switch to another if needed? His encounter with Murphy resulted in a need to continue testing the ring's capabilities and limitations.

As Rob was in deep reflection, Christine walked into the auditorium. He inadvertently looked up for a moment to see her. She looked over at him and gave him a full smile but without showing her teeth. Her eyes squinted, causing her eyelashes to form two fuzzy black caterpillars that almost hid her blue eyes. Freckles were lined haphazardly on each side of her nose but were barely noticeable from a distance. Her light-blue shirt accented her small frame. Rob did not know why he was so attracted to her. He heard through the old Rosemont High rumor mill that she moved because of something about a family transfer from a job or a death in her family, but Rob didn't really care about rumors, which he thought, were mostly incorrect ninety-nine percent of the time. He was hoping to get it straight from the source. He did not want to have her see him stare at her, so he tried looking away whenever she was, at any point, looking at him. Nevertheless, she caught him looking at her with his gentle smile, and she reciprocated with another radiant grin as she chose a seat parallel to his to watch the rehearsal.

Even though Rob dated mostly local girls because he only had a bike for transportation, he was not very experienced with girls even as a senior, whereas he thought most senior boys were quite experienced in dating rituals. It wasn't that he was too busy with playing soccer, which he was terrible at; writing for the school newspaper or being in the school musicals. He just felt uncomfortable starting conversation with girls. His uncle Bob was still dating at age forty and never married, but he always seemed to have a date even though he was bald and overweight. He used to tell Rob, "It's not about someone's appearance, but it's about their kindness, respect, openness and natural sense of humor that attracts women." *Unfortunately, that's not true much anymore.* It was difficult for Rob to start up a conversation with a girl without it sounding like a pickup line. But his uncle Bob told him to pretend it was just one of his friends and have a natural conversation with them. Many of his friends were girls, and most of his dates were just friends hanging out. But approaching Christine was different. He didn't want to seem too forward even though it was a simple gesture.

Well, here goes nothing.

Rob nervously walked across the aisle and asked Christine, "May I sit next to you?"

"Of course!" Christine answered.

"Hi, I'm Rob Shehan. We're in homeroom together."

"I know. I saw you having some trouble with that Tim Murphy man-child. I'm Christine, Christine Stewart!"

"Um, nice to meet, um, see you again." Rob chuckled lightly. "Oh, you saw that? Yeah, he's been bullying me since fifth grade. I try to avoid him, but today I decided to face him in the hall because he was harassing an underclassman."

"Wow! That was very brave of you. How'd that turn out?" Christine wondered.

"Actually, better than expected, but I'd rather not talk about it. I may be getting in trouble next week if he tells his parents and they complain to the principal," Rob sadly spoke in a subdued tone.

"Okay, I won't interrogate you any further. So are you just here to watch the rehearsal?"

"Actually, I'm in the play, but this isn't my scene. I'm just waiting for Mr. Heathtree to yell out what scene he wants to stage next. It's never in sequence, so the entire cast must be alert. Anyway, why are you here?" Rob tried to change the subject since he didn't like to talk about himself very often.

"Well, I always wanted to act onstage, but I am extremely shy in front of large groups, which cause me some serious anxiety. I like to watch actors onstage and imagine what it would be like if I were onstage someday. Does acting make your nervous, like forgetting-your-lines kind of nervous?"

"All the time, but when I practice the lines enough and immerse myself into the character, I can ad-lib a line or two that would fit into the normal dialogue until I remember the actual line in the script." He then decided to share a funny anecdote with her to keep the conversation moving. He was uncomfortable bragging about his positive experiences in theater. "Mr. Heathtree always told us he never wanted to hear dead air, which occurs when there is a very long noticeable pause between lines that makes the audience realize that someone forgot their lines. He told us he didn't care if we recited the

ABCs as long as there was no dead air. This happened last year when I played an old Asian man, Wang Chi-yang, in a play called *Flower Drum Song*.

"During dress rehearsal last year, while I was onstage during a scene, the actor who came onstage was supposed to have flowers, which he forgot, for my stage daughter and the line spoken from my stage wife was 'I see you brought flowers for Mei Li.' I looked at her and ad-libbed, 'Wang Ta, you must see the optometrist to get some glasses. Can't you see he must have left them at his house?' Without a response, the actor, Bill, who played Wang Ta, rushed offstage to get the flowers, so he exited on the right to retrieve them. But the prop was on the left of the stage. The problem arose when we couldn't continue the scene because we were supposed to exit stage left so my stage daughter, Mei Li, could meet Wang Ta. The only way for Wang Ta to get to the other side was to climb over various sets that were located behind the backdrop of the scene. While we kept hearing crashes, grunts, groans and whispers of injury, I decided to take Heathtree's advice, and I said as Wang Chi-yang, 'I have been studying the American alphabet and words associated with them. Would you like to hear them?' Well, students in the audience watching knew about Heathtree's dead-air suggestion and nearly fell off their seats, laughing. Mr. Heathtree thought it was hilarious that I could fit the ABCs into the play about Chinese-American relationships and commended me for my efforts."

Christine laughed softly and quietly, shining that lucent smile at Rob. "You make it sound easy."

"I'm just lucky I can improvise quickly," Rob said as he thought about how quickly he needed to come up with powers for the ring to grant upon him during a crisis.

"Scene 1, act 2," yelled Heathtree. "Let's go! Let's go!" Almost sounding like a football coach during practice, Heathtree yelled to get onstage. He was an amazing director whose motto was "Don't give me excuses. Give me results." No actor onstage would ever come unprepared. If they were required to donate a prop to the scene, he would expect it the next time that scene was rehearsed. And since no one knew what scene or act he wanted to practice, you could bet that every actor had that prop they needed, or he would embarrass them mercilessly.

"Oh crap! I'm in this scene. Sorry I have to go."

"It was nice talking with you!" Christine replied in a breathy voice.

"Yes, same here. Let's continue our conversation sometime soon." Rob had hoped that would not be the last time he would get to talk with Christine.

CHAPTER SEVEN

Firefighter's Carry

Saturday morning, Tommy was excited to get the scoop on what happened between Rob and Tim Murphy, so he biked as fast as he could to Rob's house and found him sitting in the breezeway, a room between the garage and house that allows the passage of a breeze to accommodate high winds, allow aeration and provide the perfect ventilation on a hot day. It had four crank-style horizontal window slats that were installed to adjust the airflow in the room. Looking at the stained pine plank walls on the garage and house sides of the breezeway dated the home and brought one back to a different era. After parking his bike right outside the entranceway, Tom knocked on the solid aluminum screen door as Rob motioned him in.

"Okay, so what the hell is going on?" Tom gasped, out of breath from his ride to Rob's.

"And good morning to you as well," Rob sarcastically said with a smile.

"Yeah, yeah, yeah! Good morning! Now spill it!" Tommy replied.

Rob reminded Tommy of the confidentiality of the situation and invited him into the kitchen because Rob was required to wash the fruits and vegetables that his father had purchased earlier in the morning from the public market. Rob's father and mother had left to run errands, and his sisters were out with their neighborhood friends. Rob didn't care as long as they didn't come home. As Rob filled the stainless-steel sink with water for washing the baskets of produce, Tommy noticed that Rob was using dish detergent in the water.

FIREFIGHTER'S CARRY

"Wait! You're putting dish detergent in the water to wash the fruits and vegetables?" Tom questioned in shock.

"My mom requires it because she says it's better to get all the pesticides off the produce," explained Rob. "Hell, she'd have me spraying them with disinfectant if she could. You know how my mom is. She'd probably spray my dad with that stuff when he came home from work if she could."

"Yeah! I understand. Your mom is really weird!" Tommy laughed. "So back to what happened on Friday in school!"

Rob went through the whole story of finding the ring, the Themadorian who appeared through his iPhone, what the ring could do and why he was entrusted with it.

"Can I see it?" Tom inquired.

"Sure!" Rob agreed as he held his hand palm down onto Tommy's open hand. "It looks like a mini whiskey barrel," observed Tommy. "What do all the symbols mean?"

"I don't know! Maybe the alphabet of ancient Themadorians."

Shocked that Rob had no idea, Tommy asked, "Didn't you ask Kralc?"

"I WAS IN A STATE OF SHOCK AT THE TIME, OKAY? I'm lucky I remembered all the details of what happened," Rob frustratingly shouted. "Sorry, I didn't mean to shout."

"That's all right. I guess I would have been shocked as well," Tom apologetically replied. "So what now? What are you supposed to do with it? Save the world from every disaster, cure diseases, fight crime or what?"

"I don't know! This is too much responsibility for me to handle." Rob sighed as he finished drying the produce. "What should I do? I can't prevent something from happening if I don't know what's going to happen. And I don't think the ring can send me to the future to learn what disasters or crimes are going to occur. And even if it could, if I changed that possible eventuality now, how would it affect people's lives in the future? Isn't that like the butterfly effect?"

"I guess you'll have to just do the best you can," Tommy calmly responded. "Maybe if we had a police band radio for monitoring."

Tommy was always coming up with alternative solutions to problems, which, in Rob's mind, was the making of an excellent engineer.

"I have too much on my plate right now, preparing for the play, homework, deciding on which college to go to with acceptance letters coming in. Then there's Christine, who I am hoping to talk with again and find out if she's going out with someone or not and whether I can get a date with her. You know, important things like that."

"More important than saving people?' Tommy spouted.

"Maybe not, but at least my plate contains small things. Saving people is way over my pay grade," Robby replied anxiously.

As Tommy and Rob tried to figure out how the ring could be of use, in the distance, a fire siren was heard. Sirens went off all the time in and around the area, and Rob never thought anything of them. He only knew trained firefighters were on their way to assist in putting out a fire or help those trapped inside a house or building, or it was the EMTs arriving and being on standby to assist with the injured.

But the sirens were getting louder, and it seemed as if the fire was in their neighborhood. Rob and Tommy dashed outside to see how close the fire trucks were when they saw one followed by an ambulance with lights flashing and racing down his street, Rosebud Drive, turning the corner and heading down the long adjacent street of Windmill Road. Since his house was on the corner facing Rosebud, Rob watched in amazement as the vehicles took the corner without skiing—where a car was driven while balanced only on two wheels. Rob grabbed his bike from his open garage as Tommy hopped onto his to race down in hot pursuit of the emergency vehicles.

They arrived at a dilapidated two-story senior-citizen apartment building across from Rosemont Elementary School, which the two boys attended years ago. By the time the boys reached the scene, some firefighters were evacuating the residents since the fire had not yet spiraled out of control. Other firefighters were dousing it with water supplied by two nearby fire hydrants. One firefighter who was supervising the evacuation of the building asked one of the elderly male residents, "How many people live in this complex?"

"I'm not sure. M-maybe twenty?" stuttered a gray-bearded gentleman who was barely supporting himself using a brass-topped wooden cane.

After a quick head count by the supervising officer, he yelled, "There may be two more people in there."

As the fire became more intense and too dangerous for firefighters to re-enter the building, a police officer on the scene tried to encourage people to move back and keep their distance. But a faint yet audible yell for help could be heard through the crackling and hissing of the flames. Firefighters heard it, but the first floor was inundated with flames as they continued to saturate the base floor with water.

"Rob, time for you to help!" Tom nudged Rob as he spoke. "Get behind this tree so you won't be seen."

"Crap! Um, time to save some people, I guess. Okay, ring! I need invulnerability, um…superstrength and superbreath, I guess," Rob choked out as the smoke began to become overwhelming all around the area. He turned the dials on the ring again as it faintly vibrated and glowed light blue.

Tommy's jaw dropped as Rob began to morph in front of his wide-open eyes. Rob looked older, more muscular and taller, with a receding hairline and a slight paunch. Tommy ran over to the fire truck and covertly grabbed a spare firefighter's coat and helmet, completing the gear with goggles and a breathing apparatus attached to a small compressed air tank, and raced back to hand it to Rob. Rob quickly put them on behind a tree. He wasn't very familiar with some of the gear, but he improvised as best he could.

As Rob ran toward the burning building, he ran past another firefighter who thought Rob was one of them and let him pass. The firefighter cried out, "That structure is deteriorating quickly. You'd better get those people out fast. Be careful, man. Don't be a hero. If you can't find them, get the hell out of there."

Once Rob was in the burning structure, he looked around for anyone trapped in the engulfing flames. Finding no one on the base floor, he took a deep breath, taking in as much air from his breathing mechanism, then removed it momentarily. He thought that he had more than sufficient air in his lungs for blowing flames out all around the area including near the first flight of stairs to the second floor. However, his breath was so cold that it not only put out the flames but also froze everything in his airstream that was covered in water, which was continuously being sprayed by the firefighters, including the stairs, which became slippery. Rob gawked at the ice-glazed stairs and carefully ascended to the second floor, where he found an elderly couple cowering in the corner of the corridor leading to the icy stairs. The results of his supercold breath had extended to part of the second floor, so few flames were threatening their exit.

"Please help us!" the old man pleaded. "My wife passed out from the smoke because she has asthma, and I couldn't lift her to get us both down the stairs. She was in the bathroom when the fire started. I tried yelling to her, but she apparently wasn't finished with her…um…business."

"I can carry both of you to safety. Don't worry!" After taking another deep breath through the mask, Rob placed it over the mouth of the elderly woman in hopes that she would be able to reach consciousness.

As Rob bent over to help the old man, who was holding on to his wife, he heard a loud crack and looked above them to see the second-floor ceiling beam collapsing onto all three. Rob, with his head down and his arms outstretched, covered the couple as best he could with his body as the burning wood hit Rob's head, back and back legs, but he felt no pain. *Holy crap! I didn't feel a thing.* Rob was able to push the beam off him and away from the couple by lifting up his body, and he pushed the burnt beam across the room. Even though Rob found it hard to breathe after exhaling, he was able to lift both of them up on each of his shoulders in a modified version of a firefighter's carry. He carefully but quickly descended to the first floor and out the main entrance, miraculously not slipping on the ice-covered steps. Two firefighters assisted in carrying each of the couple to a safe distance from the scorched building.

"Thanks for the assist, partner. I don't recognize you from our squad. Are you from another fire department?" asked one firefighters.

"Umm, yeah! Different fire department. I'll let you take it from here," Rob replied with a deep raspy smokers' voice he once again didn't recognize.

Rob rushed behind a nearby tree where Tommy was waiting impatiently. As soon as he leaned up against it, breathing heavily from his adrenaline rush and the lack of air from smoke inhalation, he began morphing back to himself. The firefighter's coat, pants and tank fell to the ground. Rob removed the suspenders that held up the firefighter's pants and took his firefighter's helmet off. He left them on the ground behind the tree. *Let them worry about it. I'm exhausted.*

Tommy's jaw dropped open and whispered, "Holy shit! That was amazing! How did it feel?"

Still breathing steadily, Rob blurted out, "Amazing! I've never saved anyone in my life!"

"No, I mean, is it painful to morph?"

"Not really! It kind of tingles when it's happening. Sometimes I don't even know when it's happening or what I look like since there are no mirrors around. Besides, I really don't care what I morph into."

"Well, I'm sure this won't be the last time you rescue someone!" sputtered Tommy.

As they sped off on their bikes, Rob observed from a distance a dark hooded figure with a shady-blue shroud and long overcoat, with four elongated fingers covered in black nitrile gloves, the orange glow from the building fire shining upon it. He thought it might have been a reporter waiting to interview people at the scene or maybe just a neighbor watching the excitement. But his curiosity got to him, and he turned and biked toward the figure.

Tommy yelled, "Hey, where you going?"

Rob turned his head for only a second and replied, "Have to check something out!" But once he turned back around, the figure was gone. He rode around the area that the figure was last seen, but his search was futile.

"Never mind," Rob told Tommy. "Let's go home! One event is enough."

CHAPTER EIGHT

Damsel in Distress

"Good evening, I'm David Myers for KOAT News. We begin tonight's newscast with a remarkable rescue from one of our local firefighters, the identity of whom is still unknown."

Overhearing the news from his bedroom, Rob sprinted into the living room to watch with his parents.

"Authorities confirm the rescue of twenty residents of the Rosemont assisted living facility in the small suburb of Rosemont, the last two of which were rescued by a fireman who, according to the Rosemont Fire Department, was not a member of their fire company. Reporting from Rosemont Fire Department is Patrick Hamilton."

"Thank you, David. I'm here with Battalion Chief O'Hara of the Rosemont Fire Department. Chief, what can you tell us about this spectacular last-minute rescue?"

"Well, we thought we had all twenty residents accounted for, but apparently, when we did a head count, two were missing. One rescued resident told us after the rescue that his wife was in the bathroom in their apartment and that he was urgently trying to get her to come out."

As the chief spoke, a video of the fire incident was playing in the background. Rob watched the footage that included the dark shrouded figure he tried to follow. *Why was he or she there? The person wasn't videotaping or using a phone to take pictures. He or she was simply watching. Who the hell is watching?*

He immediately called Tommy. "Holy crap! Are you watching the Channel 13 News?"

"Yes! Holy shit, Rob. That's you rescuing the couple!" Tommy excitedly acknowledged.

"Duh! We were there, remember?" Rob replied sarcastically. "I didn't know there were any reporters and cameras there. I guess I was too focused on helping those senior citizens. I definitely did not want any attention focused on me. I'm afraid that if they did in my morphed form, I'd end up morphing back right in front of them. Then I would be hounded by the media and eventually scientists, who would conduct endless tests. My classmates would call me a freak, and I'd lose friends and maybe even lose my job. My college of choice would reject me even after they accepted me, which, without a job, I wouldn't be able to afford supplies. I could possibly lose my lead in the musical. And you can imagine what my mom would do if she found out!"

"I would never stop being your friend. You know, for better or for worse, for richer or for poorer, in sickness and in health, until death do us part."

"Um, we're not married, Tommy. But I get it. Okay, I've got to clear my head. I'm going to work to pick up my paycheck. We'll talk later." Rob hung up abruptly.

"Mom, I'm going to get my paycheck from work." He never bothered to tell his father where he was going because his father trusted him. But his mother wanted knowledge of his whereabouts every minute of every day. She was controlling that way.

"Okay, but be careful!" Mom anxiously barked. *She was always telling everyone to be careful as if we would intentionally be reckless when riding our bikes, driving or walking somewhere.* Rob, who had completed his driving test shortly after turning seventeen, could imagine what she would say when and if she allowed him to drive their SUV: "If you put one dent in that car, you'll lose your car privileges for a week."

Rob worked part-time at the Key Drug Mart store, a very small drugstore of a much larger chain of drugstores called Keys Inc. It was the same store his Uncle Bob used to work. It was a simple bike ride from his house. He remembered one year ago placing his application with the store manager, and he would go to the store after school every day to ask if there were openings. The store manager, who was also the main pharmacist and ran the operations of the store, always replied, "No!" After the fifth day of Rob's continuous persistence, Elliot finally said, "I'm going to hire you not because I need anyone right now but because you're a pain in the ass, asking every damn day!"

Elliot was a tall man with kinky bushy brown hair, a large nose and a very thick brown mustache. Some employees were frightened of Elliot, but as long as they did their jobs and added a little humor to his stress-filled day, they would get along with him just fine. Rob worked his way up to head stock person and filled in for the floor manager, Barbara, during summers when she was on vacation. Rob liked Elliot because he truly knew who was working hard and who was slacking off when the annual hourly raises came along. He earned substantial raises per hour because of the multiple jobs he was able to perform in the course of a four-hour shift. Elliot enjoyed Rob's sense of humor and work ethic. Rob recalled one occasion when he had an upset stomach and diarrhea but didn't call in sick. Rob wasn't sure if it was anxiety or something he had eaten that had disagreed with him. He would work extra hours, take other people's shift if they couldn't make it into work due to a sickness and even asked Elliot if he needed him to work longer than his regular shift. Rob needed the money. Arriving to work in a less-than-energetic or humorous mood, he told Elliot that he might have to go the restroom frequently because of his abdominal situation.

"I thought you looked a bit peaked. Come on up here!" He directed Rob to step up to the pharmacy platform. Even though it might have been illegal to do, Elliot gave him a spoonful of an elixir that burned when it went down Rob's throat, but after a half hour, Rob was feeling much better. He thanked Elliot, and Elliot replied, "Coming to work when you have an upset stomach is admirable. Anyone else would have called in sick. I truly appreciate it!" In a hushed tone, he reminded Rob not tell anyone that he gave him medicine that only a doctor could prescribe!

Rob quietly asked, "Is that diarrhea medicine?"

"It's an opium tincture," Elliot whispered. "Don't worry. It's used in a number of narcotics, especially painkillers. In prolonged use, it can be addictive, but in your case, it's harmless. Again, it's our secret." Rob was never one to break someone's trust. His father taught him that. His mother, however, lied in so many situations, especially to save money. Rob was glad that his father was honorable.

Rob valued working there not because of the minimum hourly wages but because he got to put all the newest comics out on the black revolving metal rack on the magazine aisle. He was a natural organizer, which was unusual for someone with ADD. Rob thought that it was probably a mix of ADD and OCD. *I wonder if my new ring could help me with that.* But of course, that old Kralc rule came back to his memory. *Why am I able to stock shelves and rearrange those shelves so effectively? This disability is so confusing.* The only area he did not enjoy restocking was the feminine hygiene aisle, and those shelves needed constant restocking. He was also the fill-in for the cashiers when they took their breaks. He loved filling in for all the departments except the cosmetics counter, which he felt uncomfortable doing since he knew nothing about cosmetics and couldn't really help customers. But it was a great way to meet girls. Unfortunately, it was usually older ladies who frequented the department, most in their fifties and sixties but trying to look thirty. Rob never understood why. *Maybe when I'm that age, I'll know why.*

"I'll be back in about an hour," Rob promised his mother.

Rob always took his orange Fuji bike, which he won in a raffle at his church, through the back of the plaza where the drugstore was located. It was the very last store at the end of Rosemont Plaza. He would ride to St. Mary's Church through the short entrance to the church parking lot. A chain-link fence on the right side of the church separated the parking lot from a vacant crushed-stone lot. For some reason, there was an asphalt pathway from the fence opening to the parking lot of the plaza. Rob never understood the reasoning behind that. He hypothesized, *It must have been too expensive to pave the whole vacant lot. Or maybe the lot was supposed to be paved, but the town decided against it and that a pathway would be more economical. Who knows the reasoning?*

Rob was always uneasy when going beyond the church's parking lot onto the gravel lot because of the bad memories of one or two students in elementary school beating him up in that area after school. Rob's reasoning at the time was that if he didn't show up, he'd be called a pussy. But if he did show up, he'd get the snot beaten out of him. He figured that the beatings were less painful than when his mother used a belt to punish him for talking back or disobeying her orders, leaving welts on his sides and back. The belt hurt, but Rob was more hurt that his father never intervened to stop her.

As Rob rode down the pavement, he could hear what sounded like a lady yelling as loud as she could. Her blond-haired assailant covered her mouth, but she bit his hand. He pulled away quickly, yelling, "You bitch!" Then he slapped her with a full open arm and the back of his hand.

She turned her head, reeling from the slap, but her adrenaline kept her conscious as she screamed and kicked, attempting to kick him in the groin. "Stop it! Leave me the fuck alone! Get your fucking hands off me. Someone please help me!" she screamed even louder than before.

As Rob looked behind the strip mall's drive, where deliveries were received by each store, he saw two boys about his age trying to unclothe a young attractive twenty-something female with long flowing red hair curled to perfection. The boys had knives in their hands and threatened to cut her if she continued to struggle.

I guess this looks like a job for the ring. Rob realized the absurdity of paraphrasing a familiar catchphrase from Superman. He just couldn't believe he thought it.

Once again, he had to improvise three powers he would need to use before the lady was injured, raped or killed. Rob softly whispered, "I need the power to create and extend a force field, the power of malleability, elasticity and total body control, and, um, heat vision." The ring once again vibrated slightly, and a glow covered his hand in light blue. Rob felt that tingling feeling from the first time he morphed. He looked out at his surroundings and felt like he was on an elevator as he grew taller. He had no idea what he looked like. He just knew he was now taller. When the morphing was over, the tingling ceased. The growing stopped. Rob was never vain about his looks, and he knew there was no time for a selfie. Rob was now a tall twenty-something-year-old man with dark-brown hair, a goatee and dark-green eyes.

"Leave the lady alone!" Rob yelled in a deeper voice than his own, which surprised him even though he was used to it from his previous transformation. Rob sped up to the scene as both boys turned toward him. The woman's face clearly expressed genuine fear through her raised, almost horizontal eyebrows and widened eyes. Rob dropped his bike, extended his hand halfway out and opened it, palm out toward the young lady, to send a force field around the damsel in distress. He wanted to make sure that the two hoodlums would not threaten her life if he intervened. And that was exactly what they did. Yet they could not touch the woman, for each time they tried, each of the boys received an electric shock, similar to touching a hot wire when someone forgets to turn the power off before installing a home outlet.

"SHIT. WHAT THE FUCK WAS THAT?" one assailant shouted. "Static electricity?" He tried again, this time aiming at her legs, resulting in another electrical discharge. "No way that's static electricity!" No matter how much they tried, they could not succeed in threatening Rob with harming her. So they set their sights on cutting him with the knives in their grasps.

"Aren't you a little old to be riding a bike, asshole?" the blond thug yelled mockingly. As his fellow assailants watched, he approached Rob. "You're going to regret trying to be some kind of hero," he said and swung his knife across Rob's neck, but Rob's neck instinctively formed the letter C as it stretched backward away from the razor-sharp edge of the blade. Seeing that the leader of the trio was not successful, the second hooded punk, an overweight brunette who reminded him of Moron Murphy, tried a more direct approach by trying to stab Rob in the chest with an overhand lunge. Timed perfectly, Rob's Silly Putty chest collapsed inward to avoid impact of the knife. The boys were taken aback by Rob's newfound but temporary power that they both yelled in unison, "WHAT THE FUCK?"

"Such foul language in front of a lady!" At that second, Rob immediately focused on each of the knives, first one, then the other, and squinted his eyes to let out an invisible laser beam that heated the knives like a heating coil on an electric stovetop. His heated vision, however, burned his eyes while his tears tried compensating as a cooling agent. As the knives got hotter and hotter and glowed bright red-orange, both boys dropped them to the pavement. After each knife fell, forming a molten metal blob on the pavement, the perverted brutes were tried to cool off their hands by shaking them and blowing on them. While they were distracted, Rob expanded and enlarged both his hands to giant proportions, forming the hands of a Macy's Thanksgiving Day Parade balloon. While they were distracted, he quickly placed each enlarged hand on both sides of the boys and clapped them together, bashing the delinquents' bodies violently together, knocking them to the ground. He finally grabbed both boys in each giant hand and hurled them hard against the tan-painted brick wall behind them, knocking them out cold.

Rob's elastic hands reverted. "Oh my god! Thank you so much!" praised the lady. As the force field subsided, she ran over to Rob and embraced him tightly, still shaking from her encounter and breathing like she had run a marathon. Once she calmed down, she buttoned up her now soiled white blouse and combed and shook her hair with her fingers, trying desperately to rid herself of the stench of the two now unconscious perverts. She introduced herself as Stephanie, who worked at the strip mall's shoe store, Rosemont Shoes.

Rob, who was afraid that he would morph back to his former self in front of Stephanie, remained morphed throughout their conversation. "How the heck did you get into that situation?"

Stephanie replied, "I just finished my shift at the shoe store, and I had parked in the back behind our rear delivery door as usual. They had stopped into the store earlier and were making disgusting and vile suggestions to me until my manager asked them to leave. Being naive, never thinking that they would be waiting for me, I went about my business until my shift was over and punched out. I didn't think to have the manager walk me out to my car in case those boys returned later. I feel like an idiot for not anticipating that they would still be around. That's when they approached me and attacked me until you showed up. By the way, how were you able to do all those things?" she stuttered, still visibly shaken from the incident.

"What things?" Rob questioned as he was trying to come up with a logical explanation to his powers.

"You know, that stretchy thing you did and how you heated up their knives and how they couldn't touch me once you arrived?"

"Stephanie, I don't know what you are talking about. I think you may be in shock after this attack. You may have been hallucinating. Anyway, I'd offer you a ride home, but I don't own a car."

"Yeah, I am shaken up! I wish I could reward you for your bravery, Mr....ahhh..."

"Rob, ahh, Robinski, Cliff Robinski." It was the only name he could think of since he didn't want to tell her his real name. When he said it, it sounded like "Bond, James Bond," and he laughed to himself. *Seriously, Cliff Robinski? I am such a dweeb.*

"Well, thank you, Cliff Robinski! Would you like to get a coffee or something? It's the least I can do."

Rob loved the smell of coffee but never enjoyed the bitter taste ever since his dad let him try some. His dad drank his coffee black with sugar but never enough sugar for Rob. He had never acquired a taste for coffee ever since unless it was Starbucks. His uncle Bob frequented Starbucks and once bought Rob a skinny vanilla latte, no foam, thinking foam was like drinking suds from a bubble bath.

Presuming that Stephanie might be years older than he, he replied, "No, thank you. I'm late for work."

Stephanie asked, "Really, what store?"

Without thinking, Rob said, "Key Drug Mart." *Oh, shit! Why did I tell her that? What if she comes into the store, looking for morphed me?* "Anyway, I think you need to call the police and report this. It would keep these idiots from trying the same thing with another victim. I knocked them pretty hard when I punched them. I would suggest getting out of here when you call." Rob walked the young lady to her car, a used silver RAV4 hatchback, and strongly suggested locking her doors then calling the police to report the incident.

"Once again, thank you so very much! If you had not come along, I'm not sure what would have happened. If you need a pair of shoes or sneakers, please stop into the store and ask for me, Stephanie Young. Or maybe I can stop by Key Drug Mart sometime."

Crap! Why the hell did I tell her where I worked? Maybe because in my sociology class, I learned that people tend to tell the truth even if they are trying to cover up something. I think it was called a Kinsley gaffe. "Well, I have a nephew who could use a new pair of sneakers."

"Have him come in. We have a large variety of sneakers for such a small store."

"Are you working tomorrow even though it's Sunday?" Rob inquired.

"Yes, from nine to two," she replied as Rob stared at her gorgeous red mane of hair.

"I will let him know."

As Stephanie phoned 911, she was unaware that his morphed personage took the opportunity to swipe up the two warm clumps of steel and place them in his pockets. They were heavier than they looked, and they pushed Rob's pants uncomfortably lower than he wanted.

Rob was still shaken up by the experience, and his eyes were still watering from using laser vision. He thought he saw someone once again, this time hiding in the tall weeds beyond the back parking lot: a dark hooded figure with a shady-blue shroud, long overcoat and only four elongated fingers covered in what looked like black nitrile gloves. After he rubbed his eyes to get a better look, the figure was gone. *Maybe it's a government agent trying to get the ring or catch me in a superhero act. I have to stop watching those* X-Files *reruns. But four fingers? Maybe I counted wrong.*

He hoped that there would be no more incidents to intervene since the drugstore closed at 10:00 PM, and he needed his paycheck. He pedaled as fast as he could (without super speed, of course) to the store. No need to melt his tires too. On the way, he deposited the lumps of steel from his pocket into the corner trash can. They didn't make much of a sound since they were muffled by all the other debris in it.

Once he arrived, he locked up his bike on the rusted stainless-steel bike rack bolted against the end of the building.

Upon entering the store, he walked toward the back of the store where Elliot was working and where he received his paycheck each week. He glanced to the right of the back counter and was taken aback to see Christine sorting prescriptions by customers' last names.

After doing a double take, he exclaimed, "Oh, hello! Um… ahh…when did you start working here?"

"Hi, Rob! I didn't know you worked here too! It's nice to see you. I was just hired last week because the regular assistant to the pharmacist unexpectedly quit. Elliot found the application that I sent in weeks ago and called me. I'm surprised you didn't know."

"Well, with practice for the play every day after school, I asked Elliot for fewer hours until the play was over," Rob nervously replied. "He was surprised because I normally ask for more hours, but he understood. Once summer starts, I can get as many hours as I want to make up for lost wages."

"My break is in a couple of minutes. Would you like to join me in the break room?"

Excited but not showing Christine that excitement, Rob responded, "Sure, but it will have to be short. I have a writing assignment I have to work on." *You dork! A writing assignment over a cute girl? What the hell was I thinking?* Rob tried not referring to a girl as *hot* since his father and his uncle Bob had taught him about what women were attracted to, at least when they were growing up.

From behind the counter, Elliot smirked and told Christine she could take her break now, then he called another stock person, James, to fill in at the back counter.

While Rob and Christine were conversing, two police officers came into the drug store and strolled to the back of the store to the pharmaceutical cashier counter. The first officer, a trim, well-groomed man in his thirties, inquired, "May we speak with the store manager?"

Elliot's head shot up from finishing a prescription order and came down from the elevated platform of the pharmacy. "How can I help you officers?"

"Do you have a Cliff Robinski working here?"

As Elliot responded in the negative, Rob, from the break room, heard the officers and Elliot talking.

"What's wrong Rob?" Christine asked.

"Ah, um…nothing." Rob stuck his head out of the break room to continue listening to the ongoing exchange between Elliot and the officers. They explained what had happened, and Elliot's eyes grew wider and wider in disbelief at the victim's description of what happened.

"Yeah, well, we figured she was in shock and imagined what she saw, but there were two unconscious men against the wall behind the building. So that part of her story was true. But we found no knives in the vicinity, so we can only book them for sexual assault. But without witnesses, we may have to let them go."

As Elliot and the officers' discussion droned on, Rob began perspiring profusely and was having a hard time breathing. He went through a stress-induced asthma attack.

"Are you all right, Rob?" Christine asked, showing concern for his well-being.

I want to run over to the officers and be their witness, but how would I explain that I was there but that it was only mental me and not physically me? Sometimes I wish I had never found this damn ring.

Rob always perspired in hot weather or when he was stressed or nervous. He hated that. It was embarrassing to keep wiping his brow, especially on a date, making him look like he was always anxious. His friends would assume that since he had Mediterranean blood, he would love the hot, humid weather. He thought that maybe he had anxiety as well as his ADD, causing the perspiration. He told his mom about his nervousness so that he could get some medication to help relieve his symptoms, but his mother would always say the same thing: "It's just in your head. Just deal with it." She used the same verbiage when he complained about not being able to concentrate in school, hoping she would take him to the family doctor for an evaluation. He wanted to ask his father, but it was a useless endeavor since his mother was the decision maker. And she ignored her husband's input, calling his suggestions stupid. Rob, behind his mother's back, eventually talked with his doctor during his annual physical to get the medication he needed. Unfortunately, because he was under eighteen, it would require parental consent. Rob would have asked his father, but Rob wanted to prevent his father from receiving an onslaught of verbal abuse from Rob's mother.

"I just need some water. If you would excuse me," Rob answered as he took a large paper cup from the break room's cup dispenser and filled it halfway with water. At that point, Elliot came into the break room.

"Apparently, there was an incident behind the shoe store this evening. The officers I spoke with strongly advised that all employees be escorted to their cars when we close. If anyone is walking home, they should have someone pick them up. I will let everyone know to use the buddy system. I can go out with whomever is without a buddy," Elliot announced. Before he went to each department of the small store to share the announcement, Rob volunteered to be Christine's buddy.

"Yeah, I figured!" Elliot tittered.

"Let me call my mom to let her know I'm running late so she doesn't worry," Rob stated.

"That's very nice of you," Christine sweetly whispered.

"My pleasure. It's the least I can do after I rushed off to play practice in the middle of our conversation. Listen, are you working on Sunday?" inquired Rob nervously.

"Yes, nine to two. Why?"

"Well, play practice ends at twelve, and I have to get new sneakers because the rubber bottoms melt—um, separated from the cloth. These are old sneakers I got from the lost and found in the boys' locker room. Listen, I don't have a car, but I can meet you after your shift. And then maybe we can get an ice cream at Costello's Ice-Cream Shop near the House of Records down the road. It will be my treat, of course, unless you think that's sexist, assuming the man should pay. My dad had told me that if you invite someone for a meal, even an ice cream, it is customary for the person doing the inviting to pay," Rob timidly replied. "He also told me that gentlemen should hold doors for ladies." In Rob's mind, that was silly. *Is the door too heavy for the lady to open? I always thought to just hold the door open for whomever is following me into a store.* Rob's father always gave him good advice about being polite, courteous and respectful to whomever he was with, most importantly his dates. Rob remembered the only time his father scolded him was when Rob didn't allow his date for the junior prom to enter his father's car first. When Rob entered the back seat before his prom date, Patty, his father turned and whispered, "That was rude. Please get out of the car and allow Patty in first." *My dad was always a cavalier to ladies and my mom, but my mom was never really nice to him, as least not that I ever noticed.*

Christine giggled. "Your dad sounds like the perfect gentleman. Anyway, I'd love to! And don't worry. I have my aunt Helena's car, but we can walk if it's a nice night out. On second thought, with what the officers were talking about, maybe we should drive there," Christine questioned.

"We can walk. I don't want to impose! Besides, gas is expensive, and we can continue our conversations without my rushing off. We never seem to finish our discussions when we talk. I'm wondering if someone up there is telling us something," Rob chuckled.

"Seems that way, huh?"

"May I ask you a personal question?"

But before Rob could ask, an amplified voice interrupted. "Good evening, Key Drug Mart customers. The store is closing in two minutes. Please take your purchases to the counter of your choice," Elliot broadcasted over the store loudspeaker.

"Crap, again with interruptions!" Rob exhaustedly exhaled.

Of course, at 9:57 PM, there were no customers in the store, but protocol demanded Elliot make the announcement to give a heads-up to the employees as well as to any customers.

"Okay, people, closing time. Cashiers, match up the money you have in the cash registers and print out the readout on the totals as usual. James, man the front door. Let people know we are closed," Elliot reminded. Elliot didn't believe in using unbiased verbiage.

James was the stock person on duty that evening. Staffing the doors was another job of the stock person as well as dropping a dusting agent on the floors and sweeping it up with an old wooden-handled brown corn-husk broom. The broom's base was twenty-four inches wide. It covered half the aisle, allowing the stock person to go up one side of the aisle and down the other, sweeping up the dusting agent and emptying it into a whisk broom during double passes through the aisles.

When all the employees were heading to the front of the store with their buddies, Rob and Christine walked together. As Rob followed her to her aunt's car, a metallic-dark-blue Honda Civic Hatchback with a racing stripe down the middle and cloth bucket front seats that reclined, Rob exclaimed, "Nice car. Is it new?"

"Nope, it's used. But my dad was an aviation engineer and believed in always keeping machinery well-maintained and up-to-date. That's why he insisted on keeping my aunt's car in good shape since her husband died in the Afghanistan war. He especially loved working on new technology."

"Doesn't he anymore?" Rob wondered.

"Umm…no, he…um…died during what was supposed to be a routine surgical procedure a little while back."

"Oh, I'm so sorry! Now I feel terrible! It's none of my business."

Christine looked down and sadly said, "That's fine. You were just making conversation."

"Anyway, for its age, it's kept very well. Even though I have my driver's license, I am still hoping to get my own car, but then I wouldn't be able to afford college. My dad works hard, and we are comfortable. But I will have to take out loans, which will put me in debt until I die, probably," Rob sadly acknowledged. "Listen, I'll let you go, and we can talk tomorrow."

"Sounds great. I'm looking forward to it," Christine replied as she entered her driver's seat.

"My mom would always say, 'Be careful,' so I will say it to you even though I can't imagine you not being careful. Be careful. Just look out for the idiots who are not."

Christine laughed and gave Rob that smile that made her eyes squint and caused her long black lashes to push together as if she was staring into the sun. "I will. See you tomorrow after work."

She drove off, but Rob started to wonder if she just wanted to be friends or was interested in more of a relationship. Then Rob realized that if he were to save someone while they are out for ice cream, what would he do? He cautiously decided to improvise as he had been doing since procuring the ring.

Rob headed home, thinking about his maybe date tomorrow and hoping that no more incidents would occur on his ride home. One was enough for today!

CHAPTER NINE

The Pig and the Werewolf

Rob never liked Sundays. That was family church day. He and his family attended the ten o'clock mass at St. Mary's Church, less than two minutes from his house. Rob didn't hate church, but he didn't enjoy being told that he had to go to be a good Catholic, attending every hour-and-a-half mass on Sundays, where the priest preached the Bible but then failed to practice what he preached. It was quite hypocritical in Rob's mind. Rob had a strong belief in God and His angels, but he did not believe in organized religion. He felt that some people who would attend would act all holier than thou, only to be the first people yelling and honking at other people to get out of their way, manipulating their vehicles through the church parking lot after mass. That was Rob's frame of reference for it anyway. He chuckled to himself that the church should be named St. Hypocrite's Church of Actors.

Attending mass with Rob's family was quite an ordeal. His sisters would sit together between their father and Rob. They were not particularly interested in mass either since they would be texting on their phones secretly to their friends. His mother, completely oblivious to what they were doing, would be listening intently to the sermon, praying and believing that God forgave all mothers for whatever they did, even beating their children with belts. Rob's mother made that exact statement one day as she was slapping him relentlessly with his father's belt. He thought that God must be cringing at that false belief. His mother had loved making up things that God supposedly said in the Bible.

His father had always sat next to her and Rob at the end of the pew. The only reason his father and mother sat next to each other was so his mother could pinch his father with her sharp nails as he nodded off, which he did frequently. Thankfully, his father's arms had very little fat, but it still left bruises. He believed that his father was trying to finally get some quality sleep without Rob's mother relentlessly nagging him. *What the hell is her problem? Leave him alone.* Rob felt angry and sad that his father could not get the rest he needed, even at mass.

Rob did pray when he was at mass. He would pray for his father, who was needlessly abused. He prayed for patience with his mother and sisters. He prayed for a girlfriend who was honest and sincere, not like the ones he had a few dates with, only to realize that they had been dating him to make their boyfriends jealous. And he prayed for his mother, whom he had felt needed divine help in dealing with her emotional demons, possibly from PTSD from the Gulf War. Both his mother and father were military veterans. His mother was an ensign in the US Navy, and his father was a private first class in the US Army during the same war. Rob thought that maybe his mother felt she had outranked him in their marriage. He wondered if that was how a marriage worked, but he had no comparisons for evaluation. *It's funny that even Tommy's mother was dominating in his Italian family. Do European marriages work that way? Is it an ethnic thing? If I ever get married, I will definitely not marry someone like Mom.*

Normally, the family would ride together in the family car, but on this particular Sunday, he told his mother he was going to ride his bike to church and would meet them there. He told her that it was good exercise for him and that he had a meeting at the drugstore at 11:00 AM, which was the truth since he was meeting Christine after work. He explained that after the meeting, he would be taking a friend to get ice cream. His mother hesitantly agreed after, of course, telling him to be careful.

Besides praying that the mass would be over quickly, Rob asked God and especially His angels to help him with using the ring. He had a strong belief in God's angels. He assumed that God was too busy to help everyone who asked for His help, especially when He was being asked to have a favorite team win a game or a person win a lottery. Rob believed that those were superficial and trite. *Of course, asking for a girlfriend with the qualities I prayed for may also be hypocritical.* He trusted that archangels were God's helpers and that they would be able to assist people in their times of need or protect them from dangerous situations. That belief comforted him.

Timing would be crucial on this day. He would have to leave mass earlier than the other parishioners, then bike to Rosemont Bank, located inside a Starbucks on the other side of the strip mall, to cash his check to pay for his sneakers and have enough to treat Christine to ice cream. Then he would have to bike to the shoe store to meet Stephanie and introduce himself even though they had met with his morphed older self on Saturday evening. He would need to calculate time for trying on sneakers to make sure they were a better fit than the ones he was wearing. He needed to take into account conversing with Stephanie because he didn't want to be rude while paying for the sneakers. Then he'd meet Christine when she got out of work, which was on the other end of the strip mall. *Dear Archangel Michael, can I do this? Can you please help? It may be superficial, but to me, it's so important.*

As he was sitting with his family, he began his anxious leg bounce that slightly but noticeably shook the pew they were in. His mother gave Rob a stern look, signaling him to stop. Rob didn't understand what she was trying to signal since she always had that look, even in pictures. When she even tried smiling for pictures, it was forced and ungenuine. *Between keeping Dad awake and silently cluing me to stop my bouncing my leg, how the hell can she concentrate on praying? And why is it that she's oblivious to the texting my sisters are doing? Of course, since she's ignorant of my change of sneakers, I shouldn't expect her to notice them texting.*

Rob usually stayed with his family through the entire mass, but since he had so much to do that day, he told his mother that after Communion, he would move to the back of the church until Reverend Trout gave his parting words.

"The mass has ended. Go in peace," the reverend announced.

Before the last word came out of the reverend's mouth, Rob quickly power walked out the ten-foot-high wooden doors, its five-foot stained-glass images of St. Mary decorating the windows. He unlocked his bike and sped through the same vacant crushed-stone lot with the asphalt pathway.

Rob was thankful that Rosemont Central Bank was open on Sundays and conveniently located in the large Starbucks building across from the plaza. He pedaled as fast as he could to the bank, locked his bike up and rushed inside to the teller. A stern-looking older woman with colored hair to hide her real age greeted him. She reminded him of his mother, who was always trying to cover her gray hairs by dyeing her hair jet black. The bank associate, as engraved on her name tag, wore heavy red lipstick, her deeply tanned wrinkled skin evoking an image of an Egyptian mummy. He frantically signed his check, displayed his ID and slid the check toward her. After checking the authorization and his bank account, she handed him the meager amount of cash he had earned last week. Looking at his smartphone for the exact time, he realized that he still had plenty of time to go to the shoe store to get fitted and complete the transaction, including extra time to talk with Stephanie. That would have been simple had it not been for two masked men with pistols entering the bank as Rob turned to leave.

"Don't anybody move, and you won't get hurt!" yelled a man in a pig mask while his accomplice, in a werewolf mask, stood by, surveying the area to make sure no one made any sudden movements. Everyone at Starbucks and in the bank froze in place. "Don't even think about pulling out your cell phones unless you want a bullet through your head."

Rob laughed to himself about the man's—um, pig's—stereotypical demand, which seemed to begin most scenes of bank robberies in the movies. *You cannot be serious! Really? Now? I don't have time for this shit!* Rob was near the restrooms located at the side of the bank. He was unperceived by anyone in the building since most of them had their eyes fixated on the future inmates. Rob, this time, only spun two bands on the ring for two powers: invisibility and superstrength. *I have got to come up with more creative powers. I just am not in the mood to be creative with my choices right now. These guys are screwing up my timing.*

He checked to make sure his invisible form would conceal not only his body but his clothes as well. *Thank goodness it did. I do not want to bring attention to myself, which, at this point, I could really do without.* Invisible Rob walked behind the two men and proceeded to box the pig-masked man's ears—well, where his human ears should be—so hard that the pig man dropped his weapon, cupped his ears and yelled, "Fuck!" as blood dripped down from his ears, traveling along his neck. *I have to be a bit more careful and hold back the impact to their ears. I don't want to crush their heads.*

His associate jumped, startled at his partner's vulgar wail, and replied, "What the hell's wrong with you?"

"My ears, my ears!"

As the swine-masked man was yelling more expletives, Rob slid sideways toward Mr. Werewolf and repeated the same tactic but with a little more restraint so as not cause bleeding. "SHIT, WHAT THE FUCK!" Mr. Werewolf shouted, dropping his gun. But it did not seem to deter the two men from attempting to retrieve their guns from the floor. *Nope, not happening.* Rob placed each of his feet onto each weapon, and the offenders struggled to pick them up. While they were already bent over, with one hand on their ears and the other attempting to grab the guns, Rob placed his open hand onto both men's heads and pushed them backward with enough force to slide them about ten feet away from their pistols. One man thudded against one of the glass entrance doors, which lodged it open. The other goon slid through a large bank sign on an easel, which knocked over and landed on top of him before he hit the gray brick wall closest to the door. As two quick-thinking bank customers started to grab the guns off the floor, Rob lifted his feet off the firearms, and the patrons pointed them toward the two fallen assailants and yelled, "Someone call 911!"

Rob, who remained invisible, took advantage of the open entrance door, stepped over Mr. Pig Man and left the bank unnoticed. This was another ordeal that shook Rob up. *So many things could have gone wrong with that situation. Thank you, Archangel Michael.* Rob consistently thanked his guardian angel. *If anyone had gotten hurt or killed, I would have had to live with that for the rest of my life. This ring has been a blessing and a curse. On one hand, I was able to prevent a bank robbery, not to mention serious injuries or deaths. But if I had requested the wrong power...* Rob shook his head. He did not want to think of that possibility, which chilled him to the bone.

As Rob's powers faded, he got on his bike and started riding perpendicular to the strip mall. Shaking as he rode, the intensity of ring ownership weighed upon him, but he continued cycling. However, he felt an uneasiness, like entering a room in pitch-dark and afraid something would jump out at him. *Is this a side effect of using the ring? I felt this when I rescued Stephanie and that couple in the fire.* He decided to look behind him. Once again, his unknown friend with the four elongated fingers, dark hood, shady-blue shroud and long overcoat was standing at the side of the bank, facing him. Rob whipped his bike around and pedaled frantically toward the seemingly sinister character, but the figure had run to the back of the bank. Rob rode to the back, but the figure seemed to have vanished. *Shit! Am I imagining this?* Rob looked in every direction to predict where the figure had gone. Nothing.

In the far distance, Rob heard police car sirens screaming like banshees heralding the death of a family member. Rob did not want to be around in case the police started asking bank customers questions or the reporters arrived to interview them. He stayed behind the building, hoping the approaching police would not surround the building. Close behind the back of the building were tall weed trees that were left to grow since they didn't interfere with the bank's business. Rob took that opportunity to take his bike and hide behind them, dropping his bike to the ground in the foliage. The police entered the building while Rob was still looking for the ominous hooded character. But as Rob predicted, some officers did explore all sides of the building. One officer who explored that back of the building thought she saw Rob in the weeds since the reflector of his downed bike caught the sunlight, giving away his location.

After checking the perimeters of the building, the officer drew her pistol and yelled to Rob, "Hey, you! Get out here."

Maybe she didn't see my face. Maybe she only saw the red bike reflector. Rob looked at his ring and hoped that it would not view his impending request as personal gain. He implored his ring for cloaking power to cover himself and his bike. To Rob's relief, the ring granted his request. Rob just sat there, motionless. *Maybe protection from harm is not considered personal gain.* The officer brushed some of the weeds away, only to realize that the reflection might have come from some metal garbage thrown into the bushy thicket. She eventually continued her sweep of the back of the building. Rob was perspiring profusely, drenching his hair with sweat. *Great! That's all Christine needs to see, my perspiration soaking me.* Rob then remembered the various fans located on each support pillar along the strip mall. *I can cool myself off under those fans.*

Once all the officers were inside the building, Rob sped along the side perimeter of the bank and crossed the parking lot perpendicularly, heading to the shoe store. He arrived two stores from Stephanie's store. He did not want her to see him with his hair in disarray. He located one of the many fans mounted on steel pillars supporting the plaza's main structure. It was ironically right opposite a barbershop. He tipped his face up toward the oscillating fan. While he was cooling off, he took his comb out of his back pocket and ran it throughout his wet, bushy hair. With his peripherals, he checked his hair in his refection from the barber's window. Using it as a guide, Rob immediately thought of his uncle Al, a short mustached man with the most beautiful head of well-groomed peppered hair. *Uncle Al always told me that I needed to train my hair and that eventually, it will develop a clean part on the top of either side of my head.* Rob's hair was more like a curly mop with one curl dangling over his forehead. *Nope, that's not going to happen.*

Rosemont Shoes was just two stores away from his own personal drying machine. Rob walked his bike to the store and locked his bike around one of the pillars directly in front of it. Nervously, he entered the store. Stephanie, the only sales associate working, greeted him with a smile that accented her glossy dark-red hair. There were no other customers in the store

"May I help you find some shoes?" Stephanie asked.

"Oh, hi. Um…my uncle told me to ask for Stephanie Young when I came in. Is that you?" Rob knew full well it was.

"Yes, it is. Oh, is your uncle Cliff?"

"Yes! My name's Rob, and he told me to come in and look for some sneakers. As you can see, mine are pretty torn up, and I need something a little more durable, preferably fireproof."

"Excuse me?"

"Never mind, just kidding. I wear a size nine wide or a nine and a half, if you don't have wide sizes."

"We have many sizes depending on the type and brand you're looking for," Stephanie replied. "Any particular style?"

Rob wasn't concerned about brands or styles much. He knew how his classmates were more concerned about the styles and brands they wore so they could look fashionable and stylish. He just wanted something comfortable and similar to his original pair that burned up when he dealt with the aftermath of his fire-induced speed to the locker room.

"This may sound nerdy, but do you carry Skechers?" Rob felt like a nerd for asking for that brand, which was the brand his mother always bought because they were the least expensive.

"Actually, that's not nerdy at all, and yes, we carry that brand. So may I ask why that brand? The ones you have look like FILA."

"Oh, these? I actually found these in the boys' locker room at school because mine burned up!"

"What?" Stephanie questioned shockingly.

"Wore down and separated from the bottom, I meant to say," Rob replied quickly and without much thought. "Anyway, Skechers are just comfortable, and that was the brand I had before they wore down," Rob said, mesmerized by how pretty Stephanie was.

"Are those FILA comfortable? Stephanie asked.

"Actually, they are, but my mom doesn't know about the Skechers that ripped open. And since these look a lot like Skechers, plus, they're covered in mud, she never noticed. So I want to get another pair that are similar."

Stephanie gave an affirming grim. "It's funny. Most people our age prefer Nike or Vans or other more expensive brands. I personally wear Skechers because of their memory foam soles. Oh, sorry. That sounded like a sales pitch."

"Wait! So you're my age? Seventeen? Please don't take this the wrong way, because my father always taught me never to ask a girl's age, but I thought you were older."

"Yes, I get that a lot, but I will be eighteen in November."

"I don't remember seeing you at Rosemont High," Rob inquired.

'I was at Rosemont High but graduated early so I could take on this full-time job for a year. I'm saving for college. I took extra courses and attended summer school for two summers so I could get the extra credits I needed. The money I make will just be nearly enough to pay for books, so I'll definitely have to take out loans. But it will be worth it to become a pharmacist."

"That's cool! So how do you know my uncle?" he asked, pretending like he did not know.

"Well, I'd rather not talk about it. Let's just say he was at the right place at the right time, and I am so grateful he was."

'Oh, okay! Sorry! I didn't mean to pry," Rob said, embarrassed.

"That's all right! It's a perfectly reasonable question," Stephanie quietly replied. "Now let me go to the back and find your size."

As Stephanie walked to the back room behind the checkout counter, Rob was still thinking about the bank robbery along with the other situations that he had used the ring and wondered if this was going to be his life now. It almost seemed as if trouble was following him because of this alien band.

It's like when a new superhero comes out in a comic book. There's always a supervillain trying to kill him or her. Now that I have this ring, am I responsible for helping people at any given moment? Will there eventually be some supervillain ready to emerge to cause some disaster in order to take over the world? Besides, who the hell would want to take over the world anyway? Crap, it's a lot of work, just being the leader of a free country, let alone the world. What if they find out that I have a ring that grants superpowers? Will they try to secure it? What if the government wants it for the military?

Rob's ADD started working overtime in his brain like a bowl of alphabet soup. All the letters were there, but they didn't spell anything. Rob just wanted to live a normal teenage life without the stress of constantly using the ring, hiding it from others or worrying about the consequences of using it. *And not having ADD would be nice too.*

"Here you go. A pair of Skechers, size nine and a half," Stephanie announced as she came out of the back room. "I hope you like this blue one with the white trim."

"Holy crap! That looks just like the pair I used to own. Those are perfect. I'll just have to dirty them up a bit so my mom won't notice. Of course, she hasn't noticed that I wasn't wearing Skechers in the past couple of days, so she probably won't notice these either. Maybe I'll just tell her I washed them."

"First," Stephanie said, "let's make sure they fit." Stephanie handed Rob the pair he requested. He sat in the long backless cushioned tan bench and placed one sneaker on his right foot, tied them snugly and walked with just the lone sneaker.

"This feel fine."

"Well," Stephanie said in a soft tone, "sometimes footwear can be deceiving if you only walk with one. Place both on to make sure they are both comfortable."

"Heh, yeah! That makes sense." Embarrassed for limping with only one sneaker on, Rob put on the left sneaker in the same manner as the right, then walked around the store. "These are perfect. How much do I owe you for these?" Rob asked.

"No charge! It's the least I can do since your uncle helped me," Stephanie sweetly replied.

"No, no! You're trying to save for college. I'd feel guilty for not paying for them!" he retorted.

"It's really fine! I get one pair of shoes free every year as a bonus for being a full-time employee, so I choose these for me. But I am giving them to you."

Rob blushed. "That is really kind of you. If my family needs shoes or sneakers or boots or any other shoe-related accessories, I will highly recommend your store, and especially you."

"I'm the only other salesperson besides the manager since this is a small store, so that would be greatly appreciated." Stephanie smiled as she placed the sneakers into the black-and-white box with the insignia *Skechers USA* and the oversized letter *S* on its box.

"Oh no! Don't box them up! I'm going to wear them out of the store. You can put these old shoes in that box instead or just throw them away, if you don't mind."

"Very well. I can throw them away for you unless you want to return them to the boys' locker room at school."

"Hmmm, well, they were so far down in the lost and found bin. I think the owner had probably long given up on finding them. Besides, some of those sneakers have been in that bin for years. The owner of these is probably in college by now," Rob joked. "Um… you can leave them here for me, and I can pick them up next week. Riding a bike with a box of shoes would probably be odd or at least awkward, and I have a lot of errands to run today."

Stephanie said to him, "Sure! I'll put your name on the box and place them in the back room. I'll remember you when you come back because you look a lot like Clark Kent, that boy from the comics."

"Wait, you read comics?" Rob reacted amazingly.

"I read them at my friend Pete's house. He lives right next door. He's a real comic book fanatic. We tend to discuss them whenever I'm not working or on rainy days."

"Is he your…ah…boyfriend?"

"Oh no! We've known each other since we were five years old. We played together as kids, and we've been close ever since. He's more like a brother to me! Besides, his girlfriend is an avid comic reader too, so they make a great couple."

"Great! Ahh, I mean…that's cool!"

As another customer walked into the shop, Stephanie said, "Well, I have to get back to work." Looking over Rob's head, she softly called to the lady entering the store, "I'll be right with you, ma'am." The lady nodded.

"Oh, of course! Thanks again. I'll stop by another time to pick up the sneakers when you're not busy," Rob said as he waved and passed the woman coming in.

"I'd like that!" Stephanie shyly reacted with a smile, her head slightly down and her eyes looking up at Rob. "Have a great day!"

Rob's overactive brain started rambling again like a seven-year-old asking unrelated questions to an adult. *Wow! Stephanie is so kind and thoughtful. I'm surprised that she does not have a boyfriend. Well, I presume she doesn't anyway. However, she did deny that her neighbor was her boyfriend, but she never really told me that she had a boyfriend. I don't know why I care that she has a boyfriend. Crap. Why am I saying* boyfriend *so much? I just am interested knowing whether Christine will be available for dating. Of course, if not, maybe I'll come back here and have another conversation with Stephanie to find out more. Right now I need to focus on Christine and our maybe date. I just hope I don't have to use my ring in front of her. It's just too much for me to process or explain.*

And with his chaotic thoughts, he headed toward Key Drug Mart.

CHAPTER TEN

The Ice-Cream Date

It was almost two o'clock on Sunday afternoon, and Rob wasn't sure if he should enter the drugstore and escort Christine out or if he should wait at the entrance until she arrived. *I don't want to seem anxious.* His father had always taught Rob that when he was going on a date, he should never beep his horn at his date's residence. He was required to escort his date from her house to his car and, after the date, escort her back. Rob's father had also taught him to treat his dates with respect and demonstrate himself as a Renaissance man—cultured and polite yet humble and kind—which reminded Rob of the title of the Tim McGraw song. Coming from a blue-collar family, Rob never thought of himself as cultured, polished or refined. *I suppose that's banal thinking, whether it's true or not.* Actually, Rob was surprised at his father's etiquette. *Was he the Renaissance man to whom he was referring when he was courting Mom?* Rob had second thoughts about that because according to his father's brother, Rob's uncle Charlie, Rob's father was quite the contrary. Uncle Charlie, who could have been his brother's twin, told Rob that his father was more of an audacious, sometimes reckless, adventure-seeking athlete. Uncle Charlie shared several stories of his brother's indiscretions. Rob wondered how his father was able to give him such great advice if he wasn't a Renaissance man. Nevertheless, Rob decided to enter the store, meet her at the back counter and then escort her out.

After Rob locked up his bike, he entered the store and walked to the back counter. He saw Christine getting ready to leave. Rob checked his wallet to make sure he had enough cash to buy her whatever she wanted at the ice cream shop. He was relieved to see that he had enough since he saved so much when Stephanie gave him his sneakers for free.

"I'm all set," Christine acknowledged to Rob with a smile.

As he and Christine walked to the front of the store, the employees, including Elliot, engaged in friendly banter, including the harmless teases and occasional *woo* sounds. "Sorry about that," Rob disconcertedly whispered to Christine.

"It's fine. I'm not bothered by it. Are you? They must feel really comfortable with you to affectionately tease you like this."

"Well, kind of. I didn't think this was a big deal," Rob replied.

As they exited the drugstore, Rob was hesitant to hold Christine's hand since it was their first real date, and Rob did not want to be presumptuous. However, Christine slowly looked at Rob's hand and placed it in hers, which pleasantly surprised Rob.

"Shouldn't we take your bike?" asked Christine.

Rob did not want to stop holding Christine's hand. He replied, "Oh yeah! We should." He let go of her hand and unlocked his bike, then they proceeded to walk toward their destination, Rob rolling his bike beside them.

Rob had been on many dates before, but he still felt awkward when starting conversations or asking personal questions that he viewed to be too forward. However, it seemed as though Christine was not as shy or self-conscious about his questions. As they continued walking, Christine slowly moved her hand into his free hand again. Rob pulled his bike along with his other. Christine asked, "So how long have you worked at Key Drug Mart?"

"About a year now. I plan to work there through college. But I need to save money for my own car. During my first year of college, I will probably have to take a bus or hitch a ride with another underclassman…um…woman…um…person…um…first-year   student until I get one." *You're trying too hard not to offend. Just talk.*

"I understand. My mother and I have to use my aunt Helena's car to look for apartments so we can relocate."

THE ICE-CREAM DATE

As they walked the short distance to the ice-cream shop, Rob shared with Christine about his family, his domineering mother, his laid-back father and his obnoxious sisters. He didn't feel comfortable sharing things about himself, but Christine seemed so interested in his life that he felt less nervous. *I really like Christine, but I don't want to brag about things I've never done or talk about places I've never been. It's just not my style. I don't want to come off like some guys in the locker room telling elaborate stories about their false accomplishments to impress whomever they were dating. Then, after the weekend, they would boast about getting laid. They most likely were lying to augment their masculinity. It's just not...honest. Like Mark Twain said, "if you tell the truth, you don't have to remember anything."*

"Besides acting, what other activities are you in?" Christine asked.

"I do like to stay active, so I do play intramural sports. Most guys like playing football or soccer, but I prefer volleyball and baseball, not necessarily manly sports, according to some seniors in my class. Sorry, I guess that's stereotypical, huh?" Rob retorted.

"Actually, that stereotype gets a lot of mileage in high school. Those type of boys don't impress me," Christine replied. "I prefer kindness, honesty, a sense of humor and overall mutual respect from people, male or female. My parents taught me that. Besides, I know bullshit when I hear it. I really don't care if they play sports."

Rob was amazed at her levelheadedness and intellect. "That's what my dad says too. Anyway, I just enjoy talking with you. But enough about me. Tell me about yourself. Um...can I call you Chris?" Rob countered.

"You can, but just about everyone calls me Christine."

"Okay! Christine it is. I have a buddy who does not want to be called Doug. He prefers Douglas, so I get it," Rob said, nodding his head and slightly compressing his lips.

"Well," Christine continued, "there's so much to tell you on our first date, so maybe I can tell you some now and some on another date."

Holy crap! She already wants a second date? That's unbelievable. We haven't even finished this one!

"As I told you, my mother Olivia and I are living with my aunt Helena until we find a new place to live in the area, hopefully within the next two weeks. We came to this town in search of an artifact that was lost by my father. He had surgery in Roswell, New Mexico. He never told us where he might have lost it, so we have a very difficult task ahead of us. I found out from my mother that it's an important part of our family history. We thought he might have had it with him when he was being prepared for his surgery, but it wasn't. When we heard that he had passed, we went to Roswell to have his body prepared for burial. We searched his clothing for it, but we weren't successful," Christine explained.

"What was the artifact?" Rob asked.

"A type of jewelry. A pin, maybe, or a brooch? He never told us. He just said we'd know it when we found it. Apparently, it had some special engravings."

Rob thought about his ring and what Kralc Tenk said about Roswell, New Mexico, and that there were other rings. *Was the artifact she just described...this ring? No way. Christine is no Themadorian... um...unless she's morphed. Nah, that's ridiculous. What are the chances of a Themadorian coming to Earth? Or was there one here on Earth, and that was the one who lost the ring? Wait, maybe she's here to retrieve it. Maybe this is her father's artifact.* If Rob had not learned about the Themadorians, he would not have had any of these suspicions. However, he decided to ask Christine more incisive questions to ease his fervid imagination.

"So...your family is from Roswell?"

"Well, my aunt Helena was a scientist and a doctor on a base near Roswell. She did research and assisted in scientific military operations. We are from another...um...area."

They continued talking until they finally arrived at Costello's Ice-Cream Shop. Before trying to decipher the information from Christine and continuing his query, Rob asked her what flavor ice cream she wanted. "What would you like?" Rob inquired.

"Oh, um...I don't know. I really don't have a favorite. What do you like, Rob?" Christine asked.

THE ICE-CREAM DATE

"Cookies and cream, cookie dough, orange creamsicle, chocolate swirl, strawberry shortcake. Actually, I have a lot of favorites."

"Well, whatever you order, I'll have the same," Christine replied.

What girl doesn't have a favorite ice cream flavor? Rob's suspicions about her were elevating.

As Rob was about to ask Christine about her aunt Helena, two high schoolers from Rosemont High cut in front of Rob and Christine. Rob called out, "Hey, the line's back there."

"So? Wanna make something of it?" the insolent overweight blob asked.

What is it about bullies always being overweight? Do they grow fat by being a bully, or is there something in fat itself that predisposes a person to be a bully? Of course, my uncle Bob was fat, but he was jolly. And he was always joking. I guess this may be one of those conundrums that will never be solved.

He replied, "Look, we don't want any trouble. We are just patiently waiting our turn, and you should too. You need to move to the end of the line please," Rob angrily stated, trying not to lose control as he pointed backward toward the line's end.

"Make me!" the corpulent teen replied.

Again with this bullshit? Rob wanted to use his ring but realized that Christine and an entire line of people would see him morph if the ring deemed it necessary. This was definitely not a situation that would be considered as a personal gain, at least in Rob's perception. This situation was a defense against evil. But his better judgment prevailed. *I cannot rely on the ring to fight my battles. Might be time to take up jujitsu or kung fu, but when will I have time? I'll just have to use my power of persuasion to get them to move to the back of the line. Of course, I don't think that will work since these guys probably used an umbrella when it was raining brains.*

Christine then chimed in. "Gentlemen, and I use that word loosely, if you don't move to the back of the line, I'll have to convince you with some physical persuasion!"

"Ah, George, what's that mean?" George's half-witted partner Lenny asked.

The oversized instigator told his cohort, "You idiot! It means she wants to fight."

Rob was flabbergasted at this petite, short-haired beauty was threatening this portly menace and his spineless partner. *Why do bullies always seem to have entourages? Well, except for Murphy, but he's an exception. He never did let his brains go to his head.*

"Ha! Yeah, right, as if you could! How come your boyfriend can't defend you?"

"I am perfectly capable of defending myself, so what's it going to be?" Christine moved closer to her new nemesis. Rob had never seen Christine raise her voice or exhibit anger until now. When the dialogue got louder, people in line were pulling out their smartphones to take video of the incident.

Really? Taking out phones instead of lending a hand? What the hell is wrong with people?

George laughed. "I don't normally fight women because they are so much weaker than men, but go ahead. Give it your best shot." The crowd gasped at his statement while still recording the encounter. Women in line expressed their anger with his statement by tensing their facial muscles, compressing their lips and clenching their fists.

I think the women in line want to take a shot at him right now.

Christine, standing right in front of the menace, used her dominant hand. She bent her wrist, curled her fingers as if she was holding a bar, quickly flexed her arm forward and landed a hit directly at his nose. She then quickly recoiled. As his nose bled, she repeated the move and jabbed his Adam's apple with a closed fist. She finished her assault by swinging a sharp uppercut to his chin, then, with her right leg extended, gave him a swift upward kick to the groin.

George first grabbed his throat and his hemorrhaging nose, then he bent over in pain from the groin kick. As he bowed forward, she finished him off by lifting and bending her leg again, and using the flat of her foot, she booted the top of his head backward into his accomplice, knocking both to the ground. The crowd clapped and cheered for Christine's victory over her unmuscular Goliath. George lay in a fetal position, groaning for few minutes, then he and his colleague slowly stood and stumbled away. George was still holding his groin and his bloodied nose, still gasping for air. The crowd jeered and booed them.

"Holy sh—I mean, crap. Where did you learn those moves?" gasped Rob, astonished.

"My mother told me that a woman must be able to defend herself in all situations, especially when confronted by uncouth, chauvinistic ogres like them."

"I'm impressed, to say the least. You'll have to teach me some of those moves. They would come in so handy," Rob said, still in awe. He was thinking about how he could defend himself against Murphy without help from the ring.

"Were you bothered that I defended us?" Christine inquired.

"Not really. Well, maybe a little. I guess most guys would be upset since it's kind of conventional for the male to be the protector."

"Not from where I come from. It's important to be independent and not rely on a male to be a bodyguard for his mate," Christine paused. "Okay, so what were we talking about?"

She didn't even break a sweat. "Aren't you shaken up?" Rob asked.

"Not really! Where I'm from, the women are trained to be warriors and not take demands from men," she replied.

Where the hell is she from? Now I'm more curious, but I can't perseverate on finding out. I'm sure she'll tell me eventually. Rob was somewhat glad that Christine wanted to continue the conversation. "Okay, as long as you're all right."

"I'm fine. It seems interruptions are becoming our MO. So where were we? Oh yeah! You were starting to ask a question."

Rob hesitated and was trying to remember the question he was going to ask. "Oh! Did your aunt Helena finish her tour of duty?"

"Yes," Christine replied as she explained the situation with Dr. Stewart that resulted in her general discharge under honorable conditions, leaving out more revealing details. "She may be suffering from PTSD of sorts from her time in the military lab."

"What happened?" Rob inquired, becoming more curious as to why she left.

"I can't really say. It's a pretty sensitive issue and one that still bothers her."

"I'm sorry. I did not mean to pry."

"No apology necessary. You just want to get to know me. It's actually refreshing. You seem quite different from the other boys at school. You're authentic, forthcoming and nonthreatening. And never once did you use a pickup line on me. And believe me, you'd be amazed at some of the stupid come-ons used on me."

"Like?" Rob insisted.

"Okay! One of the guys in homeroom said, 'Are you Wi-Fi? 'Cause I'm totally feeling a connection.'"

"Ha! Did this guy think that would work?" Rob laughed out loud.

"Oh, it gets worse. While I was walking over to the auditorium to watch your play practice, this football player carrying some of his gear used this one when he stopped me in the hall, 'You look so familiar. Don't we have a science class together? I could've sworn we had chemistry.' Shall I go on?"

"No, please. I've had enough." Rob snickered again.

"That's why I've been impressed with you. No pickup lines and no bragging. You are just…you!" Christine stated.

"Dang! I was hoping to use the 'You had me at hello' line."

"No, no! But that line has been used on me as well!" Christine tipped her head slightly down while her eyes gave him a solid nod.

Finally, they arrived at the ice-cream counter. A gentle old man in his seventies greeted them with a smile and asked, "What can I get you two?"

"I'll have a cookies and cream in a bowl, please," Rob answered.

"And for you, young lady?" The ice cream man looked at Christine.

"Oh, the same. Thank you," Christine echoed.

"That will be twelve dollars," the elderly man cheerfully stated. Rob paid him. The old register rang, and the drawer popped out. "Thank you. Enjoy your treats!" the elderly gentleman said as he closed the register. Another employee handed Rob two Styrofoam bowls of cookies and cream ice cream, each with a small plastic spoon in the middle of the mound.

THE ICE-CREAM DATE

Handing Christine the bowl with the most in it, Rob looked around for a place to sit. He found a small round high table with two bar stools under a red striped umbrella that was several feet away from the counter. He escorted Christine, along with his bike, to the table. They sat across from each other, and Rob stared at her and smiled as she licked her delicacy, his thoughts running wild.

"Why are you staring at me? Do I have ice cream on my face?" Christine wondered aloud.

"No, no! I'm just truly enjoying this time with you without any more interruptions."

Christine smiled and nodded in agreement. "The day's still young. Let's not jinx it!"

He was about to continue his interrogation about her background and her father's artifact when Christine noticed the ring on Rob's left hand, which was holding his bowl while he ate. "That's a very unusual ring you are wearing. Is it a family heirloom or something you bought?"

"Oh…um…I actually found it in the woods down the road from my house. It was under some leaves. I assume it fell off someone's finger, which I found strange. How many people lose rings? Earrings, bracelets, or necklaces, yeah! They could easily break and fall off, but a ring? Ironically, it actually fit me, which I found was even stranger." Rob did not want to share his encounter with Kralc Tenk, how the ring resized itself or how he had morphing abilities. He was afraid she would think he was crazy, and that would certainly end their date and any other future dates.

I'm really getting uneasy about the connections my mind is making right now. Her father lost an artifact, possibly a piece of jewelry with engravings. I found a piece of jewelry with engravings on it. But her father's heirloom was lost in Roswell. I found this ring in the woods two hours away from there. The possibility is slim. Man, my brain is tired.

Changing the subject completely, Christine said, "Listen, Rob! I need to be honest with you about something."

Okay, here it is! She's going to say she just wants to be friends or that she already has a boyfriend and wants to make him jealous. Or she's gay. It's time to play my least favorite game, back by unpopular demand,

"Guess My Excuse" with your host, as always, Sucker Rob. Rob's back stiffened upright as he put down his bowl and lightly held the edge of the table to brace himself for her announcement. Rob replied, "Um...sure. What is it?"

Just as Christine was to answer, Rob's smartphone vibrated, since he had it on silent so that they would not be interrupted. "I normally don't like answering my phone when I'm on a date, but I just have to check to make sure it's not important. He took his smartphone out of his hip pocket and looked at the caller ID. It was his mother.

"Sorry, Christine. It's my mom. She never calls me unless it's important." He pressed the green Answer icon. "Mom, I'm kind of busy right now, can I call—"

His mother interrupted him midsentence.

Christine couldn't hear what Rob's mother was saying, but by the looks of Rob's countenance, it wasn't good.

"Wait! What?...When?" Rob asked, waiting for an answer from his mother. "Okay, yes, um...I'll come right home. I should be there in about fifteen minutes. Bye." Rob pressed the red Hang Up icon.

Christine, her visage showing seriousness, asked, "What's wrong?"

"My grandmother, Sitto, was rushed to Rosemont General Hospital. She was complaining about chest pains. I have to go right now." Rob threw what was left of his ice cream into the nearby trash can, as did Christine.

Rob removed his helmet, which was strapped to the back of his bike seat near the reflector, and handed it to Christine. "Please wear this. Do you mind if you ride on my handlebars? I'll be careful while steering so you won't fall off."

"Okay, yes, not falling off would be preferable," Christine replied with a worried tone but tried to relax the tenseness of the situation. She placed the helmet on her head, buckled the strap and mounted herself on the center of the handlebars, her body facing forward. She placed her feet on the pinch bolts of each wheel. She held on to the inner handles while Rob, with his feet on the pedals and his butt off the seat, painfully pushed his legs to gain some momentum before continuing to pedal. He gained enough speed to begin pedaling faster while balancing Christine on the center of the handlebars. He avoided most of the curbs on the way so Christine would not fall off. It only took three minutes to get to Christine's car, which was in front of the Key Drug Mart parking lot.

"I'm so sorry to end our date like this. May I call you tomorrow after play practice?" Rob said in a hurried voice. "I guess interruptions are our MOs."

"Of course, I'll give you my cell number in homeroom tomorrow."

Rob then gave her a quick peck on her cheek and took off. As he sped off, his eyes welled up with tears as his only thought now was that of Sitto.

Christine lightly bit her lower lip as she watched him pedal away.

CHAPTER ELEVEN

The Healing

Rob biked home as fast as he could, straining his calf and thigh muscles during his nervous ride. His childhood memories of Sitto distracted him so much that he actually hit the curbs, cracked and elevated concrete and potholes that he was intentionally trying to avoid.

His grandmother was the magnet that kept the family together. Sitto's heritage and her importance to his family and relatives were a fundamental part of Rob's life. Sitto was a Lebanese immigrant and was the matriarch of his mother's family. When she and her husband, Michel (*Jitto,* the Arabic word comparable to a *Grandpop* or *Grandpappy),* came into this country, they had started a candy business in a village storefront within biking distance from Rob.

Jitto died when Rob was twelve. And even though Rob was never too fond of Jitto because he feared him, Rob had always been polite to him and greeted him in an amiable way, even though Jitto spoke or understood very little English. He learned just enough to get by. Rob had always avoided hugging him, though. Always.

Jitto had always seemed very grumpy. Rob's mother had told her children that her father had been a camel herder when he had lived in Lebanon, which they had thought was pretty damn cool. *How do you herd camels?* However, since Jitto was old, they couldn't have imagined him shepherding camels. *No wonder there were so many small camel statuettes scattered throughout Sitto's house. It must have reminded Sitto of her husband.*

THE HEALING

Jitto had a short toothbrush mustache. His bald head had seemed to shine from any overhead light in their house. His peppered hair on the sides had always been unkempt, and the strands of hair hanging out of his ears had been disgustingly long, sticking out like the legs of a cellar spider. It had reminded Rob of one of his biggest fears—losing his hair at a young age. He knew that people with male-pattern baldness tended to have family members with the same type of hair loss, so having a close relative with it increased Rob's risk of developing the condition himself. *I read somewhere that the condition comes from the mother's side of the family. If that's true, I'm screwed since Dad is bald as well as all his brothers.* Rob knew very little of his father's heritage, only that he was of Lebanese ancestry as well. The only reason Rob knew that was that his mother and father spoke Arabic instead of English when they did not want his sisters or him to hear the subject of their discussions…arguments.

Most of the time, Jitto had sat in his worn-out velvet-green patterned wingback chair from the 1940s. It wasn't vintage like the ones some people bought to give elegance to their living room. It was actually an antique from the '40s.

The only time his grandfather got up from that chair was to line the wastebaskets with large paper grocery bags or go to the bathroom. He would place a seventeen-inch-high brown paper bag inside the waste bin that was located in a small alcove across from the descending steps to the side door. He would carefully tear the corners of each bag so that it would fit neatly into the can. *At the time, I had thought that was ingenious.*

All the children had been scared of Jitto. Rob was not alone in that. When Jitto had passed, Rob had felt guilty that he hadn't been very sad about it. He had only been sad for Sitto because she had lost her husband.

Sitto was the only grandmother Rob ever knew. Rob's mother rarely allowed her children to visit her in-laws. Rob would ask why they couldn't see his father's side of the family. His mother would ignore the question, or she would tell him it was too far to drive. To this day, Rob never understood his mother's aversion to his father's family. *Dad's family is Lebanese as well. What the heck is the problem? Maybe they had fought against Mom's dominance over us, including Dad.*

Sitto was very different from her husband. She was kind, sweet, loving and affectionate to all her grandchildren. Rob wondered why his mother was not like Sitto. Even his aunt Agnes and uncle Bob were reflections of Sitto's rearing, but Rob's mother was very different. *Maybe Mom did have something like PTSD from serving in the Navy, kind of like Christine's aunt, but I don't recall Mom doing anything in the Navy except clerical work. Does clerical work cause PTSD? Was her commanding officer an asshole? I really think there is another reason.*

Rob remembered a time when his mother yelled at him and his sisters while in Sitto's house. It had been the only time he heard Sitto yell in Arabic at his mother. She would scold her for treating them so cruelly. His mother had immediately stopped, but Rob and his sisters were well aware they would be reprimanded at home.

Rob's family visited Sitto on late afternoons every Sunday for early dinner. Once again, Rob's ADD kicked in. *I wonder what early dinner is called? If breakfast and lunch combined is brunch, what the heck would late lunch and early dinner be called? Luninner? Dinunch? Linner? Dunch?* Ever since Rob could remember, his uncle Bob and aunt Agnes, neither of whom ever married, were Sitto's caretakers.

In Rob's eyes, Sitto had always been old. She had salt-and-pepper hair that was pulled back from her face. It had been twisted and wrapped in a circular coil around itself on top of her head. On some of Rob's visits, he had experienced two unfamiliar hairstyles: hair spiraled down on the sides of her face or braided behind her head. No matter what her coiffure was, in Rob's eyes, she had never really aged beyond his first recollections of her. But recently, he had noticed that she had had difficulty with mobility, even at very short distances. She would hold on to any structure on either side of her to stand—stove, table, sink or refrigerator—and then stagger along. Rob realized that she was now showing her age. She would now depend on his uncle Bob to drive her to weddings, birthday parties, picnics or other family events where she could be wheelchaired around. But most recently, that stopped as well because the arthritis in her legs had become worse.

When Rob's family and relatives would visit, it was a festival of Lebanese food that Sitto cooked mostly by herself or, at times, with help from his aunt and uncle. Once prepared, all the delicacies were placed on the small kitchen table. There was tabbouleh (parsley bulgur salad), lebneh (a bitter yogurt spread), garlic and lemon hummus, za'ater (a tangy, herb on flat bread), kibbeh (spiced meat balls) and stuffed grape leaves. It had become a self-serve feast that only Sitto could produce. Rob's favorites were stuffed grape leaves, tabbouleh and za'ater. Sitto had eventually taught Rob how to make some of the traditional Lebanese foods. Za'ater reminded him of how he had tricked his buddies in the cafeteria by telling them that sometimes, when times were hard, his family could only afford putting dirt on bread—za'ater resembled dirt but with sesame seeds.

One of Rob's friends, Burt, asked him, "Are those sesame seeds in dirt?"

Rob replied, "Nope. Birdseed left in dirt. Why do you think I'm always whistling?" They all laughed as they understood Rob's weird sense of humor.

Rob looked forward to having the beautifully prepared Mediterranean delicacies every Sunday. And it wasn't just Rob's family on Sundays but all of Rob's aunts, uncles, cousins and even, every so often, some Armenian neighbors that Sitto befriended.

When Rob was younger, he recalled how her neighborhood was a multicultural smorgasbord of Germans, Lebanese, Polish, Italian, Syrian, Armenian and Ukrainian families. Fortunately, it still was, but it had been dwindling as a number of immigrants were trying to get out of the city, where the gun violence was increasing. Rob was sad about innocent bystanders being shot by stray bullets. He worried about everyone's safety at the family gathering.

Even with fewer immigrants in the neighborhood, Sitto's front porch was the welcome mat for anyone who wanted to converse, have coffee or share cultural dishes. It was a microcosm protected in a bubble of nonjudgment. Sitto was always the magnet that kept the family gatherings together, and her magnetic charm always brought in more than just the Armenian neighbors. Rob could not imagine what it would be like without her when her time came.

Rob's memories stopped as he had finally arrived home and placed his bike in their garage. His mother had been impatiently waiting for him in their car. Rob wanted to ask his mother what had happened, but he decided to stay silent all the way to the hospital. Rob's two sisters had been working, but surprisingly, his mother had informed them of the situation. They had wanted to go to the hospital as well, but Rob's mother had told them they could visit later. Rob's sisters had not been happy about their mother's demand.

Rob despised hospitals more than attending mass. He didn't want to think of people suffering, moaning and groaning in pain, vulnerably confined to a hospital room. He detested the pungent smell of disinfectant and isopropyl alcohol that permeated throughout the halls.

As his mother habitually complained about the exuberant cost of parking, she finally parked in the hospital garage. As they exited the vehicle, Rob's mother, as always, checked to make sure the doors were locked before leaving it. While walking to the entrance, Rob's mother complained about the distance they had to walk just to get to the automatic glass doors of the hospital doorway.

Rob looked at the decor of the colored walls that were supposed to be calming and restful. Instead, they reminded Rob of a cold and harsh funeral home. He and his mother arrived at the information desk to ask the attendant for the location of room C7 in the medical facilities.

With a nasal voice, the attendant answered, "Follow the blue line to the blue elevators, then go to the third floor, suite C. Once you arrive, ask one of the nurses at the center station for the location of room 7."

Rob and his mother thanked the attendant, then they headed down to the blue elevators. Rob looked down at the colored lines, grasping the need for them on a hospital floor. The hospital was an intricate maze of rooms and hallways, and every corridor looked the same. He guessed that following bright-color lines would be easier than reading panels with arrows pointing in particular destinations. Before the idea of lines was created, the system of multidirectional arrows reminded him of the scene in *The Wizard of Oz* when the Scarecrow was trying to give directions to Dorothy.

Once in the blue elevator, Rob's mother, a germophobe of sorts, pressed the C button, then immediately took out antibacterial liquid in a pocket-sized bottle and squirted some of its contents on her hands. "Put your hands out," Rob's mother commanded.

"But I didn't touch anything yet," Rob responded, but then he remembered that he had opened the entrance door for his mother.

"Did I ask? Put your hand out!" she retorted.

Rob was glad no one else was in the elevator; otherwise, her demand would be on his list of the top ten most embarrassing moments of his life. As the elevator doors swished open, the overwhelming combination of the beeping monitors, the fanning wheels of gurneys rattling, the hissing and sighing of ventilators and the continuous coughing of various patients were echoes from an out-of-sync surround-sound system. The consistent buzzing of the magnetic ballasts from the fluorescent lighting fixtures were almost stifled by all the other resonances from the hallways. *Holy crap! This would be an autistic person's sensory nightmare.* Intermittent announcements asking for particular doctors interrupted the animated sounds on the floor and added to the uneven rhythm. Rob tried to ease the tension and anxiety he felt by thinking about the *Three Stooges* scene where the loudspeaker called for "Dr. Howard, Dr. Fine, Dr. Howard." *Dad and I love watching those shorts on Hulu.* Unfortunately, that did not help him once they approached Sitto's room.

All the sights and sounds reinforced Rob's abhorrence of hospitals. *I don't like seeing defenseless patients relying on so many physicians, nurses and their assistants to help them.* Rob especially did not want to see his grandmother lying vulnerable on a hospital bed, with IVs and tubes taped to her wrists, administering anesthesia, pain medications, antibiotics, fluids or whatever other vital fluids Sitto needed. He didn't want to hear the beeps of the monitors in her room or the sensors connected to her chest and arms to check her vitals. He particularly did not want to see his aunt Aggie and uncle Bob crying around her as if she were going to die. *Why is it that when an elderly person is in the hospital, their family and friends think the worse? Don't people have hope anymore? I know people are filled with anger and fear, but what they need is some room for hope. Now I finally relate Emily Dickenson's poem "Hope Is a Thing with Feathers" from my junior year's literature class.* Rob was determined not to surrender to despondency. He trusted that his hope would not fly away.

That's not to say that Rob did not feel fear and anger but that he decided to fill himself with calming faith. *I have to put on a happy face, as the song says, to show everyone around me that I have hope that Sitto will be all right.* Rob prayed to God and His guardian angels that expressing his optimism would give her encouragement.

Normally, Rob's mother and her siblings would been tight-lipped about medical conditions in the family, but maybe his aunt and uncle could shed light on what caused Sitto's situation. But then he reconsidered asking it. He was afraid that his mother would verbally attack him in front of Sitto. Rob wanted Sitto calm and relaxed.

I remember one time when my sisters and I were younger, Mom had to go to the hospital for a week while Dad took care of us. Dad never shared the reason. Maybe he thought we would have not understood. Of course, during the beginning of my senior year, my sisters and I had found out that Mom had had a nervous breakdown. Was that another way of saying PTSD?

Sitto was awake and alert, talking to her daughters and son and just conversing about the family when Sitto had noticed that Rob and his mother were in the room.

"Hi, Robby," Sitto immediately greeted Rob as soon as she saw him. She always called him Robby, and she called his uncle Bob Bobby. Rob had guessed that it was a gesture of deep affection for her son and her grandson, which had made him smile. *If Uncle Bob doesn't mind being called Bobby, I guess I won't mind being called Robby.*

"Hi, Sitto! How are you feeling?" Rob calmly asked.

"Well, getting older is just part of life, and maybe this is the time for me to go to Heaven."

At this statement, Aunt Aggie and Uncle Bob began to tear up, but Rob's mother remained emotionless—no watery eyes and no sad face, just his mother's stoic visage. *Is Mom part Vulcan? What the hell! This is her mom. Where's her compassion?*

THE HEALING

"Listen, Robbie. When I die, I don't want you to wear black at my funeral. I want you to wear something light and cheerful. You should celebrate my life and not be depressed about losing me. I will be happy in Heaven because I will be with my other children, your aunt Mary, uncle Toffie, aunt Ester, and uncle Al."

"I promise, but you aren't leaving for Heaven yet."

"No, I think it's time."

Rob needed to say something to get Sitto thinking differently. That's when Rob thought about using his ring. *Would this be the personal gain that Kralc had referred to? Surely, it isn't a monetary gain or a gain of power but more of a rescue or helping someone live a little longer. However, it may be a personal gain. Well, I have to try.* Rob moved closer to Sitto on the right side of her bed and placed his ringed hand on her left hand as he whispered to the ring to give him the power to heal. *I hope this is not sacrilegious, since I was taught that only God can heal.* Rob might not have liked mass, but he remembered some of God's teachings. *"Don't be afraid. Just keep trusting, and she will be healed."* Rob was encouraged by that phrase. *I trust you, Lord, and I believe she will be healed. Just please don't morph me.* He held Sitto's soft hand, and upon Rob's request, the ring did not vibrate or even glow. He figured the ring didn't want his family to see it glow or agitate Sitto's delicate hand with its vibration. Since he didn't morph, he wondered whether the ring was a living organism shaped like a ring. *Now that was a strange thought. Did the ring hear my request?*

"You know why you can't die this soon?"

Sitto reacted with a gentle smile and said, "No, why?"

"Because you had promised last week to make me stuffed grape leaves and show me how you make them for my own family! You had told me that it was important to teach this Lebanese tradition to my future wife." Of course, marriage was the furthest thing on Rob's mind. Everyone in the room reacted with a smile—except Rob's mother, of course.

"I did, didn't I?"

"Yes, so I will be over next week so you can teach me how to make them. I'm sure my mother will let me use the car to visit so you and I can work together on them."

Rob's mother rolled her eyes so hard that they could be heard. She gave him a sneer because he had put her in a Catch-22 situation. Rob's mother replied with a forced smile and clenched teeth, "Yes, I can lend Robby the car for a visit next week."

"I would love that. If that's what I promised you, then I will keep my promise!' Sitto agreed.

"Okay! Aunt Aggie can let me know when you are released from the hospital, and I will let my musical director know that I will need to leave early from play practice on whatever day is convenient for you. Does that sound good?"

"Yes, I will see you then," his grandmother quietly replied as she lightly squeezed his hand and smiled.

Rob felt confident that the ring would help her heal so that she could return to her house and alleviate his family's anxiety, including his own. "I need to step out to get something to drink," Rob said, "but I'll be back!"

Sitto told Rob that he didn't have to return. "You don't want to be around all these sick people. You should go home and enjoy the rest of the day."

"Are you sure?" asked Rob.

Sitto nodded her head.

"Okay, I'll see you next week!"

As Rob exited C7, he said, "I'll be in the lobby, Mom, waiting for you."

"Rob, I need to talk with you in private," his mom whispered angrily.

Oh shit! She is going to lambaste me.

"Why did you do that? You gave her false hope."

"No, Mom! I gave her hope and confidence that she still has purpose. Once people lose purpose, they may as well be dead," Rob whispered firmly.

As his mother grumbled, "Take the car. I'll get a ride from Aunt Aggie and Uncle Bob. I want to stay a little longer. With a quick, stiff arm, she held out the car keys by the keyring but didn't let go when Rob tried to get them. "And Robbie…"

"Yeah, I know. Be careful! Thanks, Mom!"

THE HEALING

After his acknowledgment, his mother let go.

Rob left C7 and proceeded to the blue elevators, but a thought crossed his mind. *Maybe I can use the ring to help other sick people in the hospital. The big question is "How should I do that without being noticed?"* Then Rob had an idea. *As the Power Rangers would say, "it's morphing time."* Rob rolled his eyes. *I'm such a dweeb*

Rob entered the blue elevator, but instead of proceeding to the lobby, he pressed the B button for the lower floor. *Maybe there are other lives on that floor that I can help.* As he descended to floor B, he looked to the ceiling and pondered. *Am I doing God's work by healing people using my ring? I don't want to commit blasphemy by doing what only God should be doing. Maybe I'm a conduit for God. Maybe that was the reason I was given this alien ring. I don't want to be a false prophet or some fake evangelist.* His thoughts were flying back and forth like a boomerang missing its target.

Before the vacant elevator's doors opened, Rob asked the ring for superspeed even though the last time he used it, he became queasy, then vomited. He hoped that his body had adapted to his accelerated speed. He also asked the ring for the ability to heal people again. The ring slightly vibrated and emitted its usual light-blue glow. Rob felt himself morphing.

As the doors slid open, Rob noticed that suite B looked identical to suite C, with the same sounds, the same wallpaper, the same labeled room numbers and the same nurses' station at the center of the suite. He questioned whether the elevator even moved, but seeing the big letter *B* above the nurses' post confirmed it.

He exited the elevator. The two nurses who were currently at the station raised their eyebrows and conveyed a smile as if he was familiar to them. Along the elevator-side wall was a whiteboard displaying the names of the staff who were on duty along with the patients they were assigned, written in different colors. Hanging on hooks aligned across a glossy wooden four-inch board, there were full-length white lab coats with embroidered names on them. *Good. This one will be the perfect coat to cover my khakis and polo shirt. I sure hope it fits.* Rob nonchalantly took one of the lab coats monogrammed with the name Dr. Anthony Tobor. *Thank God they have full names on them. It would be embarrassing and hard to explain why I was wearing a female doctor's lab coat. It's odd that his ID tag is missing. He probably had to take it with him to get access to other floors in the hospital. I just hope he left for the day. And why did the nurses smile? Do I look like Dr. Tobor? Okay, Rob! Focus!*

As he put the lab coat on, he was surprised to see that it fit. *He must be a short doctor. Did the ring or God bring me luck? I still think the ring is actually a symbiont or has one inside it.*

Rob walked around to each patient's unit, carefully checking to see if anyone was attending to them. As he walked along the round-about, circumventing the nurses' station, he heard a patient in B1 moaning. Rob walked in to find the patient soundly sleeping, but he was intermittently moaning in pain. A clipboard was at the base of the bed, hanging on the built-in metal hook. It contained the patient's report. Rob was distracted by a slightly distorted reflection on the clip holding the medical records. Rob saw what physical features were chosen by the ring or he subconsciously had chosen. He was now a bespectacled brown-skinned male with dark eyes and wavy salt-and-pepper hair. Rob shrugged his shoulders as if he was unconcerned about his new features. *Not bad.*

Examining the patient's records and keeping a careful eye out for anyone coming into the room, he read. *A twenty-five-year-old male patient injured by a hit-and-run driver. Dang! Two cracked ribs on the left part of his chest, left hip bone dislocated and cracked and a left shoulder displacement.* Rob moved to the right side of the hospital bed, where the patient was sleeping soundly. He placed his hand on the patient's arm and held it there for about five seconds. The familiar light-blue glow filled the patient's face and hand and illuminated the room itself. Rob then moved away and walked off to the front entrance of B2. Once again checking for visitors, nurses or other doctors in that unit, he entered to find an elderly lady awake in her bed.

"Doctor, when will I be released? I would really like to go back to the nursing home to see my friends."

"Well," said Rob in a very strong British accent, "let me look at your chart." Rob read that the lady was eighty-two years of age and has had multiple strokes, severe arthritis and dementia. "I will check

THE HEALING

with your attending doctor, but in the meantime, let me check your pulse," Rob answered as he held her wrist between his thumb and index finger. He had hoped that her multimorbidity might be cured by his newly acquired healing power.

While Rob looked away from the patient, he did not notice that the ring did not glow. He was so nervous that he mistook his shakiness for the ring's vibration. He was more concerned about being discovered as an unauthorized hospital employee. *I do not want to be questioned by the authorities.*

As he was finishing up, a nurse could be heard telling another, "I'm going to check on Mrs. Madigan in B2, and I'll be right back to finish B6's paperwork."

Rob supersped out, leaving a light gust of wind in his path.

"Wow!" Nurse Hutton exclaimed. "Someone must have opened and closed a door from the lab entrance. It always seems to cause a breeze." As she shivered momentarily, she questioned her patient. "Are you warm enough, Mrs. Madigan?"

"Why, yes! Thank you. The doctor was just taking my pulse about fifteen seconds ago."

"Must have been more than that, Mrs. Madigan, since I just walked in. Let me check on your medication to ensure you've been given your dosage for today!"

Rob had sped off to the remaining eight units on the floor. He had read their charts at superspeed and used his healing power, touching all the patients before being detected by any medical personnel. The blue glow had flashed on and off like a LED rope light in quick sequence as he used the ring, but he was moving so quickly that he had not realized that the blue glow only came from a few rooms.

After finishing his rapid healing sessions, Rob was relieved that he did not get nauseous from his superpace. He then sped off, placing the white medical coat on the hook and running out of the unit toward the blue elevator. He stood nonchalantly in front of the doors as they opened. Several people had been on it, and he panicked that he would revert to his former self right in front of them. Two people left the elevator, leaving only an independent blind woman in the corner. She had dark-lensed glasses and a mobility cane holding her up on one side as she held on to the long metal bar on the other side, simply waiting for her next destination. Rob entered the elevator, still impersonating Dr. Tobor. As the doors closed behind him, Rob, with his British accent, addressed the woman, "What floor would you like me to press for you?"

"I appreciate that, but even though I am blind, I am not helpless. The buttons have braille on them, and besides, the button has already been pressed," the lady replied. "As we move, I count the dings to determine my floor. Sometimes I miscount, but most of the time, I'm accurate. We've stopped at floor B, right?"

"Yes, that's correct!" Rob replied, surprised, with his new voice.

But as she continued talking to him, Rob morphed back to his previous self. Once his transformation was complete, he replied, "I'm so sorry. I wasn't thinking. Of course, you are not helpless! My father taught me to be courteous to everyone and always offer assistance whenever possible."

The stranger replied, offering a suggestion, "Your father seems like a good man, but in a situation like this, you should only offer a disabled person help if she asks."

Rob, with wide-open eyes, replied, "Thank you. I will do that if the occasion arises again."

The blind lady asked, "By the way, what happened to your British accent?"

Rob reacted shrewdly and quickly, "Oh, I've been practicing my accent for my high school play." And with that, the elevator opened to the lobby floor. Rob let the visually impaired woman step off first. "It was nice talking with you, ma'am."

"You as well. By the way, that accent was impressive."

Rob smiled at the compliment. "Thank you!"

She exited the elevator and met her assistant.

Whew! That was close. Rob exited the hospital entranceway and headed for his family's SUV. As Rob was about to drive out of the parking lot, his mother called. Rob linked his cell phone to the car's Bluetooth connection. As the front screen indicated that his phone was connected, he answered. "Hey, Mom. Did you want me to come back for you?"

"No, I'm fine, and apparently, so is Sitto. The doctor said she can be discharged tomorrow."

"That's great news! I will call her in a couple of days to set up a time I can come over to make grape leaves!"

"Give her some more time to recuperate from her hospital stay," his mother dictated.

"Okay, Mom. I'll call her at the end of next week."

"That sounds better. Uncle Bob, Aunt Aggie and I won't be leaving until later tonight, but we will return early tomorrow in preparation for her release."

Rob began driving home. *If Sitto was healed, so were the other nine people.* Rob felt elated that he had helped more people with the ring's assistance. *I want to call Christine and give her the good news, but I don't have her cell number yet. I'll make sure I get it tomorrow.*

CHAPTER TWELVE

Lockdown

Rob was in a good mood when he arrived at school. Things were auspicious as he entered homeroom without Murphy standing at the entrance to homeroom, ready to pounce on him. Murphy was either avoiding embarrassment at his defeat against Rob on Friday or was absent because of his injuries. Rob was feeling confident that he had healed Sitto and all the patients on floor B. He made sure to remember to set an alarm on his phone as a reminder to call Sitto at the end of the week. He sensed that his relationship with Christine was moving forward as he sat next to her and exchanged phone numbers prior to the start of morning announcements. He was even grateful for the Themadorian ring, which he believed helped him demonstrate the principles and values his father had taught him.

"How is your grandmother?" Christine asked, concerned.

"She's going home this afternoon. I convinced her that she was not ready to die until she and I make stuffed grape leaves together," Rob replied.

"That's great news. You must love your grandmother very much to work so hard to get her to change her outlook on death. Stuffed grape leaves? Is that a traditional meal for your family?" Christine asked.

Rob explained, "When we have more time, I can share with you the entire Lebanese cuisine. By the way, are you working tonight?"

"Yes, from six to closing. Why?"

"I am too! I'm a closer tonight. I thought we could have some time together after work to discuss what you had said at the ice-cream shop about your wanting to be perfectly honest with me," Rob said, sounding slightly worried about what she was going to reveal.

"Sure, and you can share with me all your Lebanese traditions, especially the egg-cracking one during Easter you had told me about. That one sounds like fun!"

Rob couldn't recall when he had told her about that tradition, but with his ADD, he had probably forgotten or was distracted with something else at the time. Rob replied, "Oh, that one is not a Lebanese tradition. It was actually started by Uncle Bob's Armenian friends well before I was born. I think it was called *dzvakhagh* meaning egg-play."

She's referring to the tradition at Sitto's house during the Easter holiday where my family and relatives would play an egg-tapping game usually with Uncle Bob, who had a secret to continuously win. To play, Sitto would first color two dozen hard-boiled eggs not with the colored dye from stores but with the skins of white, red or yellow onions soaked in boiling water for a few hours to obtain a beautiful rich amber color. She would then add the eggs to the tinted water. Sometimes she would cover each egg with the skins, and then she would boil them. Once the eggs were cooled, she would place them in a large brown wicker basket, partially covered in a white linen cloth. Each person playing the game would choose one egg and hold it vertically, with either the narrow or the wide end of the egg on top. Then they would tap another person's egg with either the narrow or wide end of their egg. Whosever egg breaks, that person would have to surrender their egg to the winner. The winner could share his or her winning eggs with anyone who would like to eat them.

"I have play practice after school, then I have homework to complete. So I'll see you at work tonight," Rob reported.

"Hey, would you like to meet my aunt and mother after work?" Christine asked.

Say, what? I'm meeting her guardians already? What's going on here? Okay, be cool about it. Rob started feeling perspiration develop on his forehead.

"It depends on where you live. I only have my bike for transportation," answered Rob.

"That's okay! I'll drive you there and back. You can put your bike in my car, well, my aunt's car, and afterward, I'll drive you home."

Rob smiled as he responded. "That sounds great. I'll let my mom know so she doesn't worry. Who am I kidding? She always worries."

Christine acknowledged that comment and snickered since Rob had shared many idiosyncrasies his mother had.

Rob's mother always wanted to meet Rob's dates whenever possible, but Rob did not want them to meet her. He had actually tried not to tell her whether he was dating or seeing someone at all. His mother would say things that she thought were kind but were really inappropriate and even at times judgmental. He hoped Christine would never meet her, but he would love for his father to meet her. His father was always so polite and warm to Rob's dates and would never say anything that could be misinterpreted as unsuitable. Rob loved his father for that. Someday, Rob hoped Christine could meet his father without his mother around.

After the homeroom announcements concluded, they were off to classes. They said their goodbyes and confirmed their plans for the evening.

Rob entered Government Studies with Mr. Coughlin. He was the football coach at the school as well as one of a number of history teachers. He had a gray-haired crew cut, and he was as tough as nails and quite heavy—a heart attack ready to happen. He wore a white-collared dress shirt and a long tie that was very loose around his neck, the top of the shirt unbuttoned. He always seemed as if he was too hot to close the gap between the top of the tie and the middle of the collar. His brown pants were kept up by a belt, though the belt seemed nonexistent since his belly hung over it.

Students found him extremely funny but somewhat menacing with his deep voice and tall stature. He reminded Rob of a much taller Mugsy, the stereotypical gangster from the Warner Brothers cartoons.

Aside from his unkempt appearance, he was able to bring life's current events into perspective using historical references. Sometimes he would make up an historical event to see if any student would challenge him about it. When no one did, he told the real historical event and strongly encouraged them to question everything and not just take someone's word for it, even his. *Hmm, that's good advice. However, that doesn't work out well in other classes or with my mom.*

"In this world of misinformation on social media and the Web, it is important to get the facts based on authentic research and verified information," Coughlin emphasized. This statement avoided the habitual question that every bored student would ask: "Why do we need to learn this?" This had resulted in his commonplace answer: "So we don't make the same mistakes of the past or so we can learn from our mistakes."

I don't think Coughlin really believes that. He wasn't very sincere in his reply. Of course, he probably gets tired of answering that question.

Rob could tell from the discussions in class that there were times when Mr. Coughlin inadvertently had implied that they had learned nothing from their history.

"It seems our leaders are not forward thinkers. There is still racial injustice, gun violence, mental health issues, climate disasters and the constant political bickering and misinformation, which have caused thousands of deaths in this country. Did you ever wonder why, after decades of supposed progress, we are still grappling with the same issues? Listen, I can't get into a political discussion with you all. My views are not necessarily yours. I'm just here to state the facts of our history as best I can."

As Coughlin's lesson continued, Rob's mind began to wander as usual. *Could the ring give time traveling powers so I can make changes even though I have no idea what changes I would make?* Even though it was tempting, he believed it would set up paradoxes and maybe change his present-day life. *What if you had a phone where you could call someone in the past and make some suggestions to them? Nope! Too many butterflies to deal with. However, it would be fascinating to travel back in time to watch Sitto's journey to America or find out what event or situation changed Mom's personality.*

During his lectures, Mr. Coughlin had this uncanny ability to know when someone wasn't being attentive. He had always carried the school-issued three-inch-thick Government Studies book whenever he lectured. Upon recognizing the daydreamers or catching someone on their phone, he would proceed to lightly clunk that monstrous textbook on the head of any student not paying attention. But he did spare the females since he had the same belief about women as did Rob's father: men should not hit women—ever! Before Rob could snap out of his ADD-induced journey into his suppositions, Mr. Coughlin was just about to bop Rob on the top of his head, causing Rob to come out of his daydream. Rob flinched and put his hand on his head to prevent the possible pain he was about to endure.

I'm surprised no one reported him for child abuse or assault. Of course, his head-bopping is very infrequent since students know the consequence of their inattentiveness. It's a difficult time for students with ADD in my class since most of us with that learning disability aren't on medication.

"So, Mr. Shehan, what do you think about it?" Coughlin asked as the book hovered over Rob's head.

"Sorry, Mr. Coughlin, I was preoccupied with the notion of history repeating itself and was wondering if our elected officials bother to refer to history before making their decisions."

"That's a good question, Mr. Shehan, and nice save."

Attempting to answer Rob's question, Coughlin continued with examples of how their country had neglected to look at their history before making decisions that would affect their lives. At the same time, Rob wondered if he could use the ring to help the world change for the good. To Rob, it seemed so despairing. *No wonder so many of my friends have depression and anxiety. They lack hope, and many times, so do I.*

Rob's mundane school day continued, and he eventually approached his last class, Creative Writing 104, right before his after-school play rehearsal.

Rob had Ms. Digit, who was not only an excellent teacher but was also quite attractive as well—a beautifully figured thirty-something, soft-spoken woman with short frosted hair. She had a very creative teaching style and gave assignments that she knew would motivate even the most reluctant writer. Her assignments were more original than analytical. Rob and his class wrote at least twice a week either in their journals or as short homework assignments. *How does she correct so many essays in such a short period of time?*

With all the writing done in her class and for homework, Rob learned the concepts of rhetoric, figurative language and platitudes. She incorporated knowledge of movies, music and pop culture into her lesson because she believed that a writer writes from his or her own experiences and knowledge.

"Have most of you chosen your hero for your long-term assignment?" asked Ms. Digit.

"I have a question, Ms. D," Rob asked, his hand raised. She allowed students to call her Ms. D if they chose. "Does the hero we choose have to be real, or can it be fictional like Atticus Finch in *To Kill a Mockingbird* or from movies Rick Blaine in *Casablanca* or from comic books like *Batman*?"

"If you feel that they possess the qualities we have discussed in class, then, yes, that would be acceptable," Ms. Digit replied.

"Cool, thanks!"

Ms. Digit smiled at Rob as if to congratulate him for asking a great clarifying question. Rob blushed. One senior boy, Chuck, sitting next to him gave him a nudge with his elbow as if to encourage Rob to follow up on her flirtatious smile. Rob gave him a sneer of disgust.

Exiting from her class, Rob walked to his locker to drop off his books and notebooks and headed to rehearsal in the auditorium. On his way there, he met Tommy, who was heading in the same direction. "Hey, Robby, what's going on?"

"Nothing, just heading to practice. How 'bout you?"

"Same. Say, how are things with Christine?"

"Going well! She's having me meet her aunt and mom after work tonight!"

"Wow! That's a big step. Doesn't that seem a bit fast to you?"

"Yeah, I thought so, but it was her idea. And I have no clue as to why she moved so quickly to that level in our relationship. I didn't think we were even that serious about meeting each other's parents, and I certainly do not want her to meet my mom yet. Actually, at all. Hopefully, there will be a time that Dad will be at home alone, maybe when Mom is grocery shopping or going to the hairstylist."

"Hey, don't look too much into it. She must really be comfortable with you to skip to that level," Tom stated.

"We technically only had one date, and it wasn't, like, going to a movie or having dinner. It was just a casual ice-cream-after-work date."

"Don't look a gift horse in the mouth. From what you've told me, she may have had a longer-term relationship than what you've ever had."

Rob replied sarcastically, "Thanks for that vote of confidence. Anyway, she had said she had something to tell me. She wanted to be truthful. That always seems to mean the same thing to me. Those old standby excuses including my all-time least favorite, the 'It's not you. It's me' excuse."

"Well, it's better than the 'I can't go out tonight. I have to wash my hair' defense," Tom cynically replied. "Besides, that last one you can eliminate since she wants you to meet her mom and aunt."

"I don't know. I guess I'll just have to go with the flow of the evening and see what happens, but my guard will be up. I've been too cynical lately after having so many disappointments."

Both boys entered the auditorium. Tommy headed backstage to turn on the stage lights. Rob sat in the back with the other actors working on their lines or just socializing until Mr. Heathtree arrived.

Suddenly, behind the closed blue metal fire doors of the auditorium, students heard loud popping sounds. The sounds repeated with three loud pings against the auditorium doors. It sounded like someone was whipping marbles against it not all at once but one by one in rapid succession. *Everyone in the auditorium must be thinking someone in the physics club is conducting experiments that backfired, but why would they choose the main floor for their experiments? The club usually experiments outside, in the back of the building or near the lab itself, upstairs.* Gary, who was in the musical with Rob, slammed his body against the auditorium doors from the outside. When he did, one of the stage crew, Brian, opened the door. Gary, weak from blood loss, was leaning on the door just as Brian opened it. Gary fell to the ground while holding a gunshot wound. His left side was oozing with blood, forming a large circle on his white polo shirt. "Help me!" he whimpered.

Rob ran to Gary, thinking he might be able to use the ring to heal him. "What the hell happened?" *I can't use the ring on him now. There are too many witnesses.*

"There's a student with a gun in the hall yelling for some Murphy guy." Gary, still dripping from his left side, collapsed on the old red-flower-patterned rug in the aisle. His blood created a small puddle, darkening the rug's pattern. Once others in the auditorium saw him, some screamed, and others froze, just staring at him. But some of Rob's theater friends rushed over in an attempt to stop the bleeding.

Rob said, "Someone get something to hold against the wound to stop the bleeding." Another student ran backstage and rushed out with some cloths he had found in the costume room while another student brought down the first aid kit that had always been located backstage, in an accessible black-wired cage, in case of performance injuries. Both students hurried back with their findings. One of the two students put pressure on the wound with the clean cloth while the other tried to create a temporary wrap for the wound using a compression bandage.

"Attention, students and faculty. This is a lockdown. This is not a drill. We have an active shooter in the building. Initiate lockdown protocols."

Mr. Heathtree had just entered the auditorium before the injured student came in and had been backstage but immediately heard the announcement and ran to lock the auditorium doors.

Everyone was required to be in a classroom and out of the halls, but Rob was able to get outside the auditorium though the backstage door as it had not been locked yet. Running toward the back, he jumped onto the stage and to the right-side wall and saw Tommy locking that entrance since Tommy was authorized to have the keys to those doors. "Tommy, let me out. I think I can use my ring to help! Everyone else is in lockdown, so no one will be in the halls when I use the ring." As Tommy nodded, Rob asked the ring for time manipulation and invulnerability powers in case the shooter fired at him, but he couldn't think of a third power he would possibly need. The ring acknowledged his request by its traditional glow and vibration. "And please don't morph me!"

The stage's side door was located below the hallway level, with steps leading up to the hallway. As Rob took his last step up onto the hallway, he looked and recognized the shooter. He had been standing at the corner of the hallway, facing east toward the auditorium, and he had been pointing a semiautomatic Smith & Wesson SW99 in a shaky shooting stance. It was the freshman who was being bullied by Murphy before Rob intervened. "Hey, buddy," Rob, with his hands up yelled. "It's okay. It's okay. Easy with that gun. Remember me?"

The freshman turned toward Rob and decided he didn't care who was calling him. He just fired in Rob's direction, yelling, "Where's Murphy?"

Rob quickly raised his hand to instantly slow down time so he could avoid being hit by the bullet even though he had the power of invincibility. He figured it would be easier to avoid the bullet if it slowed down than try to explain to investigators a dented bullet in the middle of the floor if it bounced off him. He moved out of the way, then restored time, allowing the bullet's normal trajectory to hit the light-green tiled wall about twenty feet behind Rob.

I could use heat vision to heat up the gun and force him to let it go. But that may give the freshman severe burns, or the gun could go off again in another direction when it dropped. I didn't want anyone else hurt. Besides, he will have enough on his plate once this was over. I'd just have to rely on my own persuasive skills for now. I can't keep counting on the ring all the time.

Rob tried to reason with him as sirens were heard getting closer to the building. "Please stop shooting. You'll just make things worse if you hurt anyone else. Do you realize you shot a student?"

The freshman finally recognized Rob. "I don't care!" Then he hesitated. "Hey, you're the guy who saved me from that asshole Murphy, right?"

"That's right! What's your name, man?" Rob asked calmly.

"K-K-Kyle. Kyle Rayman."

"Nice to meet you, Kyle. I wish we had met formally earlier. I could have helped you. You're a freshman, right?" Rob was doing everything in his power to ease Kyle's anxiety and anger. "Where are you originally from?"

Kyle had dark-brown skin and curly hair, and his voice had a hint of an accent. "I-I'm Jamaican. M-my family had come here to get away from some of the c-crime in Montego Bay. W-we immigrated and relocated here, hoping it would be safer. I-I think we were w-wrong. Does Murphy bully me because I am an immigrant?"

"Murphy bullies anyone who is weaker than he is. It's what bullies do, unfortunately." Rob calmly tried to keep asking Kyle questions to distract him from aimlessly shooting. "Where did you get the gun?"

"Crime had been high in our area, particularly in and around certain areas of Kingston and Montego Bay, so we needed to protect ourselves. So we found guns to be necessary for self-defense. When we decided to leave Jamaica, we were able to transport our unloaded firearms in a locked hard-sided container at the immigration office. We were honest and declared the firearm when we entered legally into this country. We explained why we had them. They were legally purchased and have serial numbers, which the immigration officers checked. During their background checks on our family, the agents made their discrimination quite obvious. I won't repeat some of their comments, but the distrust in this country is nauseating. Anyway, my family has known the combination to my f-father's gun safe in case we needed it. My father has always told us to use it in self-defense only. I decided I needed to self-defend myself against Murphy. When my parents weren't home, I was able to take it from the safe and s-sneak it out of the house," Kyle stuttered.

"Umm…Kyle…that's not how self-defense works. Have you ever even fired a gun?" Rob asked.

"N-No! But I-I don't care."

"Yes, you do care! Your anger is controlling you. It's been suppressed so long that you're not thinking clearly. You just want the pain to go away. But you haven't even dealt with the pain. You just want to retaliate and not think about the consequences."

"No," Kyle shouted belligerently. "Once Murphy is dead, my problems will be over."

"Your anger is making you believe that. Once you kill someone, your problems will only get worse. There's no coming back from that. You won't have another chance to make it right because you would have caused not only his death but the scorn from your parents, his parents, and your friends."

"I just want to shoot him." Kyle was red in the face as his anger continued to rise.

"Wait! Your father said you can use the gun for self-defense, but he never taught you how to shoot it? That makes no sense," Rob trying to make sense of the illogic.

"He never had time, and there was nowhere in Montego Bay to practice," Kyle sadly responded.

"Because you've never been trained properly, you've already hurt one student whose condition is unknown right now," Rob explained. "You'll go to prison for first-degree or second-degree attempted murder or assault with a deadly weapon with intent to murder, but if he dies, you'll be indicted for homicide and most likely spend the rest of your life in jail. Have you thought this out? You'll never see family and friends and most probably be still be dealing with bullies in jail. At least that's my understanding. You don't have to do this!"

"Yeah, well, I do! 'Cause it seems like c-civility in this s-school doesn't exist, except maybe for you." Kyle tried to hold back the tears welling up in his eyes.

Seeing that Kyle was upset, Rob tried to reassure Kyle. "There are a lot of kind people in this school. I'm sorry you had to encounter one of the few exceptions, like Moron Murphy. He obviously has his own personal problems to deal with."

"I don't give a shit about his personal problems. The teachers and principal here talk a lot of...how do you say it...politically correct rhetoric about b-bullying in our school. They p-put signs up that say, 'You can't control how people treat you; you can only control your response,' or they set up 'B-Bully Busters, that asinine mentoring program for ways to prevent bullying and other crocks of bullshit they s-s-spew, making it look like they are dealing with bullying. There are no t-t-teachers, counselors or administrators in the halls to see what is truly going on in this school. I've had enough. I'm going to make sure that asshole never bullies anyone ever again," Kyle tearfully explained. "I thought coming to this country would make our lives better. It hasn't for me."

"Hey, I understand. I've been bullied by him too for over six years," Rob responded.

"Six years? How could you withstand it? He's only bullied me this year, almost every day, making me scared to come to school. But that ends today! I'm going to end his miserable life. I don't want to hurt anyone else except Murphy. It's the only way to stop him."

"There's a good chance you'll miss again and hit a second student." Rob tried to explain, "There are other ways!"

Kyle said in a shaky voice, "Yeah, right. W-what can you do?"

"For one, we can get you to a counselor," Rob suggested.

Kyle guffawed, "Why the hell should I see a counselor? It's Murphy that needs counseling. And if the counselor talks with Murphy, he'll seek me out and beat the shit out of me for reporting him. It's a no-win situation for me."

"I can meet with the administration and demand staff and teachers monitor the halls every day during each period. Maybe the student council can advocate for more cameras."

"And what happens to Murphy? Will he be punished or expelled? His bullying is technically assault," Kyle had asked, his voice still quavering.

"I don't know. Maybe we can demand he be punished, suspended or required to get anger management training. I don't know. I'm just brainstorming here."

Rob needed to keep Kyle calm until the police arrived. "But I promise I will do everything I can. Remember, it will be for my benefit and the benefit of Murphy's other victims as well. None of the sharing-your-feelings-in-a-circle crap."

Before Kyle was able to drop his trembling shooting stance, four police cruisers arrived, accompanied by the menacing screaming of loud yelping sirens. The blue-and-red rotating lights passed through the school windows and appeared on the interior walls of the building like lights from a DJ's lighting system. The officers' vehicles were parked in an obstructive pattern in front of the entrance to the building while others raced to the back and parked, in the same manner in front of the back entrances. With their guns drawn, they rushed into the building's front and rear entrances and proceeded immediately to the area in which shots had been last reported.

As he heard the sirens, Kyle frantically decided to drop his weapon. Rob told him to kneel on the ground with his hands up. The first responding officers rushed in—a team of four dressed in regular patrol uniforms, wearing exterior bulletproof vests and Kevlar helmets. The officers were armed with Glock handguns. One looked like she had a Taser in her hand.

As the police established and maintained a perimeter, one officer had her Taser drawn toward Kyle, who was already on the ground with his hands up. Rob shouted, "Don't Tase him. His weapon is down. I was able to reason with him. He only injured one student, who is in the auditorium."

"I'm Deputy Chief Maggie Maxwell. Are there any others injured besides the wounded in the auditorium?" she barked.

Rob shouted, "No, not that I am aware of."

Maxwell then radioed the EMS team, "All clear. One wounded student in the auditorium."

"Do you know of any other shooters in the building?" Maxwell asked.

"He's the only one."

As Maxwell approached with her Taser still pointed at Kyle, another officer, Sgt. Palmer, slowly approached Kyle. "Flat on the ground *now*! Hands behind your back!" Kyle obeyed each command. Palmer handcuffed his hands around Kyle's back and recited the Miranda Rights to him: "You have the right to remain silent. Anything you say can and will be used against you in a court of law. You have the right to an attorney. If you cannot afford an attorney, one will be appointed for you!"

Kyle, nervously sobbing, said, "May I call my parents, please?"

As Kyle was escorted in handcuffs, Maxwell explained to Rob, "We will need to interview you at the police station sometime today unless you have time now."

"Can we do it later? I'm a little shaken up," Rob replied. *If it hadn't been for the ring, Murphy would still be bullying me, but I never got to the point of trying to kill him. Maybe that was another reason the ring chose me. To defend and protect others. I am just appreciative that I was able to deescalate the situation without having to give away my secret.* Rob dropped his head in disbelief.

"That's fine, son. I understand, but we need to do it as soon as possible. Please leave your contact information with me, and I will call you within the next hour," she calmly but gently stated while placing her hand on Rob's shoulder. "Here is my card." She handed Rob her business card, then she had continued orchestrating the evacuation.

"Squad A, have all students and staff been evacuated from the building?" Maxwell asked through her walkie-talkie.

"There are still some in the building, ma'am," replied a voice on the other end of the field radio. "We are sweeping all the rooms, restrooms and offices to make sure."

Rob could see out the school window as he faced the corner where Kyle had been handcuffed. He saw a myriad of parents and guardians along with blaring police warning lights affixed to the top of each of the patrol cars. Parents were hugging their shaken teenagers as they exited the building while teachers and staff stayed close by to console minors whose parents had yet to arrive.

Unlocking the door from the back stage exit, Tommy opened the door slightly to see if everything was clear. Rob had been standing in almost the same position as when he had confronted Kyle. "Hey, man, are you all right?" Tommy asked in a comforting voice.

"Not really! I never thought I would witness a school shooting in our own high school, let alone persuade him to lay down his weapon."

As Tommy and Rob stood in their positions, an announcement blared over the loudspeaker.

"Attention, all remaining students and staff. This is Principal Darren Montgomery speaking. If there are any of you left in the building at this time, we ask that you leave immediately with the officers located throughout the building. Rosemont High will be closed for the next two days while an investigation is made into the incident. We will contact the news stations, social media sites and radio stations about the closings tonight. If you have any information regarding the shooter or his motives, please let one of the officers in the building know."

Rob's cell phone started ringing and vibrating in his pocket. He knew it was his mother without having to look. He had separate short musical ringtones for the most important people in his phone directory. His mother's ringtone was "Evil Woman" by Electric Light Orchestra, Tommy's was Randy Newman's "You've Got a Friend in Me," Christine's was "What I Like about You" by The Romantics, and his father's tone was "My Old Man" by Zac Brown Band, along with others including his boss at Key Drug Mart, whose tone was "Workin' for a Living" by Huey Lewis and the News. That way, he could decide if he'd answer it or let it go to voice mail.

"Hey, Mom!" Rob, trying to sound cheerful, answered after getting the phone from his side pocket.

"We were just notified by school minutes ago about the shooting. Oh my god, are you okay? I'm sending your dad to get you. He just finished a job in your area, and I called him as soon as I heard."

"I'm shaken up, but I'm all right," replied Rob. Rob was glad his dad was coming to get him. *He won't be asking hundreds of questions about what happened. If I have anything to say, he will just listen.*

"Okay, he should be there shortly. Please wait outside for him," his mom asked.

"Okay, bye!"

"Hey, Tommy, do you need a ride home?" Rob asked.

"I'm good. My mom is on her way. I'll walk out with you," Tom responded as he locked the side exit door to the stage. "I'll have to stuff my bike into her car when she gets here."

Both boys walked silently down the hall, rounding the corner to the front doors as police officers directed everyone out the exits.

As the boys stood outside among the chaos and noise of crying and talking, Rob had recurring concerns about Kyle. *He will probably be spending a lot of time in jail for his impromptu attack. I wonder if I'll ever use my ring reactively and accidentally hurt or kill someone. Dad taught me that those emotional responses to situations can only make matters worse. But it is so hard not to react immediately without thinking it through. Besides, as I continue to understand how the ring operates, I'm sure it will prevent me from doing anything stupid. Well, maybe.*

The two boys said their goodbyes as their respective rides arrived.

As his dad was driving him home, Rob's phone vibrated and then chimed with the default tone. Rob looked at the caller ID, whose number he did not recognize, but he assumed it was Deputy Chief Maxwell. *I didn't even have time to place her number in my contacts. Boy, the police don't waste any time.*

"Hello?" Rob softly answered.

"Good afternoon, Rob. I know this is soon after today's incident, but I really need to interview you today about the shooting incident at your school."

"Um…okay…sure! Can we do it over the phone now, or do I have to go to the police station? I'd have to ride my bike there since I'm on my way home with my dad, or should my dad drive me to the station?"

"I can go there if that helps. This has to be in person, and you have to sign an affidavit," Maxwell replied. "It shouldn't be any more than a half hour."

"Okay! What time?" Rob asked.

"How long will it take you to get home?" she inquired.

"About five minutes. My mom is helping with my grandmother, but my dad will be at home with me. Is that…okay? I've never done anything like this before."

"Of course, that would be fine. No need to be nervous about the questions. As Joe Friday would say, 'just the facts,'" she said quietly. Rob gave Maxwell his address. "I'll be over in about twenty minutes. See ya then."

After Rob clicked the Hang Up button, he looked at his father and asked, "Dad, who's Joe Friday?" His father had laughed with a roar.

They arrived home just as Deputy Chief Maxwell was pulling into their driveway.

Rob hoped his mother would not be coming home in the next hour. *She'd probably run into the house and think someone died and then embarrass Dad and me.*

Maxwell opened her car door as Rob greeted her with a friendly smile. Rob never really observed her personal appearance the first time they met since he was under the stress from the shooting incident, but this time he had taken notice. She had very short blond hair shaved on one side and Gwyneth Paltrow-like eyes below her officer's short-brimmed hat. She wore a short-sleeved officer's shirt that exposed lean, muscular arms. Closing the door, Maxwell said, "Hi, Rob. Thanks for doing this on such short notice."

Is it me, or are all the older female adults I encounter attractive? Dad calls it the result of raging hormones. "That's okay. How's Kyle?" Rob asked as he nodded to his father, hinting at him to leave the vicinity. His father nodded back and headed to their front door. *Dad is really good at reading signals.*

"He's still at the police station. He's quite vulnerable right now, so they are administering a mental health exam by the on-call medical professional. His parents are with him. They are shaken up as well, and they should be. He's not being booked yet until we get all the information needed to make a decision on his danger to others. A judge may consider house arrest."

"I can vouch for him. He was not a danger to himself. He has been bullied a lot by one particular student, and the pressure was too much for him. I'm glad he will be getting a mental health check. Maybe that will all come out in their report."

"If we release him, he'll have a counselor working with him, and his parents will have to hire a tutor since he will not be allowed back in school until his trial is over," she stated empathetically. "Anyway, I don't want to waste your valuable time, so let's go through the sequence of events from your perspective. I'll write them on my tablet, and you can sign it for accuracy. Does that sound reasonable?"

"Yes, ma'am," Rob politely responded, looking serious and uneasy at the same time.

Maxwell asked a series of questions, and Rob answered them to the best of his ability. He also shared what Tim Murphy had done to him all his years in high school and that Kyle had also been one of his victims. "Yes, we got a statement from his parents about that. His parents had their gun locked securely, but desperate people do desperate things. And Kyle was no exception. He was able to get his parent's gun safe combination and take the Smith & Wesson to school by hiding it in his duffel. These shootings have caused more anxiety in students than we've ever seen. Our country can't agree on how to deal with this epidemic. For now, though, this is our reality, as sad as it is."

Maxwell finished all her questions, completed the form on her electronic tablet and handed it for Rob to digitally sign at the bottom of the screen. "I hope this helps Kyle," Rob added as he signed the document.

"We'll have to see what happens next, but I'm sure it will. You may be asked to testify at his trial, which will be scheduled within the year. When it is, we'll be in touch!" Maxwell responded.

"Wait, how bad are the injuries to Gary?" Rob asked.

"He's in stable condition at Rosemont Memorial Hospital. That's all I know," she replied. "I understand this is a traumatic incident that no student should ever have to experience, but unfortunately, it's happening too often. Anyway, I hope the rest of your week goes well. I'll see myself out. Thanks!"

The rest of my week? This day has seemed like a week. Thank goodness we have the next few days off. I had better get some homework done before work. But how in hell will I be able to concentrate on that after Kyle's meltdown, Gary's injuries and my anxiety about meeting Christine's mom? Well, like Nelson Mandela said, "it always seems impossible until it is done."

CHAPTER THIRTEEN

The Great Reveal

A day that had started out so optimistically unexpectedly ended for Rob as he worked his shift at Key Drug Mart on the evening of the shooting. He was uncharacteristically quiet and not his usual jovial self. All his colleagues felt it, especially Christine, who looked worried about Rob's mental state.

Christine approached Rob and put her hand on his shoulder. Even though he was busy stocking the shelves with the amber prescription vials, which Elliot place labels on after he completed a prescription for a customer, Christine could sense his angst. "Are you okay, Rob?" Christine whispered.

Rob quietly replied, "We can talk about it on the way to your house after work. It's the only positive thing I have had to look forward to tonight. At least we won't have to worry about school for a couple of days, so we can enjoy each other's company." Rob smiled and looked up at her. Seeing her radiant beauty, he smiled. "I'll talk with you after work." He smiled again.

"I can't wait." Christine smiled back and turned to head in the opposite direction. After taking three steps, she turned back, only to catch Rob sending her a mutual smile. Both could hear the other let out slight giggles.

Rob continued to focus on his stocking duties. Rob was a motivated and creative worker. He would create a stock person's duties list, an ADD strategy recommended by his doctor, based on what Elliot wanted done each night. He initialed each accomplished task

THE GREAT REVEAL

on a laminated list—it was Rob's idea to use a page protector so erasable markers could be used—taped up on the wall of the back room, just left of the gray punch clock. With all the advancements in technology, Rob wondered why they still were using such antiquated equipment to keep track of employees' hours.

Each employee was required to punch in and out whenever they arrived or left their shift. They did this by inserting a thin cardboard time card vertically into the top slot of the machine. The punch machine—which Rob thought should have been called a stamp machine—would stamp the date and time on the card to specify a start and end time. It would make a sound much like one a nail gun used in construction makes. This kept track of starting and ending times for each employee. Elliot would then create a printout at the end of the week of the hours worked and submit it to the business office. The employees' paychecks would be based on these stamped cards. If an employee was five minutes late for their shift, they would have to make up the five minutes by staying later, or money would be removed from that employee's paycheck. Rob had learned that it was called prorated pay or docking a person's pay. It was unusually strict.

Elliot was always impressed with Rob's qualities—motivated, organized and had a good work ethic. He had told Elliot that the list would make it easier for other stock boys to know what to do during their shifts too. If the list was completed by one stock person, the next stock person would start the list again. However, if it had not been completed, the next stock person would continue the list. It always included restocking the shelves of items that were continuously in demand—feminine hygiene products, cigarettes, and toilet paper. The stockers had also been required to straighten shelves; relieve cashiers for their breaks and, at the end of the night, sweep the floors.

On this particular night, the hours had seemed to drag on—maybe because Rob was trying to deal with the afternoon's shooting incident. He felt more distressed than when he had rescued the elderly couple from the fire or after saving Stephanie from her assailants. He was aggravated by how Murphy's bullying had caused fourteen-year-old Kyle to irrationally use extreme measures and could result in jail time. *No matter how angry I got at Murphy, I would have never tried to kill him. Kyle's use of violence was impulsive and lacked an understanding of the consequences. Why did he resort to this? After seeing the violence in Montego Bay, I would have thought he'd understand what he was doing was wrong.* Rob once again thought about comic book heroes. *Batman never killed the Joker even though his archenemy killed thousands of people, killed two Robins and put Barbara Gordon in a wheelchair for the rest of her life. And though everyone around him told him that he must kill the Joker, he never did. But even though it's a comic book fantasy, I think his creed makes sense to me. Superman had the same morals.*

But Rob needed to simmer that anger before the end of his work shift. He didn't want Christine to be burdened with his irritation, especially since he must be on his best behavior in front of her mother and aunt.

The work day was coming to an end. Elliot made his announcement through the store's sound system like a self-checkout voice repeatedly reminding the customer to scan any items under their cart: "Attention, Key Drug Mart customers. The store is now closing. Please bring your items to the cashiers at this time." If customers ignored the warning, Rob was responsible for visually scanning the store aisle by aisle to politely remind them. Some customers had been apologetic, but others were too self-centered and rude to care. He and the other employees of Key Drug Mart were trained to be assertive but not aggressive toward each patron. With the day Rob was having, he could have really verbally lashed out at the nasty customers.

When all customers were out of the store, Elliot got on the microphone again. "Cashiers, match up the money you have in your cash registers and print out the summary on the total receipts from the registers as usual. Rob, manage the front entrance. Let people know we are closed and lock the doors."

After he locked the doors, Rob walked slowly to the back room to punch out and get his bike. Elliot had given permission to Rob to bring his bike into the store each time he worked his shift. He had parked it in the break area, where there was no chance of it being stolen from the outside bike rack even though his Kryptonite lock was almost invulnerable to wire or bolt cutters.

THE GREAT REVEAL

The rest of the workers joined Rob in the back, punching out and gathering their belongings in preparation for their departure. Rob, of course, waited for Christine, and they walked out together. Everyone said their goodbyes, and Elliot turned off the store lights, set the alarm and locked the door.

Christine and Rob, with his bike rolling next to him, headed to Christine's aunt's car. She opened the Honda Civic's hatchback, and Rob was able to manipulate the bike so that the hatch could close. Rob opened the driver's side door for Christine like his father had taught him, and she gave Rob that beautiful smile. "Thank you!"

Rob gave her a flirtatious wink.

As Christine began driving, Rob decided he wanted to avoid thinking about the shooting incident, so he thought it best to just ask Christine questions to get his mind off it. "So when did you get your license?" Rob asked.

"Oh, I've had it since the beginning of senior year. I passed my driver's test after the first try," she unintentionally bragged.

"Crap! It took me three tries. I was nervous all three times," Rob sadly admitted. *Actually, it was probably my ADD that caused it.*

"We live about four miles from here, so it won't take us long to arrive. My mom and aunt are expecting us," Christine stated.

"I'm really nervous about meeting them. Do they know anything about me?" Rob asked.

"Oh, I've filled them in and told them all the wonderful things I've learned about you. No need to be nervous. From what I have told them, they are looking forward to meeting you."

The drive was a pleasant one. There was an unusually warm spring breeze flowing through the car's half-open windows, like the breeze from the open window Rob felt when he spent the night at Sitto's house in the extra bedroom upstairs.

There was something liberating about riding in the dark. The street the two were driving on was hilly and largely empty of traffic, save for a few cars, with just the occasional pedestrian or bicyclist with his or her headlight shining on the sidewalk. With only the moon or the odd streetlight causing spotty illumination on the road they were traveling, Rob looked out to see houses lined up like in a standard family-friendly Spielberg movie. When passing areas of darkness, the road became licorice black again, with a long strip of dashed white or solid yellow down its center, like a strand of taunt yarn from its skein. Rob gazed up at the night sky, which looked like a blue-black blanket with minute holes in it to let in the light from the other side. Occasionally, tall trees on the side of the street would interrupt the view.

He and Christine didn't talk much until Rob asked, "So what was it that you wanted to be honest with me about?"

"Oh, we're almost there. I can share that with you then."

This is strange. Why is this something that she has to share in front of her mom and aunt? This whole mystery just got stranger. I'm feeling it's not one of the standard excuses of why we can only be friends.

Christine pulled into her aunt's driveway of a small mid-'70s two-story single-family Cape Cod home with a detached single-car garage. It was difficult to see the full exterior because of the dark sky and numerous trees in front. From what Rob could see, the house had a centered front entry, a steep roof with side gables and an overhang with a brick facade, some gabled dormers, and four front windows with white shutters. *This place makes my parents' place seem new.*

"Well, here we are. You ready?" Christine excitedly asked.

"Sure, I guess." *Ready for what? Meeting her parents or the "I have to be honest with you" part?*

"Oh, don't worry. Just be yourself. They'll love you!" she reaffirmed.

Christine and Rob walked up the uneven red brick steps, and Christine unlocked the door. The front entrance was dimly lit by a weather-damaged porch lamp that needed replacing as well as a brighter light bulb. *How old are these people?*

"Mom! Aunt Helena! We're here!" Christine affably shouted. Both ladies came out of the kitchen, her mother wiping her hands with a dish towel and her aunt bringing out a tray of cheese and crackers. Rob noticed how her mother resembled Christine, which gave him a glimpse of what his possible girlfriend would look like if she were taller and in her mid- to late forties. Her mother had short frosted brunette hair, perfectly kempt. She wore no makeup that Rob could notice, but her eyes were a stunning icy blue, the kind only a Photoshop computer generation could produce.

Christine introduced Rob to both of them. "Mom and Aunt Helena, I'd like you to meet Rob Shehan. He's the boy I've been telling you about."

Olivia replied, "It's so very nice to meet Christine's boyfriend," as they shook hands.

Okay, now we are getting somewhere. Christine must have referred to me as her boyfriend. This night is getting better.

Helena reached out her hand. "Hi, I'm Dr. Stewart, Christine's aunt, but you can call me Helena. We've heard so much about you. When Christine talked about you, I thought it was someone she imagined," she said while shaking his hand.

Rob released a light chuckle. "It's so nice to meet you both."

"Well, just by what Christine has told us about you, we have been impressed. There are very few seventeen-year-old high school students that have manners and moral upbringing out there in this world," Dr. Stewart commented.

"Truthfully, I was made of clay, and my dad molded me into a real boy!" Rob joked.

Olivia looked at Helena, bewildered.

"You know, Pinocchio, um…Wonder Woman…created from clay?" Rob tried to explain the joke, which lost its punch since it had to be explained.

"Rob loves to make people laugh," Christine added. Then Olivia realized from Christine's widening eyes that Rob was joking. Olivia produced a suppressed laugh, looking at Dr. Stewart, then at Rob.

"We can see that," Olivia replied. "Please have a seat. What would you like to drink? Ice water, ice tea, lemonade or soda?"

"Ice tea, unsweetened, if possible, please," Rob replied.

"That's exactly what we drink. No added sugars in our house! I'll be right back. Please help yourself to cheese and crackers!"

Christine and Rob sat on a large sofa printed with repeating reddish-orange-and-gold flowers. The fabric had a fuzzy velour-type texture. *How old are these couches? Do these people live in the '70s?* Rob's hands were very dry after working in the dust-filled back room of the drugstore, which caused his skin to crackle along the fabric. The chair's arms were made out of a scrolling murky wood covered in more of the same fabric, making it difficult to comfortably place his arms. He decided to keep his hands on his lap.

The room was accented by mahogany wood floors and golden pinewood paneling on the wall connected to the adjacent cobblestone fireplace. *What is it about old houses and pine paneling?* On the walnut-veneer coffee table in front of the couch was a slag-glass swan bowl and a pressed-glass candy jar filled with Peppermint Patties. On each side of the fireplace, there were two matching fabric-covered rockers with the same repeated reddish-orange-and-gold flower pattern. *Did these people raid a Goodwill store? I didn't think anyone has this type of decor in their homes anymore except Mom and Dad.*

Olivia came back with Rob's ice tea, and she placed it on a cork coaster on the coffee table. Then she sat down on one of the rockers. Dr. Stewart sat in the other as Christine moved closer to Rob.

"Rob," Christine nervously said, "there is something important we need to tell you."

We? That's so weird. My previous presumptions have to be wrong since it's usually not a family matter when it comes to discussing the status of a relationship. Besides, they called me her boyfriend. This family must be quite progressive even though their choice of decor is not.

Instead of Christine beginning to explain, she put out her palm down, opened Rob's left hand, and placed hers in his. At that moment, on her finger, a ring identical to his appeared.

"Holy shit," shouted Rob, quickly removing his hand and covering his mouth as if he shouldn't have sworn. "I'm sorry for the crude language in front of you both, but please tell me what's going on! How could you possibly have a ring identical to the one I have? Wait! Did you find this one too? Where did you find it? Did it fit perfectly? Does it work like mine? I'm so confused." *First, the shooting incident today at school, and now this. I'm totally freakin' out right now. I'm babbling! Shut up, Rob. Shut up! Crap! Here comes the sweat!*

Christine was about to explain until Olivia cut her off. "Rob, she did not find the ring. She's always had it since we, um…landed." Olivia cleared her throat midsentence.

THE GREAT REVEAL

"Oh, so you came from another country to America?"

Olivia hesitated as she spoke, "Um…no! From another planet… in a…um…spaceship."

Rob nervously laughed. "I see you like to joke too. That's funny. Spaceship. You are joking, right?"

Olivia continued, "Remember Kralc Tenk and the information he conveyed to you?"

Shaking, Rob said, "H-How do you know about Kralc Tenk? Are y-you government investigators trying to get my ring? But if you already have a ring, w-why would you want mine?" *Come on, Rob. I know I tend to jump to conclusions at times, but really? Government agents?*

Christine intervened, "Okay, Rob. Breathe slowly in through your nose and out through your mouth. Slow, deep, calming breaths. This is going to take a lot of time to explain, and we need you to be relaxed when we tell you because we are going to need your help!"

Rob did as Christine had asked, and after he had taken three cleansing breaths, he closed his eyes, exhaled and said, "Okay, I'm ready for the data dump."

Olivia said, "Now remember when Kralc Tenk told you about the possibility that Lelak Nadroj was killed based on the evidence of blood that you found on his ring?"

Rob asked, "Wait! How do you know about that conversation?"

"We have had communications with Kralc Tenk using our rings," Olivia replied. "Anyway, I'm Lelak's wife, well, widow, and Christine is my daughter."

Rob looked confused, "So Lelak married a human, and you both birthed a human daughter with no apparent alien characteristics?"

"Well, not exactly," replied Christine as she began her transformation into her true form. "My real name is Arak. I'm from the planet Themadoria, as is my mother, Lah." In front of Rob's eyes was no longer the Christine he knew but a being with light-blue skin. No more beautiful pixie-cut hair, only a hairless head similar to an average human's, black slanted teardrop-shaped eyes holding very small light-blue pupils, two nostrils without a nose, a slit for a mouth, two holes for ears and four unusually long fingers including a thumb.

Olivia also revealed herself, looking like an older version of Arak but with an aqua-blue streak that ran down the middle of her forehead and stopped at her brow. "I was the hooded figure that was following you during some of your rescues. I had to make sure you were the one with the ring."

Arak, looking very sad while looking at Rob, added, "I wanted to tell you that our friendship has been the most rewarding I have had on this planet. I care for you deeply and not just because of our mission to find your ring but because I have a true affection for you. My mom was afraid I would become too attached, fearing that you would want to begin a more serious relationship with me, possibly a romantic one, which, obviously, you do."

Rob, still in amazement at this revelation, was staring off into space.

"Rob, are you there?" Christine looked at Rob's vacant gape into nothingness.

"Um…yeah! I'm here! Just when I thought our relationship was too good to be true, you just confirmed that it isn't. Yeah, I was hoping for a more romantic involvement with you, but that is now obviously impossible. However, I have to tell you that I actually find this situation humorous because no girl has ever said to me, 'We can only be friends because I'm an alien from a planet that is light-years away from here, and I eventually have to return, so our relationship cannot get romantic.'"

Christine smiled at his sarcastic reply. *It's ironic that she is beautiful in her alien form.* His attraction to her was more than just physical. She was the kindest, gentlest person he had ever met. *Maybe that's what Dad was emphasizing. Inner beauty accents outer beauty. He told me people in today's world fall in love primarily based on physical appearance and that they never get to know the person as a person. He told me all those apps that people use now only create an allusion of physicality with its filters and fake pictures. I finally understand what he meant. I'm still wondering how he knows about apps and filters.*

"So now what? Who sent you on this mission to find the ring?" asked Rob.

THE GREAT REVEAL

"Before I answer that question, Rob, would you like us to morph back? Does our appearance make you uncomfortable?" Christine asked.

"Absolutely not. I think you are both beautiful creatures, your color, your eyes, everything, but it may be best to morph for the time being," Rob reassured them. "It will definitely be difficult to explain your identity in your current form to anyone."

"You are so sweet! We have encountered few humans on this planet, some not so kind and pleasant and others, like yourself, amiable, compassionate, thoughtful and forthright. We had hoped that the person who had possession of the ring would emulate our kind, that is, our kind before the Era of the Great Gasses," Olivia exclaimed. At that moment, both Themadorians morphed back to their human counterparts.

Christine moved in closer to Rob, turned his head toward hers and gave him a long kiss on his lips. Rob had flushed after Christine's warm kiss, "I wasn't sure how comfortable you would have been if I tried to kiss you in my original form."

"Wait! I thought this was going to be a platonic relationship. You're giving me mixed signals here," Rob questioned.

"Can't two very close friends kiss? asked Christine. "I understand from my research that there are different kinds of kisses for different relationships on this planet." asked Christine. "There's a mother's kiss, a sibling's kiss, a friend's kiss and something called a French kiss for those people in love or in a romantic relationship. I believe it's actually called a *galocher*, to kiss with tongues."

"Wow! Your research is quite...thorough!" Rob replied, surprised at her facts. *I can't believe we are talking about different types of kisses. She's definitely blunt and uninhibited.*

"Listen...can we kiss when you are in your natural form?" Rob said, half kidding and half serious.

"Rob Shehan, you are too forward!" she responded with a very serious look.

"Oh my god! I'm so sorry! I didn't mean to be," Rob shockingly retorted.

"Now I'm the jokester." Christine laughed as she pointed to Rob. "Of course, you can. I would really like that! And since I do not have lips in the conventional sense, I will do my best to form acceptable ones," Christine replied as she morphed back to her blue persona. At that very moment, Rob held her tight in his arms and kissed her long and affectionately on her thin-lipped mouth. *Do not French kiss her! Do not French kiss her!* They pulled away simultaneously.

"How did that feel? Christine asked since she had never kissed a human in her natural form.

"I never had any girl ask me how my kiss felt before. Truthfully, it was wonderful. Actually, both of them were wonderful," Rob said, "even with your mom and aunt watching us."

"Well, I've never kissed a human before now! It's great to learn from new experiences." Christine chuckled at her own comment.

And with that, they both embraced as tears came to Arak's eyes. "You are one of a kind, Rob Shehan. I will never forget you when I leave."

Still embracing her, Rob whispered, "The feeling is mutual, Christine. You will always be my first true love, well, first true platonic love…well, not strictly platonic. Um…I'll shut up now."

Again, Christine laughed. "I know what you mean, Rob. I know that it's difficult to describe what we have. It will probably be the most unique relationship we will ever have."

At this point, both Olivia and Helena became teary-eyed. Olivia said, wiping her tears with a tissue from the side table, "If we are going to complete this mission and save my son, we will need a plan. I don't trust Crumb. He truly is the embodiment of evil."

Rob looked over at Olivia and asked, "Son? Crumb? Okay, time to fill me in on the details of this mission."

Olivia, Christine and Dr. Stewart gave Rob all the details of what had happened prior to their arrival in the town of Rosemont, and they began developing a plan to get Etak back from Crumb and still retain Rob's ring, knowing full well that Crumb would not keep his word.

CHAPTER FOURTEEN

Ring Limitations

Rob was still overwhelmed the following morning. He was worried about the mission that he, Olivia and Christine were planning; Kyle's arrest and his court appearance; the well-being of Sitto; his preparation for the play and, least of all, his homework including the hero writing project, which he had still not started. The ring was the furthest thing from his mind.

Since he now had the next two days off because of the investigation into the shooting, he could take the needed the time to process everything, prioritize their importance and create a plan to carry out the best that he could. This was not easy for Rob. Since struggling with ADD, Rob always had to use the compensatory strategies he had researched on the Internet to stay focused and organized. His mind always had too many events floating, like the last ten pieces of Cheerios moving around the top of the bowl that refused to get into the spoon. The only way he could keep those thoughts in some semblance of order was to create a checklist like the one he had made at work. The checklist had to be coded in some way in case his mother saw it when she came into his bedroom and started asking questions. She was always coming into his sanctuary unannounced to evaluate the cleanliness of his room.

Why is she always checking my room and not my sisters' shared bedroom? My bedroom isn't in more disarray than theirs, but Mom seems to discriminate against me with what I am required as opposed to my sisters' obligations. The least she could do is knock. Rob resented his sisters for that. His mother kept telling him he had to earn the right to drive the family car by doing chores around the house each week, which included washing the weekly market produce. *Why can't my sisters do some of these chores? All I can figure out is that she's a misandrist by treating Dad and me differently from my sisters. The inequality in this family is pathetic.*

As he wrote his priorities on a large sheet of poster paper left over from a pointless science project, one of his smartphone's ringtones, "Opening," went off along with the accompanying vibration. It was his aunt Aggie. "Hi, Aunt Aggie! How's Sitto doing?"

"Amazingly well. She told me that if you wanted to come over, we could start making the stuffed grape leaves, but she'll need you to pick some more off the vines in the backyard. You know, I think your excitement to make grape leaves encouraged her and made her feel she was still needed in our family. Thank you for that. It made all the difference."

"You're welcome. I'll be right over! I have to ask Mom for her car. I should be there in about a half hour. Thanks for letting me know. I'm so glad Sitto is feeling better. Bye!"

After Rob hung up the phone, he was relieved and crossed that item off his list of priorities. He left the encoded list flattened out on his bed. He used single letters and short phrases to disguise his to-do list: FOTR (for play practice), OC Crumby (his mission with Olivia and Christine), HERO (homework), COG (check on grandma), and other codes. He wasn't too worried about his mother deciphering it.

"Hey, Mom! May I please use the car to go and help Sitto make stuffed grape leaves with Aunt Aggie? They are going to show me how to do it!" Rob excitedly asked.

"Yes, but you'll have to fill the tank," his mother demanded.

"I'll refill the amount I use," Rob said, knowing full well that the tank was probably low and that he'd have to use his remaining money to fill it. Whenever he used the family car, she forced him to fill the tank even though he was rarely allowed to drive it.

For the first time since Rob could remember, his father spoke up! "Take my truck. The rugs that I was supposed to install didn't arrive at the warehouse, so I'm stuck at home. There is plenty of gas, so don't worry!"

Dad just added another reason I should pick him to be my hero. His father threw him the keys of the eight-year-old black Chevy Avalanche from his coat pocket and didn't even say "Be careful," but instead, Rob said, "I promise to be careful!"

"I know you will, buddy. I trust you." Rob heard his father's reply, simultaneously hearing a *humph* sound come from his mother's direction. It was either indicating her indignation toward her husband or her displeasure at Rob not going to fill the tank of her SUV.

Sitto's house was only about three miles from Rob's house, and the streets leading there were not usually crowded. But on this day, midway to her house, there was construction on the main road leading to Arrow Avenue, the side street to Sitto's house. Cones were arranged about fifteen feet apart, and caution signs were posted, informing drivers of a traffic control person ahead. Two flag people were posted on both ends of the road where a water main break was being repaired. The repair crew was in the maintenance hole, attempting to locate the break, temporarily stopping the flow to eventually repair the damage with new ductile iron or UVC pipes. The inundation continued flooding the street with a deluge of gushing chlorinated water, creating a large ever-flowing stream. Fortunately, the traffic was not heavy, and there were only two vehicles: Rob's truck on one side and a yellow convertible slowly approaching the flag person on the other side. It was a narrow temporary makeshift section of the road to allow one vehicle through at a time.

Rob waited as the flag person flipped his doubled sided stop-slow sign to indicate for Rob to stop while others on the opposite side facing Rob's car could drive slowly through the construction zone's condensed area. When the flag person on the other side gave the all-clear on his walkie-talkie to his counterpart, Rob waited as the flag person flipped his doubled sided stop-slow sign, indicating Slow. Rob proceeded.

Luckily, no one was behind Rob's car, but when the young twenty-something female driving the yellow convertible sports car coming from the other direction decided that her texting was more important than paying attention to the road, she not only ignored the traffic control person's stop sign but also the ten-miles-an-hour speed limit sign, driving straight toward Rob. Her signal person started yelling for her to stop, but apparently, she couldn't hear him over her car's blaring music. Thinking on his feet—well, thinking on his butt—Rob hit the brakes and quickly asked the ring for phantom power and time manipulation. *Again, archangel Michael, please let these be the right powers.* He avoided requesting superspeed again since he might not be able to save the lady and the flag person simultaneously. The ring vibrated lightly and, again, emitted a faint light-blue glow. Rob felt himself morphing, but into what version of himself he did not know until he looked down at his hands. He saw that they were black. He had no time to view his full transformation, but made the obvious connection to his new identity.

Upon Rob's command, he and his truck became a wispy translucent apparition, allowing her car to go through his, which now looked like a ghostly fog except shaped like a Chevy Avalanche. As she did, Rob looked at the female vicenarian, now sitting opposite him in her driver's seat but still unaware of her surroundings until she quickly looked toward her passenger side. Shocked, she finally looked forward and suddenly realized that she was heading straight for a hydro excavator vehicle as Rob finished the pass-through. She tried to swerve to avoid it but sideswiped it and ricocheted her car toward the signal person, who could not get out of the way in time.

Once Rob's vehicle stopped, he quickly threw his dad's truck into Park. Immediately jumping out of his truck and holding his hand up as if giving someone a high five, he celebrated having successfully stopped time before the signal person was hit. He ran over and tackled him out of the way of the now motionless yellow vehicle. *Tackling him instead of simply walking over and sliding him to the side would have caused suspicion.* Before time was stopped, the flag person on the opposite side was facing away from the construction area, with his hand up to stop any other cars from passing through, so he did not see Rob's phantom truck go through the lady's vehicle. He was also perfectly still in Rob's time freeze.

Rob then had time resume. The young lady came to a complete stop as both the signal person and Rob were flat on the loose-gravel-covered road.

Rob and the signaler got up slowly and brushed each other off. "T-Thank you so much. I-I don't know how you did that, but you just saved my life. I-I didn't even see you get out of y-your truck!" exclaimed the dazed construction worker.

"Never mind that! Are you all right? I tackled you pretty hard."

"My shoulder is bruised, but I'll ice it later."

"Your other flag person looks like he's panicking," Rob said as he saw him have both the stop sign and his other hand up, using his body to block the lane to make sure no one else passed him. "I'll check on the lady to see if she needs medical attention. Please hold traffic until I check on her," Rob requested.

"Umm…y-yah…s-sure thing!" the flag person Rob had just rescued pressed his walkie-talkie. "Hey, Ralph! Hold traffic until I give you the signal," he told the other worker. "We're checking on the other driver!"

Rob rushed over to the young brunette who looked as if she was in shock. "Are you all right?"

"I-I think so. I d-don't know what happened," stuttered the young lady.

"I think the first thing you need to do is call the police and have them fill out an official police report. I could stay and explain to them what happened, but I'm late to my grandmother's house. She was expecting me ten minutes ago. Oh, and I think it would be wise if you are honest with the officer when he arrives, but that's your call. Besides, your car is damaged, and you'll need a police report for the insurance company."

"My boyfriend is gonna kill me! It's his car. I promised I'd be careful."

"Were you aware that you were texting while you were driving and were completely unaware of the construction site? You scared the crap out of me!"

The lady said, "I'm so sorry, but I-I wasn't texting!"

Rob knew she was lying.

"The last thing I remember was seeing you in the passenger seat next to me, which was impossible since I was alone in the car."

Rob tried to cover up the use of his powers. "You probably saw me trying to avoid hitting you by swerving to your left, so it may have looked like I was in your passenger seat."

"But this is a one-lane street. I don't know! I could have sworn I saw you sitting in my passenger seat but facing the other way and with a steering wheel in front of you. It was as if you were a ghost passing through my car," she supposed.

"Sometimes after a car accident, people become disorientated and imagine things that didn't actually happen. I would stay to help clarify with the officers, but I really have to go," Rob responded. "I'm sure the signal people will fill the officers in on the details."

"Um, okay. I'll call the police now, and then I'll have to explain this to my boyfriend. This car is his pride and joy. Thank you, mister," she replied, still in a stupor. Rob had no time for small talk, nor was he going to be a witness to this accident even though he knew he should. *I sure as hell hope that she or the construction workers don't describe me to the police and try to locate me. I didn't contribute to or cause the accident. She did. So I don't think I'm obliged to stay at the crash scene or provide a statement to the police. Besides, they would never find me in my present identity, since I'll morph back before getting to Sitto's house.*

As the construction signalmen re-coordinated their timing to get traffic moving again, compensating for the crashed car and the excavator, they decided to close the road completely and detour all cars to the next available side road. As the hydro excavator driver approached the young brunette, Rob got into his father's truck and slowly continued on to his destination. *I would have never survived this calamity if I didn't have the alien's ring. What if I had chosen the wrong power or didn't think quick enough? I could have been killed along with little Miss Yellow Convertible.* As he finished that thought, Rob reverted to his true self.

Rob's self-doubt was getting in the way of his ability to use the ring. *I don't mind making my own mistakes if they only affected me, but these are lives I am dealing with. Maybe I can ask Christine how she handles using the ring. She probably has more experience and can give me some pointers.*

Rob needed to concentrate on the road. *No reason to get Dad's truck in an accident too.* He arrived at his grandmother's and parked on an available side-parking area parallel to her house. Aunt Aggie saw Rob arriving and opened the side door for him. "We were worried. It doesn't usually take long to get here from your house," Aggie declared.

"So sorry! There was construction on Clinton Road due to a water main break."

"Oh, that's right. I forgot about that. It was on the news this morning that there may be delays in morning traffic. Well, Sitto is in the kitchen but needs your help with picking more grape leaves from the backyard."

Sitto had many grapevines growing on the chain-link fences along the sides and the back of her house. In eighth grade, Rob learned how to pick them when she was more ambulatory. Rob tried to recall the method she taught him, but because of his ADD, he had forgotten some of it. He asked Sitto to review it before sending him out to pick.

Even though Sitto was not physically well, her memory was amazing at recalling details for preparing Lebanese dishes. She reminded Rob, "Only select whole medium-sized young leaves about four to five inches wide with a good light-green color and no holes." She used her fingers to give Rob an idea of the size since they had no ruler available. "If you choose grape leaves that are too small, they will tear when trying to roll them with the lamb-and-rice stuffing. Avoid the larger grape leaves because they are too tough and too chewy after they are cooked. Avoid the fuzzy thick leaves. Pick only the shiny, smooth leaves."

Sitto was an expert at making all types of Lebanese foods, adding just the precise amount of ingredients without using a measuring cup or spoon. Unfortunately, Rob and his family could never get Sitto to give anyone exact measurements so they could write them on recipe cards. She would just say "a handful," "two fingers full," "a pinch of something" or "a dab of something else." *If only I could create a translation of those measurement idiosyncrasies, I would be able to replicate all the recipes and write them down. Maybe there's an app for that.* Rob chuckled to himself.

Rob headed outside through the back door, stepping onto a very small six-by-six-foot porch that could barely fit the two residing emerald-green aluminum retro rockers. One was for Sitto, and the other was for a guest. The hunter-green-and-white porch was in desperate need of sanding and a good coat of paint. Rob's mom volunteered him for the task, but his schedule would not allow any more jobs. He thought that maybe he could do it this summer when he graduated. That reminded Rob that he promised Sitto that he would come over right after graduation so she could see him in his cap and gown, in case she couldn't be transported to the tented event. Rob hoped that now that he had cured her, she might be able to attend.

As Rob picked grape leaves off the vines, his phone started singing the Romantics' ringtone. "Hi, Christine!"

"Are you busy?" Christine asked.

"I'm picking grape leaves to prepare for stuffing," Rob explained as he filled her in on how he was able to cure his grandmother from whatever it was that was wrong with her including the other nine other patients in the hospital.

"About that, you didn't cure her with the ring!"

"Why, of course I did, just like I did the other nine patients at the hospital that afternoon."

"Rob, the ring can only cure people who had injures from accidents, assaults or trauma, not genetic disorders like cancer, heart disease, or diabetes." Christine continued to explain. "Out of the ten patients you thought you cured, only six survived."

"No, that can't be. That would mean that only my persuasion caused Sitto to get better."

"That's right! Rob, I really hope that she lives much longer, but I don't really know."

"How do you know this about the ring's limitations?" Rob frantically asked.

Christine continued, "In the tunnels on Themadoria, the workers would have occupational accidents, so the medical professionals who cared for them would help them with their injuries so they could heal. But unbeknownst to them, my parents used their rings to help them heal quickly and completely as if they were never injured. They tried it on the sick and dying, thinking it could rejuvenate them, but they were wrong. A week or so later, they died naturally, some from a genetic disease and others from old age. I'm so sorry, Rob. I didn't want you to get your hopes up in case your grandmother has to go back to the hospital, nor did I want you to be surprised or feel that you were using the ring for personal gain. Didn't you notice that the ring neither vibrated or glowed when you touched some of the patients?"

"Not really. I was going so quickly with my superspeed that I didn't notice."

"Well, you would have noticed that the ring was not giving you that power for those particular patients," Christine sadly replied.

"How do you know about the patients that survived?" Rob asked.

"It was on the local news this afternoon. They talked about the six patients who were discharged and had no sign that they were ever injured. When reporters asked about the other patients on the floor, the doctor being interviewed said that those patients were suffering from inherited abnormalities or illness, like heart failure or Alzheimer's. They did not survive," she related. "I am so sorry, Rob! I know how much you love your grandmother."

"Listen, if that is true, I'm going to try and spend as much time with Sitto as I can today since we are all going to travel tomorrow."

"I understand. Are you ready for tomorrow?" asked Christine.

"Yeah, I told my mom we were traveling to visit your relatives," Rob reassured her. "I'll see you tomorrow."

"We'll pick you up at nine tomorrow morning as we agreed," she reminded Rob.

"Okay, I'll be ready. Bye!" Rob sadly pressed the red Hang Up button and continued picking grape leaves, knowing that Sitto might end up going back to the hospital to die. While that was pressing on his mind, another more urgent issue flashed in his head. *What if*

Mom wants to meet Christine? "Shit!' Rob whispered as he finished picking enough leaves for them to stuff and cook.

He returned to Sitto's kitchen with the grape leaves. Sitto noticed tears in his eyes. "Why are you so sad, Robby?"

"Allergies, Sitto. There are a lot of weeds out there. Listen, would you like me to paint the porch next week?"

"You are a very sweet boy, my Robby," she softly said, smiling. "Come over and give your *sitto* a big hug." Rob went over, bent over and hugged her for a long time, trying to hold back his tears as he held her tight but still gentle enough not to hurt her delicate body.

"I love you, Sitto," Rob said, closing his eyes tightly as tears slowly dripped down his face. She could not see the distress on his face as his head rested on her shoulder.

As he pulled away, Sitto asked, "Do you need tissues to wipe the tears? I'm sorry your allergies are acting up."

"Yes, I'll get some from the bathroom," Rob replied, sniveling.

The very petite first-floor powder room had only a white pedestal sink and a toilet with handicap assistance bars on each side. Rob walked to the powder room, closed the door and silently sobbed.

Sitto's health is going to be on my mind all day tomorrow. I know that Christine and Olivia need me tomorrow, but my heart won't be in it.

CHAPTER FIFTEEN

Mission Possible

The next morning would have normally been a routine school day, but the investigation into Kyle's armed emotional breakdown at Rosemont High was still ongoing. This morning, however, Rob did some things that he had never done before. He performed regular adult morning rituals including a morning shower, complete with brushing his teeth, flossing and putting on deodorant and cologne, which surprised his mother and father, who were having breakfast in their very small dinette, which was connected to their even smaller kitchen.

Rob even decided to have breakfast with his parents. His sisters were still sleeping like most high school teenagers would on a day off, but Rob was wide awake and reflecting on the mission with Christine and Olivia.

As he lived in a modest fourteen-hundred-square-foot home, the distance from his bedroom to the kitchen dinette area was only about twenty feet. The dinette had gaudy gray brick wallpaper on one side of the ten-by-ten room directly adjacent to the kitchen area. The worn-out wood-veneer dining table was just enough for four people, which was fine since Rob's mom seldom ate at it. She'd eat at the gray Formica kitchen counter extension protruding from the end of the countertop. Rob sat at the table, in front of the usual breakfast his mother had prepared—sunny-side-up eggs and bacon. But something was missing. In place of the bacon-soaked toast was a deviation of pancakes. Rob just hoped his father would not soak it in bacon grease. Even though his father loved fruits and vegetables, he also loved coffee, donuts, cookies and cake, so when his mother added bacon-greased toast every morning, it caused Rob to worry about his father's health.

"So to what do we owe this honor? I thought you'd sleep in like your sisters," his mother said sarcastically. "You are never hungry this early in the morning, and you usually shower the night before, which I think is gross. Don't you sweat at night?"

Rob decided to bust her chops, as his father would say, and replied, "The answer to your first question is that Christine is picking me up to visit her relatives that live near Roswell, and I wanted to impress them." Rob's father sat proud in his seat, knowing his son listened to him. "And the answer to your second question is that I don't sweat because I sleep in the buff." At this, his father, midsip, almost spewed coffee across the table. Rob had his father's sense of humor.

His mother, however, basically naive to most colloquial expressions, looked at her husband with a stare of disgust, not acknowledging that she did not know what Rob was referencing but instead trying to fake her knowledge of the expression.

Rob's mother was very limited in her understanding of the world around her. She had no interest in reading anything new, rarely read the newspaper and got her medical advice from a cashier at Walmart probably because she did not trust doctors. When her doctor recommended blood pressure medicine, she ignored it. It was probably because the family had poor health insurance, complaining about the high cost whenever the family suggested getting a checkup.

Her basic experience of today's world centered around *the Bible*, which she read incessantly, and one Pearl Buck book, *The Good Earth*, not necessarily because she liked the content but because people had told her that the author won the Nobel Prize in Literature in 1938 for it.

She believed in just about every aphorism known to mankind and seemed to intentionally relay one to Rob. His mother would use phrases like "You'll pay for that," which made no sense to Rob when he was very young. He thought he had to come up with a certain amount of cash to pay for whatever he was supposed to pay for.

Change was not something Rob's mother could handle. She was stubborn about learning something new even when Rob tried to teach her. When Rob mentioned to her the portability of a smartphone, it took him a year to convince her to get one. She would say, "This flip phone works just fine. Besides, they're expensive. Money doesn't grow on trees, you know." Rob then thought that if they did, he would have solved the problem of "paying for that" during his earlier years, whatever *that* was.

Once he announced his itinerary to his parents, Rob just sat there, waiting. He waited. And waited. And waited. And finally—"Is this the Christine at work your father told me about? Can we meet her before you leave for her relatives?" his mother said. This was the same traditional question she would ask every time she found out about a girl Rob was dating. It was always the exact same question every time. Original thought was not his mother's long suit.

There it is, right on cue.

"Sorry, Mom. We have timed the trip perfectly since her relatives will only be in town for a short time, and she wants to spend as much time with them as possible," Rob dictated. Rob remembered how he had explained to Christine when working out their meeting with Dr. Stewart and her mother of what would happen if his mom ever tried to meet her. "Mom, you always offer my friends food, and we really don't have time for a meal or even a snack. Besides, Sitto and I made sfouf when I was over at her house the other day, and I brought some home," Rob explained. Sfouf was Rob's favorite because it was a simple plain cake with turmeric, semolina, tahini, pine nuts and sometimes almonds. Since it contained healthy, organic ingredients, Christine and Olivia could eat it after he had learned of their Themadorian dietary needs. That reminded Rob to text Christine upon her arrival instead of having her come to the door to avoid the parental meeting he dreaded.

His mother had replied, "Fine," in that negative tone that his mother used when she felt she was right but didn't want to bother arguing about it.

With a sigh of relief, Rob waited for Christine's text.

His father had approached him. "I understand why you don't want us to meet her."

"You do?" He paused. "Yeah, of course, you do. It's just that it's embarrassing when Mom talks to my friends, especially girls. Sometimes I think girls avoid me after meeting her because she says stuff that would be deemed offensive or inappropriate. But they have always mentioned how much they liked you."

"Well, of course, they do!" He chuckled.

"Do you have the day off too, Dad? I noticed you aren't wearing your usual army-green work clothes."

"As a matter of fact, I do. Since I was able to take care of two smaller jobs yesterday, I thought I'd work on the yard and the garage today," he loudly proclaimed so that his wife would hear him. This was a novelty for a soft-spoken man. Then he leaned over and said, "I'm going to sneak out later to go bowling."

That was Lou Shehan's modus operandi to escape his wife's nagging. He would tell her he needed something at the hardware store—like nails to fix the fence, pegboard hooks to organize his tools or some other necessary hardware to complete a task—but as Rob had always known, he'd go bowling at the Rosemont Bowl-a-Roll, which was conveniently located next to Rosemont's local hardware store, the Rosemont Hardware Supply. Lou loved bowling almost as much as he loved his family but with one difference. Bowling boosted his self-esteem and brought a much-needed release from the tension he continued experiencing at home.

His father had been a member of a weekly nighttime bowling league that competed for money prizes including special prizes during the holiday season, like turkeys, spiral hams or tickets to baseball games. Bowling was his ultimate getaway from Matilda, Lee, Tilly or whatever name she wanted to be called that day.

To say that Rob's father was an amazing bowler was an understatement. He had won tournaments, was on local bowling competition shows and had the distinction of bowling three perfect games in two years, one of which was on the local Bowling for Bucks. But no matter what prizes his father came home with, Rob never heard his mother thank him, congratulate him or even kiss him like girls do when a jockey wins a race at the tracks. She would always complain that he could have done better, that he wasted all his strikes on practice shots or that his hair (at least what was left of it) wasn't combed. She was relentless. *Poor Dad.*

Before Rob left, he asked his father, "Was Mom always so cruel? I know you would have never married her if she were. I know I wouldn't date someone who verbally abused me." Rob waited for a quick, simple, straightforward answer. Well, it was quick, and it was straightforward. But it was not as simple as Rob was hoping.

"Not until after the miscarriage."

Rob's eyes widened. Rob whispered, "Wait! What miscarriage?"

"Let's go bowling next week, and I'll explain everything to you. Your mom told me not to tell the three of you, but I think it's important that you understand her behavior better now that you're older. Your sisters do not know yet."

Rob thought that it was bad timing on his part to asking his father a question right before leaving. It reminded him of Kralc, who stopped transmission after stating, "There are others," and he never figured that out until Christine and Olivia revealed themselves. At that point, Rob felt that he would make a terrible detective. The excitement he had about his mission with his extraterrestrial comrades faded slowly like the end of a rainbow.

Finally, Rob received a text from Christine that read, "Ready for Mission Possible!" Rob wondered if she understood her play on words. With a lot less enthusiasm and a hug from his father, he softly said, "See you guys! I'll be late, so don't wait up. I'll call if I run into trouble." Rob chuckled to himself. *How will my parents even possibly help in the situation that my alien friends and I are about to experience?* Closing the door behind him and holding his bag of treats, he could hear his mom yell, of course, "Be careful!"

Rob entered the vehicle through the back door and sat next to Christine. He had said hello with a muffled voice to everyone, with his head down after he had given Christine a kiss on her lips when she turned to greet him. Helena drove, and Olivia occupied the passenger seat.

"Okay, I know that look." Christine smirked.

"What? I'm just tired. This is pretty early for me," Rob replied quietly and with little energy.

"You realize I can ask my ring for telepathic power to read your mind, right? However, I would never do that to you because I trust you. And besides, it wouldn't work because the ring would not allow it without your permission. But if you're not ready to tell me, I understand. We should really focus on this mission. It's vital to save my brother."

"Yeah, I understand. Sorry! It's just…" Rob stopped short.

"Just what?" Christine questioned with extra attentiveness.

"I just learned before I left that my dad kept a secret from me," Rob disappointedly whispered. "I guess it was an important secret, but he was probably threatened by Mom not to tell us. Dad probably didn't understand that Mom never had followed through on her threats. Why would he do that?"

"Maybe because he respects her," Christine said.

"Why would he respect her? She never seems to respect him. She only wants to manipulate him," Rob refuted. "I think they call it gaslighting."

"We can never know. Respect means different things to different people. Maybe it's because he loves her," Christine wondered.

"Yeah, maybe. I don't know," Rob said, feeling disheartened.

"Can you tell me?" questioned Christine.

"I should have had a brother or maybe another sister," Rob disclosed with a sigh, eyes watering. "Dad told me Mom had a miscarriage. Apparently, Mom was a lot nicer prior to it, according to Dad. If I'm not mistaken, from what I understand from health class, a lost pregnancy can result in a mother having post-traumatic stress disorder, but I had always thought it was trauma from the war. I should have put two and two together."

Christine had no idea what he was referring to and asked, "Two and two?"

"Sorry, I remembered about seven years ago that Mom had a mental breakdown when we were younger. We always wondered where she was for little over a week. Dad just told us that Mom wasn't feeling well, which was true, but he only told us two years ago that she had what he called a nervous breakdown, which seems to make sense now that I know about the miscarriage. I guess it was because she has always been nervous about our safety. Maybe she felt she didn't keep her unborn baby safe. I don't know." Rob held back on saying, "It's just a theory," remembering the number of times Kralc said it.

"I'm so sorry to hear this," both Olivia and Dr. Stewart sincerely expressed.

"Okay, listen, everyone. I don't want us to be distracted by my personal issues right now. They are not as important as what we are about to do," Rob exclaimed, trying to shake himself from his funk. "So let's do this!"

During the trip, Rob, Christine and Olivia reviewed their plans and alternative plans, trying to predict what Crumb might be scheming. Their nemesis had a great deal of technology at his disposal that could be used against them, but they had the rings, which they hoped would be able to counter any attack he could instigate. Christine, Olivia and Dr. Stewart had previously shared with one another some of their observations when they were in the presence of Crumb and some of the conversations that Dr. Stewart overheard during her covert surveillance. They were trying to review his mannerisms, his discussions with his military police and his phone conversations, which were minimal and short in length. They could only theorize his end game even though he had admitted that he wanted the ring to be mass-produced for the military. He had to have assumed it was powerful enough to use militarily. Rob, Olivia and Christine understood that each ring was that powerful. They also had realized that it was possible to mass-produce the ring but had doubts as to duplicating its power no matter what type of technology Crumb used. Of course, Crumb wouldn't be able to morph even if he had the ring because Rob theoretically absorbed that ability from Lelak's blood on the ring, and the ability was not from the ring itself.

Olivia requested, "I need to get into the ship prior to the Crumb meeting so I can prepare for our assault." The others did not question her request.

Traveling from Rosemont in Lincoln County to Roswell was not necessarily a treacherous journey, but the area between Eddy

County and Roswell had major flooding in the past ten years. Rob knew that all the flooding in this area and the lack of rain in other areas around the state plus severe temperature fluctuations were evidence of climate change. Olivia looked at Christine in the back seat with a worried look.

"Your planet has a very short time before its people are wiped out from all these natural disasters," Christine said to Rob.

Rob acknowledged this with a sad nod.

"And not just the impact on natural resources, but also, your global economy will suffer a devastating loss of revenue in all areas of produce and livestock. We have experienced it on Themadoria after the Great Gasses."

As Dr. Stewart was driving and Olivia was navigating, Dr. Stewart began to notice leftover water from the flooding getting a bit deeper while they were en route. As they slowly approached Buchanan Draw Road, Rob recalled the water main break on his way to Sitto's. Large ripples of water continually flowed from the turnoff toward Two Rivers Road. "Wait! The Two Rivers Dam and Reservoir are down that road," Dr. Stewart shouted.

Rob checked the location on his phone's map app. "You're right," Rob acknowledged. "Buchanan Draw Road merges with Two River Dam Road."

"There are gates to keep people from going through. Most of the time, we never see water in the reservoir except for limited storage during spring runoff. Something is wrong," Dr. Stewart yelled.

"I just checked my phone. It was an abandoned Hondo river reservoir that the Army Corp of Engineers converted into a flood control facility. According to the map information, this area has had about eight to ten floods since 1937 caused by frequent monsoons," Rob relayed to the team.

"The floods should have been able to gradually release water into the reservoir. It may be the northern dam," Dr. Stewart exclaimed. She stopped the car at the intersection of Buchanan Draw Road. "We are too far away to be able to see what's wrong! It's at least five miles away!"

"Let me see if I can help," Rob said while looking at his ring. He turned one of the odd-lettered dials. "Telescopic vision, please."

As usual, the ring vibrated and glowed light blue. Rob squinted, and his eyes became superpowered binoculars. "The waters are coming from leaks in the flood gates in the second dam. It also looks like the hydraulic pressure control valve is rusted shut and malfunctioning."

"The water is getting too deep to drive toward the site," Dr. Helena Stewart said, panicking.

"If we can't follow County Road 145A to get there," Rob said, "then maybe Christine and I can work together to help stop the extra water and fix the cracks in the dam wall. Um...not *damn wall, dam wall*. Oh, never mind."

Christine nervously giggled. "We knew what you meant."

"Since there is water flowing along the road to keep my sneakers cool, I can request superspeed. I may also need hydrokinetic power and superstrength. Christine, maybe you can ask for—"

Christine interrupted with "Fusion power, surface manipulation and plant generation. Great minds think alike, Rob. Would you mind carrying me with you?"

Rob was impressed with her ability of forward thinking. "Sure, but prepare to feel nauseated after I stop," warned Rob.

Both rings vibrated and glowed light blue. Immediately Rob, uncomfortable about carrying Christine like a bride over the threshold of a hotel after their wedding, held her in his now superstrong arms and sped toward the water's origin.

Arriving with a sudden stop, Rob almost dropped Christine but was able to hold her tighter before she did. Christine reacted to the supervelocity the same as Rob the first time he ran at that momentum. She immediately vomited the strangest-colored vomit he had ever seen. It was light lilac in color, and it smelled of lavender. "You know," said Rob, "I usually puke whenever I smell vomit, but your vomit is, um...quite pleasant." He never thought he'd put those actual words together in a sentence—ever. But to Rob, Christine's reply had to be even stranger, "Oh, Rob, you say the sweetest things."

As they stood at the base of the dam, they both saw the cause of the dam failure. The earth embankment and the foundation had eroded almost entirely. Eventually, the huge volume of water in the reservoir, because of the recent deluge, was escaping, flooding downstream toward the intersection where Dr. Stewart and Olivia were waiting.

As the water increased in volume, Rob, thinking quickly, yelled to Christine, "I'll elevate the rushing water away from the foundation and hold it in place while you fuse the cracks in the foundation. Then use your surface-manipulation power to reinforce the base with dirt and sand."

She hollered back, "Good thinking. You should be a Themadorian!"

"Umm…thanks?" Rob questioned her compliment.

Rob concentrated, and with his hands above his head, he elevated the water over them like a large rock, redirecting the water and exposing the front of the dam. The water flowed above them and down the other side of their location. As soon as Rob was able to divert the water flow, Christine immediately fused the expanding cracks together to form a tight bond, like two pieces of a puzzle perfectly fitting together and seamlessly blending into each other. Using her surface manipulation, she did as Rob suggested, reinforcing the dirt and sand that had eroded because of the lack of foliage at the foundation. Instantaneously, dirt and sand from ten feet away began filling in the gaps and areas that were bare of any earth, like a bulldozer building debris for preliminary coarse-surface grading. She used her power to pack it tightly against all areas at the base while retrieving topsoil from other areas in preparation for plant generation, her third requested power.

"How are you doing?" yelled Rob.

"The cracks are sealed," hollered Christine.

"Oh, thanks for telling me!" Rob yelled sarcastically. "Are you almost done?"

"Oops! Sorry!" Christine shouted. "I need a little more time! Why?"

"'Cause I'm not sure when the ring will terminate all our powers or when my arms give out!"

"Almost there!" Christine bellowed.

As Christine was in the middle of growing deep-rooted red osier dogwood at the newly formed dirt base to help keep the soil from eroding, Rob continued keeping his hands out to deflect the water flow. "Can I put my arms down now?" Rob called. "I think I just lost all the blood in my arms."

"Yes! I knew there was something I was supposed to tell you. Sorry!"

Rob dropped his hands in relief. "Great! My arms were tingling from lack of blood flow." As Rob attempted to drop his arms, he realized that he couldn't fully place his vertically. It reminded him of the time he put his arm around a movie date and left it there for almost two and a half hours. He had needed to force his arms down to his sides, which caused him sharp, aching pain.

No sooner had Rob forcefully dropped his arms he received a phone call. From the ringtone, he knew it was his mom. With his hands tingling from the lack of blood in them, he grabbed his phone from his back pocket. "No, no, no, no!" Rob said while looking up at the clouds. "Please, God, don't let it be what I think Mom is calling about." He didn't want to answer it because he didn't want to hear the news, but his better angels knew he should. "Hi, Mom. I think I know," Rob spoke as his voice cracked and his eyes held back tears.

"Are your allergies bothering you?" His mom always said that when Rob was upset and teary-eyed. She gave him the news of Sitto's death as his powers subsided. He was silent for a moment. "Robby, are you there?"

"Yeah, Mom. I'm here."

"Did you just hear what I said?" his mother commanded.

"Yeah, Mom. I heard you. I'll be back home tonight. When are the services?"

His mom replied, "Not for at least four days. Aunt Agnes made most of the plans well ahead, but she has to tie up loose ends. Sitto told her to ask you to be a pallbearer."

"Okay. I've gotta go, Mom. I'll see you later tonight." Rob hung up and started bawling.

As Christine finished up, she heard Rob's weeping. "Rob, what's wrong? Is it your grandmother?"

Rob nodded as he explained everything to her. She empathically felt his sorrow. "Ring," he said unenthusiastically, trying to keep his composure as he dialed the ring, "may I have superspeed and superstrength, please?" The ring went through its customary reply with its sound and light. Holding Christine tightly in his arms as they both wept, he sped back to Dr. Stewart and Olivia's parked car, which was pulled off to the side before the corner of the intersection.

Both Olivia and Helena got out of the car when the couple seemed to appear out of nowhere and saw both of them sobbing. "What's going on?" Olivia asked.

Christine replied between her whimpering, "We'll explain on the way, okay Mom?"

"Sure! Absolutely! Let's get going. We don't have many more miles to go!"

All four returned to their previous positions in the car, and Dr. Stewart continued driving to their destination.

CHAPTER SIXTEEN

A Crumby Meeting

Rob was silent during the remaining miles of their trip. He was emotionally unraveling not only from the shooting at school and Christine and Olivia's reveal but also from his father keeping his mother's secret for so long and now Sitto's death. He wondered how superheroes coped with their emotions toward protecting their families in case their secret identities were revealed or deaths or injuries from fighting their enemies. How did they keep their mental stability? *I'm a teenager learning from my mistakes, understanding my relationships, understanding girls, anxious for college, and in a world of independence from my family. Hell, I'm still trying to understand my family dynamics. Okay, Rob! For now, clear your head for this mission. Get your head in the game. Maybe I can get back to a normal life without the ring if we are successful. Do it for Christine!*

Christine asked Rob, "I know you've been through a lot emotionally, but I have confidence in you. We are all partners in this. Of course, Dr. Stewart and my mom will be with us as well. You won't have to do this alone, okay?"

Rob nodded. "I understand. I am hoping to give this ring back to you so you can continue on to Proteus 9 to learn of their solutions to your planet's environmental situation. I've helped a lot of people with this ring, but beyond this small town, I'm not sure I could ever make a difference."

"Listen, Rob. My dad was an amazing man, kind, wise and moral even when the Themadorians' behavior changed. He never figured out why our family and many others were not affected, but he continued to be the dad who reared me. I am amazed that even with your mom's abusive behavior, very similar to the surface dwellers on Themadoria, you were able to still be the person I fell in—I mean, feel deeply for. Our mission is to get the ring and save Etak, but aside from that mission, for some reason, I was attracted to you since the first time I met you. It is what you humans call a twofer. I think it's called a BOGO. I succeeded in finding my dad's ring and, in the process, became emotionally attached to you. We thought most humans were like Crumb, and from our time together talking, sharing and enjoying each other's company, I realized that you and Dr. Stewart are not like Crumb. You never lied to me except to protect the ring from falling into the wrong hands, which really doesn't count. Your truthfulness, politeness and etiquette, which your father taught you, makes me wish you could come with us to Proteus 9 so we could protect each other. Of course, I would never ask you to leave everyone you love here, but what a team we would have made."

"So," Rob replied with his head down, facing the driver's seat, "we're just a team?"

She almost slipped and said, "I fell in love with." Freudian slip, maybe.

"Oh, Rob, we are much, much more than that," she answered, tipping his head up, turning it and giving him a long, passionate kiss.

Rob, taken aback by Christine's kiss, said, "Wow! Um…okay, then. Let's get our heads in the game, so to speak, um…team!" *Her kisses still confuse me.*

Before entering the parking area for Area 55, they went to the first of two guarded restricted area stations. Dr. Stewart, dressed in military uniform, stopped at the horizontal black-and-yellow boom gate and lowered her window to flash her military badge. She retained access to her activated ID because Crumb needed her to return with the aliens and the ring that Rob possessed. It was important that Crumb did not know of their return yet, but Dr. Stewart knew she would still be able to enter the secondary gate to get to Crumb's military intelligence facility after their quick stop to the spacecraft.

A CRUMBY MEETING

Her two Themadorian passengers used their rings to access teleportation and phantom power. Rob told his partners about the smoking sneakers incident, so he suggested they all avoid superspeed. They each teleported to the front of the hanger entrance, which, of course, had two armed guards. They easily walked through the locked hanger, then passed through the ship's closed entrance as phantoms. They procured the supplies that they needed and walked out in the same manner they had entered. Dr. Stewart was on her way to the second restricted area as Olivia and Christine teleported back into her car while it was still moving, since stopping would alert the guards and invite questions from them. Instantly they returned to their visible selves.

Slowly driving up to the second checkpoint, Dr. Stewart stopped at the second gated barrier and lowered her window to where all her passengers were now visible to the guard. Dr. Stewart flashed her badge but this time said in a very stoic voice, "We are here to see Mr. Crumb with the required asset."

"I was notified by the checkpoint 1 officer, but he said you were alone."

Dr. Stewart replied without hesitation, "Then I suggest he get his eyes checked. When was the last time he had a vision test?"

"Um...I don't know. Is that a new requirement?" he nervously replied.

"Soldier, if you don't know your current military requirements, I will need to report both of you to General Ruppel for retraining. You both do want to eventually be honorably discharged someday, don't you?" Dr. Stewart convincingly stated.

"Y-yes, ma'am, Dr. Stewart," he stammered. "I-I apologize."

"Very well, carry on!"

They arrived at the military parking area as Dr. Stewart said to all three, "I'll wait in the car in case you need me." As they exited the car, Lt. Flanagan was alerted and escorted Olivia, Christine and Rob to Crumb's barracks.

"Expected arrivals are here, sir," he announced as they entered the barracks, guarded by Lt. Gallagher.

THE ALIEN RING

"Wow! Your early arrival was unexpected but welcome," Crumb exclaimed. "Where's the ring?" changing his tone.

Olivia spoke up and shouted, "ETAK!" Etak was in hand and leg shackles, cuffed like a prisoner brought in for sentencing by a judge in a court of law and guarded by a military officer. Etak could barely walk with restraints surrounding his alien legs. She rushed to him, but the guard walked sideways in front of Etak. "Release my boy!" Olivia commended.

"Not so fast. I repeat. Let me see the ring," Crumb demanded.

Rob put out his left hand to show Crumb the ring.

"Take it off," he demanded. "No! Wait! Before you do, demonstrate the ring's ability. I want to make sure it's authentic. Let's see. How about breaking the chains that bind this pathetic creature?" Crumb pointed to Etak. "And don't try anything funny." As Crumb finished his last command, Lt. Gallagher came into the room from guarding the front door, holding a futuristic rifle by his side. Flanagan exchanged his sidearm as well with the same high-tech weaponry Gallagher handed to him.

Rob stared sternly at the firearms, which were a light-blue almost-semitransparent combination of Captain Kirk's phaser rifle and Han Solo's E-11 plasma rifle. "Fine." Rob turned a dial on the ring and thought quietly, *Superstrength and temperature manipulation.* Rob hesitantly walked over to Etak, not wanting to alarm both trigger-happy guards aiming their guns at him. Approaching Etak, he whispered, "Hi, I'm Rob. I'm friends with your mom and sister. Don't be afraid. Let me take these off you." Understandably, Etak was frightened as Rob broke both sets of chains, pulling them easily apart like the gum-wrapper chains his sisters used to make when they were younger. He threw them aside, and they clanged on the floor. "Now hold still. I don't want to hurt your ankles." He placed his fingers around the cuffs and froze them to absolute zero. Ice crystals formed quickly on the iron, causing them to crack open without hurting Etak's ankles.

"Good. I didn't think you could outsmart my superior intellect. Now hand the ring over!" ordered Crumb.

"I can't give it to you. Besides, it will not fit you. You have to be moral and righteous. The ring will sense that you are not and will refuse to modify its shape to fit you," Rob yelled.

"Are you afraid it might actually fit and work as well?" Crumb sarcastically replied.

"No, but I still won't give it to you."

"Fine! Guards!"

They pointed their guns at Rob.

"Go ahead and shoot me! You won't succeed as long as I have the ring." Rob didn't bother to ask the ring for invulnerability in case whatever resulting discharge from their weapons would ricochet and harm the others.

"Well, how brave of you! Guards, you know what you need to do," Crumb instructed.

The guards pointed one gun at Olivia and one at Christine. "I anticipated this! Now hand it over, little boy."

Rob hated being called a little boy. His mother would constantly call him Robby, and his sisters followed suit. It sounded just like a little boy's name. He didn't mind it when Sitto had called him Robby, but his mother said it mockingly. "Okay, okay! Fine, I have to dial a combination of symbols, or it won't come off, even if I request it," Rob frantically hollered. Rob turned the dials in a special sequence, knowing full well the combination had nothing to do with the release of the ring.

"Let me see the sequence you're using! You think I'm stupid?' Crumb growled.

Rob had mimicked a line he heard on an old Three Stooges rerun, "I don't think you're stupid. I know you're stupid." Rob showed the ring to Crumb while dialing the sequence. "Fine! See?"

"Don't get boorish with me. Once I get the ring, I could easily kill you."

"I told you. It won't work on you. You have no morals and no values. So here." Rob handed him the ring. "A lot of good it will do you. It will not fit you no matter if you dial the combination or not. The combination was for release only." Christine and Olivia bowed their heads and shook them side to side as Rob pulled the ring from his finger and placed it into Crumb's chubby hands.

"What the hell is your name, little urchin? I want to be able to place your name on your tombstone," Crumb demanded as he laughed.

Rob never insulted or bullied anyone in his life, but coming from a family of an abusive mother, he knew how to respond and defend himself with sarcastic intellect. Rob hoped that Christine would not be disappointed in him for what he was about to say. "First of all," Rob reprimanded, "an urchin, you buffoon, is a dirty, unkempt child. I am neither, as you can plainly see. I'm cleaner than you could ever be. Have you ever heard of soap and water? When's the last time you bathed?"

"Ah, another typically insolent teenager, I am guessing," Crumb replied as he attempted to place the ring on whatever finger would accommodate its size. "Why doesn't it go on? Is this a trick?" he fumed.

"Gee, you say you have a great intellectual mind, but apparently, it doesn't come with good listening skills," Rob said, paraphrasing something Kralc had said to him about listening.

Crumb continued to fidget with the ring, his head turning bright red with rage as he attempted to force it on any of his fingers. He bellowed, "Don't get nasty with me! I demand respect!"

"Okay, let's now review the word *respect*, shall we?" Rob continued in his condescending voice, stalling for time in hopes that Christine and Olivia would carry out their plan. "Respect out of fear or intimidation is not respect. Even though I have dealt with an abusive mother, my dad raised me to show respect, and I have given my dad respect in return. He taught me to knock before entering a room. Say 'please' and 'thank you.' Let another person take my seat if they are disabled or elderly. Help others when they are in need and not stand on the sidelines and watch other people do it. Hold the door for the person behind me when entering a building or hold a door open for my dates. Never take advantage of someone, whether it be my colleagues at work, my high school friends or girls I date. I say 'excuse me' when needed. I say 'I'm sorry' not 'my bad' when I make a mistake." *I never understood the use of 'my bad.' I always wanted to ask anyone who used it, 'Your bad what?'* "I love people, even my mom, for who they are and not what I can get from them. I was raised to treat people exactly how I would like to be treated. My mom, even when she served in the military, learned that, but due to…let's say… other circumstances, she lost that ideal to trauma. Just about everyone in the world knows what respect is despite most not practicing it. Why don't you know that? You capture a young boy, threaten to shoot me or my friends, force them to do your bidding and expect to get respect? What planet are you from?" Rob, using this colloquialism, was simply suggesting that Crumb, by his actions, was too ignorant to live on this planet.

"Ha, ha, ha! I'm so glad you asked." As the five attendants, including the two lieutenants, watched, Crumb morphed slowly into his original form: a gray Themadorian, a seemingly evil version of Lelak. His deep, sunken black eyes were more sinister, his nonexistent brow muscle forming a permanent scowl above them. His skull was a ridged railroad junction of bones and veins. The ends of his four abnormally protracted slender fingers looked more like talons than fingers. The soldiers remained alert but lowered their guns, staring at Crumb.

"That's impossible! You're a gray male Themadorian. They had lost their power to transform," Olivia screeched in disbelief. "The Unaffected Grays in the caverns retained their morphing powers but never changed behaviorally. How could you possibly be one of the Affected and still morph?"

"How? Why, my naive little scamp, it is very possible when one has a Blue's blood," Crumb laughed. "Men, I didn't say at ease. Get those guns up!" he bellowed.

"But now your soldiers know the truth. You just gave your secret away. And once they report it to your superiors, you'll be arrested or dissected or whatever they have been doing to the other alien visitors since the Proteus ship landed," Rob angrily shouted.

"Ah, but they won't. These soldiers are loyal to me," Crumb said confidently.

"Loyal to an alien?" Rob questioned. He looked at the two soldiers guarding Etak. "Come on, gentlemen. You see what he is and his intentions to use the ring. He may even kill you if he gets the chance," Rob pleaded. "Wait! Why don't you look shocked, and why are you smiling?"

"Such a gullible young man. Why would they look shocked? They were taught to play their parts convincingly. Don't you think I would bring some company when I arrived?" Just as he posed the question, both soldiers morphed to their original forms as well. "I have a lot of reserve blood, which I plan to replicate as soon as I get this ring operational."

Shocked at what they saw, Christine, Olivia and Rob stood there, frozen.

"H-how did you get a Blue's blood?" Christine questioned in a shaky voice.

"Ah, it was really quite simple. When the Affected males were at war with the Affected females, they would not accept our dominance over them. So I took the liberty of capturing a blue Themadorian for some experimentation to understand how they retained their morphing ability. I had no desire to continually fight in an unending conflict. I surmised that the blue Themadorian's blood had a larger amount of estrogen and progesterone than the gray Themadorian's blood. I theorized that it may have been the key to the Affected Blues retaining their morphing ability. So I decided to experiment on her to prove my theory and possibly regain my morphing ability by extracting her blood and injecting it into mine. I basically used myself as a Themadorian *aeniug*, or as you humans call, a guinea pig. For a couple of days, there was no change, so I thought my experiment was a failure and that my theory had been wrong, but I did not accept failure. I decided a full transfer of blood into a depository would be the solution. Then I would substitute my blood with hers, preserving the rest for future use. I disposed of the shriveled-up corpse. I thought I'd share this with my fellow Gray Themadorians, but after careful consideration, I elected to share it with these two subservients and find another planet that could easily be controlled. After researching the various inhabitable worlds, I chose this planet to begin my plan for domination and use you Themadorians to repopulate our species."

A CRUMBY MEETING

Christine and Olivia had winced at the thought of mating with this abhorrent creature.

"But first I made a trip to Proteus 9 to steal all their advanced technological schematics. After doing so, I arrived on Earth at the infancy of their atomic age, morphing into a younger version of the handsome gentleman you previously saw before you to best blend in. I was amazed at how gullible Earth people were in the late 1940s and early 1950s and enlisted myself into their military. No background check, no IDs needed, nothing."

"So you knew all along about our planet, our life cycle, our longevity, our history, everything?" Olivia realized.

"Well, not everything. I didn't know about the ring's ability and your covert caverns. With some convincing acting skills, I fooled this army division as easily as I fooled you. Of course, it took me years of practicing manipulation, deception and fabrication," Crumb bragged. Didn't one of this world's greatest writers, William Shakespeare, say that all the world's a stage and that all the men and women merely players? I was just confirming his belief, and I'd say I played my character quite well."

"How could you have gotten here undetected?" Rob asked.

"I attached to that crashed vessel the army found in Roswell, New Mexico, in 1947. It was a ship from Proteus 9 trying to retrieve the schematics I stole. It crashed because of the weight of my ship connected to theirs. When it began to nosedive, my ship detached. I used Themadorian cloaking technology when I arrived and hid my spaceship in an underground cave at the base of the Bottomless Lake in New Mexico. Their unique blue-green underwater plants covered my ship. They call it a lake, but I learned from my preliminary studies of this planet that it's actually three large sinkholes about a little over ninety feet deep. These humans are completely unaware that beneath the campgrounds around the lakes is my spaceship, filled with all the stolen knowledge I needed to slowly infuse technology into this world, starting with police car technology and military advancements in the '40s and continuing its introduction into the present time. Who do you think introduced smart technology to Steve Jobs?"

"So you faked not knowing our history and our physiology?" asked Christine.

"Well, of course, naive child," Crumb responded.

"Thanks for the stereotypical summary of your evil plot," Rob said sarcastically rolling his eyes. "This is on par with the campiest movie ever made, with you as the ludicrous villain whom everyone laughs at."

"Oh, believe me. I won't be laughed at. I will be praised for my genius."

"And there it is, the overconfident braggart," Rob disdainfully quantified.

"One more word from you, and I will use this beautiful piece of technology on you," Crumb angrily replied. "Now that I have the ring and my fingers are thinner, let's see if this miracle of technology fits." Crumb was able to place the ring onto his ring finger. "Ha, there we go. Now tell me how to activate it. It's these dials, isn't it? What are the combinations? What powers do each one control?"

"Don't tell him, Rob. He's going to kill us all anyway, so why give him the opportunity to use it?" Christine cried.

"I told you it won't work on you," Rob yelled.

"Apparently, there is a way, or your girlfriend would not have told you not to tell. And since you won't tell me, I'll have to convince you." He pointed his rifle at Etak and fired, hitting Etak in the chest and knocking him against the wall. Etak lay there, motionless.

Olivia and Christine in unison yelled, "No!"

Rob pushed through the two soldiers, causing Lt. Gallagher to knock into Crumb as both of their weapons flew out of their hands. Rob sprinted over to Etak and checked Etak's pulse—at least where he thought a Themadorian's pulse would be. He looked up at Crumb. "You killed him, you bastard." But then Rob remembered something that Christine shared with him as he was picking grape leaves at Sitto's the other day.

Olivia lunged toward Crumb in a fit of rage. "I am going to kill you!"

Rob yelled to her, "OLIVIA, DON'T." As he tried to get up from the floor, Crumb tried to reach for the gun he had dropped, only to feel Olivia's hands around his neck as she morphed her hands into a steel vise. Christine then ran to grab Lt. Gallagher's dropped weapon and pointed it at the Lt. Flanagan, who raised his gun at her. "Don't even think about it!" He dropped his gun and put his alien hands in the air. Without guidance from Crumb, his soldiers were clueless as to what they should do.

Choking, Crumb gagged out, "That's…impossible!" His raspy voice became more and more faint. "We can't partially…ack…morph! And how are your…gack…hands made of steel?"

"Olivia, use plan B. Don't kill him!" Rob hollered. Olivia did as Rob said, releasing Crumb and swinging her large metal-vise hand across the air and knocking Lt. Gallagher squarely in the head. She ran over and grabbed Lt. Flanagan's dropped weapon.

At once, Olivia, Christine and Rob executed plan B. They requested the power of molecule manipulation to form gas masks on their faces as Rob formed an additional mask for Etak…as well as for himself. While his hand was on Etak's chest. Immediately Etak's eyes opened, and he inhaled as if gasping for air after being underwater for too long. Rob whispered very softly to him, "Keep your eyes closed and go limp. I'll let you know when to get up." Etak followed his request.

Rob had previously asked the ring for elemental powers. He combined carbon, hydrogen and chlorine to form trichloromethane. His arms dissolved into the gaseous form of chloroform deadly to Themadorians, and he released it into the room, knocking out the conscious soldier and Crumb. Rob knew from his knowledge about Lelak and Themadorians in general that he could revive Crumb and his cronies afterward by administering water to them. As with Lelak, it would take at least an hour before the poison would become fatal.

Once the chloroform took effect, Rob opened the windows in the building to air it out. To be sure, Rob filled the room with oxygen using the same elemental powers so that they could all take their masks off.

Olivia apologized to Rob, "I'm sorry, Rob! He killed my son! He has to be eliminated!"

Christine chimed in, "Mom, we can't. It would be wrong to do to him what he tried to do to us."

"But it's your brother! We can't let him get away with this," she replied, sniffling. Rob agreed and shared a quote from Frank Sinatra that his father used. Rob said, "I think that the best revenge is massive success, and I think it applies here. We know that blue Themadorian blood holds the first part of the key to the remedy. Now you both need to find the second part of the cure, but I don't think you have to travel to Proteus 9 to get it. There's a possibility that it is in the stolen research from Crumb's office or on his ship, or maybe it's on the Proteus 9 ship stored on the base. In the meantime, let's find something to tie up our supposed genius and his minions, and I'll get them some water."

Olivia and Christine dropped their acquired weapons and searched Crumb's supply cabinets located behind his desk, adjacent to the single-user restroom. On the eye-level shelf, they found plastic zip ties in a small utility bin, but they also saw a locked fire safe. "Rob, look! Could the stolen documents be in here?" Olivia wondered, pointing to the safe.

"Those fireproof safes are extremely difficult to open without a combination. Of course, we can break it open with the help of our little friend," Rob said, trying to imitate Al Pacino in *Scarface*, as he pointed to the ring. Both of the ladies looked at him strangely. "Never mind! The only question is 'Will it allow us to do it?' It may sense that we are stealing something."

After grabbing a handful of the longest zip ties they could find, they wrapped them around Crumb's wrists in the front so he would be able to relieve himself shortly after getting water, and they did the same for his two military associates.

Christine suggested, "Rob, give water to our assailants. I'll break the safe open if the ring permits it. Ring, may I have powers of technopathy, the ability to psychically interface and interact with all electrical connections?" To her surprise, the glow and vibration indicated that the ring accepted her request. Christine tuned into the digital combination and was able to decode it and open the lock. When she opened it, she found a strange square yellow disk with no apparent holes or openings. "Hey, Mom. Look at this!" she called out to Olivia.

Olivia said, "Maybe this contains the digital documents Crumb stole. If it does, they are most likely encrypted. Try to use the same power to see if they are."

As Christine attempted to use technopathy again, she exclaimed, "Wow! It's working. There must be thousands of pages of research on various medical and technological discoveries from Proteus 9 on this disk. It would take us days, maybe months, to go through them for the answers. Even Talock would take months to decrypt all the files, then even more time to scan through the myriad of pages for the exact information we need."

"Okay, let's just take it with us back to the caverns. No sense in going to Proteus 9 now," Olivia concluded. "I'm sure they have the information backed up. We just have to keep this information out of the hands of the Affected."

Rob distributed water to each of the three, waking them up, and escorted each of them to the restroom. As Crumb released his liquid waste, he asked Rob, "Why didn't you kill us when you had the chance?"

Rob replied, "Because I don't kill no matter what. It's kind of a comic-book-hero code."

"But I had the ring. It fit, but I couldn't use it. And you were able to do all this without the ring. How?" Crumb whined. As Crumb staggered out of the restroom and let the other men take care of their business, Rob looked at Crumb but decided not to answer his question.

"I reminded you various times that the ring would not work for you because you are deceitful and immoral, but you did not listen," Rob replied. "And I'll prove it." Rob looked at Crumb's clawed hands and took the ring from him. He placed it back on his ring finger. "Now watch."

Rob asked the ring for levitation and size-manipulation powers. As usual, the ring responded. First, he floated the three dropped weapons off the ground and moved them next to himself. Then he checked to see if there was some type of lock mechanism on them so they wouldn't misfire. Finally, he miniaturized the guns to the size of a AAA battery and placed all three in his front jeans pocket.

THE ALIEN RING

"Well, at least I killed one of you. And once I am released, I will hunt you all down and will not hesitate to kill the rest of you."

Rob was tempted to say, "Don't underestimate the power of the ring," but he thought it too tawdry. "My dad taught me at a young age not to count my chickens before they're hatched." *Of course, at the age he taught me that phrase, I didn't truly understand because we had no chickens, and I was afraid that the eggs in the refrigerator would hatch and that the little chicks would freeze to death. He also told me never to call a girl a chick, which made as much sense as counting chickens.* At that point, he yelled to Etak, "Okay, Etak. You can get up now."

As Rob did, Etak got up and ran to his mother and sister. They embraced like two pythons, tightly wrapping themselves around one another. His mom and his sister sobbed.

"No, no, no!" exclaimed a very angry Crumb. His face contorted with rage, and his eyes blackened. "How did you do that? I demand to know."

"What, and give away my secret? I think not! I thought it was always dangerous to reveal secrets to the villain of the story, and I don't take demands from a person I do not respect. Besides, you didn't say *please*! Wait! You just gave me a great idea!"

Rob barked, "Family conference time." Olivia, Christine and Etak all looked up and smiled because they, too, felt Rob was family. Gathering together to consult with his foreign family and keeping an eye on the detainees, he turned and shared their decision with Crumb.

"You're not going to like this next power I use." Rob whispered to the ring, "Please give me the power of memory manipulation." Rob walked over, stood behind Crumb and placed his open hand on Crumb's ridged head. Crumb kept shifting his head from side to side to avoid Rob's touch, so Rob used both hands to hold Crumb's head tightly.

"What are you doing to me? Keep your repulsive human hands off me."

"Don't worry. This won't hurt a bit," Rob reassured Crumb. Removing his hands, Rob shifted to the front of the evil Themadorian but noticed nothing in Crumb's eye that would indicate a blank stare. However, his rigged brow was evidence enough to know that the first requested power worked. He stepped toward Crumb's two pawns and had repeated the same procedure. Rob was not sure how much of their memory he had eliminated, so he needed to check. "Crumb, can you understand me?" There was a lot of cooing and babbling but nothing more. He also had a very pleasant look on his face, softening the hardness of his previous appearance. The same occurred when he asked the other male Themadorians. Rob exclaimed, "Oops! Um…I think I goofed. I was trying to have them forget the last two days, but I think I wiped their memories clean. They may need to be retaught."

Olivia spoke up, "Rob, that's it!"

"What's it?" Rob questioned with a puzzled look.

"Ring," asked Olivia, "please bestow the power of age manipulation." The ring, of course, had repeated its usual color and pulsation.

"*Bestow*? Really? *Bestow*? I thought only Disney movies use that word. Oh, sorry!" Rob snickered.

Even though she had some knowledge of Disney movies, Olivia rolled her eyes, then walked over to Crumb and held her hand up with her palm open. As she did, Crumb began to change but not just a metamorphosing change—an age change. He kept regressing and regressing and shrinking in size until he became a Themadorian newborn. The fatigues he was wearing did not shrink with him, leaving the infant in a pile of shirts, pants and boots. Olivia reversed the ages of the other bound soldiers, again leaving their camouflage clothing in a pile surrounding the new toddler-sized Themadorians.

"Holy shit," Rob said then quickly slapped his hand over his mouth. "Sorry!" Rob walked over to the pile of clothes and retrieved Crumb as a Themadorian baby. "I can't believe I'm going to say this, but he's so cute."

Olivia and Christine rescued the other two babies under the pile of adult uniforms.

"Children are always cute when they are newborns," Christine said, interrupting as she held one of the baby soldiers. "Rob, I'd love to see a picture of you as a newborn. Bet you were a real cutie!"

Rob looking at Christine and responded with a crooked grin without turning his head toward her. "So what now?"

Olivia spoke up, "When we return to Themadoria, we can bring all three to the caverns and retrain them, rear them, so to speak. We won't know if your memory wipe affected their aggressive behavior until they grow older. The effects from the Era of the Great Gasses may not have dissipated when I reversed their aging. It may still be in their systems. We will have to wait as they age."

Rob laughed. "When they become teenagers, it may look like they reverted back to their uncooperative selves, but if they are anything like teenagers on Earth, it would be quite normal. Anyway, we need to find…um…diapers or at least a close facsimile."

"The fatigues on the floor!" Christine exclaimed. "Not exactly sanitary, but it's the best we can do."

As Christine suggested, the three Themadorians placed their babies on top of the uniforms, and using scissors found in the cabinet, Olivia and Christine formed makeshift diapers for each of them. They also found three military bed blankets in the supply cabinet and swaddled each of them to prepare them for travel.

They looked out the doorway of the barracks and proceeded to Dr. Stewart's car. Rob chuckled. "Can't wait until we try to explain this to Helena—um…Dr. Stewart. I may even take a picture of her reaction when we get in the car with three babies."

"Rob! Please don't, okay? This has to remain a secret," Christine asked. Olivia agreed.

"Sorry! I wasn't thinking. ADD, you know! I understand. No pictures. Besides, even if I just kept it on my phone, it would have been backed up to the cloud, wherever that is, and the whole world would know, including the media and the government. Good thinking, Christine," Rob acknowledged.

Christine and Olivia were relieved and appreciative of Rob's respect for their request.

On their way to Dr. Stewart's car, Rob and the three Themadorians, carrying their three newborns (or reborns), began making preliminary plans for repairs on their ship and their last goodbyes. As they talked, Rob and Christine looked at each other sorrowfully.

CHAPTER SEVENTEEN

We're Not Out of the Woods Yet

The parking spot was eerily empty. With Rob walking behind them, Christine, Etak and Olivia, carrying the three babies, looked around the parking area. Dr. Stewart waved them down from behind the spaceship's hanger, out of the view of any soldiers in the area. They quickly turned and power walked over, holding the babies while entering the vehicle.

Dr. Stewart was gawking at them as they approached the car. As Rob had predicted, Stewart's jaw dropped, and her eyes widened as her face contorted. A shocked and whispered exclamation of "What the hell?" came from Dr. Stewart's mouth. As Rob saw Dr. Stewart's expression, he thought, *I wish I could take a picture of her expression even though Christine and Olivia asked me not to. It's priceless, but a promise is a promise.*

While carefully entering the vehicle with their little bundles of previously evil adult aliens, Rob realized they had no car seats. "Better drive home carefully, Dr. Stewart. Without car seats, we don't want to be pulled over to try to explain where our alien babies came from, not to mention endangering the welfare of minors, um, alien minors," Rob suggested.

"All of you have some explaining to do," Dr. Stewart nervously stated. *Her request reminds me of that scene from the TV rerun "I Love Lucy" that Mom and Dad watched religiously on MeTV. Whenever Lucy was in trouble, her husband, Ricky, in a very exaggerated and stereotyped accent, said, "Lucy, you've got some 'splaining to do!"* Rob quietly giggled.

"Let's just get home safely first," Olivia replied, "then we will explain everything to you."

"Yeah, it's a long and complicated story." Rob laughed. "Maybe I'll write about it in my memoirs someday."

Dr. Stewart needed to pass the two checkpoint exits to begin their journey home. The officer at the inner checkpoint allowed her car with all its three morphed human passengers to pass, recognizing Dr. Stewart as a lieutenant colonel and saluting her as they passed.

At the last checkpoint before the exit to the facilities, the same on-duty officer they encountered previously decided to look into the vehicle to confirm that he didn't need an eye exam, as was suggested by his partner at the prior checkpoint. He did see all the occupants including the bundles they were carrying, but he had been more concerned about his vision than any contraband being smuggled out. Relieved that his eyesight was no longer in question, he sighed and let them pass, saluting Dr. Stewart as well.

Once they were off the installation, Rob felt relieved that the mission was over. "I think I can safely take this fake ring off now." As he did, the real ring on his finger appeared. "It wasn't difficult wearing two of them since the invisible one was on my right hand and the fake on my left. Thank goodness Crumb didn't notice where a ring is typically worn. And since the ring adapts its size depending on which finger it adorns, it made for an easy transfer. Our plan using the ship's replicator to create a perfect duplicate was more effective than I thought. I was able to activate the actual ring in its invisible form, which hid its routine light-blue glow. I needed to convince Crumb that he had killed Etak before I healed your son's internal injuries. I'm sorry this plan was stressful for all of you."

"It was a needed deception. And asking our rings to be invisible until we completed this undertaking and return to the car sure helped," Christine added. "I remember using that power when I was trying to hide the ring from you on our ice cream date. Sorry about that necessary ruse as well."

Rob laughed. "No worries. Actually, I had my suspicions about you when you asked about the ring. Girls don't usually notice accessories on boys, but we do notice them on girls. And besides, what were the chances of other Themadorians visiting Earth?"

Dr. Stewart retorted, "Well, maybe not Themadorians."

Rob said, "Wait! What? So there have been other alien lifeforms visiting? I've always been skeptical with all the misinformation and alien conspiracies on the Web."

She replied, "Other extraterrestrials have visited our planet. It's actually true since I've read the reports of the last eighty years. I was required to do so since moving to this installation, but this was the first time that I came face-to-face with one when we were studying it for General Ruppel.

"I knew all those fake weather-balloon reports, swamp-gas excuses or drunken eyewitnesses reporting UFOs were bogus, but it has been difficult to decipher the truth in our world," Rob confidently said, interrupting.

Abruptly changing the subject, Dr. Stewart remarked, "I had no idea Crumb was responsible for your husband's capture, Olivia. But I can tell you this. While you were with Crumb, I had gone to my superior, General Arin Sanchez, the head of medical personnel, and reported that it was General Ruppel, following Crumb's order, who killed your husband. A formal investigation is in progress. And I, Dr. Capell and Dr. Ganland will need to testify. I also have to write a formal report about what exactly transpired involving Crumb and his soldiers. So when we get home and before the Themadorians leave on their journey to their planet, I hope you will help me write it since I was not witness to any of it. Rob, I may need you to testify with me."

Rob, his mouth wide open in shock, replied in a joking manner, "Um, we have a problem, Houston, I mean, Dr. Stewart. How are we to explain the actual situation? You know, using alien rings, humans morphing back to alien form and turning aliens into babies. I thought this whole thing was going to be a secret. I agree with Olivia and Christine that we need to be discrete. Unfortunately, we will have to omit any of that information in the report."

Dr. Stewart nodded her agreement.

Olivia, still thinking about her instinctive reaction to what she thought was the death of her son, turned her head to look at Rob in the backseat and sadly had apologized. "Rob, I'm so sorry about my attack on Crumb. It was a motherly instinct to avenge my son's death. I lost control. We Unaffected Themadorians are not a vengeful, violent people. But we are a passionate people regarding family."

Rob looked at her with a very understanding smile and nodded. "We humans have the same problem, but we are, unfortunately, a violent, vengeful society brought about by so many factors, mental illness, mental and physical abuse, selfish and dishonest politicians, racial violence and so much more. I don't think we will ever learn socially what the Unaffected Themadorians have had instinctively. I completely understand. I remember presenting an oral dissertation in my eighth-grade biology class about human violence and aggression. I learned that we humans have, through evolution, inherited our tendency for violence. However, I learned that it seemed to be more environmental factors than hereditary since scientists theorized that social behavior and territoriality, if that's a word, is the cause, not necessarily our genes. And seeing how humans react to conflict, I would agree. Wow! It's amazing what I remember from doing that school presentation. I always thought it was just to stress us out or teach us technology software."

"So what's our next plan?" Christine asked Olivia sorrowfully.

"Well," replied Olivia, "we need to make preparations to repair the ship, find proper fuel for launch, figure out how we can safely transport these babies, help Helena with a report that won't give away the real incident and, of course, try to convince our underground community to accept and rear the babies."

"I still have access to the area, but getting into the ship to refuel, even if we find fuel, will be difficult," Dr. Stewart said concernedly.

"Have you ever tried using the rings' power to maybe teleport your ship back to your planet?" Rob asked.

"We were afraid that if we were successful teleporting to our planet, we may not arrive in the underground caverns. We may end up above ground or, even worse, materialize inside a mountain or other structure."

That sounds like Leonard "Bones" McCoy's anxiety in Star Trek *whenever he had to transport to a planet's surface. He feared his molecules would be scattered and reassembled into a rock.*

"Teleportation is a tricky power. We tried it here from a short distance, but we've never tried it over several light-years. We can't take the chance of being discovered by the Affected Themadorians if we reappear on the surface of our planet," Olivia replied.

"Wait! I have a friend who is a genius in creating gadgets and devices for general use. I think he's going to college for engineering after graduation. He'd know how to repair your fuel tank. I could ask him, but it would require that I expose you all and the power of our rings," Rob qualified.

"Do you trust him?" asked Christine.

"With my life!" Rob quickly replied.

"Then if you do, we will too. Is that all right, Mom?"

"Absolutely," Olivia agreed.

"Let's try to solve the second problem. I have another idea. What type of fuel is in your ship's tank?" Rob excitedly asked.

"Our scientists, prior to the Era of the Great Gasses, harvested algae, which was in abundance on our planet. We used to break down the plants' cell walls using a natural biodegradable solvent and then extract their inner lipids, proteins and carbs, which underwent a final processing step that turned them into biofuel," Olivia replied. "Then our fuel tanks were warmed to prevent the biofuel from coagulating. Why do you ask?"

"Could we maybe use some type of duplicating power to refill your fuel tank?" Rob wondered out loud.

"That's seems plausible. Once the tank is sealed, we can run diagnostics with Talock to make sure the ship doesn't have any other damage. Talock has limited self-repairing capabilities, but we do have a lot of backup parts onboard. Talock can give us instructions as to how to repair damaged areas with the parts we have on hand. Before you call your friend, we should see what needs to be done and if we have the repair supplies on the ship. No need to expose us to more humans. According to what you told us about others of your species, we should follow a trust-no-one policy, so to speak," Olivia suggested.

"The old Fox Mulder manta, eh?" Rob responded.

"Who?" Olivia and Christine simultaneously asked.

"Um, never mind. It's too complicated to explain. Let's just focus on getting your ship fixed," Rob, embarrassed, replied.

Dr. Stewart added, "I agree. That's probably our best strategy. If we enter a snag, we will have to rethink our other options."

"This sounds so much like how Themadorians cooperated in the Co-op Era, lots of suggestions, ideas and possible solutions. This is how we operated. It is so refreshing," Olivia cheerfully acknowledged.

Rob replied, "Not all humans are uncooperative and self-centered, just those who have need for control over their situations. Oh, and of course, the superrich, who are just greedy bastards."

Christine added, "My parents taught me about the history of Themadoria before the Era of the Great Gasses. There were no rich or poor because they were able to share discoveries, inventions and innovations with everyone. I learned that it used to be a utopian society until they realized what they were doing to our soil, water and air. If we can find a way to return to a New Co-op Era, we can begin developing solutions to the problems we caused. I am hopeful that we will find what we are looking for in the Proteus 9 documents once we access them."

As they were discussing strategies, Rob's phone rang. "E-evil woman, e-evil woman, e-evil woman!"

"Sorry, everyone! It's my mom. She's worried about me!" Rob's mother's continuous need to know Rob's whereabouts at any given moment was annoying to him, but with Sitto's death, it had become important for Rob to listen.

"Hey, Mom!"

"Hi, Robby. I wanted to let you know the date and times for the calling hours and the funeral."

"Okay, let me switch to my Notes app on my phone. Hold on!" Rob knew his ADD would prevent him from remembering the details, especially when he had been focused on helping his

Themadorian friends repair their ship. He swiped down from the top of his phone and chose the Notes app from the common apps he uses. "Okay, Mom. Go ahead,"

Rob typed out the exact date and hours of both the calling hours and the funeral.

His mother added, "Oh, and your aunts and uncles agreed. We'd like you to write and deliver the eulogy."

"Wait! What? You want me to write and deliver the eulogy?" Rob echoed, accidentally shouting.

"Don't you yell at me, young man!" his mother replied.

"Sorry, Mom, but why me? And why didn't you ask me first?"

"I shouldn't have to explain myself, young man. Just do as you're told, or you won't get to use the car for a month."

"Why can't one of your brothers or sisters do it? It was their mother!" Rob asked, knowing he wouldn't have a choice.

"ARE YOU QUESTIONING ME, YOU WORTHLESS PIECE OF SHIT? I SHOULDN'T HAVE TO JUSTIFY MY DECISIONS TO YOU. DON'T EVER QUESTION ME AGAIN, UNDERSTAND?" she yelled loud enough that everyone in the car could hear her. Rob was embarrassed.

"Your aunts and uncles felt a eulogy was necessary, and since you are one of the grandchildren that knew her best, you would be the perfect candidate, even though you are far from perfect." *There it is. Another excuse to berate me. Maybe it's the stress of Sitto dying. Subconsciously, I know why. She has had power over Dad, my sisters and me ever since I was little. It makes her feel like she's in control. I still think it's PTSD. I feel useless when she talks to me, but when I am with my friends, including Olivia, Christine and Dr. Stewart, I feel I am intelligent and valuable. I'm not a worthless piece of shit. I'm not. I'm not.*

"Besides, your sister Carmilla has been working on Sitto's family tree, and your sister Mariam will be singing at the memorial. You can work with your sister on details of what your grandmother went through to come to America and raise eleven children. And besides, there's no one else that has the surprisingly good writing talents you have," she said, giving Rob a backhanded compliment. "I hope it's as good as some of your aunts and uncles think it will be. As for me, it probably will be disappointing, but I look forward to seeing you embarrass yourself. Call me later. Make sure Christine drives safely. Bye."

Why would she be looking forward to it? I've never heard one person ever say that they were looking forward to a funeral or a eulogy. I can just imagine my sisters taking selfies while at the calling hours. I bet Brad Paisley was singing about them. The first stanza of that song began running through his head.

> Your grandmother's in an open casket.
> You're in a suit and shades.
> You take your iPhone out and snap it, #sadday.
> You ought to be ashamed. [1]

Nevertheless, during the trip home, Rob placed all the information from his notes to his calendar. He started to ponder about all the writing he had to do now. *Not only must I complete my writing assignment for school, which I hadn't even started, but I also have to write a eulogy for Sitto and not embarrass myself. But now I have to help Dr. Stewart with writing a report, which, technically, I don't have to write, but it still adds to my anxiety, not to mention my mom's tirade that everyone just heard.*

"Everything okay?" Christine asked with a worried expression.

"Yeah, just getting information about the wake and funeral," Rob replied truthfully. "I have to write my grandmother's eulogy."

"I heard what your mother said. It's not true. You are not worthless," she tried convincing Rob. "I wish you could come with us to our planet. Our underground would appreciate your kindness and compassion."

"I can't run away from my situation. I have responsibilities to my family, my school and myself. I just have to deal with my mom until I can muster up enough courage to show her that I'm worthwhile. Oh, by the way, my mom said to drive carefully, so I'm relaying that information to you, Dr. Stewart. Sorry! If you knew my mom, you'd understand."

---

[1] Brad Paisley, "Selfie#theinternetisforever," *Love and War*, 2017, Astra Nashville.

Dr. Stewart reacted, "Oh, after hearing her conversation with you, if you can call that a conversation, I do understand."

Christine, seeing Rob distraught, changed the subject. "I learned about funerals and calling hours when Dr. Stewart gave us information to review before we were to be acclimated to your traditions. We Unaffected Themadorians are very fast learners. It's my understanding that it's not something to look forward to, I'm sure. But you should be flattered that your aunts and uncles want you to write and deliver it. I'm sure that deep down she is proud."

"Maybe, but I'm surprised that she didn't want to write it and then make the eulogy all about her."

Shocked, Christine responded, "Really?"

"I could tell you stories, but right now, we need to focus on getting you back to your people, not that I'm looking forward to it," Rob answered.

"You are the sweetest, Rob. Neither do I, but it will be necessary for both of us."

Rob and his adopted family continued coming up with ideas for the problems that needed to be solved as soon as possible.

The alien babies—which, at this point, were quite quiet and content—all began crying at once and looked as if they were in pain. Rob watched the two babies next to him, which were held by Etak, and Christine and exclaimed, "I think I know that look on a baby's face."

Olivia explained, "It's not what it seems. It's not excretion. They are too young to have developed any waste or even gas."

Rob interrupted with "But when Olivia used the age manipulation power, there may have been waste already in their systems, right?"

"Theoretically, yes. But we never used this power before, so we really don't know," Olivia countered. Suddenly their theory was proven.

Rob explained, "Oh crap!"

"Nope, just gas!" Christine laughed.

Rob plugged his nose. "Open the window before we are asphyxiated," Rob insisted. Just then, each of the occupants of the vehicle smelled different fragrances—one citrus smell, one minty smell and the last a spicy smell. "What the heck?" They all laughed except for Dr. Stewart, who was puzzled as well. "Why are you all laughing?" Rob asked.

"Sorry, Rob. We forgot to tell you that Themadorians' flatulence usually smells like whatever they most recently ate, so in this case, maybe spicy chili, a breath mint or an apple or other fruit. We really don't know. Just be glad they didn't have cabbage before their transformation," added Christine, still snickering. "Everyone on Themadoria, prior to the Era of the Great Gasses, is what you humans call vegan."

"Very funny. Thanks for the warning! First, I find out your vomit smells like lavender, and now this. I can't imagine what the poop smells like."

"Oh, you don't want to know, but nothing like human excretion."

"Okay, good not to know. Let's not continue with this sophomoric discussion please."

As they continued traveling, the babies fell asleep, as did Christine and Rob. It had been an exhausting journey for all of them. Olivia looked at the back seat as Christine and Rob's heads tipped toward each other, forming the point of a pyramid. She smiled. As they slept, Etak secured his infant as well as Christine's tightly in his arms so they could rest.

CHAPTER EIGHTEEN

Work to Do

With all Themadorians now in their human forms, Dr. Stewart pulled her car into Rob's driveway, waking Christine and Rob from a partial sleep. Once awake, Rob's anxiety hit a new level after he had time to think about how much he had on his plate. He used many strategies, suggested by his doctor, to have some type of semblance of order in his life. He wrote notes, created lists, managed calendar reminders and tried to include an exercise routine. But the additional stress of having the responsibility of using the ring; writing a eulogy; talking with his father about his mom's miscarriage; preparing for the dress rehearsal for the upcoming play next weekend; attending Kyle's court appearance and, of course, working his part-time job, Rob was afraid that he would have a mental breakdown like his mom. *It's bad enough that I can only focus on one task at a time, but I am so distracted so easily. I feel like a dog who gets distracted by a squirrel. I can't delegate duties like at work. I just want to go to sleep and avoid it all.* These thoughts continued to race through his mind like scattered confetti shot from a cannon.

He began to prioritize everything, but he was distracted by Christine's eventual departure to her planet. Their relationship would have to end before it ever had a chance to begin. *It's not like we can be Facebook friends or privately message each other.* He decided that her safe departure had to be his first priority, as painful as it that would be for him.

"Hello? Rob? Are you with us? We've arrived on Themadoria!"

"Wʜᴀᴛ?" Rob shook his head to get out of his ADD trance.

"Just kidding." Christine giggled.

"You scared the hell out of me!" Rob said, shaking.

"Sorry!" Christine, remorseful, responded. "We are at your house. It's late, so please get some sleep. We will need to go back tomorrow to prove our theories for repairing and refueling the ship as well as figure out how to transport the babies. We'll pick you up at the same time, okay?"

"Um…sure, same bat time, same bat channel," Rob sleepily replied as all those with Themadorian origin looked puzzled. Dr. Stewart laughed. "Oh, um, Dr. Stewart will explain that phrase when I leave. Bye."

"Aren't you forgetting something?" Christine questioned before puckering up.

Rob took the hint and kissed her. Christine smiled before Dr. Stewart backed out of the driveway. Entering through the front door, his mother and father were in the living room, watching the evening news.

"Rob, I took the liberty of calling Elliot at the store and requesting that you take next week off for the play performances and Sitto's funeral," his mom told Rob as a matter of fact. "Your dad and I understand that the shooting upset you, but you need to shake it off and get your head on straight." *Mom confuses the hell out of me. One moment, she is calling me a piece of shit, and the next minute, she's concerned about my mental well-being! Does she not understand that she is contributing to the deterioration of my mental health? Mom means well, I guess. I have to be thankful that she does these things for me because of my ADD even though Mom doesn't believe in it or even understand it. But why does it always sound like military demands? She thinks these things can be shaken off like a soccer error or a missed goal. She doesn't know or understand the additional stress of dealing with the ring and the Themadorians, and I'm not about to tell her.*

"Thanks, Mom. I appreciate it. I'm going to bed now. Oh, by the way, Christine will be picking me up early again. She has to move back to her plan—um…plantation in the west. But she'll be leaving from Roswell Air Center, and I'd like to say goodbye to her and her family. Hope that's all right. Anyway, good night."

Rob heard his mother say under her breath, "Another girl he can't keep."

However, Rob didn't want to stay in the room long enough to listen to other snide and degrading remarks she planned to make. *All she does is shame me whenever I stop dating a girl. And why do I always ask for permission? I shouldn't have asked for permission to go. I should have simply stated I was going, and that would have been that. I eventually will have to make my own decisions in college. Besides, the decisions I make requesting powers from the ring should be enough evidence to prepare me for that, right?* Rob tried to convince himself.

His parents said their good-nights, and Rob went back to his regular routine of taking a shower and brushing his teeth before he went to bed. He was hoping that in doing so, he could sleep a little bit longer before Christine's family picked him up. Before he dozed off, he asked God and His angels to help him deal with the seemingly countless responsibilities coming at him all at once. His anxiety made his stomach hurt, and he spent most of the night doubled over in pain and vomiting in the toilet. He asked for a clear head for tomorrow's tasks and relief from his stomach cramps and nausea.

*****

The alarm rang the next morning. Unfortunately, Rob was only been able to get about two hours of sleep. *Shit! I was just finally falling asleep. I am so tired. Is this what a hangover feels like?* He shuffled out of bed. His stomach felt better, and he was no longer nauseated. He brushed his teeth again to eliminate his rancid breath from his night of relentless vomiting. *If it had smelled like Themadorian vomit, my mouth would have been the fragrant aroma of lilacs and lavender.*

Once again, entering the dining room, he found the usual breakfast being served, wondering whether his mom could make any other kind of breakfast. Rob just grabbed a couple of slices of toast, covered them in labneh (a Lebanese yogurt spread) and then added slices of cucumbers from a ziplocked bag that his mom had previously sliced. He pressed the two pieces of toast together to make a sandwich, cut the toasty concoction into six even slices and then headed for the door. "You must really like this girl," his mom stated. "You said she just started at school, but now she's leaving again?"

"She was only here temporarily, and we became really good friends, very close friends." Rob frantically looked out the window for Dr. Stewart's car, hoping they would arrive soon. And sure enough, there they were, pulling in. "Mom and Dad, I'll be late. Gotta go! Bye!"

"Remember, church tomorrow!" yelled his mom as he rushed out the door.

"Yeah, I know. Um, can't wait!" Rob sardonically replied. He ran to the car with the labneh sandwich in a brown paper bag and tried to enter, but with the additional baby passengers, he had to squeeze in. Once again, Olivia held one of the tightly bundled infants while Etak and Christine held the other two. Three in the back seat was possible but not comfortable for a two-hour drive. "Hi, guys—um, ladies, um, guy and ladies, and, um, babies. Um…hi, everyone!" They all laughed. "I brought some breakfast to share, but I'm not sure how Themadorian physiology will react to it. It's organic. Just milk, cucumbers and toasted bread."

"That's very kind of you, Rob," Dr. Stewart replied. "There's a small cooler in the center armrest of the front seat. You can put it in there."

Rob proceeded to raise the lid of the center console, open the cooler and place his bag inside, with the top rolled down until it formed a small handle. "I was thinking about the problems with the ship and the repairs last night. I had a hard time sleeping because I was concerned about possibly using the ring to help. If I were to use the ring to repair the crack in the fuel tank, duplicate what was left of the fuel to fill the tank or make other repairs to your ship, would it interpret is as a personal gain?"

Olivia and Christine began speaking simultaneously, but Christine stopped and let her mom explain. "That would be true if we were to use our rings, since returning to Themadoria would be a personal gain even though the only thing we would gain would be a return flight. But since you are using your ring to initiate repairs, I theorize that it would respond to your power requests as more of a rescue."

"Yeah, that makes sense. I would think that if I used it to make sure you didn't return, then the opposite would be true, right?" Rob deduced.

"Yes," said Christine, "then our rings would try and save us from what it would perceive as a danger and help us with whatever powers we requested to escape."

"Ha, ha! Nope! I'm not the stereotypical supervillain type with a handlebar mustache and a large black cape," Rob blurted out with a sinister laugh of "*Nya-ah-āhh!*" Again, the three Themadorians looked at him strangely as Dr. Stewart snickered. "Okay, never mind!"

Another long drive to the military facilities gave Rob time to think about his relationship with Christine and how he would approach saying goodbye to his dear, intimate friend. He thought of famous farewell dialogues from movies—*Casablanca*, *E.T. the Extra-Terrestrial* and *Toy Story*—but he wanted to avoid sounding like a movie cliché.

Even though Christine would have thought all of them were original, he decided on none of them. He wanted to create something that only he and Christine would appreciate.

Before they arrived at the installation again, Christine and Olivia were able to close each of the infant's slitted mouths with their fingers. As they did, each baby's nostrils increased from the size of a pencil point to the size of a nickel. Rob stared at what was happening. "Will they be able to breathe?"

Christine replied, "Of course, our mouths mainly are used for talking, eating, drinking and, in our case, kissing, but our noses are the main apparatus for breathing. Our mouths are optional for respiration and ventilation. This is how we pacify newborns."

"So you don't breastfeed?"

"Rob, Themadorians are unisex. Didn't you notice when I morphed into my original form?"

"I really wasn't looking at your chest at the time. I was too shocked at your reveal at Dr. Stewart's house at that time."

Christine snickered. "Ha, nice save, Rob. I only morphed into this shape to fit in. Our morphing capabilities can be used to manipulate any part, not just our entire body at once. I can make my mammary glands larger if you'd like. My understanding of teenage males is that they find that part of a girl very attractive. Let me show you."

"No, no, no! They look…um…perfect? Look, that's very nice that you would do that, but some boys like quality not quantity. No, I mean, sometimes boys don't look for large, um, endowments, in order to have a meaningful relationship. Wait. I mean. Look! I love you just the way you are." Rob realized he unintentionally quoted a Billy Joel song. *Crap! Did I just tell her I loved her?*

"I agree, Rob. As we admitted before, our love is unique. So yes, I, too, love you just the way you are."

"Before we conclude this fascinating but truly awkward discussion of Themadorian anatomy, I do have one question." Rob hesitatingly inquired, "How do you tell the difference in your species?"

"Oh, we have the individual gender parts, like a man's…um… phallus or a woman's…ah…genitalia, but we can mate with whomever we want. Most of the time, it's a male-and-female coupling."

"Wow! Your species is so much more advanced than ours," Rob admitted.

"Yes, from what I've learned, you humans have a lot of…what you call…hang-ups."

After moving on from that uncomfortable conversation, they arrived at the ship's hangar and made sure that they all requested phantom power once again, extending that power to Etak as well since he had no ring. He was carrying with him one of the newly acquired babies, and Christine and Olivia extended their phantom power to the babies since they had placed both infants under their coats. Etak followed suit. They entered the closed hangar, then into the ship to begin repairs. Rob realized that it would be the last time he would see Christine. As they entered the ship, the interior was vaguely familiar to Rob from the images that Kralc had shared with him.

"Talock, you fixed the cloaking device! Thanks so much," Christine cheerfully complimented Talock.

"You are most welcome, Arak."

WORK TO DO

"Call me Christine, please. It will just confuse Rob."

"Affirmative…Christine," Talock acknowledged.

Rob, oblivious to that conversation, was soaking in all the colors and reflections of the interior. It looked very different from the exterior. The floor was covered with smooth, clear quartz, reflecting all the colored crystals on the ship like a prism reflects light. There were purple amethyst crystals for controls and red agates on top of the amethyst levers—similar to joysticks but visually more pleasing. The passenger chairs were a smooth black-and-white onyx, like a very-dark-chocolate-and-vanilla pudding swirl.

As he combed the inside, Rob felt unusual, as if a burst of energy soared through his body; it was like he drank a gallon of coffee. *What the hell was that?* He shivered and shook it off. He assumed it was an adrenaline rush from the visual spectacle he was experiencing.

Olivia pressed a smooth hematite hemisphere on a slanted front panel below where there should have been windows. Slowly, with a quiet harmonic hum, three scooped dark-chocolate-colored nonpareil chairs with restraining straps rose from the seamless floor. She placed one baby into one chair as Christine placed the baby she was carrying into another chair, and Etak placed baby number three into the last seat. All babies were secured with closely knitted straps, each of which had neodymium magnetic latches on each end. Each bucket could be released through a sequence of Themadorian symbols on each chair.

The interior walls were a deep-blue color with fine white streaks crossing haphazardly in a diagonal pattern but did not have discernible windows. Rob, in awe, commented sarcastically, "Whoever your interior decorators were, they forgot to install windows."

Christine snickered at Rob's comment, then pressed one of the smooth blue celestite buttons. Rob was taken aback at the sudden melting that occurred, like a flame slowly deteriorating a sheet of paper, revealing windows that looked out at the interior of the hangar their ship occupied. Rob was mesmerized; it looked as if these were all CGI effects.

"Rob?" Olivia waved her hand in front of Rob's deadpan eyes.

"Oh, sorry!" Rob blinking his eyes.

"Are you ready to start?" Olivia asked.

"Yes, of course. This is just too fascinating. I'm trying to absorb everything I'm seeing."

Christine empathized with him, saying, "Yeah! It can be overwhelming to an outsider, but if you think this is fascinating, as they say on your world, 'you ain't seen nothing yet!'"

"Um, Christine, have you experienced Earth music of the 1970s at all?

"Music on our planet is very different from music on Earth, so I tried to listen to a diverse collection of music from all over your planet. The variety is amazing. I may have come across some from America's past. Why do you ask?"

"Oh, no reason. Just curious!" Rob replied nonchalantly.

What is it with all the song title references? Maybe it's my ADD. Now that song will be playing in my head! Crap!

Olivia commanded, "Talock, we will be using our micro earpieces to communicate with you. Please adjust your settings accordingly."

Talock replied, "Affirmative!"

Christine and Olivia, who had reverted to their original form, handed Rob his earpiece. They all inserted them into their ears. "Rob, are you more comfortable now that I have returned to my original form?"

"You never have to worry about that. Any form of you is fine with me because it's you. Wait, except the form of the Xenomorph XX121 creature that was in those *Alien* movies, yuck!" Rob distorted his face with that image stuck in his head.

"If you are referring to those scary alien movies about ugly creatures trying to kill people that I read in my human society studies, I take offense to those stereotypes," Christine half-jokingly said with a stern face.

"Oh, I'm so sorry!" Rob replied with a very scared look on his face.

"Kidding!" Christine laughed. "But seriously, why do humans think that everyone that is different from them is out to kill them or possess them or are seeking to replace them?"

"Umm, like Crumb? Or the Affected on your planet?"

"Oh yeah. Touché. I withdraw that comment," Christine replied, looking like she was trying to bite her nonexistent lower lip.

"By the way, shall I now call you Arak and your mom Lah?" Rob questioned. "This is so confusing. It's like I'm dating two people, not that I want to. I try not to deviate from my personal norm even though I did that once and scheduled two dates on the same day. When I realized what I did, I had to ask my dad what I should do."

"What did he say?"

"Let's just say I canceled with both and stayed home."

"Your dad is a wise man, Rob! Anyway, let's go to the fuel tank and see if it can be repaired from the inside. We may need to examine the interior."

"Yuck! Really?" Rob reacted.

"Rob, it's plant-based biofuel. It's organic. The walls will be covered with organic slime and maybe some natural oil residue but nothing that can contaminate you. It will be like walking through swamp water."

Isn't that how the Swamp Thing was created and where Luke Skywalker was attacked by a tentacled carnivore? Rob hesitantly followed Christine to the fuel tank. "You can access a fuel tank from the inside? I thought that was only on naval ships."

"Our ships are very different in design both in capacity and accessibility. I understand it's hard to convert human technology to Themadorian technology, so if you have other questions, I can always clarify. But then I'd have to disintegrate you."

"Ha, ha," Rob laughed nervously.

As they walked along the corridor to the location of the fuel tank, Christine began explaining. "So we usually have self-sealing fuel tanks, but something went wrong. It could have easily been a malfunction in the sensor array monitoring fuel consumption. That's what you and I need to figure out. Our first job is to check the sensors, then seal the crack and replenish our fuel supply." When they arrived at their destination, Christine said, "Here we are!"

The surface of the fuel tank's wall was coated with a smooth, shiny deep-silver-colored pattern similar to hematite but lighter in hue. "Is everything made of crystal on this ship?" Rob asked.

"Yes! We found that the crystals in the underground caverns have many rejuvenating properties. We've studied many of them on Themadoria. Didn't you feel the energy when you entered the ship?" asked Christine with a countenance of surprise.

"Yeah, like my batteries were replaced or recharged, if I ran on batteries, that is. Are all types of crystals represented here in the ship?"

"There are some we haven't used yet, but they have been stored for possible use. Why?"

Suddenly Talock was heard in everyone's ear pieces. "Attention, after completing my diagnostic as you requested before being captured, I found that this solar system's sun sent out energy waves that created EMF radiation, which disabled our fuel tank sensors."

"Bet it was a solar flare!" Rob surmised.

"All other sensors were unaltered. On the farthest edge of this solar system, as we passed Saturn, we might have passed too closely to one of the three gas rings containing debris and natural satellites surrounding the planet. A very small particle might have been embedded in the crack, or it might have entered the tank itself."

"The walls of this tank look familiar," Rob said. "Talock, what is the fuel tank made of?"

"Titanium dioxide."

Christine asked, "Why did you ask Talock that? We use titanium dioxide to coat the interior and exterior of our fuel tanks because it has an extremely high melting point and boiling point, perfect for traveling in space at high speeds. The interior is also coated with a diamond composite, a solid form of carbon combined with a mix of crystals. It's similar to your wood composites but much stronger. That's why this crack has us stumped. There should have been no fractures that would have constituted a fuel leak. Whatever hit the exterior must have exceeded terminal velocity, if that's even possible. It could also be possible that the object that hit our ship may have had the hardness of Q-carbon. It was probably from one of eighty-two orbiting satellites of Saturn."

Rob responded, "Talock, do you think whatever cracked the tank is in the tank?"

"Unknown unless I analyze it."

Rob said, "Just scan for anything that is not titanium, diamond, crystal or biofuel. I really don't want to enter that slime if I don't have to. It would smell musty or like grass, and I am allergic to it. Besides, with the cuts and scratches on my body, who knows what will enter it?"

"It's called necrotizing fasciitis, or what you humans call flesh-eating bacteria. The biofuel does not contain any of that, Rob," Christine assured him. "You are sounding like your mother."

"Oh my god! You're right. I think I inherited her paranoia. Okay, I'll enter it if necessary," Rob replied. He repeated to himself, *Be brave, but be smart. Be brave, but be smart.*

"Scanning…scanning…scanning…analyzing…analyzing. It seems you are correct. There are no other materials in the fuel tank. I also scanned for necrotizing fasciitis to ease Rob's anxiety. It was negative," Talock answered in its usual monotone, robotic voice.

"That's a relief. Thanks." Rob sighed. "So we eliminated the existing elements in the tank unless the object contained Q-carbon. Is that possible, Talock?"

"It is possible, but with the filters you specified, it is not conclusive."

"Christine, is there any shungite stored on this ship?" Rob asked.

"Yes, why?"

"Even though it might have been struck by a particle, I don't think the crack caused the leakage. I think it was those intense EMF flares damaging biological tissues of the algae by inducing changes, so I'm guessing the algae didn't leak out. I learned in earth science that the activity of algae exposed to an electromagnetic field weakened algae and lowered its growth. I'm just guessing. I'm not a computer. Talock, can you confirm my theory?"

"Checking my database. In the most simplistic terms, confirmed."

"Can we add shungite to the titanium shield to repel EMFs, Talock?"

"It is possible, but it has not been done before," Talock replied.

"There's a first time for everything, Talock. Can you develop a way to liquefy the shungite, and do you have access to a mechanical arm to spray in over the exterior of the tank?"

"Christine, what else can I do?" he asked.

"You've done so much so far. How were you able to theorize all that?"

"I cheated!" Rob shamefully replied.

"You used the ring, didn't you?" Christine smirked as she looked up with those very small light-blue pupils. "You asked to have super intelligence, right?"

"Can't fool you, my lovely friend," Rob replied, feeling comfortable enough to compliment her beauty in alien form.

"I am flattered that even in this form, you find me lovely!"

"It's the truth. I feel like I know you better than anyone. It's a heartfelt compliment. This may sound overly romantic and maybe a bit cheesy, but I found that I love you as a person, which simply highlights your outward beauty no matter what form it takes."

"So you would still love me for me if my form were the Xenomorph XX121?"

Rob replied, "Don't push it." They both laughed.

Christine questioned Olivia, "Do we have mechanical arms to do that?"

"Yes, but they have never been used. We would have to spray it by hand while we are in the hangar. That's dangerous since we don't want to be detected. Even if we use our rings to be invisible, how do we explain a floating impeller spraying liquid on a cloaked ship? We would have to uncloak the ship to make sure we accurately dispel the liquid," Olivia explained. "Our best bet is try programming the arm to apply the precise amount in the defined area."

They all agreed with Olivia's forward thinking and her hypothesis to a possible solution. "There is a possibility that we could use Rob's ring to extend invisibility onto the arm."

"I'm willing to try that," Rob agreed.

"I will work on those computations for liquefying the shungite and checking the functionality of the telemanipulator. Shall I seal the crack now since the self-sealing properties have malfunctioned?" Talock inquired.

"Wait! You can do that, Talock?" asked Christine.

"Of course."

"Why didn't you let us know? You're an AI!" Christine said, sounding annoyed.

"I can only give you information you ask for."

"Proceed, then develop a way to liquefy shungite."

As Olivia and Christine prepared for their flight, Rob suddenly found himself feeling useless, not being able to know what he could do to help. They didn't need his invisibility power anymore since Talock had been able to repair the damage.

"You have socially set a high standard for me when I return to Themadoria. I will consider you the painite standard."

"Don't you mean the *gold standard*?" Rob questioned.

"Gold has little value on our planet. Painite is a very important crystal in the mines. It's virtually priceless."

"Like a Mastercard, eh?"

Once again, Christine tipped her head and raised one hairless brow, looking similar to Mr. Spock on *Star Trek.*

"Never mind!" Rob once again felt like a comedian who had bombed onstage.

"Why don't you work on your grandmother's eulogy while we get repairs ready?"

Rob smiled. "That would be great. Do you have something I can compose with?"

"Use the digital pad on that table near the babies."

"How will I print it or save it digitally?" Rob asked. "I'm going to need to edit and revise it before the memorial."

"I can send it to you through our teledigital network before we leave."

Teledigital network? Is that like file sharing or peer-to-peer networks? I wonder how I will receive it if I don't even know how to access it. I have to remember to ask Christine before she leaves.

The Themadorians and Talock were very careful in their formulations in case they would be detected, but with Crumb and his soldiers in baby form, they were trying to be cautiously optimistic that their work would continue uninterrupted.

CHAPTER NINETEEN

My Wish

Talock had been able to seal the hairline crack on the fuel tank, liquefy the shungite and activate the mobile servicing system, which had been modified by adding in extra components from the parts storage unit. It now had two arms for faster implementation of the liquid shungite spray added onto the exterior tanks.

In the few hours it took for the others to put their plan into motion, Rob was able to write a complete draft of his eulogy to Sitto. He would have to edit and refine it prior to the funeral.

"It looks like the only thing we have to do now is replenish the fuel tanks," Christine told Rob.

"I finished the draft of the eulogy, so I can help," Rob replied. "Let's give it a try!"

They returned to the fuel tank through the same corridor. Arriving there, Christine asked Talock, "Please confirm all repairs to the tank, including the extra outer-layer solidification. Will that reinforcement withstand any other debris hitting the hull?"

"All modifications have been completed and are at optimal efficiency. Theoretically, the reinforcement should withstand an object traveling at terminal velocity. Will there be anything else I can assist you with?"

Talock's request reminds me of a technical service representative asking the same question at the end of a resolved issue. I have always wanted to reply with "Yeah, can you recommend a good sushi restaurant? Rob chuckled at the thought of the technician responding, "Of course. What city and state?"

"No, Talock. It's up to us now to test our hypothesis as to whether the ring will grant me duplication powers," Rob replied. "We have not determined whether the ring will justify my request. We believe it is not for my personal gain since I really don't want my Themadorian friends to leave, but I can only test the theory and hope for the best."

"Affirmative."

As they faced the fuel tank, Christine accessed the panel door, opening it with her alien thumbprint. She then positioned a triangular black obsidian palm stone in the center of the matching recessed wedge-shaped hole. Once it was inserted, the area around the stone glowed green like a Himalayan salt lamp cycling through its colors. They both backed away as the large egg-shaped bulkhead door opened. The door hissed as it released pressure, spewing clouds of drifting green vapor. Immediately the musty grass smell filled the corridor.

"Crap!" Rob said, covering his mouth. As the vapor lingered within the walkway, he asked the ring for molecule manipulation to create a gas mask around his nose and mouth. Rob asked Christine in a slightly echoed and muffled voice, "Would you like one too?" Christine shook her head no. They both stared at the almost empty fuel tank's base, which indicated about a foot of biofuel was left in the chamber.

"I don't think duplication power will work here. The floating algae is brown and dried. I think I need to first rejuvenate the algae mixture, then duplicate the healthy mixture to fill the tank," Christine theorized.

"That makes a lot of sense." Rob looked at her with confidence as he pointed his ring toward the waterless mixture. "Okay, then." He addressed his ring as if it were a person, politely asking, "Ring, may I have rejuvenation power and duplicating power? But please have me keep my molecule manipulation power. I need this mask. Can't do this with a runny nose and watery, itchy eyes." His last words sounded like they were part of an allergy-relief commercial.

Rob looked at his ring for a sign that said it would grant him his additional two powers since his molecular manipulation power was to protect him and not for his own personal reward. He waited and waited. After thinking that it would not work, the ring glowed light blue and vibrated as it did for his first power request. "Yes! Yes!" Rob roared as he raised his arms in the air.

He first used his power of rejuvenation by raising his hands with his palms out and concentrating. Suddenly the old brown dried algae began to dissolve and was replaced with lush-green algae with slight hints of red algae spreading throughout the tank. The transformation continued like a gentle ripple across a glassy lake. Once the conversion was over, Rob, keeping his hands up and palms out, used his duplicating powers to replicate the existing algae, lipids and microalgae throughout the fuel tank. They both watched as the levels increased exponentially. Christine was monitoring the tank's level meter so she could signal to Rob to cease the duplication process. As Rob was finishing up, Christine gave him the remaining percentage of the fuel's capacity. "Ninety-eight, ninety-nine, one hundred percent."

"Hold," Christine spoke through her earpiece with one arm up, her hand forming a gesture like a police officer stopping traffic. Rob dropped his hands, and the blood rushed out of his shoulders and back into his two limbs. "Are you all right, Rob?"

"My arms felt numb, but the circulation is beginning to come back."

Christine smiled and ran over to give him a hug. Trying to get the feeling back into his arms, Rob attempted to give Christine a hug with his arms barely wrapped around her seemingly fragile alien body. She softly spoke in his ear, "Thank you so much! I know how difficult this week has been for you, and you still came through for us. I'm sure it took a lot of emotional energy. I will never forget you for what you did for us. I consider you part of the Unaffected. You are unaffected by outside pressures because you are an independent leader. You are unaffected by vulgar people because you are chivalrous. You are unaffected by those who ridicule you because you are respectful. You would be perfect for our underground society."

Rob pulled her away gently. "Except I'm human. But thank you for all those wonderful words. I may be perfect to you, but I am far from perfect. I ridicule my mom because I don't appreciate being abused. It hurts when she continually degrades me. It's futile to yell back at her with logic and facts. She thinks she is always right and has no understanding of the damage she is doing to me, my sisters and my dad. I can't just shake those feelings of inadequacy. I don't know how my father does it, but sometimes I think that his very laid-back personality is his defense mechanism. I wish he would just fight back."

Rob, with his eyes tearing up, removed the ring and handed it to Christine. "Here, this was your father's. Keep it as a remembrance of what he meant to you and what he has done for your family."

'No," Christine said as she took his left hand and placed the ring back on Rob's finger. "We will honor him in other ways. You need to keep it as a reminder of our connection, the unbreakable bond of a lifelong and distant relationship. Accept it as symbol of the bond between an alien and a human, a friendship and love that will exist even light-years away. I know you will continue to use the ring for good, helping people who need it now and in the future."

Hesitant, Rob accepted the ring back. "I'd be honored," Rob said, his voice cracking like a bad yodeler.

"Oh, and one more thing," Christine added. "Stop watching those stupid scary alien movies unless it's about a friendly alien that falls in love with a human."

"Oh, like Casper the Friendly Ghost?" Rob joked.

"Wow, you humans can see ghosts, and they're all friendly?" Christine questioned with flat affect. "I never knew that!"

"Very funny."

Half crying and half laughing, Rob agreed. "I promise. Oh, by the way, I have something for you, but I don't know how to send it to you. I'm sure they will be beyond the distance for AirDrop."

"AirDrop? Well, whatever that is, I'll make sure you can send it to me later."

Since their repairs were successful, they contacted Dr. Stewart through Rob's phone to notify her of their departure. Dr. Stewart had been waiting in her parked car in the surveillance camera's dead zone. After receiving the call, she cautiously exited the car while looking around for the military police. She used her identification's magnetic strip and swiped it through the security door's card reader, gaining access to the restricted area's delivery. The three Themadorians waited outside with Rob.

Dr. Stewart became teary-eyed at the thought of her alien friends leaving. "First of all, my sincere regrets for the death of your mate and father," she said, directing her comments to Olivia, Christina and Etak. "I never thought in my lifetime that I would befriend three aliens in a research facility where they study extraterrestrials. Rob and I will be preparing a report that will not mention any of you, but you all will be in our thoughts as you travel back to your planet. There really isn't enough time to say everything I want to say, so I will steal a phrase from Mr. Spock. 'Live long and prosper.'"

Surprised that Dr. Stewart would quote Spock, Rob found himself lost in his own sea of farewell thoughts. He was overwhelmed with the thought of living his future without Christine. Before Rob could say anything, Christine moved closer to Rob and morphed back to her humanoid form but with one very distinct difference. Rob was flattered that she reverted to that form but was taken aback by what he saw. "What the hell!"

They all could not stop laughing as she said, "Surprise!"

Rob could not help but stare as he uncomfortably laughed with them.

"Rob, I'm up here." Christine used her hands to bring Rob's eyes up to look at her gaze. "What do you think?"

"Oh, sorry, but why did you do this?" asked Rob.

"Do you love me more now?" Christine asked.

Rob looked strangely at her, preventing his eyes from wandering elsewhere. "What? No. Exactly the same. When I first met you in the auditorium that day, of course, I was physically attracted to you, but it was your smile, your eyes, your laugh and your friendliness. Then I was attracted to your more petite features because they were more of an added bonus. But this, um…enhancement does not change my feelings for you either way. Even after you revealed your true alien self, my feelings did not change. Your beauty is so much more than, um…anatomy. I thought you knew that."

"I was just having a little fun," Christine said as she reverted back to the Christine that Rob originally fell in love with in school. "But that was the correct answer."

"Ah, man, I was just starting to get use to them." Rob laughed in disappointment.

"Don't push it!" They both laughed so hard that they cried, knowing that this would be the last time they would hug, joke and eventually kiss. "Rob, promise me this. Don't let our relationship hold you back from other close relationships. Everyone has a first love that they will never forget. Yours will always be mine. May your next love enjoy your heart, your compassion, your righteousness, your integrity, your intellect and your bad humor."

Rob interrupted with "Wait, it's bad?"

"Kidding! Well, not kidding. Sometimes it is! And some I just never understood. Remember, we've always been truthful to each other, right?"

Rob nodded.

"And if they don't appreciate the things that make you, you, then move on, because you must always be appreciated for all those qualities that you inherited from another great man, your father. Even though I have never really met him face-to-face, I feel as if I know him through you. It is so hard to say goodbye, but it is necessary so I can help our people return to our original cooperative selves, if that's even possible."

Rob, still with tears in his eyes and dripping down his cheek, said, "I'm not sure if I will ever use this ring again, but I will keep it so that you are always with me." Rob hugged Christine in an embrace that screamed, "I don't ever want to let go," their lips locked in a long and passionate kiss, leaving the others in the hangar having to pretend as though they were looking anywhere but at them.

Dr. Stewart interrupted their world-swept-away moment, saying, "You two should get a room."

THE ALIEN RING

The couple stopped for a moment and, in unison, asked, "Any ideas where?" Then they resumed their lip-lock. Dr. Stewart rolled her eyes.

The usually quiet and reserved Etak said, "At this rate, I'll be old enough to have my own children," at which point, the couple slowly stopped kissing but continued to look into each other's eyes while pulling away.

Olivia cleared her throat. "Okay, let's get this ship off the ground."

"Mom, how can we do that in this enclosed hangar? Do we plan on crashing through the roof?" Christine asked. "That's not the best way to avoid attracting attention."

Rob interrupted with "I think I may have an idea. I'm sure the ring will accept my request to project phantom power around the ship until you are out of range. Then you can activate your cloaking device for the remainder of the trip."

Olivia replied, "That's an excellent suggestion!"

"Robbbb." Christine vocally extended his name, suggesting suspicion. "Did you use the ring again for that idea?"

"No, that was all me! O ye, of little faith!" Rob expressed surprise at Christine's accusation.

"Okay, you get another kiss!" Christine excitedly said.

"How about making it short, please. I want to make sure we get home before my blood type changes," Etak dryly demanded.

Rob and Christine embraced one more time and, in answer to Etak's request, kept the kiss short. "Does that meet your approval, younger brother?"

Etak's response had been simply "Hmmph!"

Olivia, Christine and Etak entered the ship and buckled themselves in. Rob realized he had not returned his earpiece. He pressed it and spoke, "Christine, can you still hear me? I forgot to return your earpiece, but as long as I have it, I want to send you something before you sail off. But I don't know how." There was no response as the ship began to slowly hover, pushed by the pressurized air from the rocket boosters. As it did, Rob asked the ring for his phantom power again in hopes that he could extend the ability to the ascending ship. He raised his arms in front of him with palms out, as if he were blessing the ship, and to Rob's surprise, the ring glowed and vibrated. "Ring, please extend this power around the ship." The ship immediately became a ghostly apparition and floated up and through the hangar's roof. Rob and Dr. Stewart ran out of the delivery door to watch, or at least imagine, where the ship would be in the puffy white cumulus clouds. But then they actually saw a cloud distortion as the spaceship ascended beyond the roof. The ship's cloaking device was activated.

Rob and Dr. Stewart waved to the nothingness in the sky, saddened to see their first contacts go. Both of them, as they were walking toward Dr. Stewart's car, kept their thoughts to themselves. They entered the car and left the premises without incident.

Still very quiet, they both looked at each other and smiled. Then a boatswain's whistle broke the silence. It was a text message with an attachment from Christine. It read, "Here is your grandmother's eulogy. We were able to bounce our messages off certain Earth satellites until we broke through the gravitational pull of your planet. Whatever you want to send me, send it quickly." *Oh my god! She heard me. I don't know how, but she heard me.* He simply typed, "My wish for you…" and attached an MP3 of the Rascal Flatts song before pressing Send. Rob wasn't sure if Christine would ever get it.

He breathed a tense sigh in anticipation that he would receive confirmation that the message was successful. Dr. Stewart asked, "I don't mean to intrude on your privacy, but what was that you sent?"

"Christine just sent me the draft of the eulogy that I wrote for my grandmother while I was on the ship. I just stored it on my phone so I can print it out at home. I sent her a song in reply before they were out of range. I'm not sure it transmitted to her. I'm not sure I'll ever know."

"If you don't mind me asking, what song?" she inquired.

THE ALIEN RING

"This one." He opened his music app and located his playlists. He then chose the song and started playing it for Dr. Stewart as they continued on their journey home.

> My wish, for you, is that this life becomes all that
> you want it to
> Your dreams stay big, your worries stay small
> You never need to carry more than you can hold
> And while you're out there getting where you're
> getting to
> I hope you know somebody loves you, and wants
> the same things too
> Yeah, this, is my wish.[2]

---

[2] Rascal Flatts, "My Wish," *Me and My Gang*, 2006, Lyric Street Records.

CHAPTER TWENTY

Just Like Starting Over

Once again, Dr. Stewart pulled up to Rob's house. "Thank you so much for all this," Rob said. He extended his hand to give her a handshake, but instead, Dr. Stewart scooted over to give him a big hug.

"You are an amazing young man. I will not be surprised when you find success in whatever endeavor you choose. Don't forget what Christine said. You need to move forward. Cherish her in your memories and try to return to a normal life." She sat back into the driver's seat. "I know that will be difficult."

"After this experience, I know it will be. I'm uncertain I want to continue helping people using the ring's powers."

"Rob, you have already helped many just in this little town. Imagine what you could do when you go to college next year and help that community," Dr. Stewart conveyed.

"What about our world? I can't possibly help everyone."

"I don't think you were meant to. That wasn't even possible for Superman," she replied.

"It's frustrating. We have been so caught up in our everyday lives, including me, because we tend to wear metaphorical blinders. We can only focus on their part of the picture until those problems affect us. The Themadorians had the same problem. The difference was that the Themadorians were oblivious to what they were doing to their planet because everything was going smoothly in their society. Our world does not run smoothly. Constant conflicts between countries, even within our own country, are preventing us from creating any meaningful solutions. Why are we so oblivious to what our scientists have been warning us about for over thirty years? Even when plausible solutions are offered, those possibilities never come to fruition because some deem them unprofitable. I want to help open people's minds and educate them. I learned in my history class that Plato said, 'Ignorance is the root of misfortune.' Our future misfortune has been predicted by those who are educated. Sometimes, even with the power of this ring, I feel hopeless," Rob sadly replied.

"Rob, in the military, many of the sergeants, during infantry training, commonly use a quote from Franklin D. Roosevelt to motivate future troops. He said that we must always hold to the hope, the belief, the conviction that there is a better life, a better world, beyond the horizon. After my experience with you and our alien family, I believe with all my heart that it's true," Dr. Stewart thoughtfully expressed.

This time, Rob initiated a hug from Dr. Stewart.

She continued, "You may be the person to break those blinders so the rest of the world will see that big picture. I think you will achieve that, Rob. Don't let anyone discourage you."

"Thank you, Dr. Stewart. It will be a challenge since those blinders are made of stubbornness, ignorance and pessimism."

"Call me Aunt Helena," she replied with a smile.

"Thank you, Aunt Helena," he repeated.

Rob exited the car, then Dr. Stewart began to back out. She and Rob waved to each other, and then he turned toward the front door. As he was about to open the door, his phone rang. It was Dr. Stewart. "Hi, Dr.—um…Aunt Helena. Is everything all right?"

"Well, in all the rush and excitement of our success, you forgot the snack you had prepared for us. We were so busy that we never had a chance to share it."

"That's okay. You may have it. It's one of my favorite Lebanese sandwiches," answered Rob. "It's an acquired taste. Think of it as a tarter version of yogurt cheese with cucumbers."

"It sounds delicious. I've never had one before, though I have had yogurt. I'm looking forward to having it for my late dinner tonight."

"Remember to prep your mouth," Rob replied, laughing.

"By the way, we will have to come up with a report that will be believable to the US Army Medical Research and Development Command. Will you be available sometime in the next two weeks?" Dr. Stewart reminded Rob.

"Well, my school's musical is next weekend from Thursday through Sunday evening. I could meet with you the following week."

"I'll create a draft of the incident report, then you and I will modify it to make sure we left all the extraterrestrial details out except, of course, General Rupple's killing of Olivia's husband. Anyway, we'll figure it out somehow. I don't like lying on an official report, but we have to protect our Themadorian comrades," Dr. Stewart stated confidently. "I'll outline the report right up to the disappearance of the ring. We can connect that with the missing ship and Crumb and his alien associates' disappearances," she said.

"Okay, thanks! I do have a lot going on, so that would be very much appreciated."

Rob hung up as he walked into the house. His mother and father were in their usual places at this time of the evening, like creatures of habit, watching the evening news.

"Good evening, I'm Samantha Marvis for CBA Evening News in Washington. We begin tonight's newscast with the disappearance of an aircraft from the supposedly closed Walker Air Force Base. An unknown source revealed to the Pentagon that an aircraft, which they would not identify for us, has gone missing. They also reported that a veteran Army officer and two of his military police have gone missing. Are the two linked? We'll have more after this."

"Hey, Mom and Dad. I'll be in my room, writing the eulogy and finishing my homework for Monday. Oh, by the way, I have to work the afternoon shift tomorrow at the drugstore. Then after the weekend of the musical, I offered to help a friend write a report. She's in need of my editing skills."

"I thought Elliot told me you wouldn't be scheduled because of the play," his mother said, confused.

"He was short on help. Two workers called in sick. He always relies on me for helping him out," Rob countered. "I don't want to disappoint him."

His mother then replied, "Does this friend you're helping happen to be another girl?" She never waited for an answer. "You don't waste any time, do you? First, this Christine, then another girl. They seem to quickly lose interest in you. It figures. Apparently, they don't think you're anything special. Seems to me they're just using you."

Before his mother could insult him again, Rob interrupted, "Mom, I will not dignify that insult with a response. I'm going to my room."

His father had looked up disgustedly at her insult. "Leave the boy alone for once, will ya? Maybe he just wants to date a lot of girls until he finds the right one."

Holy crap! Dad just reprimanded Mom. Way to go, Dad!

She looked at him angrily, "You and I aren't finished with our discussion as to why you took off to bowl for three hours today instead of doing the chores that needed to be done around here. This place is falling apart because of you!"

"Leave Dad alone! And don't call it a discussion. With you, it's never a discussion. It's a one-sided belittling where you make demands. A discussion requires at least two people. He works hard for this family, and you have no appreciation for him."

"You can't talk to me like that!" she shouted.

"Why? You have no problem insulting Dad, my sisters or me!" Rob watched his mother's face turn red. Her clenched fists tightened, and her teeth started to grind, but he was not able to wait for another affront from his mother. Rob dragged his tired body down the short hallway.

That's the first time I stood up to her. My God, she doesn't even realize she insults us. Does she even think before she opens her mouth? Well, I need to get to work on editing that eulogy. This is going to be rough. I need encouragement to writing it, and the only encouragement I get has been from Dad, Dr. Stewart, Olivia or Christine. Even aliens give me encouragement. But I'm too tired to edit. I just want to sleep. Am I procrastinating like Mom said? No, I just need a fresh start tomorrow evening. Rob dragged his tired body to his bedroom, stripped down to his boxers and fell backward onto his bed as he collapsed into a much-needed sleep.

*****

The next morning was set up to be another routine Sunday, except this one would be the first Sunday not visiting Sitto with the rest of his relatives. Once again, he entered the breakfast nook and told his mom he was going to ride his bike to church and that he would meet them there.

"Remember, you have dress rehearsal this week. You've been out late two nights in a row, doing who knows what, and the funeral is Tuesday at ten o'clock in the morning. I've already called school two days ago to let them know you'll be out Monday and Tuesday. I figured you would procrastinate on the eulogy like you've done on all your other assignments."

"How would you know that?" Rob asked, using this opportunity to catch his mother in another lie.

His mother sternly shouted, "Your teachers had told me at the open house." Rob doubted that happened too. "Just remember, your senior year's grades will be on your permanent records. Oh, and remember to ask all your teachers for your assignments and get your friends, few that there are, to take class notes for you."

Oh no. Not the dreaded PERMANENT RECORD. Who knows what evil lurks in the hearts and minds of those who write the permanent transcripts of students worldwide? The shadowy hooded spy knows. He's the one who skulks around every corridor and every corner of every school in the world, writing in every permanent record worldwide and storing them in the all-mysterious permanent-record cloud. I wonder if my puking on Murphy is now in my permanent record. That shadow spy may have been around the corner when it happened. Rob chuckled to himself. Rob had absolutely no idea what his permanent record looked like, what was on it, who was keeping it or where it was stored. And personally, he didn't care. It had been just another one of his mother's idle threats. "Mom, I know what to do. You do realize that I actually know what I'm supposed to do even with my ADD, right?"

"Again with that ADD crap. There's nothing wrong with you except your laziness," his mother retorted.

"Not according to my doctor."

"Doctors don't know anything. You know I heard from a cashier at Walmart that doctors like to diagnosis their patients and prescribe needless pills so they can get kickbacks from the pharmaceutical companies," Rob's mother added. "If I had authorized that ADD medication, he'd get a nice commission even though he probably knows you don't need it."

There may be some truth to that for a small minority of doctors, but I'm not about to get into a discussion about information she got from a Walmart cashier. Mom doesn't even know how to use the Internet to even check on the information she gets, let alone know what the Internet is. She calls it that Web thing.

"I don't have time for this!" Rob shouted. "I have to get ready for church. I'll meet you there."

"We are going to the earlier mass at eight thirty this morning because I have to meet with Aunt Agnes to help with the funeral arrangements."

"Fine, I'll be there." He left the dining room full of anger, grabbing his toiletries and his bath towel from his bedroom and heading toward the bathroom. Since there was only one bathroom, no one was allowed to keep their toiletries in the bathroom except the females in the family. He placed his towel on the only towel rack, which was located above the toilet, then placed his necessities on the sink and entered the shower.

While showering, Rob began to theorize possible uses for the ring's power. *If this ring can help people who were physically injured, maybe it could alleviate mental injures like Mom's PTSD. She wasn't born with it. It isn't a disability from birth. It was a result of trauma when she miscarried. I think it could work. Physical injury is traumatic, but it's also mental trauma. I was able to heal those patients in the hospital, which, I would guess, relieved their mental anguish. But would the ring perceive this as a personal gain? I guess I'll just have to put trust in this extraterrestrial Aladdin's lamp, minus the genie. If it doesn't work, I'm none the worse for wear.* His senior writing course spent a week on idioms, and Rob was proud he could use it. In actuality, it was his father that used the phrase when he was trying to solve a unique situation while installing a neighbor's carpet. Rob continued to reassure himself. *But if I'm going to try this, I will need to be able to touch her. She hates being touched. Poor Dad. That has to be hard, not being able to touch your own wife. She doesn't even like being kissed. She's afraid of getting germs. Maybe if the ring helps her, it will make Dad happier, and the happier they both are, the longer they'll live and the happier my sisters and I will be. If it glows and vibrates, I'll have to explain why. I hope I can think of something. Since I'm able to improvise onstage, contriving an excuse for the ring's behavior should be a breeze.*

Rob exited the shower, dried off and commenced his hygiene routine. He rushed into his bedroom, quickly dressed and walked into the living room, where his sisters were already prepared to leave. He whispered to the ring and asked for healing powers. "Hey, Mom, I thought you'd appreciate something that Christine gave me before she left. Take a look." He held his hand out, and she placed her hand under his, like a doctor examining an injured hand.

"Ouch," his mother winced as the ring glowed and vibrated.

"Sorry, Mom! It must have been the static electricity from these rugs," Rob ad-libbed. "Now that we have discharged all the static, take a closer look. Check out how these dials move. I thought it was pretty cool!" Rob let his mother hold his hand longer so she could squint at it since she had always refused to wear her prescription glasses.

"Why, it is very attractive. Some guys don't wear rings unless they are married, but this one with the strange symbols engraved in the wood is so unique. It actually looks good on you. Where did she get it?" she said, surprisingly fascinated.

"Christine gave it to me before she left. She only told me it came from a place far away," Rob pleasantly responded. "The symbols must be some type of numbering system or maybe their alphabet."

"I know you miss her, Rob. You always date such wonderful girls. I'm sure you're sad she had to leave," his mother complimented. "They will never realize what they've lost."

"Wait! What?" Rob stood, shocked at her comment. It wasn't demeaning, insulting or degrading.

Holy shit! It worked. It really worked. I thought it would have taken a little longer before I would see the results, but it worked! It healed mom's PTSD.

"I bet she was sad too," his mother added, seemingly empathizing with her son.

She complimented how nice the girls looked and how well-groomed Rob was. His sisters looked at each other, stunned. Rob, moving his eyes back and forth between his father and his sisters, just smiled. Rob's father, standing with his mouth open, looked shocked.

"What's wrong, Lou? Are you all right? Are you having a stroke?" his wife responded with concern.

"I'm…um…fine! Are you all right?" Lou replied.

"I feel great! Let's get to church!" she answered.

On their way to St. Mary's Church, all the family members except Rob and his mother were trying to figure out Matilda's sudden change of personality. Even while they were taking their seats in their usual pew, no one questioned her behavioral transformation. The only thing his sisters and father could do was stare at her.

As Rob sat with his family, he began to pray.

Dear God, please bless Sitto as she is at peace in the afterlife. Please bless my second family, my alien family, that they successfully arrive back on their planet and find a cure for their species' planet's chaos. Please bless my family so we can begin a better relationship with my mom and her newfound relationship with my dad and my sisters. Please bless the people of Earth that they will finally realize the environmental issues we will be facing in the near future. And finally, I want to thank You, dear Lord, for giving me the ring so that I could heal my mom as well as those that I rescued or healed. Just like in the movie It's a Wonderful Life, *I was able to touch others' lives in ways that I thought were unimaginable, but I'm sure You had my guardian angel with me all those times.*

With that, Rob felt a new appreciation for his belief in God and His angels, not necessarily agreeing with many of the man-made laws in orthodox Catholicism.

Rob repeated the church procedure he used when he bought new sneakers, prevented the robbery at the bank and met Christine for ice cream. When the celebrant said, "The Mass has ended. Go in peace," Rob dashed out the church doors, grabbed his bike and sped off.

Riding his bike to his first stop before his work shift, he thought about the day he humorously called the day he defeated a pig and a werewolf. He was amazed at the number of accomplishments he had been able to achieve in an hour. This time would be different, though, since he arrived at the strip mall much earlier than the previous Sunday.

Dr. Stewart's words, "You'll find success in whatever endeavor you choose," echoed in his head as he arrived at his first stop: Rosemont Shoes. He was hoping that Stephanie was working so he could pick up his old sneakers and dispose of them properly. He spotted her through the shoe display's glass window, which exhibited all the latest men's and women's footwear. He couldn't have missed her red flowing hair, perfectly styled like Starfire, the exotic alien princess from the *Teen Titans* comics. He took a deep breath for confidence and entered the store.

She had been working with a customer that was trying to make a decision on which pair to buy. Rob caught Stephanie's eye, and she smiled in recognition and said, "I'll be right with you, sir. I'm working with this customer at the moment."

Rob replied, "Please, take your time. No rush."

While Rob looked around the store, picking up shoes from the display rack on the right of the back counter, examining one and placing it back, he wanted to make sure her customer didn't know he had no interest in buying shoes, only to pick up his old burnt sneakers, which she had held for him for a week.

Is it too soon to be asking another girl out immediately after my relationship with Christine? Of course, that was an alien in human form, but still, it was a relationship nevertheless. But Christine, aka Arak, and I were not in a committed relationship even though we did have a strong affectionate relationship without the sexual intimacy. And even if it were sexual, what would that have been like? Would she be in human or alien form? Rob shook his head to get that intrusive thought out of his mind. *Okay, Rob, start thinking straight. It doesn't matter. That was then. This is now. This is no time to live in a what-if-istic kind of world. Back to life. Back to reality. Crap, another song reference. What the—*

"Rob?" Stephanie asked, waving her hand in front of him to catch his attention.

Rob blinked his eyes, snapping back from his fantasy world and still having a shoe from the display rack in his hands, and reacted. "Oh, I'm so sorry! I was in my own world."

"But they know you there, right?" Stephanie snickered.

"Ha, all too well," he laughed along with her.

"I presume you're here to get your old sneakers back, right?"

Rob replied, "Well, yes, but more than that. I was wondering if you'd be interested in getting coffee or tea with me after you get out of work. I am working at the drugstore until 6:00 PM, but we can do it anytime you're available."

"Sure," Stephanie answered with a large smile on her face. Rob noticed how her bright eyes and large smile accented her red mane. "I am off work at six tonight, but I have to be up early tomorrow to do it all over again. These hours are exhausting. The coffee shop is open until eight tonight, so maybe we can meet for a little while."

"That sounds good since I need to have time tonight to edit a eulogy for my grandmother," Rob responded.

"Rob, I am so sorry to hear that. Were you two close?"

Rob said sadly, "Yeah, very close, but let's talk at the coffee shop tonight! I have to get to work. Oh, and I think I will take those sneakers and toss them."

"I can do that for you with no problem."

"Really? That would be awesome. Thanks so much! I'll meet you at Starbucks at about 6:15 PM or so. I have closing duties," Rob explained.

"I do as well. Sounds perfect. I look forward to getting to know you better," Stephanie excitedly replied.

"Yes, and you as well!" Rob agreed as he exited the shoe store. *If she asks me about former girlfriends, I'll have to be imaginative about my relationship with Christine. She doesn't need to know about the whole first-contact scenario. Since Mom called me in for Monday as well, I can work on the eulogy late tonight. It's basically written. I just want to make sure I give Sitto the recognition and adoration she deserves. In the meantime, I'm really looking forward to getting to know Stephanie. I do still think about Christine, but she told me not to let our relationship hold me back from other possible relationships. Besides, sitting around and feeling depressed about her departure will not help me move forward.*

CHAPTER TWENTY-ONE

A Fresh Beginning

Starbucks was surprisingly crowded, despite the bank being closed on Sundays. Many of the tables were occupied, but few people were in line for drinks. Rob entered the front door and saw that Stephanie was already seated, with her decaffeinated coffee on her table. He approached her, saying, "I thought inviting you to have coffee with me meant I would pay for your coffee," remembering what his father said to do when inviting someone for lunch, dinner or even coffee unless they insisted on splitting the bill.

"Oh, that's fine! You can get me one on a future date." Stephanie smiled.

Is this déjà vu? Isn't that what Christine told me when we first met? Or did she mean a calendar date? Why am I so nervous? Maybe it's because I'm worried that Stephanie, too, will reveal herself as an alien. Even if she did, I would think it would be in a private place and not in public. Of course, stranger things have happened to me lately, like gaining morphing abilities and finding this ring.

"That sounds good, but I'm hoping that when we come here again, you'll wait for me before you order," Rob suggested. "No pressure, though. You don't have to. I'm just…um…trying to be considerate."

"It depends. Who's inviting whom?"

"Touché," Rob replied.

"I'm kidding. I promise. Girl Scout's Honor!" Stephanie said while holding up the three-finger sign and laughing quietly.

"I'll be right back," Rob replied. "It shouldn't take too long since no one is in line now."

Rob walked to the counter and politely requested, "A grande skinny vanilla latte, no foam, with almond milk please." The barista wrote it on the standard store cup and gave Rob the total. Rob pulled out his wallet and handed her five dollars, leaving the rest for her tip. He walked back to Stephanie and sat down. "We can talk now while they prepare it," Rob said.

"That's a very unique ring you have. It looks exotic."

I really need to make this thing invisible. It's difficult to lie and remember the lie I told. I remember from seventh-grade literature class Ben Franklin's quote, "A lie stands on one leg, truth on two!"

"It was a gift from a dear friend's father," Rob truthfully replied but tried to change the subject. "So tell me about the colleges you hope to go to."

Stephanie started, "First, you promised to tell me about your grandmother."

The barista from behind the coffee counter shouted, "Skinny vanilla latte, almond milk, no foam, for Rob."

"Excuse me...again." Rob rolled his eyes and curved his mouth slightly.

Upon Rob's return, he and Stephanie conversed for almost an hour and a half, which seemed to Rob like merely minutes. They laughed a lot and shared funny stories. He shared about his family background, Sitto, his job, school activities and his apprehension about college, and Stephanie shared the same along with why she wanted to be a pharmacist. They even discussed former relationships, which for Stephanie were few because of her work schedule. She told Rob about a long-term relationship with her high school sweetheart, and Rob had shared about his short-term relationship with Christine. Of course, he left out the close-encounter-of-the-third-kind events since that would have been a future date breaker in Rob's mind.

"I'm surprised. I thought you would have had many more boyfriends. If you don't mind me saying this, especially if it sounds insincere or like a pickup line, which would be a bit silly since we are having coffee together. I find you extremely attractive, easy to talk with and very witty. I would think you would have gotten lots of calls from, as they say in the literary realm," Rob said, doing his best stuffy British accent, "eligible suitors."

"Well, first of all, I appreciate your kind and sincere words, but my experience has been that most of the boys who are interested in me lack any type of sophistication. Think of the 'football is my life' type. Please don't take my bluntness as not ladylike, but they were always trying to get into my—"

Rob quickly interrupted with "Explain no further. I get it. But you do realize that all boys are not like that, right? It's like when we watch the dishonesty in politics, the racist language and the inhumanity to others on the news. I think we make the presumption that the world has no redeeming qualities. It reminds me of the movie *The Goodbye Girl*."

"Is that the one with Richard Dreyfuss?" Stephanie asked attentively.

"Yes, that's the one. I'm so surprised you know that. It's a very old movie that my parents and I watched one night on one of the cable channels. His character was a struggling actor. He fell in love with his actor friend's ex-girlfriend who had been abandoned. When he decides to leave out of town for an acting audition, she stereotyped him as a fly-by-night kind of guy when she accused him of abandoning her as well. I love what he says to her. 'I hate those guys that walked out of here. I hate them. I'm the only one that's coming back, and I'm getting all the blame.' It's really the same thing here. Not every guy is a sexist pig who tries to overly emphasize his masculinity."

"I guess you're right. You know, your honesty is refreshing." Stephanie sighed as she looked at her watch. "Wow! I can't believe how late it is. Oh, please don't take that the wrong way. I really am enjoying your company. We must do this again soon."

"I am swamped this weekend with the play and all, but..." Rob replied.

"And I work the whole weekend as usual," Stephanie sadly responded.

"How about Wednesday this week?" Rob timidly asked.

"Wednesday is my day off, so maybe when you get out of school?"

"That's the night of our dress rehearsal. Would you like to come and watch? Then we can go out afterward." Rob wondered if that was too childish since she was a high school graduate.

"To watch an actor in action? Can I give you an unbiased critique?" She grinned, half kidding.

"Um...ah...sure," Rob sheepishly replied.

"I'm kidding. I just want to enjoy your performance."

Christine would do that all the time to me, then tell me she's kidding. If Stephanie turns out to be an alien, I am really going to lose my shit. Either that, or maybe I am destined to date an alien. Maybe she's from Proteus 9, trying to retrieve the documents Crumb stole. Maybe she was hiding on the ship in the Bottomless Lake in New Mexico. Maybe that's why she agreed to have this date and was fascinated by my ring. Why do I do this to myself? I have to stop this assuming. It's simply a date. Focus, Rob. Focus.

"Dress rehearsal starts at five o'clock," Rob told her. They both walked out together, and Rob grabbed his bike and walked Stephanie to her car.

"That's funny." Stephanie observed Rob's bike. "The bike you're riding is just like the one your uncle was riding the night of the... ahh...incident. I don't know why I would have notice that since I was in shock. I was convinced by your uncle Cliff that I was imagining things that really didn't happen. The police agreed with your uncle Cliff's assessment."

"Oh, his car was in the shop, and I lent it to him." *I hate lying to her, but I really feel that I need to keep my secret under wraps. Maybe in time, she can know the truth.*

"Listen. Once I really get to know you and we have some more dates, I can share with you about the whole situation that your uncle saved me from. You're a sweet guy, Rob, and I had a great time just talking with you. I'll be looking forward to seeing you in your starring role," Stephanie said as Rob held out his hand to shake. She clasped his hand with both of hers, almost like a politician. However, hers was different. Her left hand was staying on Rob's, making it more sincere. While holding his hand, she gently kissed him on his cheek.

"'Night. I'll see you Wednesday." Rob waved and blushed. As she drove away, he started his short journey home.

Wow! Okay, that was unexpected. Anyway, I really need to edit that eulogy. It's still early, and I'm not too tired since I forgot to ask for decaf.

Rob arrived home, placed his bike into their single-car garage and let his parents know he was home. He grabbed a bottle of water from the refrigerator and headed to his room to begin editing Sitto's eulogy.

*****

Monday morning came too soon for Rob. He had been nervous about delivering the speech, but since it had been written down, he wasn't as nervous as he would be for the upcoming play, especially since Stephanie would be there. He, however, remembered what Mr. Heathtree told all his actors and actresses: "The more nervous you are the better. It means you are always thinking about what to do next."

Now that I finished the eulogy, I really need to choose my hero and begin this outline. Rob spent the rest of the day in his room and started outlining what he felt were qualities of the hero he charted on his computer. His definition had changed over the course of the past two weeks and even had been different from the qualities that had been discussed in Ms. Digit's class. *A hero is not someone in a comic book, and most of the hero's qualities have nothing to do with their superpowers. It's the way they live their lives, more of a way of life, like helping others, being honest and trustworthy and having dignity and moral integrity.* Rob added one more quality to his chart: courage to face one's fears. Rob began his outline and realized that his hero was someone he had decided earlier not to use. He continued working on it throughout dinnertime and prepared the final draft, which he decided to revisit before submitting it, as all good writers do.

*****

The day of the funeral arrived. His aunts were crying excessively, not that Rob could blame them. Sitto had been an immigrant from Lebanon, or what she referred to as the "old country." He remembered her talking about how she and Jitto had started a candy store when they arrived in the United States and how they had raised eleven children. *I can't even imagine having eleven children in these turbulent times.* Rob also remembered Sitto had told him not to wear dark colors. Rob respected her wishes and wore a light-tan suit, which some of his aunts frowned upon because it wasn't the traditional black, but they never said anything about his attire. Sitto had also wanted to be cremated, but her children believed that it was against the orthodox Catholic religion, which it was not, according to Rob's research. *Am I the only one who respected Sitto's wishes? Didn't they even check to see if cremation is acceptable now? Catholic rules change as often as our traffic lights.*

All of Sitto's grandchildren were pallbearers, which was a first for many of them. Each of them was very young and was not accustomed to funerals. They simply followed the funeral director's instructions and proceeded to the front of St. Mary's Church. They stopped at the first pew, then filed into both the left and right front benches.

Rob noticed for the first time that his mom was crying. The ring had allowed him to eliminate her PTSD, which had been so devastating to her over the years. Usually, she would never cry at anything, whether it was a death of a friend, a relative or even her oldest brother, Toffie, who died when Rob was only seven. At that age, Rob had been confused as to why she had not cried for her own brother.

The mass went on as all Catholic masses did with the same sequence—the blessing and incense around the casket and then the delivery of the homily. It was getting close to Rob's speech, and his right leg, as if precisely on cue, started bobbing up and down but without a stern corrective word from his mother, who had been behind him this time. Instead, she put her hand on his shoulder and whispered to him, "I know you're nervous, but we know you can do this." And for the very first time, Rob's mother made a failed attempt at a joke. She said, "You're shaking your pew like an unbalanced load in a washing machine."

Rob apologized and stopped. He was shocked and even proud that she could even think of a joke since she never joked before.

"And now," the monsignor announced after he completed his homily, "we will hear from her grandson, Rob." Rob rose from the pew, and after being careful not to trip on the stairs while walking to the pulpit, he carried his prepared speech. *I'm not going to tap the microphone like so many do and ask if it's on. Of course, it's on. The monsignor just spoke in it.*

As he placed his transcript on the lectern, he began. "I've never written a eulogy before, but I'm honored that my first one will be for Sitto," Rob said after clearing his throat. "Some adults think that a seventeen-year-old knows nothing about death or dying, and they are correct. But I can tell you what I do know. There are things that this world has been lacking for a long time, kindness, integrity, acceptance of diversity, cooperation and morals. However, these all existed in Sitto's world. I don't mean some alternative world but the world within her own house, her own neighborhood.

"Hers was a world where we learned what it meant to be human. Sitto's world showed me how to make good decisions, and if they were not the right ones, she taught me to accept the consequences of them, then make a different choice and try a different pathway. Sitto's world showed me to never blame others for my own failures. Living in Sitto's world taught me how to be honest with others because it elucidated integrity, and that integrity would lead to trusting relationships. Sitto's world showed me how to accept and celebrate different races, cultures and religions. Sitto's world showed me to revel in our cultural heritage but also honor the culture of others by being respectful and open-minded about those who were different. Her world demonstrated how to be neighborly and welcoming by inviting neighbors of all nationalities and religions over for coffee and Lebanese cookies on her porch. And they, in turn, would bring their traditional delicacies. Sitto's world taught me how to find harmonies in others' heritages and focus on our similarities, not our differences, especially when it came to food and music because she said they were the core of all cultures. Sitto's world taught me how to self-evaluate what I do and how I do it. Sitto's world taught me how to share in friends' and relatives' accomplishments. Sitto's world taught me that working hard and never taking shortcuts was the key to success. In Sitto's world, we would find common ground with others even if they were aliens from another planet. We should welcome them without suspicion or distrust."

Rob paused for a minute as his eyes teared up not only from missing his grandmother but also from his friendship with the Themadorians. He continued as his voice began to crack. "In Sitto's world, we respected others, and in return, we received their respect. Sitto's world sheltered us from our currently divided world as if her alternative world was the real one. You see, when we lost Sitto, we also lost her world, a utopian world where humans respected and cooperated with other humans. As we lay her to rest today, I have hopes that her world will not fade but melt over and blanket our world today so we can start fresh, like a new coat of paint over a battered wall. Yes, I'm a seventeen-year-old boy who doesn't know much about death or dying, but I do know a lot about living. Everyone here should promise one another that we begin living in Sitto's world and start a new world as its painters."

There was not a dry eye in the church, and as Rob wiped his tears away, he saw that others were wiping theirs as well. He walked down from the pulpit; and after he sat down, his mother and father, from behind his pew, placed their hands on his shoulders, one hand over the other, and, almost in unison, whispered, "Perfect." Rob placed his hands over theirs and nodded his head as an acknowledgment of their praise. From the end of his parents' pew, his sisters gave Rob a unified thumbs-up. This time they were not texting on their phones. He realized that his family would be very different—actually, better—thanks to the Themadorians' gift. But his experience with Arak's family had not just been about the ring. It had been about the tenderness of their commitment to him and his to theirs.

In essence, they wanted to begin the process of returning their world to its previous harmony, similar to his grandmother's world.

*****

Wednesday morning was unusually tough for Rob; he was feeling exhausted from his last two weeks of mayhem. Rob moved slowly to prepare for his return to school. He readied his homework including his finished hero essay for Mrs. Digit. He entered the kitchen, and as usual, his mother was making the same breakfast for his dad and asked if Rob wanted some. "Tommy will be here in a couple of minutes, so may I have some toast with almond butter and honey please?"

His mother, who never liked anyone in her kitchen preparing anything except what she made, replied, "Help yourself. Everything is in their usual spots."

Shocked, Rob began toasting two pieces of bread. Just as he finished creating his almond-butter sandwich, like clockwork, Tommy rang the front doorbell. "I'll get it," his father said as he wiped his mouth with a paper napkin and walked to the door. Opening the door, he greeted Rob's usual guest. "Morning Tommy! Want some breakfast?"

"No thanks! I already ate. I brought some extra food with me since the dress rehearsal is tonight and I won't be going home after school," Tommy said.

"I never thought to do that," Rob responded in a surprised voice. "Mom, is there anything quick I can make so I can eat before dress rehearsal?"

"Take the leftover honey, and I'll fill a small container of lemon juice as well," his mother calmly announced. "Oh, and take these protein bars and two cans of ginger ale."

"Huh? Lemon juice, honey and ginger ale?"

"The honey for your throat. It's going to soothe it. And the ginger ale cuts through any mucus that may build up in your larynx since the stage still has some dust from those last-minute set constructions," she explained.

"Wow! Thanks, Mom. You really thought this out."

"With the stress of missing school and writing and presenting the eulogy, which, by the way, the family is still talking about, I thought I'd help," his concerned mother said.

Rob decided to hug his mother, which would be a true sign that the ring had cured her of PTSD. She accepted the hug and squeezed him tight. "Break a leg," she said.

His father added, "Let your whole cast know we said to break a leg. Ha, maybe that's where they got the idea for casting a broken leg."

Rob rolled his eyes and snickered. "Sure, Dad. Sure!" At that, both boys headed to school. "I'll be going out after the dress rehearsal. I shouldn't be too late."

Tommy looked at Rob in shock as they went out the door. "What the hell was that? Tommy was referring to Rob's mother's personality.

"Oh, it's a long story. I'll fill you in sometime."

"How about the condensed version!" Tommy insisted.

"Okay, ring minus PTSD equals…"

"Oh, that helped. Not!" Tom sarcastically replied.

*****

School was different today. Christine wasn't there. Murphy hadn't been seen for days. Students were still apprehensive and anxious about another shooting. Rob, though, was more excited. Tonight he was hoping for a bad dress rehearsal. That might sound strange, but Rob remembered what Mr. Heathtree told his cast and crew: "A bad dress rehearsal means a great performance." Rob understood. Mistakes in a dress rehearsal would be shared with the cast since Mr. Heathtree would debrief the cast after each act to ensure a smooth performance each night. Heathtree's notes were meticulous as he observed all minuscule details of errors, but his focus was on the positives, especially when ad-libs had the audience laughing.

Rob loved working with his cast and crew. It reminded him of how Lah, Arak and Dr. Stewart worked together for a common goal, sharing ideas and solutions to problems. Rob's adrenaline was heightened not just for the performance but from knowing that Stephanie would be attending.

*****

The school day was quick and uneventful. There were no major interruptions to the day. Rob handed in his hero essay to Ms. Digit as she walked around to collect them. She looked down at the title of Rob's essay, "A Different Kind of Hero, My Father."

"I love the intriguing title. Looking forward to reading how he's a different kind of hero." She had the habit of complimenting every student in one way or another as she collected papers. If a student did not hand one in, she would place a typed note down on the student's desk without saying a word and move on to the next student. They all knew what the note said since gossip is rampant in high school. The note was actually not unique to that student but more generic. "Please see me after class" was typed on a laminated index card, and she had a number of different-colored ones at her disposal. No one could figure out what the reason was for the different colors.

*****

The end of the day arrived, and Rob, Tommy and the rest of the cast and crew gathered in the auditorium to get notes from their last regular practice. However, all of them knew there would be many more notes after the dress rehearsal. Mr. Heathtree would make all students responsible for remembering his verbal notes prior to performance. He expected no repeated errors.

No one was allowed to be seen in costume in the auditorium before dress rehearsal and definitely not before a performance. The cast had to arrive at school at least an hour early for makeup to be applied before they were allowed to be in costume. The makeup crew was comprised of student volunteers and was coordinated by a local parent hair stylist and a mother of one of the cast members. The technical crew had to arrive as early as the cast to make sure all lighting and sounds were working properly.

A FRESH BEGINNING

The cast and crew were now ready. The musical needed to start right at 5:00 PM as a practice for the premiere night, which required everyone to be onstage as the curtain opened at 7:00 PM. If they weren't ready, the curtain would open anyway. If the cast and crew were not ready, they would have only embarrassed themselves, which was a key motivator that Heathtree used to ensure their readiness.

Peeking out of the small opening of the curtain, Rob was amazed at the number of people, which comprised of mostly parents and friends of cast members or students who couldn't get tickets for any of the five performances since the show was sold out. He looked for Stephanie and spotted her with another guy. *Must be a friend of hers or maybe someone else she's dating.* Rob then threw that suspicion out, knowing that Stephanie was not seeing anyone at the time. He also realized that she technically was not exclusive to Rob. His mother's comments when she had PTSD of how no girl would be interested in a long-term relationship with him was an indelible stain on his self-esteem. Rob decided to focus on his opening scene, which would be the essential theme to the entire production. The orchestra began the opening melody of songs as the curtain opened, and the show began.

The intermission was brief since it wasn't the actual scheduled performance. Mr. Heathtree, of course, met the cast in the gymnasium that was adjacent to the backstage entrance, and he shared his notes with them. Surprisingly, he had few. He even commented and laughed about the incident with the rooster and the chicken. Heathtree had a habit of making his stage as authentic as possible. In *Fiddler on the Roof*, he used a rooster and some chickens during the opening scenes of the dress rehearsal to see how the cast would react and how the birds would behave. However, it wasn't the cast that he had to worry about. During Rob's scene of "If I were a Rich Man," one of the chickens jumped out at the front row of the audience. An eruption of laughter and a scream from a lady whose lap was the landing spot of the uninvited guest forced one of the stagehands dressed entirely in black to go out to the front row to retrieve the flapping fowl while the dialogue continued.

"Excuse me. Excuse me. Excuse me. Excuse me," Brian, the dark-dressed stagehand, whispered as he crossed a number of occupied seats to get the escapee. "Gotcha," Brian whispered. He then carried the chicken back across the same row of seats, excusing himself again. "Excuse me. Excuse me. Excuse me." No sooner had the chicken been returned to the stage than a rooster started walking up to one of the various microphones lined across the front of the stage. Right in the middle of Rob's "If I Were a Rich Man," the rooster crowed a breathtaking *cock-a-doodle-do*. The audience once again roared in laughter. But Rob kept his composure and continued his song, trying not to laugh. Heathtree mentioned that in his notes. As a result, they decided not to use them and returned them to the farm the next day.

So much for realism onstage.

After the finale, the cast was once again briefed and told to be on time for makeup and last-minute preparations for the premiere performance on Thursday. The cast was allowed at this time to enter the auditorium and greet any friends or relatives in attendance.

Rob found his red-headed beauty and approached her. "I'll just need some time to take this beard off and wipe all this makeup off so we can go for coffee." Looking at her male companion and holding out his hand, Rob introduced himself, saying, "Hi, I'm Rob Shehan."

"Nice to meet you, Rob. My name is Pete. I'm—"

"Stephanie's next-door neighbor." Rob finished Pete's introduction. "It's nice to finally meet you."

"That was one hell of a performance, Rob. Better than Leonard Nimoy's Tevye on Broadway. Your comedic timing was impeccable. And that mishap with the chicken and rooster was hysterical, as if they were added for comic relief."

"Wow! Thanks!" Rob was blushing but proud. "Well, those animals will not be returning. Their debut did not impress our director."

"Listen, Stephanie, I have to meet Monica at the library. We have to study for midterms," Pete explained.

"Thanks for keeping me company, Pete. Coming to a place by myself is a bit nerve-racking, so I very much appreciate it," Stephanie

A FRESH BEGINNING

replied. "But could you stay just a little longer until Rob cleans up? I just feel uneasy since the incident."

Rob knew what the incident was, but he refrained from bringing it up. "I'll just be five minutes," Rob said as he rushed off to transform from Tevye, the Jewish milkman, to Rob, the Lebanese romantic.

Upon returning, Rob and Stephanie met in the back of the auditorium with Rob's bike in tow. They walked out the back of the school building and to the parking lot. Rob loaded his bike into the back of her silver Nissan SUV, and they got into their respective seats.

"I was impressed that you didn't jump to conclusions about Pete at the dress rehearsal. You see, most guys, after one date, would presume that I was dating them exclusively. Then they'd become angry and rude without knowing the facts," Stephanie shared.

"Since we only had one date, who you date besides me is your business. I just enjoy your company, and I hope that we can get to know each other better. So those types of assumptions can never happen. To be honest, I hope we will have more dates in the future, that is, if you don't mind driving. I'm hoping eventually that my mom or dad will lend me one of their vehicles for some of our dates, if you're game," Rob said, smiling and hoping for a positive response.

"Yes," Stephanie acknowledged, "that sounds great." And with that, they headed out to what would become their usual hangout.

As far as the ring is concerned, Rob could not be sure of what the future would hold for him in his relationship with Stephanie, his college years or his possible travels. And as they walked, Rob recalled from his Government Studies course. a quote by an old British governor "Great power carries with it great responsibility, and great responsibility entails a large amount of anxiety."[3] *Isn't that the truth!*

---

[3] 1879, Sir Hercules G. R. Robinson

ABOUT THE AUTHOR

Bob lives in Upstate New York with his wife, Carol. He is a retired language arts teacher whose dream is to write and publish a novel. He used his knowledge of adolescent behavior and his love of science fiction to write *The Alien Ring*. Besides his teaching talents, he was also a singer, actor, coach, department head, and an entrepreneur and operator of a disc jockey service. He continues to be an avid comic book reader, collector and seller and is currently selling his many collectibles from the past fifty years.

CPSIA information can be obtained
at www.ICGtesting.com
Printed in the USA
BVHW042230020723
666613BV00001BA/79